HELEN'S PASSAGE

A portion of the author's proceeds from this work
will be donated to
Literacy Volunteers of America, Inc.,
a national, non-profit organization of trained volunteers
dedicated to opening the worlds of reading and writing to others.

HELEN'S PASSAGE
DIANA M. CONCANNON

CAVATICA
PUBLISHING
Publishers of Science Fiction & Fantasy

Redondo Beach, California

Published in the United States by Cavatica Publishing Company
1262 Beryl Street, Suite 30
Redondo Beach, California 90277
310-371-1036

Library of Congress Catalog Card Number: 97-95002

ISBN: 0-9662199-0-2

First Printing: April 1998

Concannon, Diana

Acknowledgments

It has been noted that the writer's path is a solitary one.
I am deeply grateful to the many individuals who kept my journey
from being lonely as well.

To Tad Crawford, writer and publisher, without whom this project
would not have come to fruition.

To Professor Angelos Chaniotis of the Department of Classics
at New York University for his painstaking review of the manuscript and
his detailed input on various historical points.

To Hilda Brown and Louise A. Wetzel for their careful proofreading.

To the friends, family and colleagues — Glenn Baker, Virginia and Charlie
Bufano, Bob and MaryAnn Concannon, Chris Concannon, Danny and
Maura Concannon, Victoria Marie Concannon, Tom Dessereau, Carol Levy,
Dafna & Dave Nidorf, Kristin Robbins, Liz West and Jan Wetzel — who
endured my constant rambling about Ancient Greece in particular
and about writing in general.

Finally, a special thanks to Christopher Wiley, for his patience and love.

PROLOGUE

*A*lready, *they say the light that illuminated Greece died
with the death of Troy. They say too that I, Helen of Sparta and
of Troy (and Troezen, Attica and the Pharaoh Land, for these
shaped me as well) am responsible for the darkness.*

*The priests of the Olympian gods are always quick to judge
that which they do not understand.*

*Look at what they did to the Great Mother, calling Her idol
of the simple folk, a fantasy borne of the imaginations of the ignorant. They dismembered Her essence and scattered Her aspects
among their own goddesses — and even their gods — calling this
one virgin and that mother, calling one a god of war and another
a god of artistry. They patterned their deities after men who do
not understand the contradictions within their own natures. And
men, weary of the internal struggle to understand, embraced these
false gods. It was only a matter of time before the priests denied
Her existence totally, annihilating Her with the force of their lies.*

*They could not do likewise with me, though I daresay they
wished to.*

*Instead, they judge me shallow and whore, a selfish woman
who brought destruction to satisfy her own lusts.*

*I fear their lies about me will be held as truth, even as their
denial of the Great Mother is. The truth is this: Long before the
coming of the Olympians, the world worshipped in accordance
with the Goddess and each man and each woman fought the personal, inner battle to live in harmony with Her ways.*

I fought for the freedom to continue doing so.

*Judge me then on my failure, for the freedom I sought has
been strangled by greedy hands. But for one last time, judge me
based upon the truth. Not upon the lies the priests would have
you believe.*

i

PART ONE
SPARTA & ATHENS

CHAPTER ONE

Leda was dying of course. Life was taking life.

There must be balance.

Ironic that the words of her mother would haunt her now.

Pain burned her skull, scorching feeling in its wake. She thought her sight would blur as death seeped through her. Instead it cleared, became painfully clear. Her hearing, her sense of touch, her ability to smell and to taste, gave their power to her eyes, a last grasp at vitality.

She is the womb of life and the hand of death.

She looked at the tranquil beauty of the waves and dolphins and water shells painted upon the room's surrounding walls. She glimpsed at the depiction of a blue-green-white-yellow sea, framed by a thin line of pink at each wall's uppermost reach, which changed with the shadows of day and night.

She is the breath of light and the heart of shadow.

Pain sliced her again, mercifully severing the tenuous bond between body and spirit.

Leda had expected death to be black, a thick veil of obscurity slowly rising. She had not expected the radiant colors that danced before her, through her, within her, bringing ecstasy, communion, contentment.

Within Her all things meet and opposing aspects join as one.

Images of her mother chased themselves before eyes: Eurythemis leading a group of maidens to the placid river vein for purification. Eurythemis, great and terrible, swaying mindlessly as smoke carried the sacred herbs burning upon the central fire. Eurythemis' patient gaze upon her:

Serve Her, for by so doing you serve yourself.

The spirit of Eurythemis loomed in the Otherworld. Leda

felt her own spirit shrink to the child she once was and she turned so the tears of rejection that flooded her eyes would not be seen. *Even at the moment of my death, mother cares only for the Goddess she worships.*

In this place, her thoughts moved her forward, allowing her to flee her mother and search for her father — the man who had patted her upon her cheek and laughed when she raised the wooden sword with her brothers; the man who had promised to marry her to a strong and wise king.

Father!

She stopped as a figure approached, shrouded in the mists that cloaked the Otherworld, drawing the light that danced in the air. A woman, Leda thought, desperate to find her father, unable to move beyond the apparition before her.

The figure continued Her approach and Leda felt a warm breeze surround her.

"Daughter, I am with you and in you and of you, as you are in, with and of me."

Leda drowned in the warmth of Her breath, floating in a storm of erotic tranquillity.

No!

Surely it was as the priests of her husband said: Only the ignorant still believed in the Great Goddess. Life had many aspects and many goddesses and gods to attend them. Each deity represented an aspect of nature and all bent to the will of their king, Zeus, even as all men subordinated themselves to mortal kings. Zeus, the Thunderer, the lord of many goddesses and gods. Zeus who, Leda knew, was real. This figure before her was nothing more than a tale for the simpleminded and for mothers who did not care for their children.

You are not real! she screamed.

Once more, her thoughts had the power of action, for the apparition of the Lady vanished, leaving only a small ache that Leda ignored.

She fled again, her spirit growing from the essence of a little girl into the queen she had become. Long auburn hair framed her delicate features and large, emerald eyes. Her search changed as well. She forsook her father and sought her lover, the father of her children, her god. She searched the colors, between spaces, seeking the power she remembered when *he* looked out from her husband's eyes.

The past appeared before her once more.

"Leda." His whisper was lighting, his form illuminated. The man who was her husband wore the semblance of the god, moving toward her in the open air of the palace courtyard.

As she watched the scene unfold, her spirit could almost feel the thunderous pounding of her heart, which abruptly stilled to breathless silence. The god pulled her close, violence and gentleness merged. Her night shift fell about her feet in soft, luscious folds.

The past vanished and she was left, once again, to wonder if she had dreamt the luminous beauty.

Surely not. Surely he would meet her now, as her spirit made its final passage through the Otherworld.

Her spirit ran and ran until pain she should not have felt sliced her side and she fell to her knees. Her vision blurred, the mists collapsed.

Her spirit met the flesh of her body.

"You clumsy, useless thing! Run and get additional bowls. And you, stop your gawking and get more linens!"

"What has happened? Leda whispered, pained anew to be back within her all too familiar chambers.

A woman approached her, drawing the light that danced about the room to her obscured form. The apparition, returning for her...

"No!" Leda screamed, her raw throat producing no more than a whisper.

"Rest quietly, my lady," the woman said and Leda recognized Rhemnesia, her senior attendant.

She sunk further into the feather pillows that held her agonized body.

"Your babes are fine and protesting the new distance from one another," the woman continued.

The colors are so dull here, Leda thought, willing herself to care that she had just given birth.

"Congratulations, my lady. A family fit for a king," Charisia the midwife said, beaming just like Leda thought a new mother should. She walked toward Leda with an infant carefully cradled in each arm. Leda's heart quickened as the children were placed to her breasts and life reasserted itself.

Twins. Beautiful little maidens in possession of the right number of fingers and toes, a rosy pink upon them. She hoped the king would not be too disappointed that the first of his children were not the sons he craved.

A second woman stood above her, cradling two more infants. "And your sons, lady."

Sons? Two more children?

"Who would have thought the king to be so potent," Rhemnesia said dryly.

The said king burst into the room. He looked upon his wife with aching tenderness, which quickly became confusion as he surveyed the mob of babies surrounding her.

"Your family, my lord."

Tyndareus moved forward, stopped, stepped again.

"They won't hurt you," Charisia offered.

The king worked his mouth, failing to draw words from his muddled brain. He shook his head impatiently, drawing breath and the mantle of kinghood upon him. "The sky god has truly shown his favor upon my home," he said at last.

"I'd say your god needs some lessons in the abilities of women's bodies," Rhemnesia remarked.

Tyndareus ignored her and approached his wife. "Are you well, my beloved?" he asked softly.

Leda nodded, attempting to smile beneath the tears that washed her cheeks.

"You'd better name them," Charisia said, drying her hands and anxious to move the process along. Charisia knew fathers.

"Of course."

"The little one to the right was the first born."

"Helen," Tyndareus said definitely, regaining his authority.

He turned to the remaining children. "Clytemnestra. Castor. Polydeuces."

He stood then, looking at his family with hesitation and toward the door with longing.

"You may leave now, " Rhemnesia prompted.

Tyndareus fled.

"No doubt, he'll boast of his prowess from here to Crete. As if he did anything beyond what any farm animal could do."

Perhaps not even that much, Leda thought and searched her children's faces for a sign of her god lover.

The messenger waved an impatient hand at the woman who offered him wine and a bath. His employer had clearly ordered him to deliver the message in all haste, and he knew she expected him to forgo even rudimentary hospitality. Indeed, it seemed he was expected (though how this could be, he did not know) for a second young woman emerged from the darkened stone corridor and beckoned him forward. He followed her lithe form beyond the limestone pillars to a small room, which she indicated he enter.

The other woman was there, waiting. He did not allow himself to dwell on her beauty, nor to wonder at the power which emanated from her slight form; his body, however, acknowledged both and he gave a graceful bow in homage.

"She is born," he said, quickly, pouring strength and pride into his words in a futile effort to overcome his unease.

She looked through him in that uncanny way and then, surprisingly, bowed her head humbly.

"So it must be."

CHAPTER TWO

"It's over warm for this season," Charisia complained, peeling her sweating bottom from the wooden stool.

Another spring, Leda thought. *Years spent in longing pass quickly.* She looked up from the summer tunic upon which she placed the finishing embroidery and let her eyes drift to her daughter Helen. She could not but look to Helen. Her daughter's beauty was too great for simple senses to comprehend. Surely, this was *his* daughter, the offspring of her union with the greatest of the Olympian gods. For the ten winters since her children's birth, Leda studied each, looking for some echo of the power she had felt, once, long ago — a power which she could neither comprehend nor deny, but which she longed to experience again with every cell of her being. Castor and Polydeuces grew into fine handsome boys — one fair, one dark — and each bearing the faintest echo of Tyndareus' features in the curve of their eyes and the length of their noses. *They are boys to make a mother proud*, Leda reminded herself. Strong, intelligent, adventurous.

But not remarkable.

She was not overly heartbroken when, at five, they were taken from the women's quarters to be raised with the other palace youth.

Nor was her daughter Clytemnestra particularly unique. Clytemnestra's auburn hair and green eyes marked her as her mother's daughter, though the stubborn thrust of jaw was all her daughter's own. Still, though she was as beautiful as Leda, Clytemnestra was not endowed with that undefined something that would demonstrate the hand of the god.

Unlike Helen. Words of Helen's beauty were spoken as far north as Thessaly and as far south as Crete. Her golden hair flowed generously about features seemed carved from alabaster, their creamy smoothness interupted by impossibly blue eyes that tilted slightly upward at the corners. At ten, her body began to hint at generous curves that defied the awkwardness of a typical growing girl. Surely, Helen was the god's own. Leda wondered if *he* came to her daughter, sharing with her the power that forever changed Leda's own life. *Perhaps I will ask her*, she thought, as she had countless times before. She returned her eyes to the cloth on her lap, knowing she'd keep silent. She would not admit her fear that her daughter would not know the god of whom she spoke.

Helen ignored her mother's surreptitious glances and focused on the pattern taking shape on the linen beneath her hands.

"She thinks you're born from a god," Clytemnestra had sneered the first and last time Helen had asked her sister about her mother's curious looks. "Although you can't be without all of us being so," her sister had added.

Leda was the matriarch of the women's quarters; the peculiarity she sought in her daughter was searched for by the waiting women and various maidens fostered at the palace. Helen found herself entering circles of conversation that went abruptly silent, raising her eyes to meet those of others which slipped away.

"It is Amazon weather," Rhemnesia remarked in response to Charisia's complaint about the heat. The women looked up from their work expectantly, awaiting Rhemnesia's tale. Helen did the same, though she felt an ignoble pang of jealousy. Rhemnesia alone spoke with her, seeking her out when the other waiting women and palace maidens shunned her presence. But then, Rhemnesia did whatever she pleased, heedless of the secret pacts of others.

"Who are the Amazons, lady?" Phoebe prompted politely.

All the young girls called Rhemnesia "lady," though they did not know why. Perhaps their respect was due to the haughty mystery that surrounded her. No one knew whence Rhemnesia came, only that she arrived immediately before the king took Leda as his queen. No one, not even Leda herself, questioned Rhemnesia's place as the queen's senior waiting woman, nor as guardian of the princesses. Perhaps their respect was in silent obedience to Rhemnesia's eyes, which were a curious black, bespeaking shadows that saw into the very soul of the one they sought. No one contradicted those eyes.

"The Amazons are the women of the battle ax, who keep the ways of the sacred Mother and roam the plains of the east," Rhemnesia responded, leaning back upon her stool and letting her bone needle lie idle on her lap.

"Where is their palace?" Clytemnestra asked.

"Ah, but they have no palace, no walls of men to enclose them." Rhemnesia replied, her tone sharpening slightly as it always did when she addressed Helen's sister. "Now keep your peace and I shall tell you all. The Amazons retain the rule of the Queen, who is ruler and priestess both, and keep men only as slaves or to make babies."

Clytemnestra's eyes widened.

"They have horses as strong and swift as the best bred of Sparta and learn to master them before they walk."

"They are the daughters of Poseidon, then?" Clytemnestra interrupted, forgetting the command of silence.

"No, no child," Rhemnesia replied impatiently. "They follow the great Goddess, who proceeds the gods of men."

She looked to Leda, who started at the last. The two women remained locked in silent conversation until Leda bit her lip anxiously and returned her attention to her work once more.

"They are the greatest of warriors," Rhemensia continued, bringing her attention back to the room's occupants. "You know how they came upon the King of Attica, Theseus, when he abducted their queen, Antiope? When he refused to return her and she refused to bring the dagger to her own heart as was proper for an Amazon stolen by a man, they marched upon the city and struck her down, sparing Theseus only after he vowed to aid them in times of need."

"I would like to be an Amazon and ride as well as men and take a dagger in my own defense," Clytemnestra announced.

"Indeed, I believe you would do well in their tribe," Rhemnesia replied blandly.

Clytemnestra's peers agreed, loudly imposing their imagined ideas of an ideal Amazon's life.

"Perhaps you can content yourselves with running in the garden for now," Leda suggested, relieved that Rhemnesia had concluded her tale.

A cluster of girls leaped in unison.

"Fold your work first," the queen admonished.

"Today we'll be Amazons," Clytemnestra announced, taking charge despite her smaller height and younger seasons.

Helen took more time than necessary folding her linen, creating distance between herself and her peers. Rhemnesia noted it and raised an eloquent eyebrow in Leda's direction before preparing to join her charges.

The queen shrugged. "Helen's always been different," she said.

"Children are what their parents expect of them," Rhemnesia retorted, annoyance dripping in her voice.

Leda assumed the dreamy expression that so exasperated her senior attendant. "Indeed they are," she said at last.

Helen has always been different.

The words wrapped themselves around Helen's body, a foggy weight that further slowed her steps and increased the distance between her and the other maidens.

"Phoebe, you play Queen Antiope," Clytemnestra ordered.

"Why Phoebe?" another asked rebelliously.

"Because she's the oldest and the prettiest."

Phoebe cast her dark eyes downward and tossed a lock of wavy hair over her shoulder. Leda said she resembled her mother, a woman who was beautiful enough to be the king's mistress before he married the queen. Phoebe wished her mother had stayed alive long enough for her to remember her face. "Helen is far more beautiful than I," she said at last. Honor required that the truth be spoken.

"Ah, but Helen's too good to be a mere Amazon," a younger girl said viciously as the beautiful princess approached.

"I have more important things to do than play childish games," Helen answered.

She turned and walked away from the group and the pain that they could inflict upon her, making her way through the women's garden and its rows of blooming trees, matched for size and an order of riotous color.

The perfection choked Helen.

She wandered beyond the courtyard. A river of sage grass parted for her passage and she came at last to the olive tree that stood in gnarled beauty beyond the garden's grounds. She climbed the branches that extended through time to form cradling arms. Her arrival was marked by the yellowed bellied birds who flew from the upper branches, raining sunbursts above her. One of the flock deemed her harmless enough to return to a branch a safe distance away.

"Did you ever see an Amazon?" she asked the undoubtedly well-traveled bird.

The creature cocked its head but made no reply. Helen sighed and looked about her.

The palace rose on a small hill, transmuting distance by offering a clear line of sight over the houses of merchants and farmers and slaves which surrounded it. It ruled over a fertile valley nursed by the Erotas River, protected by the huge ranges of white-capped mountains that lined its perimeter. Sparta needed no walls for protection.

Her first born princess was not so fortunate.

With a child's instinct for survival, Helen surrounded herself with a wall of indifference to deflect her mother's dissatisfaction. Leda wanted something from her, an elusive something that Helen could not identify. When she was younger, she had sought to understand her mother's desires, and shape herself into the daughter her mother needed.

She was rewarded by flaming looks of approval and punished with burning scowls of disappointment that did not coincide with her behavior; the reactions she received were based on a pattern Helen could not decipher.

Leda's scowls grew more frequent than her rewards, wounding Helen again and again and again until a scar formed and toughened and became the first layer of her defenses.

Walls were easy to build on such a foundation.

She created them with a single-minded determination that ceased only during those surprising moments when tears would flood her eyes and dissolve her fortifications and make her forget why her protections were necessary.

"Does our mother know you still wail like a baby?" Clytemnestra had demanded when she happened upon his sister during one such episode.

Where Helen built walls, her sister built advantages. Clytemnestra shared Leda's disapproval of Helen to win their mother's approval. When they were younger, Clytemnestra's efforts took the form of pulling viciously at Helen's hair or pinching her white flesh until dark marks appeared. Clytemnestra was particularly fond of stealing one of their brother's wooden jousting sticks and extending it in Helen's path when she walked behind their mother. Predictably, Helen would topple headlong at their mother's feet, earning another of Leda's blistering frowns.

The torment went on for many years until Helen's despair hardened to anger and she shoved her sister with surprising force, realizing for the first time that she had grown larger than her twin. Clytemnestra winced in pain as the bottom of her spine connected with the stone floor. Her killing look stopped Helen's breath. But the action also stopped Clytemnestra's abuse, at least temporarily.

Her sister soon replaced physical taunts with verbal ones, rallying the palace maidens, who were growing increasingly envious of Helen's looks, to join her. It was not long before the already confused princess found herself friendless and isolated within her home. She pretended not to care, building stronger defenses against her mother and sister, not realizing that the walls she constructed further isolated her from those around her.

Except Rhemnesia.

"Maybe I should be a priestess," Helen said aloud, wondering briefly why her thoughts of Rhemensia would lead her to ponder this vocation.

Rhemnesia would not have wondered; children were far more intuitive than the adults who surrounded them.

Helen heard the rustle of sage grass and turned to see her guardian approach.

"It is time to continue our lessons," Rhemnesia said as she drew near.

Helen swiftly forgot her misery and her family and scampered down the tree with an agility that made Rhemnesia sigh with envy. The waiting woman sat her slender body upon the earth, heedless of the dirt that could soil her garment. Helen started to do likewise.

"Remember that the flow of your body is a celebration of Her," Rhemnesia admonished.

Chagrined, Helen slowed her movements, striving to feel her feet move in her light sandals, her knees bend to the earth, her spine support her. She raised tentative eyes to her teacher and relaxed upon meeting Rhemnesia's encouraging smile.

"Everything is within you," Rhemnesia said, as she had many times before. "As we grow, learning some facets of life — like walking and talking — our awareness of other aspects — like grace — diminishes. Practice brings that which has been forgotten back into awareness until it becomes an active part of us once more."

Helen, looking at Rhemnesia's perfect posture and the ease with which her delicate neck held her head high — even with the complicated braids that weighted her hair — wondered if her guardian was overestimating Helen's own natural abilities.

She nodded, though she suspected Rhemnesia's bottomless black eyes saw her doubts anyway.

"The chief priest Glaucus was present at lessons again this morning," Helen began. Instruction from the temple of Artemis, patron goddess of Sparta, was frequently part of the maiden's daily lessons. "Glaucus told us the story of Niobe, whose children were killed because of Niobe's excessive pride. Is not the celebration of one's body excessive pride?"

Rhemnesia hid a sigh. Her lessons with Helen had begun several moons before, when she found the beautiful young girl seated upon the olive tree. Rhemnesia had been pleased with the opportunity Helen's isolation afforded her to fulfill her mission and delighted that the child had chosen the solace of open spaces — although she suspected Helen's motives had more to do with putting distance between herself and her sister than finding communion with the natural world. As the moons cycled, the girl slowly began to trust her and, through her, to know of the Goddess.

Initially, Helen had been tentative about questioning anything Rhemnesia said, causing her guardian to wonder if Helen lacked the wit necessary for inquiry. It soon became apparent, however, that Helen was filled with questions which, until now, she had not been encouraged to ask. Her mother's peculiar behavior, her sister's taunts and, later, the lessons of the temple priests, were to be accepted without comment. It took some time for the girl to understand that Rhemnesia actually welcomed her questions. Rhemnesia did not show her annoyance at the temple teachings, rightly fearing that Helen would misinterpret her irritation and believe herself the cause.

"Niobe," she said slowly. "It is frightening how history can be distorted to serve the poets."

Helen offered a small, ironic smile that pleased her teacher immensely.

"Well, since the priests have told you their truth, I will tell you mine. Niobe was a beautiful woman who celebrated the Great Mother in all aspects of her life. As a result, her blessings were many: she was married to a loving man of unsurpassed musical accomplishment, lived in a luxurious palace, amassed great wealth, which she generously shared with her neighbors.

"But her greatest joy came from celebrating the act of fertility. She bore seven sons and seven daughters, whom she cherished beyond all else. She and her children could often be seen running about their lands to the accompaniment of the melodies sung by her doting husband.

"Her life was an inspiration to the people around her, who

strove to follow her worship of the Great Mother and share similar blessings.

"It was at this time that the order of Olympian priests came into being. Insanely jealous of the worship accorded the Great Mother, they roamed the land in an effort to discredit those who followed her ways. Naturally, Niobe came to their attention. They dispatched a young girl, who they claimed was a seer, into the city where Niobe resided.

"'Women of Thebes,' the girl shouted, 'Your city is graced by the temple of Leto. Weave laurel leaves upon your heads and prepare offerings so you may receive the blessings of she who bore Artemis and Apollo to the great Zeus.'

"Many of the women who heard her had grown tired of introspection. 'How much easier,' they said to themselves, 'to make a simple offering and receive the gifts of our heart's desires.' And so off they went to the man-made temple, bearing gifts of grain and livestock and gold.

"Niobe, hearing of this, was outraged. 'Our misguided friends will impoverish themselves to attain that which can only come from within.' She decided to go to the temple herself and set things to right.

"When she entered, she was appalled to see so many women gathered, dragging the fruits of their labors beside them.

"'Are you mad?' she shouted, creating a stunned silence throughout the temple precincts. 'You cannot purchase the blessings of the Goddess like some trinket from the marketplace. Her gifts are bestowed upon those who work in their hearts to deserve them. Yet here you stand, attempting to bribe a man-made goddess to get what you want. What can this goddess offer compared to the example of my own simple life? She is not even honored as wife to the man she calls the father of her children. And what has she but two of those? Do they compare to my own blessings, to my loving husband, to seven times her offspring?

"'Stop this foolishness right now, I say, and work upon your hearts.'

"With that, she turned in a rush, stomping from the temple. The women whispered to each other quietly and at last obeyed. They tore the laurel from their heads and turned their backs upon Leto's altar and the furious priest who presided there, taking with them the offerings with which they came.

"The priest was indeed furious." Rhemnesia continued, "and was heard to scream his curses down upon Niobe.

"Shortly thereafter, Niobe's husband Amphion was engaged in teaching his seven sons how to ride and race their beautiful horses. Proudly, they made their mounts raise their hooves as they demonstrated their skills.

"The eldest son, Ismenus, raced ahead of the others; he was stopped suddenly by an arrow that tore at his heart. The second son, Sipylus, pushed his horse to his brother's side, riding into a hail of arrows that claimed his life as well.

"Slowly, the other brothers realized what was occurring and rode forward with all haste, despite the warning shouts of their father. Each met a similar fate as the arrows rained down upon them. Only Amphion was spared this particular death; he was found with a dagger plunged into his heart.

"Niobe, learning of this, went wild with grief, throwing herself upon each dead body in turn and kissing it tenderly as an embarrassed crowd looked on. She rose with a grace much older than her years. 'She tests me as She does each of us. I am grateful the Goddess saw fit to spare me my daughters,' she said with quiet dignity, causing the crowd to ripple with awe.

"She did not notice the man who did not share the crowd's respect, but rather seethed with an anger that brought his body's blood to his otherwise pale face. The man was, of course, the priest of Leto. Niobe returned to her home, silent tears pouring down her cheeks in due tribute to the Goddess' death face. She sat in a great wooden chair in her beautiful garden as her remaining girl children ran about her, striving to cheer her with the compulsion children have to make their parents happy.

"It was then that the ultimate horror struck. One by one, she watched her beautiful maidens hit by the points of arrows. She ran to frantically to cover their bodies with her own and to shield them from certain death. But time and again, the marksman defied her attempts until at last only her youngest remained.

"'I beseech you,' she screamed, thinking herself speaking to the Goddess, 'spare me my youngest.'

"There was a moment pregnant silence when she believed her plea to be answered; it was broken by the hiss of an arrow's flight that ended its course in the back of her child.

"Rage overcame her and Niobe ran past the courtyard to the grove of trees from which the weapons of death issued. Her speed gave her glimpse of a retreating figure, wrapped in the robes of a priest.

"'Murderer!' Her voice rang through the trees, echoing like the accusation of the Goddess herself.

"The figure ceased his flight and melted into the shadows. 'In the name of the goddess Leto, all you love shall perish,' a very clear, male voice answered.

"Niobe stopped her pursuit, horrified at the thought that

her children and her husband were killed for such petty vengeance. Her thoughts raced to her many neighbors and friends
and distant family members.

"'I will not see you murder again. In the name of She who
is, I curse you!' she screamed, a terrible cry that echoed beyond
the little grove and spilled into the nearby town. The people
stopped at the sound, pulling their shawls closer about them as
if a blustering wind had battered their spines.

"Niobe cared not for her neighbor's reactions, but cared
deeply for their safety. She resolutely lifted her skirts and quit
the forest and Thebes, never to return.

"How could the poor woman know the full extent of the
Olympians' treachery? With her retreat, the priest went on to
murder the people just as sure as if he loosed his deadly arrows
among them. He let it be known that it was the children of Leto
— Apollo and Artemis — who killed Niobe's children because of
her pride and defiance. When Niobe's brother sculpted a beautiful image of his sister in the whitest marble, the priest claimed
it was in fact the spirit of the irreverent woman, condemned
forever to weep in atonement for her arrogance.

"The people, not knowing otherwise, believed the priest's
words, and flocked to Leto's temple with a host of offerings. And
thus it was that the Olympians gained a stronghold in Thebes
that they hold to this day. Tales of the supposed power of their
gods spread far, while the Thebans slowly impoverish themselves
to appease the goddess they are told is true."

Rhemnesia's anger rose, as it always did when she recanted
the tragic tale of Niobe. She held it in check to attend the stricken
child before her.

"Why do they hate the followers of the Great Mother so?"
Helen whispered.

"People often hate what they do not understand, not realizing that by so doing, they become despicable. The Theban priest
hated what he believed was dishonor and pride on the part of
the priestess Niobe. Yet in doing so, he brought the greatest dishonor upon himself: He became a murderer of innocent babes."
Rhemnesia forced herself to brighten, fearing the depressing tale
was overwhelming her student. "I suppose the priest told you
his tale in preparation for the Anthesteria festival," she said, as
cheerfully as she was able.

"Yes," Helen responded, her own disposition darkening.

Each moon, the normal routine of lessons and needlework
was interupted by festival, celebrating some aspect of the gods.
Helen previously welcomed these times, as they offered her
blessed relief from the unwanted attentions of her mother and

sister. Now she saw them as an intrusion upon her time with Rhemnesia. Her guardian was, as far as Helen knew, the only person in Sparta who absented herself during celebrations.

Rhemensia knew the reason for Helen's unhappiness and looked forward to the day when she could include the girl in her own rituals. But though she knew this to be an important part of Helen's education (and, truth be told, she looked forward to sharing the rituals of her home with another), she was wise enough to know the time was not yet. Even if Helen, as princess of Sparta, did not have to stand beside the king and queen during some of the more formal parts of the Olympian festivals, Leda would undoubtedly think her daughter too young to be beyond her mother's watchful eye at such times. Rhemnesia would have to settle for showing Helen the echo of the Goddess in the festival of the male gods.

"Like all festivals of the new gods, Anthesteria is based upon the celebrations of the Goddess," she explained, shifting her hands to rest more comfortably upon the earth. "Not long ago, people everywhere would gather to celebrate the coming warmth and ask Her blessing for the seeds they sowed. Food saved from the previous harvest was shared by all in appreciation for the year's bounty. By fully enjoying what has been given, She grants us more. When planting was concluded, the queen, who was also priestess, beckoned her consort and led the people in the fertility rites, the sacred marriage of sun and earth."

Although a princess, Helen grew up surrounded by animals kept by the palace. She was quite familiar of the joining of male and female and knew that offspring resulted from such unions. She remembered Anthesteria festivals past, when the adults went off into the groves beyond the farms and the children were led away by the elders. She never understood, nor had anyone bothered to explain to her, what had been transpiring. She reviewed her experience, searching for other similarities and differences with the spring rites of the Goddess.

"As you participate in Anthesteria, seek the distant echo of the Mother's rites," Rhemensia directed, as if reading Helen's thoughts.

Helen nodded. Perhaps by so doing, the festival would not be quite as onerous as she anticipated.

And so it was that she joined the other girls in waiting for her mother at sun's rise the following morning, her mind occupied with studying the celebration as her guardian suggested.

The distraction was almost sufficient to deflect Clytemnestra's nastiness.

"You look like one of the flute girls father hires for the men's dinners," her sister jeered, provoking supporting laughter from the clique of maidens who surrounded her.

Helen, not usually concerned with her clothing, looked down at the light blue shift her mother ordered her to wear and was aghast to see how the sheer material clung suggestively to her maturing body.

Without word to her sister or to Anaystana — the waiting woman Rhemensia assigned to watch the girls in her absence — Helen returned to her rooms and grabbed a cloak to place over her immodest garment.

Predictably, Leda had joined the girls in her absence. Upon Helen's return, her mother narrowed her eyes to show her annoyance at the delay before turning abruptly to lead the girls beyond the palace walls. *At least,* Helen thought, *she did not wonder why I am wearing a cloak in this weather.* She ignored Leda's disapproval and her sister's satisfied smirk and followed the women's group out-of-doors.

The most obvious difference between the Anthesteria festival of the new gods and the fertility rites described to her by Rhemnesia was that Anthesteria focused upon wine, rather than all foods given by the mother. Helen wondered if this was because wine was so important a part of Sparta's wealth or because the priests found it easier to incite the crowd to gratitude through its spirits.

The throng of people who surrounded them outside the palace walls certainly seemed grateful for the upcoming celebration. Helen took advantage of the press of the crowd to separate herself from the royal party. Her escape brought her beside a man whose sun-worn face marked him as a farmer.

"It's about time we tasted the fruit of them long hours in the field," he was complaining.

His wife jabbed an indelicate elbow in his side. "Hush now. It's for the priests and the king to decide when the festival begins. And the princess stands not three paces from you," she added in a voice unaccustomed to whispers.

The man's deep brown eyes locked with Helen's own. "Aye. She's just a child like any other."

Helen offered him her most grateful smile. *A child like any other*, she thought, pleased.

Pithoigia, or jar opening, began day one of the festival. In carefully orchestrated chaos, the populace brought clay vessels filled with wine from the vineyards scattered across the countryside. The king supervised the procession of wine to the temple, while the queen ushered royalty to the palace for washing and purification.

"All festivals of the Goddess begin with the purification," Rhemnesia once said. *"With Her water, we wash away doubts and fears and open ourselves to wisdom."* In this, it seemed, the festivals were similar.

"This must be the longest day of the year," the king grumbled when he returned home for his own washing.

"Ah, but we shall be well rewarded," a guardsman reminded him, his eyes in dreamy memory of festivals past. His thoughts were interupted by the sight of the princess who entered the palace before them. "Your Helen grows into a beautiful woman, even if she is a bit, uh, distant," he said.

"Beautiful women must keep their distance," the king responded with a wave of hand that dismissed both admiration and criticism.

When the sun at last descended beyond the mountains, the community gathered to the east of the temple, where they could impatiently view the rights. Helen stood to the right of her mother as custom demanded and watched as her father handed the first jug to the priest. She noticed a tall string of a man, garbed in the robes of an initiate, staring at her lustfully.

"The priests defile the holy gift of lovemaking by requiring that all their initiates remain celibate. Even the greatest priestess, who saves her life force for the oracles, does not remain chaste during the festival of Her gifts," Rhemnesia had said. *"It is one more way in which the Olympians separate themselves from nature."*

It seemed that the young initiate was not pleased by his own separation. Helen gave him a cold stare, which caused an unflattering shade of pink to color his cheeks as he momentarily averted his eyes. When he returned Helen's look, hostility was clear in his eyes. *Why does he look at me so?* Helen wondered. *I am not the one who made him take his senseless vows.* She shrugged off the question, returning her attention to the ceremony.

"We honor the gods first," the king intoned.

"And may they recognize your gift," the priest Glaucus replied. He stood behind a brick altar whitewashed with lime. The altar was abutted by a metal tablet upon which the sacred fire always burned. Glaucus splayed the wine across the altar's surface, causing the flames of the fire to burst forward dramatically. "The gods accept your gifts. Return to your homes to await celebration on the morrow."

The exhausted mass murmured its appreciation and sought their beds.

One needed to be well rested for Choes.

Choes — wine jugs — began at first light the next morning. One by one the members of the community returned to the temple to receive their wine-filled containers. The sun had reached its zenith before all the provisions were made. A trumpet signaled.

"Begin," the king commanded. Men and women and children dove into their jugs, each striving to be the first to finish their portion.

Silence was filled with a chorus of gulping.

"I've finished," came a cry from a grizzled old warrior whose throat had the most practice. He promptly fell across his table.

Helen sipped her wine carefully; though she wanted to celebrate her gratitude to the Goddess, she disliked the vulnerability she experienced when she drank too much. The others emptied their drinks enthusiastically then swayed to their homes to paint them with fresh pitch.

"Choes is a day of defilement," the priest had explained the previous night, while roping the entrance to his sanctuary. "Your irresponsible merrymaking must be balanced by industrious activity."

Rhemnesia had said nothing about celebration being irresponsible but the priest's tone hinted at unspeakable consequences if balance was not maintained.

Fresh pitch lined the front of the homes.

"Watch here!" the smith's wife yelled at her husband. "You've thrown a whole bucket through the doorway."

As the sun set once more, the partially pitched homes were gratefully abandoned and the disorderly populace, emptied jugs in hand, made its way back to the sanctuary.

"Just leave them outside," Glaucus said, failing to hide his panic that one of the drunken throng would enter his temple. From behind him, fourteen sober women carrying lit torches emerged.

The heat of the flames ignited in the eyes of the crowd.

Helen watched the women intently. This, Rhemnesia had taught, was the reenactment of the sacred marriage, when the consort would lie with the priestess to encourage the fertility of the land. Men and women left the children in the charge of the elders and followed the priestesses with inebriated dignity. Helen moved closer to get a better view of the procession and nearly collided with her sister.

"They're going to couple like animals," Clytemnestra giggled with drunken certainty.

A small girl, overhearing Clytemnestra's remarks, stared wide-eyed as she watched her mother walk to the woods with a man who was not her father.

Helen, annoyed by the vulgar interpretation and the effect on the young girl, turned on her sister. "They are not. They're reenacting the sacred marriage," she hissed.

"Same thing," Clytemnestra said in dismissal, and turned her bright eyes back to the procession.

Helen backed away, wanting distance between herself and Clytemnestra, and stood beside the wide-eyed girl and her older sister.

"Pardon princess," the younger girl said politely, pulling slightly on Helen's cloak. "But what *are* they doing?"

Helen looked down at the innocent brown eyes and up to frankly curious ones of her older sister. "They are paying homage to the Goddess," she responded, mustering a confidence she did not feel. "They celebrate the fertility granted us by the Earth Mother."

The little girl looked puzzled. "Which Goddess?"

"They are all one," Helen said, then quickly regretted her words. The tale of Niobe still haunted her thoughts. Not even Rhemnesia spoke openly against the priests in public!

But the younger girl did not seem startled and the older one nodded sagely. "I suppose this is true, though I doubt the priests would like us to say so," the older girl said, voicing Helen's thoughts.

The two girls shared a smile.

"My teacher speaks of such things all the time," Helen said, wanting to continue conversing with this girl who looked to be about her age. Then, impulsively, she grabbed the girl's hand. "You could study with me," she said quickly.

The girl started but did not pull away. "I help mother in the fields all day," she explained and Helen's heart sank. "But I do get a break at sun's peak for a small meal. Can I bring a friend?"

Helen could not remember feeling such happiness. Friends. Maybe they would be friends with her too.

She told the girl to meet her at the tree behind the palace grounds. "There's a break in the garrison wall that you can slip through." She did not want them to enter the palace and pass by Clytemnestra and her friends on their way. Clytemnestra, she was quite sure, would steal the girls for her own group.

"We'll see you the day after festival then," the girl said and grabbed her sister's hand to return home.

Only after did Helen realize she did not know the girl's name. Nor, she thought belatedly, was she certain that Rhemnesia would agree to sharing time with common folk. She thought again about the prospect of her own friends. No matter what the girl's name was or what Rhemnesia thought, she would study with these girls, she decided. She could not wait for festival to end.

The final day of festival was overlong for all the participants. The tentative populace made its way to the open field where cauldrons were already lit by luckless servants. Each family contributed its share of grain to be boiled in oil and honey. The sun rose too early and pierced the eyes of the wine-headed crowd.

Chytroi, or pots, offered the first meal following the spirit's defilement. The community gathered to digest their new beginning. Food burned fog from the brain. Children were the first to recover.

"Let's go," Clytemnestra said, leading her peers to the swings set up for the occasion.

Helen looked on enviously but then remembered her own engagement scheduled for the following day and smiled. She joined the others who watched the young people contest to see who could sway highest. Wine had cleansed the blood; the movement of life prevailed and, fortunately, the day soon ended.

CHAPTER THREE

The following day, Parthenope and a young maiden named Melite, joined Helen and Rhemnesia beneath the olive tree. Helen had postponed telling her guardian of their anticipated arrival for fear that Rhemnesia would forbid it. She was delighted when the woman embraced the young girls as if expecting their presence all along.

It was not long before word of the meetings spread and the branches of the great olive tree shaded twelve young girls from the heat of the burning sun.

"Sound is the air that is Her breath, joining all Her creatures. Close your eyes and listen. Listen beyond the flow of the river, the sway of the breeze upon the leaves, the rhythm of your individual breath. Hear only the voice that joins all in the one song, the uni-verse."

Helen joined the others in closing her eyes and trying to do what Rhemnesia instructed. Her unruly mind would not obey, insisting upon identifying the song as coming from the gathering birds or from the distant rustle of a cloak as a maiden shifted at the far end of the circle.

"Focus upon the breath that connects all," Rhemnesia said again.

Helen's body began to relax and she no longer listened diligently to her mind's rattling. Slowly, the sounds around her began to blur, becoming a continuous song that flowed from within Helen's own body to those around her, to the tree, the birds, the water, the sage grass. She felt herself expand until she thought she would burst with the air of the world.

Helen opened her eyes and met those of Parthenope, seeing her own wonder reflected in the eyes of her friend.

Parthenope smiled and Helen reached her hands to the girl she first met at the Olympian festival.

"I did not hear anything different," complained Henioche, a younger girl with riotous brown curls. Helen and Parthenope moved toward her and enveloped her in a generous hug.

"Practice. Practice brings to awareness that which has been forgotten," Rhemnesia reminded them. The girls began hugging each other, recognizing the familiar words as the end of their lesson.

Helen watched wistfully as her friends departed to return to their labors. Rhemnesia moved beside her. "We too must go to our work," she said.

Helen made a face. "How I wish our work did not involve endless sewing within walls with my stupid sister and her friends."

"Your sister is also part of the one song," Rhemnesia reminded her.

Helen's grimace deepened. "It would be easier for me to seek communion with the river toads than with Clytemnestra."

"Remember, you must embrace that which you despise. Otherwise it will forever remain a barrier between you and She who created all."

Helen nodded, secretly thinking that there were some things even Rhemnesia did not understand.

⌘

The maidens flowed passed him, unseeing, and Kalchas was able to regain his vantage point in time to see the princess nod to her teacher.

Corrupter of youth! Godless heathen!

The cries screamed through Kalchas' cluttered brain as he watched the princess bow her head to the older woman. His large lips pulled upward in a distasteful sneer that further accentuated his beaked nose and bulging eyes and added even more lines to the permanent creases of his forehead.

He watched as the princess and the woman turned to the palace, wishing (not for the first time) that his place of observation allowed him to hear more than a few tantalizing words cast his way on the summer wind.

Not that the initiate needed to hear what was actually said. A few discreet inquiries here and there and (he told himself) instruction from the gods, informed him of all he needed to know:

The seemingly harmless group of maidens came to worship the very deity his gods were determined to destroy.

It was his role, his destiny (so he told himself) to stop them. Then, then...

Kalchas knew he was destined for greatness. Why else would he have been born third son among handsome brothers to a struggling wool merchant and his wife rather than within the opulence of a palace? For what other reason was he tormented by those same brothers, large, beautiful boys next to whom he seemed a pathetic, drowned cat? And why else would his very existence be ignored by the father his brothers resembled and barely tolerated by the mother who bore him.

"You must be nicer to them," his mother had said when he complained, her attention quickly returned to the girl child she birthed almost immediately after thrusting Kalchas from the womb.

Nicer? He needed to be no such thing. He needed a place where his ample talents could shine and where his great worth was recognized.

After considering soldiering and pirating and thievery (all of which posed too great a risk to his special person), Kalchas was led (so he told himself) to the temple of Artemis.

Even within its precincts, the gods challenged him. The chief priest Glaucus and the elders did not immediately recognize his gifts and set him to the mundane tasks undertaken by common novices. *If only I had a vision*, Kalchas told himself as he had many times before. The thought brought him abruptly back to what he had seen beneath the great olive tree. The heathen woman had led the girls in a trance. Even from the distance Kalchas was forced to keep, he had seen the princess rise and take the hands of the tall, dark-haired farm girl. The look on her face had been wondrous.

She had a vision! Kalchas suddenly realized, momentarily humbled by the greatness he participated in from afar. Humility quickly changed to outrage. She had a vision! She, a mere girl, a simple princess and a follower of the dead Goddess had a vision, while Kalchas, a priest (soon to be) and destined for greatness (soon to be recognized) had not.

His anger moved him from the rock behind which he hid and his feet kicked at the dry sage grass that tumbled before him. A vision! She had a vision! His feet kept time with his litany, casting up balls of dust from the dry earth. She had a vision!

Mocking laughter floated through the clouds of dirt he created. Kalchas stopped to see two old women, carrying jugs filled with water from the nearby river. After attracting his attention, they continued past him, amused smiles beaming from their wrinkled faces.

Suffering this new humiliation, Kalchas' frustration rose, and with it, suspicion grew. Women. The old women shared their smile. The Goddess shared Her vision with a girl princess. His mother shared the love she denied him with his sister. Women. Women stuck together, sharing secrets with one another that they would utter to no man. And he was pledged to a woman!

Kalchas' breathing slowed to normal as this new information came to him. Artemis was a woman. Of course she would not share a vision with him — a mere man to her eyes — no matter what his greatness. It became incredibly clear, as if the hands of the gods led him directly to what he needed to know. He needed to demonstrate his worth. Without visions. For now. Then, when his greatness was realized, the temple priests would fund his travels to a temple of a god — Apollo perhaps — and Kalchas would have his visions.

He thought again of the heathen women beneath the ugly old olive tree and stomped his way back to the temple to see Glaucus.

The temple Artemis Orthia stood between visiting ships arriving at port Gythium and the palace. The huntress goddess was believed to provide protection from guests who were less than friendly. *She would have to. The humble temple*, Kalchas thought in disdain, *would not intimidate a sheep herder.* Placed upon a foundation of stone, its baked mud bricks formed columns that supported an open porch and the walls to the cella chamber. Its roof face was ornamented with an artist's vision (that word again!) of Artemis' head.

To one side of the temple were the even humbler quarters of the women and men dedicated to its service. To the other, was the building that housed the temple elders and, standing alone, the residence of its chief priest.

Kalchas hastily made his way to the last, taking advantage of its slightly ajar door to gain audience.

He found Glaucus seated behind a wooden desk, his ample features in peaceful repose as he studied a scroll. Glaucus looked up and smiled benevolently at his initiate; his effort was lost on his agitated guest.

"There are over ten of them now!" Kalchas blurted. "Ten girls gathered about that heathen woman listening to lies about the dead Goddess!"

Glaucus noted his initiate's blazing eyes and dirt smeared cloak and felt a disharmonious ache in his stomach. "Do sit down,

Kalchas, and speak normally. You're making my head itch."

Kalchas reluctantly grabbed a stool and perched upon it. "Over ten of them," he said again. "I tell you, they are plotting to overtake the new gods!"

Glaucus' eyes regarded Kalchas levelly, making the initiate distinctly uncomfortable.

"How is it you know this?" the priest asked.

A guilty flush spread across Kalchas features. "The gods have shown me," he insisted.

Glaucus reminded himself that temple worship flourished because of young zealots like Kalchas. He hid a sigh as he also reminded himself of his responsibility to ensure that such passion was well directed.

"The Goddess has been worshipped from the beginning of time and yet the Olympians have still successfully won the hearts of the Greek people. If She was going to avenge Herself, I daresay She would have done so before now."

"But she is doing so. Can't you see! And that heathen woman is her vehicle!"

"I find it hard to believe that ten young girls pose much of a threat to our temple," Glaucus responded.

The initiate's eyes widened with outrage that lifted him from his seat. "Today it is ten. By tomorrow it will be more! We must silence them."

"No matter how many there are — and please do sit down Kalchas — I trust that they will come to the feet of the gods as their parents have done before them. It is by education, not tyranny, that the truth is known."

"So you say," Kalchas retorted. "And yet even in this very temple we compromise truth. Artemis is our patron and yet we lend her temple to any minor nature deity who wants to borrow it. And even her own festivals are compromised. Once, this was the temple where boys came to be men after they were flogged by the cutting leaves of the orthia to prove their strength. Some would argue that the ceremony is now no more than a token, a mockery where boys are lightly stroked, their manhood assured."

The fanatical look in Kalchas eyes' told Glaucus who the "complainers" were. His patience was diminishing.

"Some would say, quite accurately" he responded, holding anger in check, "that the ceremony to which you refer is an adaptation of an earlier heathen time when boys were lashed with the orthia and their flesh thrown into the fire as sacrifice!"

Kalchas' eyes gleamed brighter and the ache in Glaucus' belly grew. "Kalchas," the priest began again, keeping his voice level, "your concern for the temple's influence is admirable. And perhaps there is some truth to what you say. We have focused our instruction upon the nobles but have ignored the common folk. Is it any wonder that these children turn to those who value them?" He let an official note creep into his voice. "I put you in charge of arranging educational forms for all of Sparta's youngsters. I myself will speak to the royal family and request the princess and her entourage attend." *Perhaps by teaching you too will learn*, Glaucus thought, hoping this would be so.

Kalchas replayed the priest's words in his head to ensure he heard the him correctly. Him? Teach the common folk? Any additional duties to his already belabored schedule was, as far as he was concerned, a poor solution. And to teach commoners? How appalling!

But as he reviewed Glaucus' words, another thought struck him. The priest said he would ask the children of the royal house to attend. If Kalchas taught such classes, his unquestioned intelligence would be recognized and his presence would become a familiar, trusted one in the palace. Technically, priests were chosen from among the temple elders in conference with the goddess. In fact, the elders were often influenced by the preference of the royals. If he provided a proper education for the members of the palace, perhaps he could win the king's support. Glaucus was old, after all, and could not live forever. And if Kalchas was chief priest, no one would question his funding of his own travels...perhaps to a temple of Apollo.

He realized that Glaucus still awaited his reply. "As always, I am servant to my priest and the goddess I serve," he said quickly and rose to take his leave.

Glaucus watched him depart and decided the ache in his belly had grown too large to continue his reading.

Clytemnestra walked alone — a not altogether pleasant experience for one accustomed to being at the center of others, but the only way she could think of to undermine her sister. She had snuck away when it was time to return to the women's quarters, easily moving past the dozing Astyanassa, whom Rhemensia had successfully petitioned to assist her in watching the palace maidens. Leda, she was certain, was unaware that Rhemensia had placed Astyanassa in charge of Clytemnestra and the others, while the supposed guardian went off with Helen and her unsanctioned friends. No matter: Rhemensia would be called to task for Clytemnestra's disappearance. And if Rhemensia was undermined, so too would Helen be.

Helen.

Clytemnestra walked passed the two-story homes where merchants shouted to one another from their shops and onto the dirt road that separated the farms. Once or twice, a farm hand would raise his head as she passed, but the work before him and the unrelenting summer's heat kept his curiosity to a minimum. Clytemnestra did not mind their lack of attention; she needed time to figure out what to do with Helen.

From her earliest memories, Clytemnestra found her sister an insufferable inconvenience. Royal guests, visiting dignitaries, even waiting women would look over the children with the sweet, distracted faces adults always assumed when confronted with the children of their hosts.

Until their eyes found Helen and polite smiles turned to genuine awe.

"My, but isn't she the most beautiful baby born!"

"Look at those perfect cheekbones," or nose or hair or toes.

"Why, she has got to be the most special child I've ever seen!"

From the earliest time, Helen turned Clytemnestra's stomach.

Leda's rapture with her first daughter sickened Clytemnestra most. Leda decided her beautiful daughter was the child of a god or some other such nonsense. This absurdity led to the only time Clytemnestra agreed with Rhemnesia.

"How could a god have possibly caused you to conceive one child without seeding you with the other three as well?" she had overheard an exasperated Rhemnesia demand.

Her mother's eyes took on the characteristic dreamy look she affected whenever she discussed Helen. "Just look at her."

Rhemensia had withdrew, disgusted. Clytemnestra had done the same from her hiding place.

Something unacknowledged rendered Clytemnestra unable to direct her hurt and anger toward her mother; it was much easier to launch her resentments at her sister.

She began by taunting Helen mercilessly, tugging and pulling and tripping her until Leda reproved her perfect darling for her clumsiness. This proved quite effective until Helen had grown unexpectedly larger than her twin; Clytemnestra's spine still ached when she remembered Helen pushing her upon it. Her next approach — taking charge of the other maidens and alienating Helen completely — had been simple. The growing girls, already jealous of Helen's charms, were more than willing to exclude the beautiful girl from their games. Helen was forced to go off by herself, alone, isolated. It was the perfect punishment as far as Clytemnestra was concerned; her sister was the center of attention in far too many circles.

Clytemnestra's efforts proved most successful, until Rhemnesia spoiled them. The woman to whom everyone deferred, despite her obscure origins, had always taken a special interest in Helen. It was bad enough when Rhemnesia called Leda to task for her unreasonable treatment of her child, worse when she became thoroughly disgusted with their mother and began mothering Helen herself. But now she arranged for the common maidens to come, surrounding Clytemnestra's twin in loving adoration once more. And, perhaps most horrid of all, Clytemnestra's own carefully cultivated group now wanted to join the informal teaching circle that surrounded her sister.

It was intolerable. Clytemnestra's scathing disdain for the discussions of her sister's group was loosing its power over her peers.

It was time for more drastic action. She thought of going to Leda and informing her that her daughter was cavorting with commoners. But Leda would probably think it wonderful — as she did everything Helen was involved in — and authorize Rhemensia to serve refreshments. She considered approaching her father. But the king was never about and made an unspoken agreement not to be involved with the lives of his female children; he'd probably just refer her back to Leda anyway. No, her parents were not the solution.

If only I could get rid of Rhemnesia, she thought.

Her concentration kept her from seeing the figure hurrying from the temple until she was upon him.

"Watch where you're headed," the man growled.

Clytemnestra looked up, ready to supply an angry retort. The man saved her the trouble. Recognition and something Clytemnestra did not immediately identify as ambition spread over his face.

"Forgive me, princess. I just left conference with the high priest and I was deep in thought," he said hastily.

His manner was not as obsequious as Clytemnestra would have liked; certainly a mere initiate, as his dark gray robe proclaimed him to be, should demonstrate more respect. "I too was deep in thought," she said haughtily. "But you don't hear me offering it as an excuse."

Surprise at being spoken to by one so young was evident on Kalchas' face, pleasing Clytemnestra immensely.

Kalchas did not share her pleasure. Moments earlier he was

pondering the advantages of currying royal favor and now he found himself exchanging words with a royal brat.

He feigned his most polite tone. "Please do not take offense princess. You and I will, after all, be seeing a great deal more of each other when I begin instruction about the true gods."

Clytemnestra had little interest in the gods and even less in seeing this initiate on a regular basis.

"I do believe you are mistaken," she said, matching his tone. "We already receive instruction from the chief priest before the festivals." She moved to pass him and end this meaningless discussion.

Kalchas had the temerity to block her path. "It seems there is need for that instruction to be expanded — and not to just to yourself and the other royal maidens but also to all Sparta's young people." A fanatical light shone from his eyes. "It has come to me that some of the younger girls are being led astray and falling to the ways of the dead Goddess. But I shall set them right. I shall save them from their folly!"

Clytemnestra wanted nothing more than to get out of this madman's presence. Still, his words stopped her. "You would, perhaps, be referring to the lessons offered to my sister and some of the common maidens by the woman Rhemnesia?"

The fanatical light burned brighter. "That heathen will be exposed for what she is."

Clytemnestra regarded Kalchas thoughtfully. "You are a fool," she said at last.

Kalchas, who knew himself to be no such thing, paled.

"The only way to triumph over Rhemnesia is to get rid of her." Clytemnestra continued. "Always her influence has been great, though I can't imagine why."

"Then I will get rid of her!" Kalchas pronounced.

"And how would you propose to do that?" Clytemnestra asked with false sweetness.

Kalchas mind worked furiously, tripping over the tangled possibilities. At last, a plan emerged.

"Brilliant," he said aloud.

Clytemnestra arched a skeptical brow.

"The woman is in charge of the palace maidens, correct? Well, perhaps she can be proved incompetent in her duties in such a way that the king cannot ignore."

Clytemnestra's skepticism turned to genuine interest and Kalchas went on to detail his plan.

Let her know that I am inspired by the gods, Kalchas thought. *Let them all know.*

CHAPTER FOUR

Helen was happy. Every day, it seemed, her perceptions expanded under Rhemnesia's teaching. She heard the one-song with greater frequency and saw the continuous pattern of life which flowed beyond the sunlight and shadow and touched all things. The phases of the moon echoed the tide of emotions in her body, filling her, peaking in brilliant ecstasy, quieting in darkened reflection.

As she grew, so too did the circle of girls she learned to call friends, and especially her connection to Parthenope. Petite, with the sun-kissed skin of a farmer's daughter, straight brown hair, dark eyes and a ready smile, Parthenope was as opposite Helen as any of the girls present. And yet from their first meeting, their spirits entwined as the sisters they were in the eyes of the Goddess.

Helen sat beside her friend at each of Rhemnesia's lessons and ran off with her during every festival.

Parthenope is my true sister, she told herself again and again. The pain of her relationship with her sister by birth slowly ebbed away. With Parthenope, she could share everything.

So it was Parthenope whom she sought when her woman's courses began, despite her fear that she would be rejected for being different from her peers once more.

"Why, now I'll have someone I can really talk to when my time comes," Parthenope whispered, hugging Helen warmly and assailing any doubts the princess had of losing her friend.

Parthenope's reaction had made her mother's significantly more bearable.

"It's so soon!" Charisia the midwife exclaimed.

Her mother lifted a knowing brow. "Helen's different."

The sense of belonging she attained within her new circle of friends almost compensated for her mother's peculiar response.

As was the custom under the Olympian gods, Helen was secluded in the guest chamber for the duration of her first woman's cycle and was not permitted to wash. Food was left outside her doors at regular intervals.

She spent her days watching the sun's light rise and fall on the square patterns that lined the walls and listening to the shouts of her sister and Clytemnestra's peers, which rose on broken waves from the courtyard below.

If I was not so different, I would mature with the other girls. Perhaps one of them would even be in the room beside mine, she thought miserably. When she felt despondency begin to overtake her, she would remember Rhemnesia's promise.

"It would be unwise to disobey the rites of your mother," her guardian had said. "But when you have completed their doleful ritual, we will celebrate your womanhood in the manner of She who gives such gifts."

Rhemnesia explained that the isolation ritual was another way the priests of the new gods sought to undermine a power they did not understand. "They fear the power of creation that flows through women. Rather than face that fear, they have proclaimed first blood to be unclean and have decided that a woman experiencing her first courses must remain isolated lest she corrupt others."

The rites of first blood celebrated in the name of the Goddess were a marked contrast.

"A woman honored by first blood is helped undress by her peers and then taken to the river so she can add her blood to the flow of life. When she steps from the river, she is clothed in garments made by the hands of her friends to signify her elevated status. A small feast ensues, in which all celebrate, as this is one of the greatest mysteries of life."

Thoughts of the beautiful ritual kept Helen sane during the lonely days of her courses and carried her to the last day of her confinement. At last, a knock rang at the door, indicating the end of her isolation. Helen rose sluggishly from the bed upon which she spent most of her days. She opened the door to find her mother, accompanied by Charisia and several women carrying washing bowls. She hid her disappointment that Rhemnesia was not present — reminding herself that her guardian never participated in the rituals of the new gods — and allowed the women to bathe her under her mother's direction.

When her body had been cleansed and adorned in a chiton of soft linen, she was led from the room, carried along by a tide of women whose ranks swelled as they made their way through the palace. Guards and warriors averted their eyes as the women passed; under the dictates of the new gods, men had no part in this mystery.

Fresh air welcomed Helen as she stepped out of the doors and followed the female crowd to the temple. Merchant wives and even some women from the farms stopped their work to join the procession. The mob reached the entrance of the temple and Leda appropriated a dove from a young attendant, handing it to her daughter. The bird flapped angrily in Helen's hand. *We share in blood spilled to the Goddess*, she whispered, running a finger along the creature's delicate chest. Its wings quieted in agreement to the sacrifice.

By previous arrangement, the male servants of the temple had absented themselves, leaving the women priestesses to conduct the rites. Helen looked to a tall woman dressed in deep blue. Her eyes sparkled with a light Helen associated with the Goddess; Helen wondered how the woman felt serving the male gods. She pulled her awareness back to the task at hand, murmuring a prayer of thanks to the bird she held, before drawing a knife across its throat. Blood washed her hands. Helen felt herself expand, connecting again with the one-song. *"Why, She is in the ceremony of the new gods as well,"* she thought, amazed at this surprising revelation. *I must speak with Rhemnesia.* She wiped her hands hastily on the cloth offered her and joined the women returning to the palace.

"Is Rhemnesia within her chambers?" she asked her mother, preparing to run ahead of the group and join her mentor.

Her mother's unexpected look of embarrassment stopped her. "She has gone," Leda said, turning to begin the walk back to the palace.

Gone? Where could she have possibly gone?

Helen moved into her mother's path. "Where has she gone?" Her voice rose with the beginnings of panic, drawing curious looks from several of the women beside them.

Leda gave a furtive glance at the crowd. "Rhemnesia has left us. She has failed in her duties. We will speak of this no more," she said, summoning the authority of the queen. Her royal power did nothing to shield her from the shock that flushed her daughter's beautiful features. *My god child!* she thought. Unable to bear her daughter's pain, she moved passed her and hurried to the palace.

Helen was frozen in place. Rhemnesia gone? She stared unseeing as the crowd moved passed her until her eyes rested upon the face of her sister.

Clytemnestra's mouth was stretched in a malicious smile.

Helen did move then, running away from her pain and the sister she was certain was its cause. *It is too much,* she thought, heading thoughtlessly to the great olive tree that had shaded her happiness. Tears streamed down her face as pains past and present joined to ring her heart. Rhemnesia. Her guardian. Her teacher. Her friend. Gone. Her sobs intensified as she sat alone beneath the great tree. *The maidens will not come now. They have no reason to come now that Rhemnesia is gone.* Better that she had remained lonely than be left alone after finding friendship.

"It's time for your real woman's ceremony," Parthenope's gentle voice called from behind her.

Helen turned and looked into the faces of the maidens she had come to think of as friends, all smiling at her now in warm sympathy.

"Come," Parthenope said, extending her hand to help Helen rise. The remaining girls fanned about her like a guard of honor.

Helen's tears began anew as she walked with the girls to the marshy grass at the river's edge.

This time she felt joy mix with her pain.

The group stopped uncertainly before the running water.

"We must help her undress," Parthenope said, assuming command despite the fact that she did not know how to proceed any more than the others. The maidens, relieved to have someone to follow, began to gently undress their princess, allowing their hands to linger upon the smooth stones of her girdle and the soft linen of her chiton. A collective gasp of awe issued from the group when she stood naked before them.

"You'll grow into womanhood much the same," she said defensively.

"Not likely," Parthenope responded dryly.

One of the maidens giggled, followed by a second. Helen looked to Parthenope's laughing eyes and answered in kind, feeling fear and pain drain from her body. She assisted the others to undress and ran with them to the cool water, where they splashed each other mercilessly.

"Enough," Parthenope yelled, her face assuming the mask of solemnity she thought the occasion demanded. "Kneel," she said to Helen, who did so without thinking. "Helen of Sparta, today you are a woman in the eyes of the Goddess. Open to Her wisdom," She leaned down and grabbed a fist of water, which she allowed to trickle upon Helen's head. The others repeated her gesture.

When the last had performed the act, Helen stood and once again saw awe in their eyes. This time she did not reprimand them, knowing the same was in her own.

Silently they left the cool water and pulled some of the marsh reeds to dry themselves.

As they dressed, Helen turned to Parthenope. "How did you know what to do?"

A flicker of mischief passed over her friend's generous mouth. "I made it up."

The giggling started again, carrying them back to their resting place. Helen noticed that they left Rhemnesia's place vacant and became serious once more.

"What happened to her?"

The girls looked to Parthenope, who had become their unspoken leader, to answer. She shrugged. "They say she allowed one of the palace maidens — Phoebe, I think it was — to couple with the princes."

"How could they possibly prove that?" Helen asked, thinking quickly. If she could argue against the vicious rumor, perhaps she could bring Rhemnesia back. Her hopes crashed with Parthenope's next words.

"It is no rumor. The king found Phoebe with your brothers in the stables. Apparently, he happened upon them when walking with an initiate of the temple — Kalchas is his name. The king was angry, of course, but the initiate was outraged. From what I hear, he raved about the king's reputation, and said no visiting royalty would leave their daughters in his care or some such nonsense. Kalchas insisted that the king demonstrate his concern for the girls under his roof by sending both Phoebe and her guardian — Rhemnesia — away. I suppose the king felt he had no choice."

She shrugged again but her nonchalance did not hide the pain that etched her taunt features.

"Would that the king and that stupid initiate been elsewhere that morning," a girl named Laothoe said, tossing a handful of stones to the base of the great tree.

Helen's mind saw her sister's malevolent smile once more.

"Clytemnestra," she whispered aloud.

The girls about her looked puzzled.

Parthenope eyed her intently. "She does seem to enjoy Kalchas' lectures," her friend said at last.

"What lectures?"

"Apparently, Kalchas decided we commoners worthy of instruction with royalty," Parthenope answered sarcastically. "He's begun classes for all the young people in the countryside — dull lessons about the Olympian gods. We're supposed to be there now." She continued, answering the unasked question she saw on Helen's face. "He has spoken to our families, virtually ordering our attendance."

Anger replaced Helen's puzzlement. "Kalchas and the priests might influence the king but they don't yet overrule a request from the palace." She stood, knowing they needed to return to their farms. "Go to Kalchas' meeting tomorrow," she said decisively. "I'll fetch you there."

A small smile lit Parthenope's lips, eliciting a similar response from those around her. When they left, Helen turned and stormed into the palace.

Clytemnestra. Helen's mind filled with satisfying visions of strangling her sister with her long auburn braids. Her sister would have arranged a meeting between Phoebe and her brothers and then somehow had the initiate lead the king to the stables at the most opportune moment. How in the world Clytemnestra became cohorts with a temple priest Helen could not imagine. She put nothing past her sister; Clytemnestra would do anything to ruin her happiness.

Not this time, Helen vowed. *Not again.*

Once more the messenger waved away the young priestess who would offer him water and wine. Whereas before, impatience and obedience to his employer prevented his accepting the proffered hospitality, now his own nervousness did so.

As during previous visits, a second priestess came immediately forward to escort him to the lady's chambers.

Messengers are sacred to the gods, Aeslop reminded himself. Even if the woman was angered by what he said, she would not berate him for it. His anxiety reminded him that he was not, in fact, a messenger.

Nor, he thought glumly, was he very successful in the profession to which he was trained. Despite his father's diligent and often abusive instructions, Aeslop could not breed and train the horses that were his family's legacy. The great beasts — with their powerful muscles and large nostrils and hoofs of stone — terrified him. The animals instinctively knew of his fear and did not hesitate to bite at his arms, his hands and his clothing whenever he came near. Aeslop fancied them laughing at him when he turned his back.

He fancied his wife doing the same, hers the bitter laughter of a woman who had married into wealth only to watch it flow away within a few short seasons. She had married Aeslop for his charming smile and the strength of his position. The former no longer moved her and the latter was fast becoming a lie. Aeslop believed himself doomed to a life of endless nagging until the day a woman from the royal palace had knocked upon his humble door and requested his service. Soft of voice and gentle in manners, she explained that she needed someone trustworthy to deliver messages to Troezen from time to time. She would pay handsomely, she said, to any man who would do so in complete secrecy. The job suited Aeslop perfectly, allowing him much needed escapes from both wife and horses, while providing wealth to keep his demanding woman sweet. Beside that, the woman who visited him had the most uncanny black eyes; he felt she was commanding his very spirit.

He accepted the position happily.

Now it was threatened by the message he was about to deliver, which his own honor, rather than gain, demanded. He was escorted to the room in which the beautiful lady sat, her auburn hair flaming about her delicate face, her piercing gray-green eyes regarding him levelly.

It occurred to Aeslop that he should have prepared a message before coming before her. He licked the salty moisture that beaded on his upper lip. "I have no message," he blurted, then stopped to regain his composure. "The lady Rhemnesia has been banished from the palace."

The woman nodded as if he was merely confirming what she already knew. He wondered if she had other messengers upon whom she relied — messengers (probably horse riders) who were quicker than he. The thought irritated him greatly and his nervousness was replaced by a desire to prove his worth to the woman whose name he did not know.

"They say she allowed a young woman in her charge to become corrupted by one of the king's sons," he said, rightly presuming she already knew this. "It is rather hypocritical, if you ask me," he continued quickly when it looked as if she would dismiss him. "In another moon, the young woman could do what she wished and the priests would forgive her action as part of Kronia."

The woman leaned slightly forward. "Kronia?"

Aeslop smiled his charming smile. *The are some things only I think to tell you*, he thought, proud of his cunning. "Kronia is the festival in which men and women relive their mania. All the lustful deeds of the year are re-enacted — to a reasonable degree — and then the priest says his blessing and offers atonement. During the nine days of atonement, no coupling is permitted, no fighting may occur and all battling ceases. But before..." he left off with a careless shrug of his hands.

The woman sat back once more and considered Aeslop's words silently. "What happens if Sparta is attacked during those nine days?" she asked finally.

"Gestures of peace would be made. Of course, if a full army were to attack the people, the soldiers of Sparta would have no choice but to break Kronia and defend the populace," he added, suddenly suspicious.

"Of course," she said mildly and smiled.

Aeslop relaxed. *She is only a woman, after all.*

"You have done very well," the woman continued. "You have demonstrated sound judgment in coming here when not explicitly directed. If it would please you, I'd like you to continue in my service, reporting anything you believe might be to my interest. You will, of course, be compensated."

Aeslop beamed. *I bet she didn't offer that to the others.*

The woman bowed her head in dismissal. As he walked beyond the chamber doors, Aeslop heard her familiar words echo in the empty room: "So it must be."

Kronia, the Olympian priests said, was the festival of balance. For nine days and nine nights, the populace took a blessed respite from working in the heat of the summer sun to re-enact their excesses and then atone them.

The former was especially embraced.

Youth and young girls gathered in erotic and intricate dances. Warriors participated in mock battles. Merchants argued vehemently with their customers. Slaves stole from their employers. Tempers flared. Greed flamed. Lust exploded.

Kronia would atone all.

Helen walked to the group of spectators who ringed the arena, seeking her friends. She watched as contestants bursting with life lined up to join the sword play and javelin throws and archery contests. Two men of equally large size broke from their assigned places and began a heated wrestling match in the small space available to them.

No one protested as muscles danced and limbs tangled and

dust rose in choking clouds.

Everyone understood mania.

A second, small group moved from the line and began a slightly more organized boxing tournament. Helen continued to seek Parthenope in the crowd; her attention shifted when her brother Polydeuces joined the boxers, surprising her. Except at formal occasions when the women joined the men for meals, Helen had not seen Polydeuces since he left the women's quarters to be raised among the men. She remembered him as a gentle boy, quick to cry and eager to avoid confrontation. She wondered why he chose to enter this particularly aggressive contest. She saw the king across the circle, clearly wondering the same thing. Her father stepped forward to intervene but was stopped when her mother placed a delicate hand upon his arm, restraining him.

Tyndareus need not have worried about his son's safety.

Polydeuces quickly triumphed over youth and men, striking them with a viciousness that exemplified mania at its best. The spectators' breath grew louder, their eyes glowed with primal appreciation. Helen's heart kept beat with each blow, her blood raced through each limb of her body, her fists balled. The familiar expansiveness of her meditations on the Goddess stole over her, laced with a violence she had not felt before. *Is this too, then, an aspect of the Goddess?* Her heart ached with the desire to ask the guardian who was with her no more.

Despite Rhemnesia's absence, Helen had fetched her friends from Kalchas' lessons the day after her woman's ceremony. She derived great satisfaction from the shock that registered on the faces of her sister and her initiate consort. It was almost as satisfying as seeing the forlorn looks of Clytemnestra's own group as Helen and her friends took their leave. Apparently, Kalchas' educational sessions were not a success.

She and her friends resumed their lessons under the olive tree, practicing the exercises Rhemnesia had taught them and studying nature for clues as to what more they should learn. Their teacher's absence was sorely felt, however, and there were many frustrating days when the informal lessons raised more questions than granted enlightenment. No one was more frustrated than Helen.

One more unanswered question, she thought, breathing deeply until her normal awareness returned. She looked up and saw Polydeuces doing likewise as Castor threw his arms around his brother, stopping him from killing the man he had long since downed.

Mania. Is this too of the Goddess?

The low note of a horn chilled heated blood and beckoned

the crowd forward.

The priest Glaucus waited — at a distance — for his populace to gather around the naked boys who lined the dromos. When the people stilled to the limited extent he knew was the best he could expect, he stepped forward, clasping the arm of young man weighted by fillets of wool.

"You have agreed to be chased by your fellow runners for the length of the dromos," he said, addressing the youth in a ringing voice that carried to the crowd. "If they catch you, we will expect good for the city, in accordance with local tradition. Run to Eileithyia."

As Kalchas had complained, the goddess Artemis often shared her sanctuary with minor deities, as the festivals dictated. Glaucus thought this fitting, for the gods as he knew them were generous. It was only right that the virgin huntress to whom he pledged loyalty would offer her place of worship to Eileithyia, the deity who represented the new life that would be granted to those who repented their year's mania. Not that Eileithyia's presence was anything but symbolic. Hindered by his garments, the runner did not get anywhere near the temple before he was swarmed by a mob of his peers, ensuring the year's prosperity.

The crowd cheered as if the outcome of the race was not anticipated.

Glaucus' smile beamed satisfaction. "The gods will accept your repentance. Go now and reflect upon your ways." The populace let loose a collective sigh of relief and scattered peacefully. Only the initiate Kalchas, standing beside the chief priest, scowled. *Perhaps*, Helen thought viciously, *the initiate resents having to atone his ways.*

She turned with the others to walk in solitude and begin the days marked for inner reflection. Atonement. During Kronia, all excesses of the previous year were forgiven, the priests taught. For once Helen did not require Rhemnesia's presence to know how her guardian would respond. *Every individual must face the consequences of her own actions and decide for herself whether her deeds align with the will of her spirit. Forgiveness lies only within the self and only when one changes her future actions to fit her new understanding.*

The priests of the new gods would, undoubtedly, scoff at Rhemnesia's beliefs. Some acts, they said, were wrong, regardless of the individual's will or intention. It was these actions that needed to be atoned and then forgiven by the gods who had such power. The gods were, to say the least, quite generous in their forgiveness. A man who killed another, abducted a wife or stole the goods of his employer was completely absolved during

Kronia.

Helen stopped suddenly, causing a young boy who had been walking behind her to collide with her back. She turned and met his startled face with a silent smile of apology that seemed to shock him further. She moved passed him, making her way quickly to the temple. By their own rules, the priests would have to atone Phoebe on this day. And in granting absolution to the girl, they would have to atone Rhemnesia as well. She ran the last several paces to the priest's quarters, oblivious to the curious stares that followed in her wake, and stopped before the humble brick building she knew to be Glaucus'.

As always, the priest's door was slightly ajar in welcome to any who sought his counsel. Helen took a deep, calming breath and scratched respectfully upon the door before entering.

Glaucus stood with his back to her, rustling though some scrolls that contained lettering Helen had never seen before. She cleared her throat. "Your pardon, chief priest."

The startled priest dropped several of the scrolls he had been clutching and turned quickly to face Helen.

"I am sorry I have surprised you," she said quickly, then added, "I did knock."

The priest did not seem angry. "Like all else," he said, "my hearing is not what it once was." He took a small cloth from atop the table and mopped the perspiration that dampened his large face while gesturing Helen to be seated on one of the room's small stools. He himself sat upon one of the considerably larger chairs. "How may I assist you, princess?"

Kindly blue eyes twinkled from the fleshy face; Helen felt herself relax.

"I would ask you about atonement," Helen began.

Glaucus leaned back in his chair and regarded the young woman thoughtfully. He looked beyond the dazzling blue eyes that tilted slightly upward, the proud cheekbones and generous blonde curls. He noted the intelligence and poise of her face, as well as the tension that emanated from her young body. He saw something else as well, at once familiar and elusive, and puzzled at it for a few moments before realizing that she was patiently awaiting his reply. ☀

"Atonement is rather complicated," he began slowly, pausing to collect his thoughts. "Personally, I like to call it reflection myself — a time when men and women can look within, review their deeds and see the opportunity available to them for change."

Helen was sure her shock showed on her face, which was confirmed by Glaucus' next question. "Have I surprised you in some way?"

Helen lowered her eyes. "It is only that your words echo those of a teacher I once had," she said softly.

"You refer to the lady Rhemnesia, do you not?"

Helen looked up again, suspicious. "I do."

"I had the pleasure of meeting the lady but once," he said slowly, wanting to disarm the young woman's distrust. "She did not make herself seen very often. I found her a kind and learned woman, like to many who follow the Great Mother."

Confusion replaced Helen's suspicion. Rhemnesia had taught that the Olympian priests were dedicated to eradicating all traces of the Great Goddess. Certainly the initiate Kalchas had proven this so. Yet here sat the chief priest of the temple, speaking of Rhemnesia as if he admired and respected her. "I thought surely you'd despise those whose faith proceeded your own," she blurted.

Glaucus threw his head back with a hearty laugh. "Ah, so that is why you looked as if you were about to stab me with a cutting knife."

Helen blushed.

"Be at peace, princess," he said quickly. "I suppose there are many in the temples who feel as you fear, and make your suspicions warranted."

"But you do not?" she asked boldly.

Glaucus' eyes moved beyond her and his face lifted in a small smile. "I do not. But then I have experience many within the temple do not." He looked at her once more. "I'll tell you a story, princess, that I have not thought about in many years." He shifted his bones to a more comfortable position. "As you may be aware, many initiates of the Olympians travel in solitude before becoming priests — much like the priestesses of your Goddess."

Once more, the chief priest startled Helen. *How does he know this when I do not?*

Glaucus was considering his words as well, looking as if something had suddenly became clear to him. He spoke not of it and continued his tale. "At the minor temple to which I was pledged there were an over abundance of initiates — far more than the modest precinct could house. The priest there, a kind man named Polydectes, spoke a place for me here and suggested I travel alone to fulfill the requirements of the priesthood." He laughed then, taking twenty winters from his face. "I think I was less concerned with fulfilling my vocation than with satisfying the wanderlust of my youth. I set off to seek adventure and that, much to my chagrin, was what I found.

"I decided to scorn the comforts of the city and spend my nights under the open stars. With the foolishness of the young, I told myself that, as a pledged follower of the huntress goddess, I could walk freely amid the wild creatures of the open spaces. I even fancied that, if need be, I could communicate with the beasts. That conceit earned me a tusk in the shoulder; the wild boar I attempted to speak to was apparently not learned in the language of my goddess." His tone was dry and Helen laughed with appreciation. "I was sure that I was for Hades. After the boar attacked, I scrambled up a tree to avoid his killing charge. My strength was spent and my arm was bleeding profusely. It was only a matter of time before I lost consciousness and slipped from my place of safety, where the boar or some other predator would find me and finish me off.

"I prayed fiercely to the goddess who was my protectress but had little hope in my heart. At night fall, I resigned myself to my fate and moved down from the tree, unable to hold its branches any longer. I slipped into the sleep of the dead. When I awoke, I lay upon a straw bed and looked into the eyes of the most beautiful woman I had ever seen. I fancied the goddess had come to greet me as I fell into the Otherworld." He smiled again, a slow smile laced with sadness. "Perhaps I was not wrong. I soon learned that I had been in the care of the priestesses who fled the temple of Delphi when the god Apollo took up residence there. They had happened upon me when returning from their rituals for the departing sun. The few priests among them carried me to their makeshift quarters and their healer priestess worked upon me until my life was safely returned to my body.

"As you can well imagine, it took several moons before I was well enough to travel again. During that time, I shared in their worship of the Great Mother, learning of their wisdom as would any novice who happened upon them. They seemed to respect me as I did them, for when I was able to depart, they invited me to join their sect.

"It was a turning point in my life and even now I wonder what I would have accomplished if I had chosen their path."

His eyes settled on Helen once more, recalling her presence.

"Why did you chose as you did?" she asked him.

Glaucus sighed. "I can say that I was young and prone to seek joy in places yet unseen and that would be so. But I think also I believed, as I do now, that the world was becoming too complex for the teaching of the Great Goddess. Whereas once men lived off the fruits of their labor, able to spend time seeking the complex inner wisdom your Goddess demands, today they work for others and their time is spent in worry for the preservation of their bodies. Men need the mysteries to be simpler, explained to them by another who has gone before. They have not time, and I fear, little inclination to seek wisdom within themselves. The Olympian priests keep them tied to the forces that are greater than they."

Despite the wisdom of his words, Helen was appalled. If men did not spend time on inner mysteries, how would they have the power to change their own lives, to answer the worries that plagued them? Another thought occurred to her. "You are clearly a learned man, priest Glaucus," she said carefully. "But what of others of your station who would seek to teach the common man without having gained that inner wisdom themselves?"

The priest issued another sigh. "Your concern is valid, of course. We do our best to train our initiates carefully, providing every opportunity for inner wisdom to grow. And yet, as I am sure you yourself have found, such knowing does not come automatically with the utterance of a ritual formula or participation in a rite." He shifted his bulk uncomfortably. "I believe we have now come to the true meaning of your visit."

Helen regarded the priest levelly, as he had previously done with her. "I will say nothing of your initiate Kalchas, who must find wisdom or not as his own spirit wills. I ask only this: Under the laws of you own gods, Kronia grants atonement for the excessive acts of the people. Will you grant atonement to the girl Phoebe and to her guardian Rhemnesia and inform the king that you have done so?"

Yes, Glaucus thought, *I recognize that which is familiar about this young princess. She is alike to those who cared for me, alight with the honesty of inner knowing.* He wondered if she herself knew of her power and what it meant that a princess of a powerful city should come to the wisdom of an older time.

"You are generous to hold silence where Kalchas is concerned," he said at last. "As his mentor, however, it is my responsibility to see that he is corrected when he strays from the road of wisdom. I believe he has done so in the matter of your teacher." His tone took a formal note. "I grant atonement for the maiden Phoebe and the lady Rhemnesia. I shall repeat these words to the Spartan king Tyndareus and formally request the exiles' return."

He praised his decision as he watched the solemn young woman before him transform into a delighted child. Helen jumped from her stool and gave Glaucus a swift kiss upon his cheek, leaving before she saw the pleased smile that stretched across his face.

Rhemensia will return! The ache that had grown within her during her mentor's absence melted as Helen skipped from Glaucus' quarters to the small grove beyond the temple. Her giddiness would be unseemly amidst the multitude of introspective people who wandered Sparta's countryside. Still, she could not contain her joy. *Rhemnesia will return!* She danced amid the oak trees, sharing her happiness with their birds and host of small animals which sought refuge in the grove. *Rhemnesia returned.* Surely the Goddess favored her.

She never heard the two men approach; her eyes fell in darkness a moment before her mind.

CHAPTER FIVE

As on all festival days, men and women of the palace joined together for the meal. Unlike other feasts, the supper served during Kronia was sparse, consisting of baked fish and boiled roots. It was scheduled to begin when the king re-entered the palace grounds for the evening.

Clytemnestra, aimlessly wandering the dusty, sun-drenched roads with the rest of Sparta's populace, kept an eye on her father and wished he'd hurry homeward.

Mania and atonement; Clytemnestra had no inclination toward either. The forced silence of reflection caused her thoughts to wander down well-tread paths, leaving a state of agitated frustration in their wake.

Helen. As long as she could remember, Clytemnestra was forced to contemplate her sister's demise in order to garner the prestige that was rightfully due her. Nothing seemed to work. Her childhood taunts, her alienating sneers, even her successful plot to rid the palace of that troublemaker Rhemnesia did not destroy her beautiful sister. Worse, the last was nearly costing her her own circle of friends — as unremarkable as they were — who were now forced to listen to Kalchas' dull babbling day after day after day.

Clytemnestra cared not a wit for religion. She worshipped power. She thought she recognized a similar reverence in Kalchas. His unpolished mannerisms marked him as a man birthed into the lowest ranks of society; the priesthood was a natural arena for him to satisfy his self importance. Clytemnestra had not counted upon him being a witless fanatic.

Nor had she predicted her sister's bold counter move of pulling her own circle of admirers from Kalchas' lessons. How could Clytemnestra have foreseen that her doll-like sister would have the cunning to retaliate?

Helen knew, of course, that Clytemnestra would not go to Leda for intervention. The queen was so distraught over the anger her precious, favorite child showed since Rhemnesia's banishment that she would grant her daughter anything — even the right to mingle freely with the peasants.

Helen had won this round in their unspoken war. Clytemnestra was growing tired of the game anyway. Her sister would always be the center of their mother's attention, more beautiful, more adored. The battle against Helen was proving as tiresome as it was useless. And Clytemnestra's own group of admirers was growing increasingly dull. Why should she be satisfied by ruling over some insignificant bastards and a couple of visiting princesses anyway? She needed a game worthy of her talents.

She continued to walk aimlessly amid the unharvested crops that danced gently on the undulated land. The people she passed saw her no more than she saw them; contemplation during Kronia turned eyes inward. It was one of the few times she had permission to walk wherever she would without fear of being accosted or questioned. As with leadership over the palace maidens, the lack of challenge drained her journey of its appeal.

In one of the few strokes of fortune to enter her life, it appeared that her father found contemplation equally dull. She caught sight of her mother and ran to her to follow the king within the palace.

Leda was dressed in a becoming chiton of summer green, simply adorned by the girdle of gems in a darker shade. Her thick auburn hair fell in a single braid down her back.

Clytemnestra moved to her side, looking ahead as a man in the ceremonial robes of a visiting dignitary approached her father. "Who is the man walking with the king?"

"Where's Helen?"

Clytemnestra ignored her mother's predictable question and with the patience of long practice, pursued her inquiry undaunted. "Who is the man?"

Leda looked beyond her own thoughts to her husband and his guest. "Tantalus, son of Broteas and king of Mycenae," she said finally.

King of Mycenae? Clytemnestra looked at the man's receding back with greater interest. The gold that was liberally laced throughout the purple of his heavy cloak made him easy to see; he shimmered like a gaudy gem beside the plainly dressed king. The regal presence he affected was compromised by the hurried pace he was forced to assume to keep up with her much taller father. "What does he want with the king, mother, to have traveled in the worst of heat?"

Leda waved a dismissive hand, lowering her voice as they passed through the main gates to the palace grounds. "I have heard that summer burns hotter to the north, so perhaps for him our air seems mild. As for what he wants, I'd dare say it's to trade the abundant gold said to be mined in his country."

"Has the king said what he might trade in return? Perhaps horses. There are no finer horses than those bred by Castor," Clytemnestra whispered.

"If the kings thoughts run thus," the queen answered, "he has not shared them with me.

Nor would you pay attention if he had, Clytemnestra thought with contempt, following her mother to the great audience chamber.

Harried servants were already abustle, bringing oat cakes and wine to the small round tables that filled the long room. The tapestries along the walls, which artfully depicted Sparta's many battle victories, insulated the room from the worst of the summer's heat and kept it moderately warm during the winter months. Additional heat, when needed, was offered by the large fire pits placed at either end of the room. Clytemnestra followed her mother to the tables at the room's far side, which were raised above the rest by a stone platform. Tyndareus, who already stood beside his table, beckoned them forward.

"King Tantalus of Mycenae," he said formally. "I present queen Leda of Sparta."

The visiting king made an elegant bow in her mother's direction. His heavy cloak billowed about him and Clytemnestra noted the faint stain of perspiration that beaded his lip. As he regained his upright stance, Clytemnestra saw that he was a full head shorter than her father. His face had the fleshy countenance of one used to pleasure, but his level dark eyes bespoke of a willingness to work to attain it. His black hair curled in thick waves atop the collar of his cloak; Clytemnestra wondered if it grew so naturally or if he had it pressed with hot tongs.

"May you feed well and rest content within this house," Leda said, offering the ritual greeting.

Tyndareus drew his daughter beside him. "And my daughter, the princess Clytemnestra," he continued.

Clytemnestra started; her father had never called her so that she could remember. She recovered as Tantalus offered her another of his elegant bows, only to be shocked anew as her father indicated she share a table with the guest. He seated himself at his own small table with her mother beside him. Even

Leda was surprised at the arrangements. On festival days, women ordinarily shared the two-person tables, while the king shared his plate with any guests. Still, the queen made no move to protest and Clytemnestra was forced to sit meekly upon the stool indicated.

"Where is princess Helen?" her father asked after graciously assisting her mother to her seat. Clytemnestra looked as if seriously interested in her mother's response to avoid meeting the intent eyes of the stranger.

"Helen is late returning from the temple," Leda announced, unwilling to acknowledge that she had no idea where her daughter was.

"It is often like women to dawdle so," the king replied.

Tantalus turned his bulk to better face the king. "Ah, but in what better place to linger than at the hands of the gods," he interjected smoothly. "As with you, the temple within my country seems, at times, more significant than the palace itself. And our great citadel, guarded as she is by the cyclopean walls and watched over by the likeness of lions and the strength of men, is not easily surpassed in splendor."

Not very subtle, Clytemnestra thought, forcing a polite smile.

"Indeed, it is just that the house of the gods is more splendid than that of men, even if they are kings," her father responded piously.

The servants came round with freshly baked fish, an abundance of cooked vegetables and flat barley cakes.

"But you are eating nothing," Tantalus protested, skewing a large piece of the flaky fish on the point of his cutting dagger. Clytemnestra murmured something about losing her appetite to the heat and turned her attention to the jugglers and flame throwers entertaining the guests. The servants returned once more to collect the dinner plates and present a delicious display of sweetmeats to finish the meal.

The entrance of a guard to the hall interrupted the king as he reached for a fig pastry. Tyndareus nodded and the guard made his way to the king's table. Curious dinners pretended to continue their conversations, while straining to hear the guard's announcement.

"What?!"

The king's bellowed response broke Clytemnestra's already taunt nerves, causing her to send her wine flying across the table.

Tyndareus stood, addressing his guest. "My dear king Tantalus, I beg you to continue your meal in comfort, while I take my leave to confer with the guards."

Clytemnestra looked to her mother, whose blood-drained face made her appear to be a ghost of herself.

"King Tyndareus, if the matter is not secret, please share your need with me so I might pledge my assistance." Tantalus' voice was like water running over honey and Clytemnestra again wondered about his motives for visiting the palace.

"The princess Helen has been stolen," Tyndareus responded reluctantly.

Tantalus made the appropriate murmur of shock and outrage, echoed by those throughout the hall. Clytemnestra saw her brothers, who she had not noticed seated to the other side of her parents, rise in union.

"Know you the traitorous abductor?" Tantalus asked, calmly mopping away the wine Clytemnestra had spilt on the table between them.

"Young king Theseus." The king spat on the ground. "I daresay the king will find he has overstepped his adventuring this time."

"I quite agree, Tyndareus," Tantalus said, rising. "But it seems he chooses his timing well. As I recall, the men of Sparta cannot pick up arms during the Kronia festival."

"It is so," Tyndareus growled, suspicion kindled in his eyes.

Tantalus, recognizing his mistake, recovered quickly. "As we discussed earlier, Athens grows overbold. Did I not say upon my arrival here that we need unite against her and her young upstart if we are to avoid war and devastation?"

How convenient, Clytemnestra thought and assessed for herself the possibility of Tantalus' involvement in the abduction. Negligible, she decided; the man was not crafty enough to be involved in such a scheme.

Her father seemed to agree, for he said, "Perhaps your proposal is a wise one."

Curiously, he and Tantalus looked to her before Tyndareus turned and started across the dining hall. Tantalus bowed slightly in her direction before following her father and brothers.

She left off trying to puzzle the meaning of their attention as the hall door opened for a second time, admitting the initiate Kalchas. He did not wait for the king to beckon him forward but rather stated the reason for his interruption from across the room, effectively ensuring his audience.

"King Tyndareus, I am sorry to interrupt you," he said smoothly. Kalchas seemed many things but Clytemnestra would not have numbered apologetic among them.

"Is this about princess Helen?" Tyndareus demanded.

Kalchas' was not adept enough at state craft to hide his surprise. "Uh, no my king." He squared his shoulders and regained his composure. "I have come to regretfully inform you that the priest Glaucus is dead. It seems that his heart..."

Tyndareus waved a dismissive hand, halting Kalchas' carefully planned speech. "We shall pay the homage he is due. Unfortunately, I am unable to see to it just now. We have suffered a minor problem."

"Of course, sir. We will await the funeral upon your pleasure." Kalchas hid his glee; the gods were surely shining upon him that the king was too occupied elsewhere to focus upon his news.

"Are you prepared to take over his duties?" the king asked, already returning his attention to the audience chamber.

"Indeed sir," Kalchas replied quickly. "Glaucus has groomed me for the role." The lie came easily; Kalchas convinced himself that he served a higher truth where minor lies were of no great consequence.

"Then please do so. And see to whatever arrangements are appropriate."

The king left the hall without waiting for Kalchas' submissive bow, allowing the initiate to flee to a more private place to celebrate his victory.

Leda, left alone, slumped in her seat. Clytemnestra moved beside her and absently held a wine goblet to her mother's lips. A detached part of her mind reviewed the dinner's shocking events. Her sister was gone (*Gone! Actually gone!*), Tantalus came seeking alliance with Sparta, the priest Glaucus was dead and Kalchas was given the king's approval to serve as head priest. She quickly dismissed the possibility that Kalchas had anything to do with Helen's disappearance; if he had considered such a thing, he would have contacted her. Besides, he did not have the audacity to arrange for a princess's abduction. But for the death of a priest...Clytemnestra's eyes narrowed shrewdly. Yes, she could imagine the ambitious initiate having a hand in that, especially if the priest had ordered Kalchas to cease his senseless classes or had otherwise tried to thwart the initiate's teeming ambition. And it was odd that a mere initiate should report the priest's death to the king. Clytemnestra knew little about temple life, and cared even less, but even she knew there were elders who were responsible for conferring with the king in times of crisis. For that matter, wasn't it the elders who presented the king with their choice of successor, requesting his approval of their carefully considered choice? *Well, Kalchas effectively side-stepped that bit of politicking*, Clytemnestra thought with grudging admiration.

None of this seemed to have any bearing whatsoever on the way Tantalus and her father looked to her before quitting the hall. She added up the spoken and unspoken words that transpired between them, coming to one irrefutable conclusion: Tantalus wanted to form an alliance with Sparta through marriage with one of its princesses.

She slammed the goblet she had been holding to Leda's lips upon the table. "You'll do her no good by sitting here swooning," she snapped at her useless mother.

Leda started at her daughter's shocking tone.

Clytemnestra ignored her; she no longer cared for her mother's approval.

CHAPTER SIX

Moisture sucked warmth from her bones and a vortex swirled her belly. Her nostrils flared, searching for air laced with earth and trees and dung. The air she found was washed clean, was too pure. The wind beat at her from all sides, unobstructed, undirected. The ground beneath rippled, demanding she follow its sway.

She was trapped in a world her mind did not know.

Helen opened her eyes and the weight of the sky pinned her down, holding her hostage for the white-capped waters that lapped toward her in delicious anticipation. She pressed against the wood behind her, willing it to splinter in her skin and accept her sacrifice of blood.

"I didn't know your mother had taken a liking to beautiful young girls."

A large man, well developed muscles rippling through his tattered clothes, moved before her. He was pushed against the boat side before Helen got a clear look at his face, pinned there by a man of much smaller size whose gray eyes sparkled in angry intensity and whose gleaming dagger was poised to seek retribution. Helen shut her eyes once more, wishing away the violence of the men and waves surrounding her.

By the waters of Her living womb...

Rhemnesia's words rung in her mind, reminding her that the flow of life was carried on the very waves she now feared. It was small comfort. Always, the waters were represented by the gentle river that lined her homeland or the cleansing drink that washed her throat. Never had Helen been exposed to the turbulence that now surrounded her. She felt the power, yes, but it was beyond her, outside of her. Against her. Perhaps the Goddess had left the world and chaos trailed in her wake...

The voices of men were carried to her, closer than farther, and she felt a shadow loom before her.

Helen forced herself to open her eyes.

Along the length of the great ship, men pulled upon oars in perfect unison. The largest of them, the one who had been pinned against the boat's side with a dagger to his throat, was walking back and forth, shouting incomprehensible orders to those battling the water's will. The man who had threatened him stood before her, watching her with those intense gray eyes. He was indeed short — shorter certainly than she — his beardless face framed by a halo of blonde curls. Was this small man, no more than a boy really, in charge of the ship?

He turned his unwanted attention upon Helen. "Take my cloak," he barked, wrapping a garment around the princess' shaking shoulders. He grabbed at a passing deck hand. "Bring her some hard bread to settle her belly."

"Who are you?" Helen demanded.

The gray eyes hardened dangerously, wiping all traces of youth from his features. "King Theseus of Attica," he said. Helen felt her blood flow to her toes. "We will arrive at the dock of my city shortly," he said to her before turning and ignoring her completely.

Theseus.

The storytellers spoke of the young king's adventures with sparkling eyes and musical tongues. His abductions of innocent maidens were well known and much admired.

Ariadne of Crete. Antiope of the Amazons.

And now, Helen of Sparta.

Helen closed her eyes once more, ignoring the bread left beside her, the shouts and curses of the men around her. Her attention was demanded by the waters that bounced and carried her, moving her in a merciless and independent rhythm. She sought to use the momentum to reach the familiar comfort of trance state.

I am between the worlds, I am between the worlds...

But the violence of the waters kept her firmly rooted within the world her body found itself.

"We will deboard now," a voice informed her.

Helen ignored it, focusing upon the relentless sway that held her in its grip.

She felt herself lifted and carried from the ship. Her feet touched ground and were re-acquainted with land, slowly overcoming the motion that still rippled through her lungs and her stomach.

Theseus waited impatiently for his captive's body to right itself. "Welcome to my land — the greatest in the world."

The earth beneath her lent her strength and, with it, came anger.

"If it is so great, why are you forced to steal princesses from others?" she retorted, regretting her words as Theseus' eyes hardened dangerously once more. She made herself look beyond him, surveying her surroundings. Apparently Theseus was not the only one to think his city the greatest in the world. An endless mob of bodies rippled from the harbor. Men compared swords and argued feats, women chattered in high-pitched voices, jewelry singing with every nod of a proud head or lift of an expressive hand. Children ran squealing between their elders' legs, chasing bleating goats, watched by dignified oxen. Smell and sound and people and animals attacked the space around them, gleefully eliminating every free handspan.

No wonder Theseus took to the sea.

The suspicion that had seized her upon the water journey grew menacing larger: perhaps the Goddess had fled the world. Even the priest Glaucus had stated that the complexity of the new cities came between Her and humankind. Helen sought desperately for the feeling of comfort that flowed through her when she called upon the Great Mother. Nothing! No comforting shiver laced her spine, no quieting soothed her beating heart.

Helen swayed again, this time in panic.

"The chariot will take us to the palace," Theseus said, placing an aggressive hand upon her arm and lifting her into the elaborate wicker basket.

A young charioteer swerved expertly through the crowd, avoiding those he could, pushing past those he could not.

Slowly they made their way through the mob of bodies that challenged their path. Theseus' palace was set atop a large hill that commanded a view of the surrounding countryside — or, rather, what would have been a countryside. Houses swallowed the land, rammed together to ensure that it did not reemerge between them. Cattle grazed the grass they trampled. An unrelenting stream of feet and hoofs beat the sparse, unclaimed earth into submission, forcing it to serve as roadways for the endless chariots and carts that rushed to get somewhere undoubtedly better than the place from which they came.

Helen felt her panic rise and forced herself to calm. *Whether the Goddess dwells here or not, I need to retain my wits*, she told herself sternly.

The palace was guarded by a chaos of soldiers with smart uniforms and prideful postures, a wall of humanity determined to keep the common folk from entering the esteemed building behind them. They saluted Theseus' chariot and moved aside to allow him entrance.

The space within the palace was as cramped with bodies as the world outside it. Servants swarmed their king, plying him with goblets of wine and washing bowls and hand cloths. A team of horseman moved forward to relieve him of the chariot. Helen stepped from it swiftly, having no desire to be carried off in the harried bustle.

"Theseus, at last you are home!" A young man, dressed immodestly with single cloth around his waist and a burden of jewels around his upper body, pushed through the crowd and kissed the king's cheek.

"Taursas, my friend, I thought to find Marinsa able to run beside you by my return."

"Alas, the babe knows a good thing when he's in it and seems content to remain snug in his womb," the young man returned. "Where have you been?"

"Sparta," Theseus growled and ignored the questions visible in his friend's eyes. He turned his attention to Helen. "Inside," he ordered, looking as if he would grab her again.

She hesitated, a momentary resentment tempting her to remain rigidly where she was. The look in his eyes dissuaded her. What power had she, if she could not call upon the Goddess she served? She followed him through a corridor, ignoring the opulence of the tiles beneath her feet and the delicate patterns that covered the walls. She stared resolutely at Theseus' back as he led her up a wide stairway, down a corridor of rooms and before a heavy oak door, which he pushed open.

"These will be your chambers," he said, waiting for her to enter.

She passed before him and the door closed behind her.

Prisoner!

The rooms in which she found herself were unlikely prisoner's quarters. The large space was dominated by an oversized bed, its headboard inlaid with rosettes of bronze. The dyed blue fleece which covered it matched the rich tiles of the floor. Murals covered the walls from floor to ceiling and light blue fabric hung over the windows. Every corner held pottery glazed with unfamiliar designs. Apparently, empty space offended the Atticans.

"I am here to serve you."

An old woman separated herself from one side of the room. She was simply dressed in a gown of faded blue which matched the eyes that looked questions toward Helen from amid a mass of smiling wrinkles. Her white hair stood in disarray about a face well worn by time. "You're chilled from the journey," the woman explained, stepping forward and taking Helen's arm. "A warm bath will fix you right up."

"Am I a prisoner here?" Helen demanded.

The woman dropped Helen's arm. "Gods no! The king 'eeps his prisoners in the cell below ground." She let loose a slightly unbalanced laugh. "Attica must 'ave a greater reputation than I thought if ya think we house prisoners like this."

Helen walked to the doorway that opened beyond the bed. Within was a bathing chamber which shared the blue patterning of the sleeping room. "See, your bath is fixed for you," the woman said encouragingly.

Helen was suddenly aware of the dirt and sea grim that plastered her hair and body and clothing. She would better face what was to come if she was clean, she decided, and allowed the woman to undo her clothing and ease her into the bath water.

"Eh, you're as knotted as a horse master's rope," the woman pronounced. "You just breathe and relax and let me work some of this from your muscles."

The woman was stronger than she looked. Expert hands moved along Helen's back and neck, seducing tension from her taunt body. Helen felt herself slipping into a space devoid of pain and worry, a place where abductions and gods and sea journeys were less than meaningless. She straightened abruptly. "Why am I here?"

The old woman jumped backward.

"Eh, me can't take much of that anymore." She grabbed a cloth to dry her hands and took several breaths to calm her galloping heart. "You are here because king Theseus wants you here," she replied with certainty.

Helen gave up on gaining information from the woman who was serving her. The bath that cleansed her body also helped clear her mind. She allowed the woman to dress her and stepped into the sleeping chamber, walking to the door to discover if, despite her lavish surroundings, she was indeed a prisoner within the palace. To her surprise the door was unbarred; she was not at all surprised to find it guarded.

"I think you'll be wanting to remain inside, princess," the guard said.

His lewd stare, more than his words, convinced her to follow his advice. She closed the door firmly behind her and moved a heavy stool before it. The light furniture would be useless in

keeping anyone out but at least it would alert her should someone try to enter.

When she turned, the old woman was gaping at her. "Come
sit and I'll get ya your meal," the woman said quickly. She indicated that Helen should seat herself at the small table and carefully circled around the princess to reach the room's doors.

"I'll just 'ove this a moment," she said, looking at Helen
nervously as she slid the stool aside and opened the door, conferring with the guard beyond it. A few moments later the guard
returned, carrying a heavy tray. He handed it to the old woman
slowly, using his time to stare at Helen.

"Get out!" the woman yelled with the startling authority of
the aged.

The man quickly obeyed. The woman watched his retreat
with a satisfied smile and walked languidly over to the table,
placing the tray upon it. She turned then, making her way back
to the door, replacing the stool before it. She returned to Helen's
side with a self-satisfied grin.

Helen turned to her meal, which was indeed as generous as
the old woman promised. An entire side of roasted kid, swim-
ming in its own fat, was surrounded by a wide assortment of
highly spiced roots and vegetables. Despite her hunger, Helen
ate sparingly, her attention caught again and again by the sharp
edge of her cutting dagger.

In a single moment, she could thrust the point to her heart,
puncturing the life held there, releasing her from her captivity
and answering her doubts about her Goddess' existence. Surely,
she would meet Her in the Otherworld and be freed from the
suspicions that threatened to torment her. One swift, strong
thrust, one strike in the center of her breasts.

Coward!

The voice that screamed in her head sounded suspiciously
like Rhemnesia's. She let the knife fall to the table.

At the room's far wall, a window was curtained with light
silk. She walked to it, parting the fabric to reveal an expanse of
unmolested land, a valley of tall grass and gentle hills and riotous olive trees, guarded to one side by the palace, and the other
by a massive temple.

"That is the temple of Athene, patron goddess of our city,"
the old woman explained proudly. "The great lady worked hard
for our city. Fought the earth shaker Poseidon for us. He was
able to create a spring of water at the very center of the temple's
precinct. But she 'ave us the gifts of olive and oil. She 'ave us
wealth and we celebrate in her honor."

The tales of the new religion are so fantastic it is a wonder anyone believes them. But they do, she reminded herself, and their beliefs have the power to destroy the truth they deny.

Her shoulders slumped in resignation.

"Come, child, let us prepare you for bed," the woman said kindly. She ushered Helen to the bed, turning back the coverlet for Helen to slip beneath.

"I will return to ya on the morrow," she said, patting Helen's shoulder absently. Helen watched the door close behind the woman, satisfied that the stool was still in a position to warn her if anyone tried to enter.

She forced herself to focus upon her breath, to connect with the life that was stronger than the fear that lingered at the edges of her heart.

If I manage to get beyond the guard at the door or jump undamaged from the height of the window, it is unlikely that anyone in the outlying villages will give me shelter or that the boatman will take me home — not when I have been seen with the king. I cannot expect help from my homeland; even if they know of my abduction, the men of Sparta will not lift arms during the atonement of Kronia, believing the gods will curse them if they do so.

Truly, she was in the hands of the Goddess now. But would She come to this land that surely had forgotten Her? The fear loomed closer and Helen thrust it aside, striving once more for the calm that would open her to the comforting presence of the Great Mother.

The stool shattered against the tile, interrupting her efforts. She jumped from the bed as a familiar voice cursed aloud and she found herself face to face with Theseus.

"What do you want?" she demanded, fear hardening to anger once more.

His laugh reminded her of the old woman's. "As if what I want matters," he replied and paced to the windows, hiding his face and his thoughts. "My counselors think I'm a fool," he said aloud. "They're wrong. They don't see I had no choice. No choice at all." He pounded a fist upon the table and Helen took a step backward.

Was he mad then?

Theseus wondered that as well.

Memories and admonishments and commands he dare not disobey rolled freely in Theseus' head.

You are not to harm her in anyway, his mother had said, using the same tone that had cowered him in his younger years.

I supported you to attain your current position; I will not hesitate to rescind that support.

The threat had been annoyingly unnecessary. Theseus avoided his mother to the best of his ability; it was part of the tie that pulled him to distant shores. But he had not once gone against her will. His imagination supplied him with fantastic consequences should he pursue such defiance. He had faded memories of his mother playing with him when he was younger, a beautiful woman who held him upon her knee, bouncing him until he rewarded her with a giggle that she effortlessly matched with her own. Perhaps his memory was no more than fancy. His memories of brooding silences and foreboding words of darkness were far clearer.

It is necessary that you continue the tradition, she had said in that tone he had grown to hate.

Then she showed him the exact spot to insert the marble wand she had commissioned to move the rock. Beneath lay the sandals and sword that belonged to king of Attica, placed there for whichever youth in Troezen proved strong enough to obtain them and claim his place as heir.

It was for this that he hated her most. She had taken away his ability to demonstrate his own strength, replacing it with her cunning.

He journeyed to Attica to place distance between them, as well as to rule after the great king's death. His efforts to preserve the traditions she spoke of were no more than token. Instead, he set out to prove himself, successfully breaking tyrannical Crete and its barbaric demand for youth to feed the beast within its labyrinth, successfully demoralizing the Amazon women who roamed the plains by capturing their queen.

If his current adventures were not quite so heroic, at least they were interesting. Pirating distant shores won his people prestige and respect.

He almost felt he had earned his kingship. Almost.

The small doubt that remained caused him to embark upon this senseless journey to kidnap a quivering princess from a powerful land. In some way, he felt he owed his mother still. And he resented it terribly.

He turned those paralyzing gray eyes upon Helen, looking through her to the demon in his own mind. "I may have started a needless war for you. All because of you and your plans and your schemes!"

"What are you talking about? What plans?" Helen heard her fear break through her voice and took another step backward to distance herself from the unhealthy gleam in Theseus' eyes.

The madman smiled maliciously. "Unharmed, you say. Well perhaps I can do something that even you can't detect, mother mine."

Helen had no time to ponder his puzzling words. He closed the space between them in an instant and grabbed her hair, yanking it mercilessly. "This won't show, will it?" he said, tugging harder.

Helen struggled frantically, willing herself to find a voice to scream at him.

"And I don't think you'll see this." He ripped her bed dress and grabbed the nipples of her breasts, pinching and pulling them simultaneously.

At last she did scream, realizing his intent.

Her love and life is celebrated in the ecstatic union between man and woman.

Theseus grabbed a piece of material and pushed it down her throat. The tears that burned her eyes seemed to excite him further. She kicked him before his hand reached between her legs.

"Oh. You witch!" He raised his hands to her and then stopped himself. "Oh, no, you won't get me that way, clever one. The bruise would show, wouldn't it?" He chose instead to rip the remainder of her dress, exposing her pale skin.

"So fair," he murmured, before placing the blow intended for her face in the sensitive area between her legs.

The pain was unbearable, sending hot waves through her entire body. She fell back on the bed, willing herself to die.

She was not granted that much mercy. Theseus threw himself atop her, using his knees to pry open her legs and expose her bruised sex.

The pain increased tenfold, extending inward as he pushed himself within her, breaking her resistance in one merciless thrust. The heat of the explosion in her body was scorching. Darkness descended upon her before he left her body.

*H*elen *continues...*

I had been taught that life follows the pattern of the seasons, each happenstance yielding its opposite. Thus sorrow yields to joy yields to sorrow and birth to death to rebirth and light to darkness to light.

The merciful darkness that enveloped me did likewise yield to the painful light of the sun and I found myself aboard Theseus' ship once more.

Would that this learning of the seasons was as false as I had found the other teachings I had previously believed.

The bruises deep within my body pounded in painful reminder of the thrusts inflicted upon me. No Goddess shared my union with Theseus; that was a godless agony of pain and hatred that I could scarce comprehend.

My memories swelled in the whirlwind of that horrible moment and I lived anew the peculiar rejection of my mother, the active hostility of my sister, Rhemnesia's departure...

In my twelve winters, I experienced the peace that comes from the gentle breeze singing along my skin and from the sweet bird song speaking to my heart. I felt wonder at the tales contained within a candle flame and at the healing within the petal of a wild flower.

And I experienced the hatred of those I loved, the mindless aggression of one I did not know and abandonment by one I trusted.

My inner reality — the peace and beauty of the Goddess upon whom I had come to rely — was negated by an outer reality of inequity and confusion and violence.

I did not care that Theseus had carried me as he would a pile of wood logs, dumping me to one side of his ship's deck and ignoring me completely. Nor did I care that the merciless waves threatened beyond the vessel's meager walls once more. My own despair had already drowned my spirit and I would gladly lhave left my bludgeoned body.

The Goddess did not exist. Or if She did, She was powerless to change the ugly events of the world She created.

I did not then know that She is but co-creator of the tragedy that lines one's path. The knowledge of this mystery was one of many that awaited me on the next step of my journey — within the city of Troezen, at the hands of the high priestess Aethra.

PART TWO
TROEZEN, MYCENAE & SPARTA

CHAPTER ONE

"We will deboard now," Theseus barked at her, putting out his hand to help her rise.

Her hatred of him twined with that she felt toward herself for flinching at the sight of his outstretched arm. She forced her beaten body to rise unaided, stabbing Theseus with a glare as she did so. She felt a small satisfaction when he shrank from her.

Beyond him, she saw their destination, a small port defended from uninvited traders and unwelcome pirates by a jutting headland that separated the calm shallows from the unforgiving waves beyond it. A few small fishing boats were anchored in the shallows; the fisherman raised their hands in greeting and returned to their nets.

A single man came forward to supervise the beaching of their vessel. "Aye, my lord Theseus. It has been too long." The man pounded Theseus with one large fist.

Theseus became charming. "Faustinus. Not long enough for you to create a real port, I see."

Faustinus grunted. "Our little sand dune keeps away the pirates we don't want visiting." He turned his attention to Helen with a raised eyebrow. "And is this the bride we've been hearing so much about? I'd say marriage was never a more welcome ceremony."

Despite his great bulk, Faustinus awarded Helen an elegant bow.

Helen glared at him as she had previously done at Theseus.

"Not my wife, no," Theseus interjected, his calm slipping. "I am here to bring her to my mother. We must go quickly."

Faustinus' sensitivity for the pull of the tides and the change of the seasons did not extend to the moods of those around him. "I'll bring your horse, my lord," he said cheerfully. "And a chariot for your lady." He offered Helen a second bow before leaving them, returning a moment later with the promised transportation. Theseus directed Helen to board the simple platform before setting himself beside her.

"A good day to you both," Fauntinus called, slapping one of the sturdy horses on its ample haunch to send their chariot along its way.

Helen clenched her teeth at the chariot's rocking motion, keeping her eyes fixed upon the trail ahead. It was not long before the path ended. The home of Theseus' mother was a humble, single structure with only a small stable off the inner courtyard. Flowering vines climbed the walls and wild blossoms lined their paths.

Helen kept her body stiff as Theseus helped her alight and led her to the home's megaron.

"Wait here."

Fine marble benches were placed at random intervals around a central hearth. Fresh and painted flowers flowed along the wall in exquisite harmony. Helen felt something deep inside her stir in response to the simple beauty; she resented it greatly.

"You are princess Helen."

The strong voice behind her jolted the stressed muscles of her body. She turned swiftly and the sight of the woman who said her name gave her a second surprise. A slender, almost fragile face held deep gray-green eyes that tipped slightly downward, giving the woman a look of lazy concentration. Her skin was flawless ivory, concealing her age. Her delicate build seemed too slight for the heavy copper hair that fell from her head, and much less so for the jewelry around her throat and waist. She was dwarfed beside her son, who was not a large man, but the room seemed to shrink in her presence. Though power rippled from the woman's small frame, Helen could detect no malice from her.

"I am princess Helen of Sparta," she responded, reminding herself that this beautiful woman was her new captor.

Her emphasis on her homeland went unregarded. The woman stared intently, looking through her. Shame ran unaccountably through Helen's blood.

"You may leave now," the woman said to Theseus, without lifting her eyes from Helen. "Come with me," she added, the last clearly a command to Helen, spoken with a faint but decidedly familiar accent.

How dare the stranger treat me as a dumb farm animal to

be herded upon demand. Let her know that the one she would claim as captive is not so meekly led!

Memory of her inability to fight Theseus violated her thoughts, replacing her defiance with fear.

"Who are you?" she forced herself to ask, despising the betraying quiver in her voice.

The woman's intense look did not waver but Helen thought she saw the face soften with something akin to sympathy.

"Aethra, high priestess of Troezen."

The woman turned then, moving with the grace of one born royal, from the room in which they stood. Helen had no choice but to follow.

High priestess Aethra of Troezen knew her charge followed; she did not look back to confirm this, nor did she slow her pace along the smooth stone pathway that bore her.

She did not wish Helen to catch up to her and see the turmoil that she was sure marred her mask of calm.

It is she! her mind screamed, with the mixture of awe and relief that always welled when that which she had only seen in the water's surface appeared in the flesh.

Not quite appeared...

She resisted the temptation to look backward at Helen's face to confirm that she was the woman. To do so would be an unnecessary indulgence; no one alive looked like the woman in her vision except the child her son brought to her. She had thought that she had embellished her vision's heroine with unrealistic beauty. Yet Helen's face was, if anything, even more spectacular than she envisioned.

But there were some things Aethra's vision had not shown her. The girl's eyes held a hardness she had not foreseen, an anger that boiled from within.

It reminded her of the anger that roiled her dreams, the message that she had not sought but had ruined her sleep night upon night.

The fields were blighted, animals undernourished, people toiled without energy. A male face appeared, shadowed in darkness. "The gods speak to me alone," he intoned. The face shattered, dividing again and again, its multiplying pieces cast throughout the whole of the land. "The gods speak to me alone," each new voice intoned, chanting louder, louder. Men and women and children were roused from their homes, their heads bowed in supplication, their eyes devoid of the spirit of life. The chanting faces grew, feeding off the strength of their followers.

The gods speak to me alone.

Darkness, black and empty, blanketed the space between the raving faces, covering the masses who joined before them.

No! Aethra had ran frantically in the enveloping dark, shaking at those caught within its wake, throwing her useless body against the threatening, lying faces.

To me alone.

Angry eyes turned upon her, directing her to the widening black void.

"I will not!" she screamed, beseeching the Goddess whom she revered.

It was then that she saw the light, small and distant. She found strength and hope and ran to it, putting distance between herself and her homeland and all she had cherished, striving to outrun the darkness. She stumbled, rose, ran on, desperate for success, certain of failure.

A woman's face appeared in the light. She collapsed before her, exhausted and relieved.

The face was that of the girl behind her. Princess Helen of Sparta, whose angry eyes gave her pause.

She is the one, Aethra reminded herself sternly.

The dream had persisted until, at last, fatigue threatened to paralyze Aethra completely and she forced herself to take the trance-inducing herbs to find the woman of the light.

She was from Sparta.

Despite Aethra's best efforts, this was all the information her sight would yield. She detached women from the temple to find her, to comb every house, every hut in the foreign land. "When you see her you will know her," she had said, "for she is more beautiful than beauty itself."

They had left, obedient and skeptical. Their skepticism turned to disbelief when they returned to report no such maiden existed. Aethra remained adamant.

"Perhaps she is not yet born," the priestess Rhemnesia suggested.

Aethra knew this to be true as soon as Rhemnesia uttered it. She dispatched the priestess immediately, ordering her to insinuate herself in the palace, where she could learn of all births that took place within the city. Rhemnesia's breeding, coupled with the haughty arrogance of a seer, won her an unquestioned place among the palace women.

Winters passed, children were born in bunches, the king took a wife.

And still the child of Aethra's vision did not appear.

Then the Spartan queen, who confided in Rhemnesia as she did in no one else, became pregnant. The priestess reported Leda's unshakable conviction that she was impregnated by a male god who took her husband's form. Rhemnesia's initial response was to presume the queen had bedded a man other than the king and was concocting a story in the event that the child looked like someone other than her wedded husband. But the priestess knew the queen well; if she were having an affair, she would have confided it to Rhemnesia, if only for the sheer pleasure of expanding her guilt.

"Perhaps she was seduced by an Olympian god," Rhemnesia reported. *"She has come to believe in these ridiculous figments, despite the teachings of her mother. As we know too well, such beliefs often shape the reality of their holders."*

Would the child they sought come from such a birth? Rhemensia believed so and Aethra hoped it were true. Her dream left scars of fear that were not healing and with each passing day she felt increased urgency that the child be found.

She ordered Rhemnesia to locate a messenger to send information. Her emotional turmoil was too great to trust visions alone.

Helen's birth confirmed Rhemnesia's intuition. Among the four children given life, one girl held unsurpassed beauty. Rhemnesia's work as teacher began, her success in winning Helen's sympathies to the old religion an unmitigated success.

"I am aided by a dubious occurrence," Rhemnesia reported. *"It seems the new gods still possess some understanding of balance for, with this child of light, comes a child of undeniable darkness. Clytemnestra swims in a muddied pool of jealousy and hate and revenge. Her efforts are primarily aimed at her sister, whom she alienates from others with unhidden glee. Becoming the lonely girl's ally was easy; strengthening her spirit was easier still, as she has sharpened her wits against the blade of her sister's cunning."*

Scrying upon the water's surface showed Aethra that Helen would live within the temple of Troezen. She set upon the plan to bring the princess to her. Would that her vision had told her how to deal with the girl once she arrived!

Ah well, the Goddess gave us strong minds as well as guiding visions. She would doubtless find some way to communicate with the girl.

Still, Aethra was glad when they reached the steps to the temple and she could beckon one of the priestesses to them.

"This is Helen, who is joining us," she explained, not looking to her captive's face. "See that she is assigned a room and given instruction for joining the others."

The solemn priestess nodded. Aethra felt Helen's angry eyes upon her but once more resisted looking in the girl's direction. She turned and not quite fled to the sanctuary of her own rooms.

Helen was furious. With little welcome and less explanation she had been ordered to follow the Aethra woman to this humble temple and was then left in the charge of a stranger. The fear that had threatened her earlier was swallowed by anger and sheer frustration.

The tall, plainly dressed woman to whom she had now been assigned walked from the large room down a corridor opposite from that which Aethra disappeared.

"Where are you taking me?" Helen demanded, stubbornly staying where she was.

The woman turned, a puzzled expression on her thin face. She placed a finger to her lips in a silencing gesture that annoyed Helen greatly and turned once more toward the corridor, beckoning Helen to follow.

She is tall but very thin and probably not over strong, Helen reasoned. *If I do not like where she takes me I shall push past her and leave this place.*

With that small resolution, she followed. The hall into which she was led boasted the same beautiful simplicity as the room in which she had first met Aethra. The walls were a smooth, brilliant white, as if made entirely of marble. On the uppermost reaches were frescos of budding flowers and delicate birds, elegantly wrought and washed in the same white as the walls. The sun came through several small windows, gently reflecting off the polished oak doors on the hall's left.

It was before one of these that her guide stopped, lightly rapping upon the wood and then pushing it open.

Within was a humble room containing two small beds with a chest between them, a small stool, a table and several shelves. Some of the last were covered with goblets and clay figures which Helen presumed belonged to the girl seated upon the first of the beds.

The girl jumped up at their entrance, bringing her hands together before her chest and bowing easily to both the woman and to Helen.

Her brown hair was braided and looped beside her round face, which was sprinkled with freckles. Her hazel eyes regarded Helen cheerfully.

"Are you new come?" she asked excitedly.

Helen looked at her guide, expecting her to offer the girl

some explanation. When it was clear that she would not answer, Helen responded. "Yes, I have just arrived at this place."

The girl, who was slightly younger than Helen herself, squealed delightedly.

"We have not had a newcomer for seasons and seasons. I wondered if I would ever get a chance to share my room." She turned to the woman. "Should I help her dress and bring her to the evening ritual?"

The woman nodded and bowed her departure to both Helen and the young girl.

"I'm Clarisa," the girl informed Helen while pulling her toward the bed chest. "The priestess filled this draw several days ago in anticipation of your coming. Here, you'll want this one."

The girl handed her a blue chiton similar to the one she herself wore. The dye was without flaw and the texture so soft Helen could not begin to know how it was worked.

"Beautiful, isn't it? Although the garment you wear is equally fine, if a bit travel worn," Clarisa said shyly.

Helen looked upon her dirtied shift and cloak and noted the same grime coated her hands and sandaled feet.

"I'll go fetch you a washing bowl," Clarisa offered, bounding from the room before Helen could protest.

Helen collapsed upon the small bed. A high priestess greeting her, garments awaiting her, a girl her own age striving to befriend her.

What was this place?

Clarisa returned a moment later, carefully cradling a copper bowl in her arms. "Here, let me help you," she offered after carefully setting the bowl atop the wooden chest.

Helen ignored the watered cloth offered her. "How long have you been imprisoned here?" she demanded.

The girl looked puzzled. "Imprisoned? Not at all. Who could have told you such a thing? I was the third girl born in a family of nine. My parents knew they could not afford to feed me and doubted they could make me a good marriage — few boys were borne to our village at that time — so they sent me here. I'm very glad for it. I enjoy the learning of the Goddess and would much rather be here than working in the fields."

She knelt then and began washing Helen's feet herself. Embarrassed, Helen took a second cloth to her hands and face.

"Is this a temple of the Great Mother then?"

Clarisa looked upward, her large hazel eyes holding her own questions.

"Of course it is. Didn't whoever brought you here tell you that you would come to the great temple of Troezen?"

"No," Helen responded bitterly. "I have been told nothing at all. The woman — the priestess, I suppose— who ushered me to this room would answer none of my questions."

Clarisa giggled. "That is Ashtara. She is under vows of silence. Come, let's get you into this garment. The sun is already setting and we'll be reprimanded for being late."

Clarisa helped her change into the appropriate clothes and hurried her down the corridor beyond the room. The far end of the hall opened upon a large courtyard that was blanketed with soft grass and wild flowers and peppered with large oak trees. Clarisa led her beneath one of these, where upwards of thirty girls and women already sat. The oldest gave them a curt nod and then began her ceremony.

Setting sun

Lion of fire

Mother of flame

May the light

that is your life

Burn brightly with us this night

The woman walked about a cairn as she chanted and one by one the girls rose to follow in her wake. Clarisa grabbed Helen's hand and led her likewise. When the circle was complete, a girl separated herself from one side, holding a lit torch, which she dropped within the fire pit. Kindling was quickly added to keep it alight and the circle chanted in words Helen did not understand.

"May the spark of the Creatrix burn bright within our hearts," the older woman said, leading the girls about the flames once more and then back into the temple.

The ritual silence was quickly broken when they entered the precinct walls.

"Goddess I'm hungry," Clarisa whispered beside her.

Helen's stomach ached in sympathy, reminding her that she had gone the day without food. The girls were led to a long room dominated by a large table and benches. As they took their seats, several of the group separated themselves and went to the kitchens, returning a moment later with serving bowls and large platters of bread and cheese. The simple fare was augmented with a rich stew containing vegetables and spices Helen could not identify.

"Ismar is cooking this moon — which means the soup is wonderful and the bread is as coarse as a mare's hair."

The soup was indeed delicious and the bread as dry as she was warned. Still, Helen's aching stomach accepted the food gladly and she washed it down with some of the clear, sweet water that made its round.

With her hunger sated, Helen tried to focus upon her surroundings, fighting the sleep that sought to overcome her.

"You must be very tired," Clarisa said solicitously when Helen swayed where she sat. "I'll take you to our rooms. The excitement of first encounter with the temple always leaves one exhausted."

Helen knew it was not the temple that had wearied her so but forbore to say anything, allowing Clarisa to lead her back to her room and to the bed that awaited her.

Tomorrow. Tomorrow I will plan my escape. But her spirit soared in the gentle peace that surrounded her and she fell into sleep with the beginnings of happiness tickling her thoughts.

CHAPTER TWO

"This is truly beautiful!" Clarisa exclaimed.

Helen looked with critical eyes upon the cord she braided. The green dye she had so carefully set was the color of leaves budding with spring. The wool was silky and fine and her braid tight and sure.

Yes, it is pretty enough for the Goddess.

She gave Clarisa an acknowledging smile and continued working the cord that would bind her to the Goddess. A small part of her mind wondered at this still, but it was like the soft echo of the wind off the sea. In the three moons since she arrived at the temple, Helen found the home she had not known she sought.

She had awoke from her first night in the temple walls with thoughts of escape imprinted upon her mind. These were quickly interrupted by the morning ceremony she was required to attend. With the rest of the temple maidens, she had welcomed the sun into the sky and saluted the leaving of night, feeling her energy drained by the pull of the group and then returned to her tenfold. When the ceremony was complete, she was ushered to the dining hall for a brief meal of nut bread and cheese before returning to the temple garden once more to join the lessons that she soon learned structured each day. All her thoughts were consumed by the strict concentration needed to memorize the various uses of the strange flowers and leafs and roots put before her.

Next came lessons given by an elder priestess named Castalia, whose disapproving face softened as Helen and a group of younger girls, including Clarisa, were drilled again and again in the rituals of sun and moon and stars. The older maidens — those past their woman's making — had retired to the temple's precincts to accept offerings and hear the petitions of the city's populace. They rejoined Helen and her group for the noon meditation and an open discussion, during which experiences were shared and questions answered. The exercise of the mind was followed by exercise of the body as the girls split up to perform the various tasks of gardening, harvesting, hunting or cooking assigned to them.

Helen was relieved to be assigned to harvesting with Clarisa, who quickly taught her how to determine which fruits were ripe for picking and the invocation of gratitude to be said over each.

Thoughts of escape faded with the day's light.

It was easier to keep focused upon the information she was required to absorb, the tasks she had to perform, than to focus upon returning home; the last triggered memories of her journey to the temple and with them, feelings of pain and shame and loathing too great to examine. Still, her hurt remained an unnamed presence, standing between her and the girls and women surrounding her.

Like Clarisa, many arrived shortly after their births, knowing no other life but the peaceful existence in honor of the Goddess they served. No tragedy had ever shaken those beliefs to dust, no larger events tested their power.

At moments the envy Helen felt for the innocence of those around her wracked her body with bone crushing pain. Would that she could be like them, seeing only wonder and beauty, feeling the power they attributed to their Goddess run through her body, reminding her of her place within the Mother's heart.

Events had stolen that innocence from Helen and in one of life's many paradoxes, she longed for its return in equal measure to her acceptance of its loss.

Perhaps that was why she sat beneath one of the garden's glorious oak trees, braiding the rope that would serve as her girdle and her pledge to the Goddess.

As the only newcomer to the temple, tonight's ceremony would celebrate her pledge alone. For the days before the pregnant moon, she had been excused from the physical tasks of the temple to prepare the symbol of her service. She wondered what tonight's ceremony would hold for her. Her questions to Clarisa and the senior priestesses had elicited frustrating, vague responses. She knew only that she had to complete her cord this day, fasting while others ate, and return to her rooms by nightfall to await summoning.

Maybe I should have asked questions of Aethra.

For the first moon of her stay, the woman who had met her

upon her arrival to Troezen was curiously absent.

"Do you know the high priestess Aethra?" she had asked Clarisa.

The young girl was surprised. "Of course. She is the one who ordinarily conducts the afternoon lessons. And she stands as the voice of the Goddess at all important ceremonies. How is it you know of her?"

"She brought me here," Helen said simply, foregoing a more detailed explanation.

Clarisa's surprised face sparked with awe. "Are you the chosen daughter?" she asked, her voice barely above a whisper.

"Surely not. I don't even know what you're talking about."

Clarisa was not convinced. "Every high priestess must bring a daughter to the temple, born of her body or chosen by her hand. Aethra is also queen of Troezen. They say she never married because she did not wish her kingdom to become akin to those elsewhere — where kings grow hungry for power and insist the people worship the Olympian gods, forgetting the laws of the Great Mother. She gave birth to a son once — Theseus — who is now king of Attica." Clarisa looked beyond Helen, missing the uncontrollable flinch that swept her friend's body. "No one knows the child's father. Many say that he was borne from a sacred marriage between priestess and god."

Helen's body jerked again, this time with annoyance. Would she forever be surrounded by women who believed themselves impregnated by gods?

"Anyway," Clarisa continued, "She gave birth to no other child and it is unlikely that she shall. So she must chose a daughter to be trained to her place. Ordinarily, such a choice is made among those already serving in the temple but sometimes the Great Mother will direct a choice to be made from without the temple walls. It is said that such a choice from without indicates exceptional ability on the part of the candidate."

"Well, that alone proves that I am no such choice," Helen said sharply.

Clarisa regarded her skeptically. "You have learned more in one moon with us than I have in several years of living here. Almost, it as if you are merely remembering what was learned long ago. And you are certainly possessed of exceptional beauty."

The look of admiration — not unmixed with jealousy — that spread across Clarisa's features brought Helen's annoyance to the fore. "I have come to the temple at an age when my mind is practiced at memory. That is all. And they certainly are not going to chose a priestess for her looks."

Clarisa still did not look convinced but her sensitive nature responded to the steel in Helen's voice and she said no more, returning her attention to gathering berries for their evening meal.

The conversation continued in the silence of Helen's head. She did seem to learn easily all that was taught, absorbing herb lore and ritual with ease. She also experienced the silence of mind and attunement with nature far more readily than her peers ....

Still, she was not as heartwhole in her faith as the least accomplished temple maiden. Surely, the Goddess would chose one who was not as tormented by doubt as she.

Aethra's return to their daily lessons further confirmed her knowing that she was not the chosen one to whom Clarisa referred. The noon discussions remained open to questions by those in training but, by silent agreement, the maidens became more thoughtful in their asking, more respectful in their listening, as if the presence of the high priestess placed their words on guard. The casual conversations Helen had grown accustomed to were now dressed in formality. Aethra herself did nothing overtly to cause this change; she smiled readily in response to a meaningful question and looked with stern disapproval upon those she thought frivolous. Her answers had the strength of law and were taken as truth.

Helen found herself resenting the priestess' authority even as she clamored with the others to win a rewarding smile.

The last were bestowed upon her quite sparingly indeed. Certainly Aethra did not give her any of the special favors she presumed would be accorded a chosen daughter. Indeed, Helen received even less attention than the others. She was rarely called upon to carry out one of the many tasks Aethra assigned to those around her nor was she called to serve the priestess in silent attendance as others took turns doing. Helen told herself she was relieved by the formidable woman's lack of attention toward her, but her true feelings were far more complex. Resentment. Fear. And yes, when Aethra served the rituals, even admiration and something almost like love. In those sacred moments, Helen fancied the beautiful, powerful woman to be the embodiment of the Goddess she had lost.

Well, tonight I will be the focus of the priestess' attention sure enough.

She tied the final knot upon her braid, looked as if for the last time upon the setting sun and rose to return to her rooms to await the summons.

It seemed a long time before it came. Helen sat upon her

bed, the braid held loosely in her hands. Her stomach had protested fiercely at the lack of food, quieting as her mind slowly
shifted in the way of one of the verge of dreams.

When the knock came upon her door, opened moments later
by a group of robed and masked figures, she was certain dream
time had taken her in truth. She floated into the fold of the group,
neither frightened nor intrigued by the grotesque masks that
covered all but the centers of their eyes.

They carried her along, down the now familiar corridor, out
into the courtyard beyond. The cold of midnight air chilled her
bones, while the light of the full moon warmed her blood.

Onward, forward. She went where led, beyond the familiar
grounds, beyond the gardens and pastures that lined them,
through the grove unclaimed by man. Forward again, beneath a
canopy of branches that allowed no moonlight to enter, but which
was framed the distant torches. Onward, forward, until she stood
before an assembly of masked figures whose bodies and faces
moved in the uncertain light.

The chanting began, a low rumble that accosted her from
all sides, entering every pore of her body, demanding surrender.

A small woman walked forward, her mask of battered gold
catching and tossing the light offered by the surrounding flames.

Aethra, Helen's mind said, but the name meant nothing.

The figure of the gold mask helped Helen to remove the
gown she wore. The cold of the evening air did not touch her.
The figure held a goblet to Helen's lips, forcing her to drink of
its contents. Her throat opened easily to the quenching liquid,
relishing the ease of thirst.

Fire! So suddenly it changed, water becoming fire that
scorched her tongue and throat and belly. She doubled over, falling hard upon the ground as the chanting grew, swirling around
her to assure her death.

Downward, downward. She sunk into the ground beneath,
burying herself within the cool soil.

"Mother!" The cry was ripped from her scalded lungs, echoing to the earth's very center, ringing through the trees, released
into the sky.

Rain answered her, surrounding her within wet gray clouds
that claimed the fire.

Forward, onward, she walked through the mists, searching
for something she could not identify

"Where are you?" she demanded.

The mists cleared in response, showing her tree and river
and sky, predator and prey, bird and insect.

I am everywhere.

The voice spoke in her heart, bringing her to her knees once more, this time in a longing that was beyond pain.

"Where are you?" she asked again, a plea.

Her heart tingled with a warmth that radiated through her body, filling her, saturating her.

I am everywhere, the voice repeated.

In her vision, a small pond appeared. Helen's spirit crawled forward and lay against the grassy bank to look upon the water's surface.

Her reflection looked back at her, showing the features that others found so pleasing.

I am everywhere!

The voice was louder this time, calling forward a light that flared in the reflection of Helen's eyes, blinding her.

Everywhere.

The voice echoed as the mists closed about Helen once more, lifting her in a swirling circle, carrying her nowhere.

Everywhere.

The mists cleared and she looked into the reflection once more. Before her was a man with hard gray eyes and a halo of blonde curls.

"No!"

Everywhere.

The reflection of Theseus rippled, changed into the scowl of the initiate Kalchas.

Everywhere.

Helen's spirit rose in protest; the mists pushed her down once more.

Everywhere.

The surface changed again, showing her the land she had traveled and beyond.

Everywhere.

Faces appeared once more, this time of carved stone, beautiful, grotesque, tossed along a great expanse of land, streaming a suffocating blackness in their wake.

"No!"

Helen's scream was now laced with fear as land and water and animal, villager, merchant and nobleman fell to the noxious cloud that emanated from the grotesque masks.

She reached out her hand, slashing the waters surface again and again and again. Unbalanced by her own efforts, she fell into the water's depths.

Downward, downward. *I am with you always. Everywhere.*

The voice in her heart echoed once more, wrapping her in a cocoon of silence as she drifted down the watery abyss and returned to the simple grove.

Competent hands wrapped a cord about her waist and carried her gently down the corridor she once knew.

"She who is everywhere is within you."

Helen did not know if the words echoed from the depths of the sea or from the women who surrounded her.

❧

Ravenous hunger awoke her. Helen opened her eyes to the familiar surroundings of her room with the temple. Clarisa's bed was empty, the bed fleece neatly smoothed. From the position of the sun beyond the small window, she noted that it was far past the time she was to rise.

She lifted herself slowly, for her limbs felt weighted and battered. Pushing back the fleece, she noticed the braided cord she had so carefully woven was cinched about her night dress and that a small sheathed dagger was coiled in its dangling length.

Bound to the Goddess.

Thoughts of the night crashed upon her but she hastily pushed them aside; her need for food was more immediate.

She rose and drank greedily from the water pitcher placed upon the small table. The quenching of her thirst eased some of her body's discomfort and she felt able to wash before seeking food. Choosing a fresh gown from the worn chest, she made her way to the bathing room assigned to her. Quickly, she undid the knot which held the girdle about her waist, careful to study its workings so that she could re-tie it when she was through.

The cleansing water was a further restorative. Helen dried her body and quickly dressed and replaced the girdle, leaving the room to search the kitchen stores.

A tall woman whose name she could not remember intercepted her in the corridor. "The priestess Aethra would see you now," the woman informed her.

In all the moons of Helen's stay, the priestess had not once requested her presence. Surely she could have prolonged her entreaty long enough for Helen to eat. Helen hid her irritation and followed the expectant priestess to Aethra's rooms, trying to school herself to the expression of respect she knew was expected of her.

If Aethra knew her composure to be contrived, she gave no indication. The priestess was in her receiving room, seated upon one of the four throne chairs that it contained. To each side were chambers similar to the one Helen slept in. Beyond was yet another door, which led to a private bathing area.

"Thank you, Ianthe" Aethra said and the priestess who had summoned Helen bowed obediently and left the room.

"Sit and eat first," Aethra said, indicating a throne chair to the room's left.

Beside it was a small marble table holding a generous platter of bread and cheese and fruit.

Under Aethra's watchful eyes, Helen gave a moment of thanks before eating to her full. When she finished she positioned herself to face the priestess directly. She returned the woman's thoughtful gaze, astounded anew by the height of power that grew from the petite body. Aethra's beautiful face grew a hint of smile, making her seem younger than the seasons she must have lived.

The smile vanished. "Tell me of your vision."

The command jolted Helen and words pushed their way past her resentment, until she spoke in detail of all that had transpired in her vision to the Otherworld.

The priestess sat straighter at the mention of the masks and the darkness, but did not interrupt. At length, Helen finished sharing her memory. To her surprise, Aethra slumped backward as if Helen had wounded her greatly.

"I too have seen the darkness of the male gods, although it was not offered to me to banish it." She straightened and her smokey eyes narrowed. "That task has been given to you."

Helen stared at her, dumbfounded. For a brief moment, she entertained the thought that the woman before her was deranged. It was quickly replaced by a swelling pride that she should be so chosen. She drank of her power, feeling it grow with each sip until she was dizzied by her own potential.

Practical common sense crashed upon her.

"Even within the vision, I was not able to part the darkness," she said cantankerously. *Nor will I ever be able to see the Goddess in the likes of Theseus and his kind*, she added to herself.

The priestess was unmoved by her protest. "It means only that you have more to learn."

Aethra stood as if in dismissal. "This is why you will serve me now. Your things will be brought to the room beside mine. In my service, you will be called to do many things and will be lessoned in many others. You will obey me even as you would obey Her to whom you have bound yourself." She looked pointedly at the girdle about Helen's waist, reminding. "You shall ask no questions, nor speak unless spoken to. Of course, this does not apply during the afternoon training nor anytime when you work with the others. We must join them now for the session."

She turned as if to go, stopping mid-stride. "I want you to know this: There is nothing that does not happen but by your will and Hers. Your task is to discover that which you truly desire and bring it forth — for such desires are an echo of Her will. Then you must trust the path that carries you forward."

With that she did turn, leaving Helen to ponder her words and follow in her wake.

Time in Aethra's presence heightened Helen's already mixed feelings for the woman. There were moments when her resentment flared so great she had to restrain herself from shoving the bone clip which she fastened to the priestess' hair into her ear instead. Other moments the familiar awe would overtake her and unshed tears of gratitude and love burned her eyes.

The opposing nature of her emotions kept Helen in a near constant state of tension. Her only relief came during those times when she was released from the lady's service to join Clarisa on some task.

She particularly enjoyed those times when she and Clarisa could stand naked and free within the river's waters, cleaning the temple linens while splashing as much water upon each other as upon the clothe beneath their hands.

"Enough," Clarisa had pleaded on one such occasion, shaking her head in a futile attempt to dry her unbound hair. "You are far bigger than I."

Helen walked with her back to the grassy bank, carefully laying the clothes to dry before flopping herself down. Clarisa joined her shortly and peered a look at her friend.

"Temple food suits you," she remarked.

Helen opened one eye to her friend then looked to her thickening waist. "It's odd," she said, "I'm quite certain the food is plainer that at home."

"Oh, you need not worry. The extra weight becomes you," Clarisa responded, not without envy.

Helen turned upon her stomach and noticed Aethra watching them for a distance. The priestess' normally calm composure faded rapidly as she came within calling distance.

"Helen, attend me," she snapped.

Helen swallowed the lump of rebellion that rose to her throat. If Aethra called her in such a manner, there must be an important reason for her to do so. Helen met Clarisa' eyes. The other girl shrugged but Helen saw that she too was surprised at Aethra's tone. Helen hastily pulled her shift about her and hurried to where Aethra waited.

"This way," the priestess commanded, leading Helen to an isolated glen beyond the garden.

When they arrived, she confronted Helen immediately.

"How long have you been pregnant?"

The absurdity of the notion hit Helen first, generating a laugh that began at the base of her throat. It was choked back by horror. She had been in Troezen for five moons. Five moons without bleeding. Five moons since Theseus.

"Your waist is thickening," Aethra went on relentlessly. "You have a stomach ailment most mornings that disappears by mid-day. You've been drinking so much water, we'll need to drain the river soon!"

"No!" Her feeble protest was blown back to her on the morning wind.

Aethra advanced upon her. "You lay with a man before you came here, didn't you?"

Helen's racing heart sucked the blood from her face. *He was ripping her clothes, prying her legs open, thrusting himself inside her.* She shoved her fist into her mouth to keep from screaming.

"How could you not know this would happen?" Aethra demanded, continuing her merciless advance.

With relief, horror turned to rage. "How could I not know? How could I know? I was carried away from my home, dumped aboard a ship, taken to a strange palace and then your son — YOUR SON..." She would not go on, could not go on. The remembered trauma stole her voice, her mind was captured by visions she did not want to see.

How dare Aethra bring this back to her? Helen took sadistic satisfaction in Aethra's stricken look.

"My son? My son did this?"

It was Helen's turn to advance, closing the small space between them so Aethra would breath her hatred. "Yes. Your son. Cruelly. Maliciously. He beat me and then and then..."

Helen raised her hands to strike the woman, ready to pummel her as she had been pummeled, hurt the woman she had come to love and fear and respect, as she had been hurt.

"You poor baby. You poor, poor girl." Aethra grabbed hold of Helen's arms, a gesture of comfort rather than defense, and pulled her into an embrace. "I am so sorry."

The priestess cried astonishing tears that flowed from her small face down Helen's arms, beckoning forth Helen's own tears in a deluge of released pain.

They stood there for an eternity, grieving until their tears were spent and the voices of the maidens beyond the grove drew nearer.

"We must prepare for your coming child," Aethra said, gently extricating herself from Helen's arms.

Their eyes met, lapis blue to smokey green, reflecting healing and a burden shared.

As soon as it was detected, the child within Helen's body grew unchecked, shape changing Helen from slender maiden to voluptuous adult.

"She's kicking again, isn't she?" Clarisa leapt from her place on the grass and pressed her ear to Helen's protruding stomach.

Helen was more grateful than ever for Clarisa's friendship. Her impending motherhood, coupled with Aethra's insistence upon Helen's service far beyond the usual time proscribed, had increased the gulf between her and the other maidens. The latter situation convinced Clarisa that Helen was in fact Aethra's chosen daughter, although Aethra had said nothing of this to Helen.

Still, she had no time to mourn the loss of her potential friendships. The confusing changes of her body absorbed her attention utterly.

She had planned to hate the child within, conceived from the pain and horror of her past. But the creature who grew inside flooded her blood with an aching innocence which her heart expanded to protect.

She saw her former misery carried in the orbs of Aethra's eyes. Beyond that, their relationship continued as before. The priestess was tender and irascible by turns, continuing the education of Helen's spirit despite the distractions of her changing body.

Her petite shadow fell upon the two girls, announcing her presence. Clarisa jumped from her resting place and bowed respectfully. Aethra acknowledged her and turned a critical eye toward Helen.

"The babe will be born by moon full," she announced, as if her very words could command the life to spring forth from Helen's body.

Perhaps they had.

Within a fortnight, Helen's middle screamed in pain, claiming the air from her lungs.

"Help me!" Her plea was no more than a whisper echoing off the stone walls of her sleeping quarters. With the long ears of the Goddess trained, Aethra heard her cry and came running to the room, lit torch in hand.

"It has come," Aethra said, officially marking the beginning of Helen's labor.

The priestess stood in the doorway, the flames of the wavering torch alternatively casting light and shadows across her face, her unbound hair and the folds of her nightdress.

Like the spirit of the Goddess come forth from the Otherworld, Helen thought irrelevantly before pain attacked her body once more and she closed her eyes to everything outside her. She felt Aethra approach, and the touch of her expert hands moving firmly along her sides.

"I will beckon Ianthe," the priestess said and left before Helen could protest.

Time expanded as Helen lay alone, a sticky wetness rushing down the inside of her thighs and the tempo of her pain gaining intensity.

"My!" Ianthe exclaimed pointlessly, entering the room and feeling about Helen's body as Aethra had done a moment before. Her jolly manner turned abruptly brisk. "Set water to boil and bring fresh thrash to place in the room's corner," she ordered to the high priestess.

Helen flinched in response to the woman's tone, anticipating Aethra's reprimand. Who would dare speak so to the Goddess' chosen?

But Aethra handed her authority to the one charged with bringing forth life. She hastily set the torch to the room's hearth and fled, returning a moment later with a kettle of water that she secured on a pole above the flames. A second time she scurried from the room, returning with a bundle of thatch that had been set aside in anticipation of the birth.

"Help me," Ianthe ordered and Aethra moved once more to do her bidding. Together, the two women freed Helen from the bed covers and led her to the thatch-covered corner.

"Stand behind her, Mother, and hold her upright."

Helen could scarce feel the priestess' delicate frame support her. Pain blurred her senses and fogged her awareness.

"It won't be long now. The Goddess shows mercy to this one."

Mercy? The agony that wracked Helen had lasted since the beginning of time. "Call upon Her power within you," Aethra reminded, smoothing Helen's sweat-drenched hair away from her face.

Helen focused her awareness on the space above her heart, feeling the familiar expansion that portended the Goddess within. The presence was as soothing as a kernel of corn to a starving man's belly. Pain dominated her awareness, claiming her totally.

"Oh!"

The cry left her lips as the pain shifted lower, urging her to expel it. She grunted and focused and pushed the resisting life from the confinement of her body.

"We're almost there!" Ianthe screamed.

We? Helen promised herself she would rip the woman's lying tongue from her mouth.

"Push harder."

She did, straining against the life that sought to crawl its way back into her womb.

Release came and a constellation of stars burst behind her eyelids. Aethra eased her head upon the straw bed, while the healer attended the space between her legs.

A lusty cry cut through the silence.

"A beautiful, healthy girl," Ianthe said proudly, placing the child to Helen's breast.

A small mouth closed about her nipple, joining the world through the nourishment Helen offered her.

"She is beautiful," Aethra breathed, wonder fresh upon her face. Within one breath and the next, she re-assumed the mantle of power. "I have read the stars in anticipation of this birth and have learned that this child carries an important destiny. She too is a messenger of the Goddess."

A chill finger of fear traced its way down Helen's spine and she drew the babe closer to her breast. The child's warmth reached her heart, dispelling her unease. Time enough to worry over destinies.

"What will you name her?" Aethra asked, her tone blessedly informal once more.

A name buried in the recesses of Helen's mind burst forth. "Iphigeneia."

Helen, excused from her temple routine to care for her child, sat in contented silence against the sheltering body of an oak. She looked compulsively toward the sleeping form of the child who lay upon the blanket next to her.

"The life of the temple suits her," Clarisa remarked.

Helen had to agree. Some babies, she knew, were fussy and demanding. Iphigeneia, however, showed herself to be easily contented, sleeping often and deeply, feeding at regular times, crying infrequently.

She is perfect, Helen thought, as she had so many times before, her body awash with a love so great it squeezed water from her eyes. She watched the steady breathing of her child, at once anxious to hold her again and fiercely protective of her sleep.

Her mind supplied her with the image of another woman whose kind hand stroked the heads of she and her sister with equal affection. It was ironic that the birth of her child would open the doors to her past, clearly showing her own mother's forgotten affection.

There was a time when Leda cared for me — cared for each of her children — without expectation. The memories were a revelation, and not a totally pleasant one. *Once, Leda felt toward me as I do toward Iphigeneia. Will my love change as radically?* She hardened her heart against Leda's forgotten love, building a wall to prevent her past from influencing her future.

Aethra is more mother to me than Leda ever was, she told herself firmly. Thoughts of the high priestess caused the lines of her forehand to wrinkle with worry. Aethra had said nothing to her, but Helen knew the priestess was deeply troubled. Though she presided over rituals and supervised the temple's everyday activities as she always did, there was no spirit behind Aethra's words. It was as if some vital part of the priestess was occupied elsewhere. From her adjacent chamber, Helen could hear the woman rise in the night and knew she walked outside beneath the stars, as if searching for answers.

Helen longed to ask Aethra what was wrong but knew she would not. Despite her suspended duties, she was still pledged to Aethra's service. The injunction against speaking without first being spoken to still held. And Aethra did not confide her thoughts to Helen. Indeed, since Iphigeneia's birth, Aethra rarely spoke with Helen at all, except for an occasional distracted murmur of one sort or another.

She is high priestess, chosen of the Goddess. No doubt there are a great many things to occupy her thoughts. You are not her only concern, Helen told herself firmly.

She looked once again at her child and shrugged off her worry, missing the sight of the priestess walking beyond the clearing into the shade of the grove.

Aethra was glad Helen had not seen her. The dreams that once again stole her sleep made it difficult to look into the young woman's eyes. She walked slowly along the ground that supplied life to the trees around her, imploring the earth to replenish her vitality as well.

As before, her dreams enveloped her in a blanket of darkness that threatened to turn her fragile body to muck and steal the spirit housed within. But this time, the light she sought was not found in Sparta. Rather, it wrapped itself around the princess she had stolen, who stood proudly at the prow of a ship, ignoring Aethra's futile attempts to swim to the safety of the vessel.

Despite the summer's warmth, Aethra shivered and raised her eyes to the sky. She could anticipate the night and the waning moon it contained. Too many days until it turned dark and was reborn. Too many days until she could scry upon the water's surface and learn the message of her dream.

Until then, fear and the training that forced her to honest self inspection offered their own interpretation. Had she already lost Helen to her own machinations? Again and again, her mind replayed the horrid day when Helen disclosed that Theseus had attacked her. The revelation was a wound to Aethra's soul. Her son, her son had defiled the Goddess in this way! Beyond that horror was another: She had ordered the situation that allowed him to do so.

She had cried as Helen has cried, as much for the poor girl who had been violated as for herself. She did not reveal that she was responsible for Helen's kidnapping. Nor had she yet explained that she had set Rhemnesia to be Helen's guardian.

The girl's training is not advanced enough to understand the necessity of such actions, Aethra told herself firmly.

You are a coward! another part of her screamed.

She knew both were true.

As she knew her dream could be borne of her guilt and anxiety as easily as it could portend the unfolding future.

Would that she could learn the latter without having to wait upon the moon's movements.

As if in answer to her plea, two men of incredible beauty stepped from behind the concealment of bushes and stood in her path.

"Where is she?"

The demand was made by the shorter of the two. He was blonde and menacing, with a wrestler's build and no-nonsense blue eyes.

The man beside him was equally good looking with curly dark hair and large brown eyes. They looked nothing alike yet had the similarity of brothers. That and the rich texture of their clothing told Aethra who they were.

She locked eyes with the blonde, guessing him to be the more shakable of the two. "You mean the Princess Helen of Sparta, I presume."

Her guess had been accurate; the blonde man's eyes widened in surprise and he took a small step backward.

"Well, that saved us some time," the darker of the two said languidly.

Aethra looked to him with what she hoped was her most intimidating stare.

The dark-haired youth was surprisingly unmoved. "She's been kept hostage here. We've come to take her home," he explained with calculated patience.

Years of training kept Aethra's face unreadable. "Hardly a hostage. But," she said when the man would speak further. "perhaps you'd like to speak with her and determine this for yourself."

She noted with satisfaction that the man's tranquil composure slipped a bit. *This one is used to fighting to gain his demands*, she rightfully surmised. She turned abruptly, frustrating them further by calmly walking through the shade of the grove, leaving them to follow.

Her satisfaction melted before the reality that faced her.

So this is what my dream portrayed. Have I ensured Helen's loyalty enough to keep her here? Or did the dream speak of my failure?

Against her will, she walked faster, fearful of Helen's reaction to the men's arrival, impatient to see what it would be.

They entered the garden in which Helen sat, contentedly braiding flowers that would be used for ritual garlands, as Iphigeneia slept beside her. The princess looked to Aethra and smiled tentatively.

Her smile vanished as the two men entered her sight.

"Castor? Polydeuces?" She jumped from her place, careful not to disturb the sleeping babe.

With rising hope Aethra noted that Helen did not run to embrace them.

Helen could not embrace them for she could no longer move. Her brothers seemed like spirits returned from the Otherworld, the shapes of men, hinting at the boys she once knew. Of their own volition, her eyes sought her child.

I must seem similarly strange.

It appeared to be so. Castor and Polydeuces looked at her, then scanned the tranquil surroundings before looking back again. Castor threw a furtive look at his darker twin.

"We've come to take you home," Polydeuces announced.

Helen just looked at him.

"We're rescuing you," he explained further, his voice hardening.

Helen could not stop herself from laughing at his arrogance. She opened her arms to indicate her surroundings, simultaneously drawing their attention from the sleeping child who lay a few paces behind her. "This is what you came to rescue me from?"

Polydeuces looked pained and Helen felt instantly remorseful. They could not, after all, have known the conditions under which she lived. They probably imagined her in some squalid hut, deprived of luxuries of any kind.

"I am grateful to you for your concern," she said softly. "But truly, I am more happy here than I could ever be at home."

They looked to her as if she had gone mad. Castor turned an unbecoming shade of red and broke his silence. "Nonsense. Your place is at home and we mean to return you there."

He advanced upon her and grabbed her arm roughly.

Helen's remorse vanished. "How dare you lay rough hands on me?" she screamed angrily, pulling herself free. "I will not leave with you."

For a short instant, she had thought she might go with them, returning to a homeland that, if not perfect, was at least familiar. But their assumption that she could just be carried off like some errant child irritated her beyond reason. She would not leave now no matter what they threatened.

"You must come," Polydeuces said with certainty. "We cannot have the other kingdoms believe Sparta will simply standby and allow a princess to be abducted!"

Helen wanted to strangle him. "What do I care what other kingdoms believe?"

"You should care." Polydeuces responded, his calm voice rising. "It is your duty to care"

She looked from Polydeuces to Castor and back again, seeing the same hard looks in each of their eyes. *They care only for the reputation of Sparta and not at all about me*, she thought. Her eyes moved to Iphigeneia, who had, amazingly, slept through the entire exchange. She walked to her child and gently lifted her into her arms.

"And will Sparta be pleased to welcome an unmarried princess with child," she said, softly and spitefully.

The shock that appeared on her brothers' faces was deeply satisfying.

Castor turned on Aethra. "Do you run a temple for heirtias then?" he demanded.

The priestess remained cool in the face of his insult. "Princess Helen was pregnant by Theseus, king of Attica, before she arrived here."

Helen knew her brothers did not see the small lines of pain that appeared around Aethra's eyes; it was enough that she had.

"Theseus." Castor spat upon the ground. "Would that he had not fled his kingdom so that I may have seen him safely to Hades to continue his havoc in the Otherworld."

"When he returns, he will meet death from the hands of he who now holds the throne," Polydeuces reminded him. To Aethra, he said, "Your son has been replaced by a more worthy successor and I'm certain Menestheus will not easily yield to his rule again."

Aethra's face was unreadable. "He has gotten only what he deserves."

Helen's heart broke with empathy. Though she could not help but agree, she knew how painful an admission this must be for the proud priestess.

"Enough," Polydeuces said, returning his attention to Helen. "You shall leave the child and return with us at once."

Her arms tightened involuntarily around Iphigeneia, who cried out in protest. "I will not go with you," she said calmly, her body daring her brothers to take her forcibly.

Polydeuces was implacable. "If you do not return of your own volition, we will let it be known that the city of Troezen refused to release you and declare war upon them."

Troezen was a small town on the sea, populated by fisherman and sheep herders who lived in peaceful service to the temple they honored. They relied upon their location and simple lifestyles to protect them from the greedy hands of other kingdoms and, if necessary, would fight to the death to protect their home. Still, they were no match for an army the size of Sparta's.

"You cannot!" Helen cried, appalled, rocking her child in a feeble effort to calm her from the upset Helen was communicating.

Polydeuces was unmoved. "We can and we will."

Helen found that she hated him. She looked to Aethra.

The priestess was stricken but defiant. "The kingdom of Troezen will do everything within our power to support your decision," she said to Helen alone.

Helen knew she could not allow this. The kingdom of Troezen gave her refuge from Theseus, a good life, meaningful work and, she realized as she looked at Aethra's face, love. She would not subject them to sure ravishment.

"You have won," she said bitterly to her brothers. "But I will not leave my child, no matter what you threaten. If you insist on attacking Troezen for that, I will flee before the army arrives and you will be exposed for the barbarians you are."

Once more, a brilliant red flashed across Castor's face and he began to advance upon her. Polydeuces held him back.

"Fine. We will take you and the child to Mycenae and discuss the situation with Clytemnestra. Pack your things immediately."

Helen turned and entered the temple, feeling Aethra follow behind her. Clytemnestra. Helen hugged her babe tightly, as if to hold together the shards of her splintering life.

They left that afternoon, boarding a ship with Helen's few possessions, the babe and Aethra.

"It is my destiny," the priestess said simply.

She had convened a meeting with the temple maidens, designating an elder priestess to oversee temple functions, appointing another to serve as queen in her absence and even making a proclamation to her people — all with the efficiency that Helen had grown to admire.

The only indication that the priestess was shaken by the sudden departure was her peculiar insistence that she board the ship before Helen.

CHAPTER THREE

The spoils of war.

Massive shoulders moved delicately to avoid waking
Clytemnestra from feigned sleep. With hooded eyes, she watched
the naked figure slip silently into a silk robe before departing
her chambers.

A victorious smile melted Clytemnestra's full lips. So little
time to savor her success! She allowed herself a luxurious
stretch, her well-used body sighing in tribute to the strength of
the man who had just left her.

Agamemnon's reputation was well deserved.

Her new husband easily took the great citadel of Mycenae,
killing the guards loyal to Tantalus and swarming the great
palace with remarkable speed. It was testimony to his military
prowess and strategic cunning, they said. Agamemnon, most
powerful of men. Agamemnon, king of Mycenae.

And Clytemnestra, his queen.

She thought of her dear, dead late husband and wished him
well in whatever Otherworld he now inhabited. No doubt
Tantalus was grateful for the permanent rest granted his spirit.

Tantalus had been an absolute sloth in life, preferring boasting to action and dice to ruling. Clytemnestra's smile widened
to a feral sneer as she recalled her first moons at the palace.
How appalled she had been by her husband's lack of interest in
the kingdom he ruled! For him it was a mere inconvenience. As
was his wedding to the daughter of the powerful king of Sparta.
Clytemnestra soon realized that his visit to her homeland was
one of the rare times Tantalus exerted himself in any way. He
himself viewed it as a necessary exception: Once a powerful
alliance with Sparta was made, he spent even less time on mili-

tary matters, relying instead on Sparta for any necessary defense of his homeland.

So he wed the Spartan princess, installed her in his great palace, bed her once and then returned his attention to dice and the scrawny, brainless women who were his preference.

Of course Clytemnestra hated him.

During the first several moons of her Mycenaen reign, she drowned in a pool of despair so uncharacteristic she had thought she would die. She considered returning home, but could not bear the humiliation she thought would greet her there. She also could not remain confined to her bed for long; her own passionate character would not allow her to wallow forever. She sought relief from her bitterness by issuing strict orders to the lazy servants who roamed about the palace. Disappointment turned to anger when they ignored her completely.

"The king likes it this way," they replied again and again.

Her impotent fury gave her visions of lining them up against the nearest wall and severing their heads.

The most satisfying image was of dealing a similar fate to the man she had wed.

Seething, she had forced herself to speak with Tantalus instead.

She had been surprised to find the door to his chambers, behind which he was assuredly gambling with his underlings, slightly ajar.

"...and so, my lord, I need your recommendations for the festival offering."

"I leave the procurement to your discretion," she heard Tantalus reply.

"But my lord..."

"Surely you can decide upon how many sheep or whatever need to be slaughtered for a festival that occurs every spring."

Typical Tantalus. Opportunity embraced Clytemnestra like a lover.

"Perhaps I can be of assistance," she said, pushing the door open and stepping inward.

Immediately, the guards scattered around the floor began to rise. Tantalus waved them to stay where they were and they sank back to their circle, amid trays of half-eaten foods and round discs Clytemnestra assumed were used for wages.

"You don't need to trouble yourself, my dear," Tantalus said.

Pretending civility at that moment was the greatest challenge of her life. "It will be no trouble, my lord," she said calmly.

Her husband was having a difficult time pulling his attention from the game. "As you wish then. The queen will assist you, priest Iapetus."

Iapetus' ugly face was a comical mixture of trepidation and relief. Large brown eyes, spaced wide to accommodate a bulbous nose, regarded her cautiously while his thin lips puckered with a most revealing quiver.

A perfect tool, Clytemnestra thought. Vitality pumped in her veins once more.

She exercised the authority denied her in the palace freely within the temple walls, insinuating herself in the planning of festivals and the coordination of lessons for the children. She still cared not one wit for the gods but knew well the power of religion; it was a power she intended to exploit to her greatest advantage. She considered adopting the religion of the Great Mother but dismissed it quickly. The Great Goddess preferred the open fields to impressive temples, the gift of spirit to the offering of jewels; Clytemnestra found such preferences intolerable.

Still, she knew the faith practiced by her hated sister and Helen's loathsome guardian made the queen the central ruler of the land and the king a merely expendable war leader. Such beliefs had a necessary advantage over the king rule promoted by the Olympian gods. Clytemnestra spent several nights worrying over her choice, weighing her limited knowledge of the Olympians against her even more limited understanding of the Great Mother, seeking the greater opportunity to be had.

Her decision came in a moment of sheer brilliance. She would combine the religions, slowly instituting Mother rule, while continuing to demand the wealth of offerings preferred by the Olympians. She would even continue the worship under Artemis, as the people had grown accustomed to. Wasn't that goddess already a leader? She began hearing petitions, placing herself as the voice of the goddess Artemis. Iapetus was appalled; only those initiated to priesthood or women sworn to live as priestesses could offer counsel from the gods. Clytemnestra informed him that the goddess told her otherwise...right after Artemis ordered her to build larger sleeping quarters for the temple's head priest.

Iapetus voiced no further objections.

Day upon day, she built a citadel of power by rendering judgments to those seeking divine assistance. The people grew to revere, respect and sometimes fear her. Her words became the cornerstones upon which many built their lives. But her word was not law. Too many people — particularly the nobles — sub-

mitted their desires to Tantalus for judgment. She worried over
this problem as she prepared for the Thesmophoria festival, a
senseless three-day affair in which all the women gathered in
seclusion to speak with the goddess. To liven things up a bit,
she planned a variety of shocking events — pig sacrifices, phalli
ceremonies, pits rippling with snakes. She smiled in anticipation of the noble women's response to such sights. Perhaps by
impressing the wives, she would gain some influence over their
husbands. She left the palace shortly after the sun's peak . During festival's past, the women met at any point during the mid-
afternoon, depending upon when they completed their fieldwork
or finished nursing their children or finalized meal preparations
for their husbands. Clytemnestra, refusing to wait around, ordered them to assemble at a set time.

She was greeted by a tense mob. Throngs of women stood
about uneasily, flagged by a good many men who had come to
glare their resentment.

This was a mistake, Clytemnestra thought, her brain frantically searching for ways to handle the unexpected situation.

Then a miracle occurred.

The formerly vapid, blundering women looked at each other
to avoid looking at their men. A slow smile was passed among
them, spreading with smug pride. The men shifted uncomfortably; the women's smiles widened. Peasants and noble women
and merchants locked eyes and their bodies straightened with
shared power. The men began to move backward.

Clytemnestra moved to the front of the crowd, throwing the
men a look of calculated innocence before adding a smile of her
own to the women before her.

"To Thesmophoria," she said, turning to lead the march,
feeling power radiate from the women's procession, direct itself
to her, bolster her.

It was intoxicating.

Careful, her cunning brain warned. *You have won the power
of the women but you need the men as well.*

She considered this new challenge as she led the women
who laughed with uninhibited lust to the river to begin the purification ritual. She kept them moving to the temple courtyard,
where a pit was dug and snakes slithered in echoes of primal
memory. Distracted, she lit the herbs to bring about visions,
knowing that any seeing would result more from the fasting the
women did that day than from the herbs. Some of the women
began stamping their feet on the solid earth. More and more
joined in and they began swaying. Clytemnestra continued to
consider her problem as the earth beneath her rumbled and the

sacred smoke burned her eyes. *The men must be loyal to me as well*, she thought, knowing she could not rule half a kingdom, knowing that when she had won the support of all her people, she would need to expand her rule and conquer lands beyond Mycenae. She needed a consort. Loyal. Obedient. Ambitious at her command.

Her vision blurred further, smoke obscuring her clarity of thought. She stood transfixed by its curling tendrils, watching pictures form and release.

And then she saw him. A man of surpassing beauty, delicate features surrounding deep granite eyes, strong arms outstretched from his powerful body. His eyes met hers and he bowed in supplication.

Clytemnestra screamed.

Over the next few days of the festival, she hardened herself against the vision and thought rationally. She needed a king who would be strong and submissive. He would win the loyalty of the men and bow to her command. He would engender fear in neighboring peoples and follow her orders.

He would be someone other than Tantalus.

Someone like the man in her vision.

It was not possible, she told herself firmly. The man she saw amid the smoke was a fanciful composite born of her mind to lead her to the actual solution to her challenge: ridding herself of Tantalus and setting up a man to whom the Mycenaen men would pledge their loyalty and who would, in turn, pledge his loyalty to Clytemnestra.

By the end of the festival, a plan was forming and she was able to return her attention to the women. Now that she had empowered them and won their servitude, she would have to hold their interest.

Stay with what works, she told herself. "We will hold an abbreviated Thesmophoria during each moon full," she announced at the final day of the current festival.

The women cheered.

Having taken care of them, she returned to the palace to begin her next move. She called a messenger to her chamber. "I wish for you to go to Sparta and speak to priest Kalchas. You are to say the following: 'The queen Clytemnestra remembers the assistance she gave you and is very pleased at how far you have come. She requests a private visit with you to reminisce the success of the past and share wine in anticipation of an even more promising future.'"

Clytemnestra awaited Kalchas' visit, confident he would

come. Over the last season, as she gained authority in her kingdom, she had not forgotten the initiate's fortuitous arrival to
announce the death of Glaucus. She was certain he killed the
priest and she suspected he knew she knew. He was about to
pay for her silence. She received him in her private chambers,
which were a magnificent display of wealth. Silk curtains covered the windows that overlooked the expanse of Mycenae. Heavy
furniture, beautifully adorned with gold in the likenesses of lions and flowers, was scattered artfully about. Her own chair
boasted soft feather cushions of exquisite embroidering. Kalchas
entered, unsuccessfully hiding his awe at their surroundings.

"Kalchas, how wonderful to see a familiar face." She showed
him her most gracious hospitality, offering chilled thick wine
and fine figs, reminiscing idly about Spartan life and making
inane comparisons with that of Mycenae.

Kalchas relaxed. Clytemnestra noted it.

"And how is it to be high priest?" she asked sweetly.

Tension poured through Kalchas' veins, altering his posture. "An honor I strive to fulfill," he said curtly, then covered
his face with his wine goblet.

Clytemnestra hid a smile. Before her invitation, she had
ordered messengers to Sparta to observe Kalchas and the workings of the temple. The information she received was well worth
the brooch she paid for it. Kalchas was in trouble. His high priesthood was not officially conferred, despite the king's approval.
The station was technically granted by the temple priests themselves, with whom Kalchas was as popular as a wart. The most
generous thought him young and foolish. The rest believed him
a manipulator and a liar.

Clytemnestra pressed her advantage. "I understand your
position has not yet been conferred. Has a date been chosen?"

Seeing the facade of calm melt from Kalchas' face was
uniquely pleasurable. She could almost hear his thick brain
weigh the advantages of speaking plainly or continuing the farce.
He chose a path between the two. "Actually, your invitation was
like a portend to me," he gently replaced his goblet on the table
beside him.

Clytemnestra admired his smoothness. "How so?" she asked,
enjoying the game even as she recognized that it would soon
become tiresome.

"There are some older men within the temple, wise men,
who — forgive me — have lived beyond their service to the goddess Artemis. Unfortunately, they are swayed by one man called
Iarbus, who I suspect wants the position for himself. His self-
interest makes it impossible for him to support me."

One of countless possible reasons, Clytemnestra thought. She kept her expression interested.

"His influence is great and he is very single-minded."

"Ah, that can be a problem."

"The only influence upon him," Kalchas continued, ignoring her hint of sarcasm, "is that of his mentor, whom he speaks of highly and often. His mentor is Iapetus. I believe that you know him."

Clytemnestra hid enormous pleasure as he mentioned the Mycenae priest. How wonderful that she did not have to mention him herself. "Indeed. We are quite close," she made herself say blandly.

"I believe that if I can convince Iapetus of my superior claim to the position, Iarbus will adhere to his mentor's judgment and the priesthood will be rightfully conveyed to me."

Clytemnestra pretended to consider his problem. "That is quite a task. You know — or perhaps you don't — that Iapetus is a bit of, shall we say, an isolationist when it comes to the affairs of temples outside his homeland."

"Everyone can be influenced," Kalchas said positively.

"True," Clytemnestra said. "In fact, I am quite certain that, I, for example, could easily influence Iapetus to support your cause."

Kalchas remained silent.

Shrewd man, Clytemnestra thought. She reminded herself that she would not be wasting her time with him if he were not.

"Perhaps we can help each other," she suggested. "There is information I need as well as assistance. Of course, I must be able to trust the provider of each implicitly."

They each moved their lips in what were supposed to be smiles.

"I believe I can prove most helpful," Kalchas beamed, assuming the confident pose Clytemnestra expected. His reaction to her next words shocked her utterly.

"I have had a vision..." she began.

Kalchas' posturing disappeared completely. He leaned forward nervously, his eyes alight with an eagerness other men reserved for women or wine.

How interesting. But at the moment, she was far more uncomfortable than intrigued. She would ponder his reaction at some later time — preferably when he was far from her presence.

"I need a powerful man to attack Mycenae and become king

in Tantalus' place," she said with more bluntness than she would have liked.

"Your vision told you this?" he asked, leaning still closer.

Clytemnestra's body sunk involuntarily backward, while her mind alerted her to new possibilities.

"Yes," she said slowly. "You played prominently within the vision."

Kalchas clapped his hands in undignified delight, his homely features stretching with what Clytemnestra could only describe as joy. "Almost, then, it is as if I myself had the vision," he mumbled, no longer seeing her. "I have the power...but it was a woman who spoke after all, woman to woman." The joy was fast changing to a dangerous bitterness.

"I was shown your importance in serving the hands of fate," Clytemnestra said quickly. Then, because it would not serve her if he held his own importance too highly, "That is, I think it was you I saw. Perhaps it was not, if you do not know the man I seek." She issued a dramatic sigh, foretelling her anticipated disappointment.

Kalchas melded nicely under her manipulations. "Agamemnon is the man you seek," he said quickly, with what may or may not have been certainty. "He is a young lord who has consistently proven himself in battle. Indeed, he has won many followers among the landless men." His enthusiasm with his choice grew. "He himself has only a small holding so he doesn't have a great deal of power as a ruler. But I take it this would serve you quite well. He will no doubt be willing to abide the wishes of a competent queen."

He smiled, satisfied with his understanding. Once he articulated her plan, Clytemnestra discovered that she did not like his knowing.

"The vision also indicated that you could be trusted to contact him without revealing my involvement. I trust that this part of the vision is accurate as well. No doubt Artemis will attend to you herself if you break such a confidence." She issued a careless shrug and hid relief as Kalchas face paled remarkably. *How easily manipulated are those who believe in this gods nonsense*, she thought disdainfully.

"I will tell him I knew you in childhood and am concerned for your welfare," he was saying. "I will tell him that enemies threaten Mycenae's borders and I fear the current king cannot defend against them. I'll tell him that I want to be sure the king of Mycenae is capable of safeguarding the current queen."

"Yes," Clytemnestra replied. "And in return for assurances that he treat me well, you will provide him with detailed information about Mycenae's defenses so he can easily breech them."

Providing information to Agamemnon meant sharing it with Kalchas, which Clytemnestra was loath to do. Still, such action was necessary. Her spies in Sparta would ensure that Kalchas was never in a position to take advantage of the knowledge himself. "Agamemnon's victory," she continued. "will be so decisive that his reputation throughout Greece will be secured. And, of course, by marrying the current queen, he will demonstrate his generosity and win the support of the Mycenae populace, who adore her."

The power of Clytemnestra's vision was quickly losing its hold upon Kalchas as he considered his involvement in so dangerous a plan.

"I am confident in your powers to persuade Agamemnon to our cause," Clytemnestra said smoothly. "As I am equally confident in my own abilities to convert Iapetus to your cause. I guarantee Iapetus will support you, as I recommend."

Kalchas knew a wall when it was pressed against his back.

And so it began.

Clytemnestra spent the battle in the temple, with a small army and a large group of women, ensuring her protection. Even if Kalchas had convinced Agamemnon to take Clytemnestra as wife, she could not be certain the warrior wouldn't change his mind. The knowledge that he would have to kill the women, overcome potentially loyal men and invade a temple to kill her would surely forestall any wavering he might experience. No matter how ignorant he was of politics, he would not violate these basic rules of war.

He was not in the palace long before sending a messenger to request her hand in marriage.

The ceremony took place immediately. If anyone wondered why the bride had a wedding dress stowed away in a temple while she hid from the conqueror, they were wise enough not to ask.

As Clytemnestra was wise enough to bury her disappointments that man she now bed had brown eyes and not gray, jutting features instead of delicate.

She became equally adept at hiding her resentment that Agamemnon was not proving the malleable consort she anticipated. Kalchas had been accurate in his report of Agamemnon's strength. The man had overtaken Mycenae with brilliant efficiency, appointing his men to his top positions and granting lesser positions to Mycenae natives to instill their gratitude and loyalty. The men adored and feared him in turn, praising his fairness and remaining mindful of his wrath, which could be quite formidable when he was crossed.

His physique added to his power. Over a head taller than most men, his arms, torso and legs were large and in perfect sculptured proportion. His features were strong — boulder cheeks, large eyes and a powerful jaw that seemed to grow even larger when he was displeased.

He was not what one would ordinarily consider attractive but he was exceptional and that gave him a certain allure. So too did his leadership abilities. In this, Kalchas had been wrong. Despite his relatively humble upbringing, Agamemnon possessed an intuitive grasp of justice.

It was a real problem.

When he had usurped Tantalus' throne, Clytemnestra intended to assume the powers of magistrate — hearing the petitions of merchants and noblemen, as she did peasants and farmers, through her unofficial position in the temple.

"You need not worry about listening to their tiring pleas," she had informed him sweetly. "I'll oversee their petty complaints to free you to make our kingdom strong."

"Defense is only one of the strengths a kingdom has," Agamemnon informed her pedantically. "It is my responsibility to ensure that our subjects are loyal and abide by the decrees that keep us powerful."

The best she could arrange was to preside over the petitions with him, which, curiously, he seemed to welcome.

In fact, it seemed as if he actually liked her and enjoyed her company, relishing pitting his wit against her own. Such acceptance had been denied Clytemnestra so long that she had no place to put it. To cover her discomfort, she focused upon ways to use his affection. So far she had not been successful.

He proved annoyingly reticent when it came to expanding Mycenae's wealth. She had carefully presented him with plans to conquer neighboring cities — Cornith, Nemea, Tegea— outlining the goods that would augment Mycenae's own stores.

He took polite interest in her plans, then ignored them completely. She persevered and he became irritated. She persisted and he exploded.

"We cannot just go around attacking our neighbors without provocation! Word will get out that the Mycenaes are no better than pirates. And how long do you think it will take for them to unite against us with an attack we cannot withstand?"

He was right of course, although Clytemnestra was loath to admit it. Still, her ambition was not cooled. Mycenae seemed to grow smaller as her thirst for power grew more intense.

❧

It was then that she decided to use what power she did have: the temple religion. She planned carefully, relocating initiates loyal to her to neighboring temples, moving whole families whose wives she had converted during her women's rituals.

She stressed the power of the goddesses Artemis and Athene, warrior maidens who Clytemnestra fancied gave orders and offered strategies in much the same way she did. She had her loyal women speak to their men of Ares, the mindless war god who would fight where he was told. She placed less emphasis upon Zeus, whom she felt was a useless philanderer, capable of undermining a woman's authority. Similarly she ignored Poseidon who was, in Clytemnestra's opinion, too wise and rational to be a man. No mention was made of Aphrodite; Clytemnestra had no use for love.

As her followers spread her interpretation of the gods, she gained the reverence of those within her kingdom as well as those beyond it. Such reverence loosened tongues, which brought Clytemnestra valued information. She envisioned a time when her religious spies would influence the decisions of their new kingdoms' rulers, perhaps even launching the provocation Agamemnon needed to fulfill his rule as warrior consort.

But she needed to move slowly and carefully. If her lackeys assumed authority too quickly, they might arouse suspicion and Clytemnestra's plans would be in ruins.

Of course, she dispatched one of her first and most loyal initiates to Sparta. Kalchas had indeed proven quite useful and Clytemnestra felt he deserved the influence she exerted to make him high priest. Still, she did not trust him for as high as she could lift a cow.

He would know, of course, that he was spied upon. Clytemnestra didn't care. Such knowledge would keep him anxious and divert his attention from the priestess who Clytemnestra also moved to the Spartan countryside.

She was quite content to wait for her system of religious contacts to be fully operational. Already, their minor influence was proving highly beneficial. She knew, for example, when a kingdom was experiencing a drought or a crop short fall or was preparing a minor skirmish against another.

She began presenting such information to Agamemnon, who begrudgingly acknowledged her accuracy when she was proved right often enough.

She, of course, credited her knowledge to the visions granted her by the gods. Agamemnon was skeptical but said nothing; he seemed to have less use for religion than she. Her people accepted her supposed powers without question and credited her with the voice of the gods. She had no doubt that this would prove useful one day.

In the meantime, she focused her attention on strengthening an alliance with Sparta. Of course, as Sparta's former princess and daughter to the king, she could count on her father's support in the time of crisis. (Indeed, during her planned takeover of Mycenae by Agamemnon, she was sure to send carefully deceptive messages to her father's palace to keep him from interfering). Unfortunately, her father's stance, like her current husband's, was primarily defensive. A powerful alliance between an aggressive Sparta and Mycenae would give Clytemnestra control of a large portion of the Greek mainland.

Fortunately, her father could not rule forever. Clytemnestra had spent the past couple of winters carefully cultivating her brothers' loyalty. The crown would inevitably pass to them anyway — especially now that Helen was not a contestant — and Clytemnestra wanted to make sure they were under her influence.

Unlike her father, her brothers were easy to manipulate. Castor had a reputation as a wrestler and was graced with more muscle than brain. Polydeuces, though smarter by far, was possessed by an unquenchable wanderlust. Most of his considerable talents were spent planning his next adventure.

They were perfect candidates for the Spartan throne; they would be adventuring for much of their rule, allowing Clytemnestra to appoint a steward loyal to her to sit on the throne in their absence.

Two problems stood in the way of her plans. She had learned from her sources that Polydeuces was still in love with Phoebe, the girl Clytemnestra had used to get rid of Rhemnesia. Phoebe would remember that Clytemnestra had betrayed her.

Her installation at the Spartan palace would be intolerable.

Clytemnestra used her contacts in Messenia to arrange a marriage between Phoebe and a minor lord, but she could not be sure that the marriage would be enough to dissuade the stubborn Polydeuces from going after her.

Her second problem was far more serious. Her sources said that there was a rumor that Polydeuces and Castor were going to rescind all rights to the throne in favor of their adventuring. With Clytemnestra already queen of Mycenae, that meant that Helen was in line for succession. Of course, if Helen was dead, this would not be a problem. Still, if her brothers rescinded too soon, the king could appoint whomever he wished to succeed him and there was no guarantee Clytemnestra could influence his choice.

Of course, if Helen was alive, it would be disastrous.

A scratch at the door, followed by the entrance of her husband, interupted her thoughts.

"What is it?" Clytemnestra said, annoyed to be interupted from her rare time for reverie.

"A rider has informed me that your brothers will arrive for a visit on the morrow."

Clytemnestra started. She fabricated her abilities to know what was to occur so often that she was unsettled when events took her by surprise.

She recovered in time to see Agamemnon's faintly amused look.

"We must prepare to give them a heroes welcome," she said, rising and giving him a tantalizing glimpse at her body before wrapping it in silk. Let Agamemnon have his amusement. Her brothers arrival was most timely; it would give her the ideal opportunity to dissuade them from abdicating the throne, while also giving her a chance to showcase herself as sister to heroes, one of the privileged children of the gods.

"They bring your sister with them."

Clytemnestra's image shattered as the luminous beauty of her sister drowned her own importance. Helen.

"We must receive them quietly," she amended.

Agamemnon's question spoke from his raised brow.

"My sister has just survived a horrid ordeal. We do not want to exhaust her further," Clytemnestra snapped.

"I'll defer to your judgment," he said dryly.

CHAPTER FOUR

Helen's stomach had not yet settled from the sea journey when her shaking legs were forced to carry her to the Mycenae palace. During the voyage, she had huddled Iphigeneia to herself, sitting beside the silent Aethra and promising herself that her future in Sparta would be different from her past.

With each wave, she captured a memory from her time at Troezen — lessons beneath the Mother oak, Aethra's alternating stern and gentle commands, Clarisa's easy friendship — and held it fast. Now that her time at the temple was ended, she realized how truly precious it had been.

It is a part of me, she reminded herself fiercely. The tug of home was surprisingly strong, as if she were returning to the place where her breath came more naturally. She resented its power. How could a palace in which she had been so alienated still snag her with fantasies of comfort?

"We're here," Castor announced unnecessarily.

Helen shifted her focus from her inner world to the palace before her. Thick, oppressive walls packed with small stones and clay held the crushing weight of two limestone lionesses, their paws resting protectively on a wide pedestal. Bold terracing led the party upward to a columned porch, which was exquisitely decorated with frescos of elaborately dressed women and colorful lotuses and rosettes. The carefully painted stucco doors were colored with linear designs that beckoned one further within the castle.

To Clytemnestra.

Helen had easily forgotten Clytemnestra during her time away from Sparta and carefully avoided thinking of her during their journey. Brief glimpses down that corridor of her mind reminded her of the animosity she had previously experienced.

Better to avoid thinking of her sister altogether.

When Clytemnestra emerged from one of the many doorways, a large, dark man at her side, Helen could ignore her no longer.

"Sister, I welcome you to my home." Clytemnestra's powerful voice echoed off the stone walls. Helen found herself wrapped in a rigid, scented hug. She stepped back and looked into eyes that flared without warmth. "I see you survived."

"Despite all expectations to the contrary," Helen responded. *At least I know now that nothing has changed between us.*

Clytemnestra's lips issued a smile that was unanswered by her eyes. "Let me introduce you to my husband," Clytemnestra said, "King Agamemnon of Mycenae, I present my sister, princess Helen of Sparta."

Helen nodded in formal acknowledgment of her sister's husband. He acknowledged her in kind, his eyes offering the warmth Clytemnestra's lacked — an offering of friendship, devoid of the lust that often flickered in the pupils of other males she encountered. She felt herself relax then tense tenfold. This man was her sister's husband; it was quite likely that his friendship was a role played for one of Clytemnestra's schemes.

Despite this probability, his next words seemed sincere enough. "Your sister suggested you might appreciate a quiet family meal. We'll forgo the usual ceremony that accompanies your brothers' arrival." He turned to greet Castor and Polydeuces.

"I, for one, would forgo all matter of ceremony for a wash and some fresh roasted kid," Castor responded with easy familiarity.

"And you shall have both." Agamemnon called servants to care for the twin's horses and to escort the men into his mammoth castle.

"And you shall come with me, sister." Clytemnestra ordered.

Helen resented it. "I'd like to first introduce you to the priestess Aethra," Helen interupted.

Aethra stepped forward with Iphigeneia in her arms.

"Be welcome in my home," Clytemnestra said, matching her tone with a frosty smile.

Aethra's own mouth stretched slightly in answer.

"I see you've had a child for the temple," Clytemnestra remarked.

"The child is mine," Helen said.

She was rewarded when Clytemnestra's composure slipped, her eyes bulging with undisguised shock.

Agamemnon gracefully interjected himself into their midst. "As you said, my queen, your sister has survived a harrowing circumstance. I am sure she and the priestess would like an opportunity to refresh themselves before we discuss it."

Aethra looked at him thoughtfully. "That would be most welcome."

Clytemnestra recalled her composure. "But of course. Please follow me."

She led them to the most impressive guest chambers. "A serving woman will come to assist you shortly," she said and closed the door behind them before running down the stairs in time to intercept her husband and brothers.

"Tell me about the child," she said, without preamble.

Agamemnon stepped forward. "Clytemnestra, surely this can wait."

"It certainly cannot wait!" Clytemnestra snapped, focusing her attention on Polydeuces.

Her brother let loose an exhausted sigh. "She's probably right. Let's go to a reception chamber."

Clytemnestra hid her impatience and ushered them all into a small room. "Now..." she said as soon as the door was closed behind them.

Polydeuces sank into one of the elegant chairs. "Apparently, Theseus fathered the child upon Helen after he abducted her. He then deposited her with his mother, the priestess Aethra."

"Why did you not leave the child and the priestess behind?"

"We tried," Polydeuces replied. "Helen insisted she would go nowhere without the child and the priestess insisted on joining us."

Clytemnestra wondered how her brothers could be so successful as adventurers when they could not even dictate the terms of a simple rescue.

"We stopped here before going to Sparta, hoping to find a solution to this unexpected problem" Polydeuces finished.

"The babe should be killed," Clytemnestra said immediately and was surprised when Castor jumped up in protest.

"She shall not." They all looked at him and he blushed. "She's of our blood. And, besides, I held her often on the journey here," he added sheepishly.

Clytemnestra began to pace.

"Helen and whomever she marries will be the successors to the Spartan throne," Polydeuces said. "She cannot return with a bastard child."

In the times of the Goddess religion, women birthed children in accordance with their own readiness and desire. Like many others, this custom changed with the coming of the Olympians. Though it was a sign of potency if a man had a bastard, for a woman to birth a child without being wed was considered a disgrace.

"You and Castor will just have to assume rule then and have Helen married to some lowly lord," Clytemnestra announced, singularly pleased with the notion. She caught Agamemnon eyeing her suspiciously.

"That's out of the question," Polydeuces responded with a firmness that surprised Clytemnestra. "We've already informed father that we wish to live the lives of heroes and not be chained to the throne."

"You can be kings as well as heroes," Agamemnon said softly, his thoughts clearly on his own fate.

Polydeuces shook his head. "It is not the same. Father agreed that if we returned Helen, he would appoint her as ruler."

Clytemnestra stopped pacing. She could not believe what she was hearing. Helen, queen of Sparta, hateful Helen over whom she had no control, except....

The plan came to her, beautifully complete. "She'll have to leave the child with me to raise as my own."

The three men stared at her.

"We'll let out that the babe is mine and Agamemnon's. Our servants are loyal; no one will gainsay us. Then Helen can return to Sparta and father can provide her a husband." *And Helen will bend to my will if she wants her child to remain safe,* she added to herself.

"It's a good plan," dimwitted Castor said needlessly.

"I don't know if she'll leave her child here any more than she would leave her in Troezen," Polydeuces said doubtfully.

"I'll take care of that," Clytemnestra said, walking to the door. "I'll leave you to refresh yourselves."

She left quickly, before they changed their minds. She knew exactly how she would part Helen from the child. She went to the kitchen and grabbed the arm of a serving woman. "Come with me," she ordered. The startled servant scampered at Clytemnestra's side.

They stopped before the stairwell. "Listen to me. You will accompany me to the guest chamber where I will hand you an infant. No matter what I say within the rooms, you will take the babe to my inner chambers and bolt the door behind you. Do not open it for anyone but me. Do you understand me?"

The girl went wide-eyed and nodded. She was as stupid as a barrel of shells but she could handle children and take orders.

"Let's go."

Clytemnestra entered Helen's chambers without knocking and found her sister seated before the serving woman, having her hair oiled and brushed. Her dazzling beauty choked Clytemnestra. Pregnancy had rounded her sister's ample body and softened her features. She was luscious.

And about to be childless, Clytemnestra thought, carefully melding her hatred until it formed the weapon with which she would execute her plan.

The priestess had obviously gone to the adjoining room. Clytemnestra was relieved; the woman reminded her too much of Rhemnesia. She noted that the babe was cooing softly in the center of a large bed.

"Leave us," she said to the servant beside Helen. "I would like to speak with my sister alone." She turned to the woman she brought with her. "Take the babe to the nursery."

Helen rose as if to protest. Clytemnestra affected her most innocent look and her sister returned to her seat.

Fool! Clytemnestra thought viciously.

"It must be a relief to be back in the civilized world," Clytemnestra said, seating herself at the end of the bed.

"Troezen is quite civilized," Helen responded coldly.

"Yes, Troezen. That's the small fishing village that still practices the dead religion, isn't it?" Clytemnestra told herself to station a priestess in Troezen as soon as possible.

"Actually, they worship the Goddess in a tradition far older than that of the cities. It seemed quite alive to me."

She's grown more confident, Clytemnestra observed, not at all happy with the realization. It was time to bring her sister to her knees.

"You will leave the child here to be raised with me."

It was a pleasure to see Helen's rosy cheeks pale as she jumped from her chair.

"As I have told our brothers," Helen said, losing a battle to retain her control, "I will go nowhere without my child."

Clytemnestra had not realized this would be so much fun. "Actually, you will. You'll either go and the child will remain here and be raised with all riches Mycenae can offer or you will go and the child will be suffocated before you leave the palace walls."

Helen ran to the door.

"You need not bother looking for her," Clytemnestra said before Helen opened it. "I assure you she is, by now, safely hidden in a place where you will not find her."

Helen walked back to the room's center and Clytemnestra prepared to collect her sister's look of defeat. The slap that rung her ears was a complete surprise.

She raised her hand to her burning cheek. "You are doing nothing to dispose me to let your child live."

The look Helen gave her was of hatred instead of defeat.

"Well," Clytemnestra said, rising gracefully from her position on the bed. "At least now we can have an honest relationship."

She turned her back to her sister and left the room.

Chapter Five

The journey to Sparta was not long enough. Following her loss of Rhemnesia and her abduction and rape by Theseus, Helen had kept connection to life through the dubious strings of despair and agony, striving to understand the incomprehensible. Now even that bond was broken; her pain ran beyond tolerance, searing her spirit and numbing all that she was.

She did not wish herself dead. To do so would require some notion of being alive. Instead, she wished those around her would vanish, leaving her to fade in a cocoon that contact could not breach.

"You must eat now," Aethra would say and Helen would pass bread through uncaring lips.

"You must rest," the priestess would command and Helen watched changing colors swirl behind her eyelids.

She grew comfortable in the vast expanse nothingness.

The cloths Aethra placed upon her brow did not heal her heart; the fresh cooked bread did not nourish her body; the cacophony of cheers that greeted their arrival did not reach her spirit.

Her cocoon was impregnable.

"My beautiful baby! Unharmed! Returned to us!" Leda pulled free from the crowd and smothered Helen in kisses. Helen's cloak of isolation was punctured by the special anger her mother alone could illicit.

"Tonight the countryside will feast for the return of our princess and the victory of the princes. All are welcome in the hall," her father announced.

A cheer rang through the crowd, shared by those gathered beyond the gates as news of the king's proclamation spread.

"I'd like to go to my rooms now." Helen's toneless voice sliced through the gaiety. She made her way into the palace.

"Helen's always been different," she heard her mother explain.

Yes. Different. Helen returned to the rooms of her childhood.

She swung on a pendulum of irritation at her mother and guilt at having dragged Aethra to this dreadful place. The illusion of home that had tugged at her heart was pulverized by the force of reality. Most of her time was spent within the confining walls of the women's chambers, weaving and stitching, listening to Leda's senseless chattering and the useless comments of her mother's vapid attendants.

"That red dye!" Leda exclaimed. "I don't think I've ever seen anything like it! However is it made?"

Aethra answered Leda's meaningless questions.

"It is simple really. The color is released from the common safflower plant. When set with salt from the plant's ashes, the color remains true red, instead of turning orange."

"Why that is amazing! How did you ever stumble upon such knowledge?"

"It is part of the priestess training to study the natural world in which we live and celebrate the gifts given us by the earth Goddess."

"The priests say the old religion is for simple folk," Leda said tactlessly.

Aethra was not offended. She paused from her stitches and looked to a distant place to formulate her response. Helen remembered the gesture from her time at the temple, when Aethra would instruct the maidens on the natural mysteries. The memory brought a stabbing pain.

"Unraveling the natural mysteries takes a great deal of dedication," she explained at last, "and an attunement to the natural world. There was a time, not long ago, when kings and queens farmed the land and cared for the herds directly. They had, as the common folk still do, a reverence for the land and the seasons. Wars and battles were fought only against enemy people, who had violated respect for peace. Now, many a kingdom's wealth is founded upon the goods it has stolen from its neighbors or the food it has received in trade. The ruling class no longer claims its wealth from the work of its own hands; their attunement to the larger forces around them is compromised. Once, the priests were dedicated to bridging the gap between the new way of life and the older forces of nature. Now, most priests find it easier — and more to their personal advantage — to help the ruling class revere the pursuits most pleasurable to them. They have created false gods who honor the hollow pursuits of man — war, strategy, commerce, lust. They are blind to the inevitable destruction that lies down such a path."

Leda grew uncharacteristically pensive. "You call them false," she said slowly. "But some would say they are quite true." She looked at Aethra directly. "I myself have felt the influence of one such god."

Helen's irritation was overcome by deep longing she barely understood. At last her mother spoke directly to the circumstances of her birth.

Aethra's voice was surprisingly gentle, as if she, too, knew Leda alluded to a long harbored secret. "As the ruling classes have moved away from nature, they have also moved away from their own natural impulses. There was a time, for example, when the urge to kill was honored in ritual so that man might test his battle prowess without unnecessarily destroying weaker peoples. There were also rituals for the celebration of lust, when one could fornicate with unabandoned pleasure, without pretense or decorum. The new religion would deny that such urges exist. Their denial has been — fortunately — unable to eliminate these impulses. Instead, they have proclaimed that one filled with incredible battle lust is possessed by this god and one overcome by love lust is possessed by another.

"Under the new gods, men and women have to deny their own longings and believe such longings are the products of a god, not their own hearts. It seems to me that it is a short distance from denying one's own desires and denying one's power."

Leda turned away, saying nothing. Helen wondered if her mother would abandon the fantastic notion that she was impregnated by a god.

And if it would make any difference to their relationship if she did.

Her mother appeared to be thinking similarly. "Well, whether I was visited by a god or simply experiencing a depth of passion that I had never before felt within myself, I rank it as one of the greatest experiences of my life. I only hope you will have similar experience in you own marriage, Helen."

Helen was so stunned by the uncharacteristic directness of Leda's comment that she did not immediately credit her words.

Their meaning hit her like a storm wave. "What marriage?"

"Your father has let out that you are seeking a husband," she said. "He's decided he would like to retire to the villa in the years remaining to us."

Somewhere, a part of Helen's brain registered that her marriage was inevitable and not Leda's fault. The rest of her seethed with fury that her mother would so casually mention such a horrid event. She found herself standing, allowing the cloth within her hands to fall carelessly to the floor. "How dare you!" she screamed.

Leda looked more confused than offended. Helen ran from the room before her tears betrayed her.

"I'd say she's a bit upset," Aethra said dryly, giving Leda's hand a gentle pat before rising to find the princess.

The tree beyond the courtyard was massive. As Aethra expected from Rhemnesia's reports, she found the girl she sought cradled upon the lower branches.

She slowed her steps, expanding time so she could balance her own conflicting emotions.

Impatience. With every passing hour, Aethra felt the new gods tightening their stronghold on the spirits of mankind. She needed to act — to act quickly — to loose their choking grip if the Goddess was not to disappear from the hearts of man.

Compassion. Helen had suffered so much — a distant mother, poisonous sister, the rape by Theseus (curse the boy), the loss of her child.

Impatience reared again. Aethra knew many losses of her own; perhaps those who made an impact upon the world needed to understand suffering. It was part of Helen's destiny.

She reached the tree before finding any semblance of equilibrium.

Helen's face was heart-wrenching. Tears fell from her eyes, unchecked, washing her cheeks as she stared intently to the horizon. Aethra surveyed the tree before her. Its thick lower branches offered a kind of stairway to the place where Helen sat. No doubt the younger girl scrambled upward with ease. Aethra was not confident she could do the same. She took a deep breath and began the climb, reminding herself that she had successfully overcome more daunting challenges in the past.

After nearly losing her balance once, and cursing poetically twice, she made it to the branch upon which Helen sat. She positioned herself close to the trunk — the girl could very well turn around to speak with her.

Helen did not turn.

"I am truly cursed," she said at last.

Aethra could have wept at the angry resignation of the girl's voice. *She is too young to be so old.*

"We often believe so when we don't understand the reasons for the circumstances in our lives."

Helen did turn then. "Tell me those reasons."

Aethra was startled by the intensity of the girl's gaze. Helen needed to know what Aethra did and would settle for no lesser truth.

"That truth is locked within your heart," the priestess said simply, feeling wholly inadequate.

Still Helen said nothing, her intense eyes waiting patiently.

By the Goddess, she's a priestess, Aethra thought, the revelation taking her breath away. She pushed it aside for later inspection.

"I have told you that in my younger days I had a powerful and disturbing vision. My sight showed me the temples of Greece, from the sky, as a bird might see them. On their uppermost reaches, I saw men dressed like priests, screaming and throwing the bloody flesh of sacrifice upon innocent and horrified creatures. The priests changed, assuming the likeness of the Olympian gods, each of whom wore the crowns of kings. They no longer threw flesh. Rather they cast a thick darkness like the muck at the bottom of a dirty pond upon the people before them, blinding innocents with agony. They cast their darkness wider and wider until it nearly stretched the whole of Greece. Only a single light was visible. It came from a small crib in Sparta. The vision offered no words but somehow conveyed its secrets to me. I knew a child would be born here, under mysterious circumstances, and that she would assist in kindling the light during the time of approaching darkness. It was said that your mother believed herself impregnated by a god and the common folk said she mated with a swan — either of which would be an unusual circumstance indeed. I knew you were the child I saw."

Helen's face revealed nothing of her thoughts. "My mother gave birth to four children, two of whom are girls. What makes you believe it is I and not Clytemnestra who holds this light?"

"I have met your sister," Aethra responded dryly then realized that Helen was in no mood for wit. She continued more seriously. "The way of the natural world is to move toward balance, every condition containing two opposing aspects. Within life is death, within love is hate, within courage is fear. Darkness and light are similarly paired. The ignorant see conflict in these aspects, the wise see harmony. Born with the child of light is a child of darkness. You can decide for yourself whether or not Clytemnestra contains the darker aspect."

Helen had decided long ago that her sister did, although she had not characterized it quite that way.

Aethra shifted nervously. *Now she will wonder how our paths have crossed. I cannot lie before those eyes*, the priestess thought, bracing herself for the inevitable wrath she would incur when Helen learned that Aethra had spied upon her lifelong and arranged the abduction that led to her rape.

But Helen did not ask after these things. "What am I to do to foster the light?" she asked.

Aethra's body slumped as tension left her. *Coward!* she screamed at herself. But perhaps fate did not want Helen to know just how long Aethra had played a role in her life. She attended Helen's question.

"The vision was unclear. Though I have sat in silence for many years over that very question, no definitive answer has presented itself. My own limited intelligence says that the people must be strengthened, their connection to the natural world bolstered. Perhaps then they can withstand the onslaught of the power hungry gods and their corrupting temples."

Helen looked past her, working the solution through her own mind. *Whether a curse or the workings of fate, I have spent far too long awaiting a force beyond me to influence my life. It is time to take control of my own actions.*

"The temples are spread throughout Greece and already are powerful. Those sacred sites that once stood as centers of the natural religion, such as Delphi, have been overtaken by the Olympian gods. How can one princess and one priestess overcome such power from one kingdom?"

"I don't know," Aethra admitted. "I have fostered the religion in Troezen and you yourself have seen the results. The people there are strong and content. Warfare does not touch us as it does other places. Our land is prosperous. But Troezen is not important enough to make an impact. Sparta is."

Again Helen considered Aethra's words in that disconcerting way, her face a mask, her body perfectly still.

"Perhaps you are right," she said at last, smiling for the first time. "I believe that I already began strengthening Sparta's tie to the Goddess before my abduction. My nurse maid, Rhemnesia, was wise in the ways of the old religion. We would gather beneath this very tree, with a circle of maidens from throughout the countryside, and discuss the mysteries. You would have liked her I think."

Aethra forced a smile to hide the torture she felt inside. *Tell her now*, a voice within ordered.

"We should get back now," Helen said, rising easily on the sturdy branch. "I will think more upon how we can best accomplish our task. One good thing about having this marriage forced upon me is that I shall be queen. I'm sure we can use that influence somehow."

I will not tell her, Aethra decided. *Not now. Not when she has so readily accepted the role fate has placed upon her.*

"You'll have to go down first," Helen added, "I cannot safely move around you."

Aethra looked down the tumble of branches she had climbed. "We may have to stay here forever," she grumbled.

"... and then, Ajax, son of Oileus, offered to conquer lands in Helen's name. As if a gentle princess would leap at the notion that innocent people would be ravished in her honor! The man apparently believes that anything requiring strength will be a welcome gift — one that he is uniquely qualified to bestow. Lampus says that as the gods provided him with an abundance of brawn to compensate for a severe lack of wit, it is probably no more than prudent for him to believe thus." The waiting woman Astyanassa paused to giggle.

Helen did not find her stories the least bit amusing. She sighed and glanced at her mother, who listened attentively to Astyanassa's prattling, silently encouraging the girl to continue.

Leda herself had not spoken of the marriage since Helen had screamed at her and stormed from the women's quarters.

The king, however, had. Incessantly.

Men crowded into the audience chamber and spilled into the hallways. "Did he invite every eligible man in Greece?" Leda had exclaimed upon seeing the mass of bodies overrunning her palace. Helen had smiled at that, startling the queen. For one brief moment, mother and daughter had looked at each other in shared understanding. But that brief harmony rested upon a crumbled foundation incapable of supporting it and quickly sank into the rubble between them.

Leda learned that Astyanassa was being courted by a guard who stood within the king's chamber during the proceedings. Apparently, the guard believed he could win the stupid girl's heart by regaling her with tales of the marriage interviews. Apparently, he was right.

Astyanassa beamed under Leda's attention.

"The king said Ajax would rip this land from one end to the

other and dismissed him."

Well that is something at least, Helen thought.

"The next man he interviewed was Idomeneus of Crete. They say he has little to offer in ways of riches or prestige. I asked Lampus why the man thought the king would consider him and Lampus told me — reluctantly — that he was extraordinarily good looking. He figured the prospect of attractive grandchildren would entice the king."

Astyanassa let loose another hapless giggle, which Leda joined.

Helen thought she would go mad. The senseless gossip, coupled with the high level of noise resulting from the presence of too many people within the palace, was grueling. Speculation on Helen's marriage and the endless complaints of servants and guards who had been turned out of their quarters so the multitude of guests could be housed, grated the nerves of everyone. Already, one guard had lost a hand to a sword fight that erupted in the little village of tents and tarps that rose beyond the palace gates.

Helen stood before Astyanassa drew her next breath. "I'm going out."

Leda waved her to sit down. "You can't, dear. If the men learn you are out of doors, they'll riot in an effort to see you."

"I'm not even married yet and already I'm a prisoner!"

Aethra rose slowly. "I'll accompany her. We'll take one of the side entrances and be safe enough."

"Alright then," Leda said immediately, her attention already returned to Astyanassa.

Helen and Aethra exchanged wry smiles as they left the room. "Does she think you can make me invisible?"

"Perhaps she believes I can turn any potential attacker into a toad."

They walked down the servants wing into the kitchen and beyond, making their way to the women's courtyard.

"There's a break in the fence beyond the tree," Helen explained. "The girls from the farms used it to enter the courtyard when we gathered to discuss the mysteries. I doubt we'll run into any of the visiting nobles going this way."

They walked in silence and Aethra wondered what Helen might be thinking about her impending marriage.

But Helen's thoughts were elsewhere entirely.

"There is a girl named Parthenope who studied the mysteries with us. Rhemnesia was banished during the time of my first women's courses. I was in isolation as is the custom here." Her brow wrinkled in recollection. "I thought I would go mad but for the anticipation of participating in a women's ritual of old, which Rhemnesia was arranging to take place when I was released. When I learned she had been exiled, I think I was initially more upset that I would not undergo the ritual than because she was gone." She allowed herself a small, sad smile. "Parthenope gathered the maidens anyway and we performed our own ritual in the river. It was nothing like the rituals you taught me, but it was beautiful nonetheless."

Aethra said nothing, rightly assuming that Helen was heading to Parthenope's home. The priestess was curious to meet this brave young girl who led an impromptu ritual for a heartsick princess.

They walked over well-worn streets lined with fancy villas which Aethra presumed were the residences of the nobles. Flowers bloomed in riotous colors and trees were well placed. People were nowhere to be seen. As they continued through the town, the villas became less grand and their owners were more evident, watching their children run about freely and sharing gossip amongst themselves.

They turned down a narrow path and were assaulted by noise. Merchants and customers screamed above the cacophony of blacksmiths and horse breeders and sculptors. Those working amidst the turmoil would stop as Helen and Aethra passed, giving curt nods of recognition before returning to their transactions.

"They certainly aren't affected by the presence of a princess in their midst," Aethra shouted, making herself heard above the din.

Helen waited until they moved beyond the center of the marketplace to respond.

"The merchants here are quite prosperous. Goods not traded locally are shipped to Crete. Their wealth allows them independence from the obsequious behavior often displayed by the nobles and the peasants. It's rather a relief really."

"That is how all people treat royalty in Troezen. It is not wealth that gives them independence but rather their understanding of the power of their individual spirits."

Helen's smile was disconcerting. "Well perhaps someday that will be the case here as well."

The landscape opened, revealing gentle hills covered with corn and simple houses that were spaced further and further apart. *These are the people who are truly wealthy*, Aethra thought, reveling in the open spaces and the natural quiet after the noise and confusion of the city.

They had not walked far before Helen turned down a wide pathway and headed toward a farmhouse. A large, sunburned man lifted his eyes from his plowing and grunted his hello. He immediately returned his attention to his task.

"It would seem the farmers here do not fawn over royalty either."

"His reaction is peculiar," Helen responded, a puzzled frown worrying her brow. The man's greeting was barely courteous.

They walked up a few stone steps to the entranceway of the small house. The structure was in an appalling state. Planks on the doorway were rotting and had not been replaced. Several holes pierced the front facade, where mortar had cracked and stone was permitted to fall away.

Helen's frown deepened as she knocked on the door.

"In a moment," screamed a crackling voice from inside. "I told you I was simply takin' a short rest....oh!"

The woman had clearly been expecting her husband. Her wide-eyed stare at finding a well-dressed princess and priestess at her door changed into something very akin to anger, which was quickly hidden behind a formal blandness.

"May I help yer two good ladies with somethin'?"

"We have come to call upon Parthenope," Helen said, attempting to hide her growing discomfort.

The flash of anger returned to the woman's eyes and was once more quickly extinguished. "Well she ain't here, sorry to say."

Helen wanted to thank the woman graciously and turn and flee from her hard eyes. But something in the woman's tone alarmed her. Was her friend in trouble? "Can you tell me where I might find her please? I mean her no harm. We were friends when we were younger."

The woman's face became an unflattering purple. "Aye. Don't I know it," she barked and then remembered she was speaking to a princess. "She married young Archelaus — the only man who would have her. They live in the farm down the ways. Not that I 'ave time to see 'em much."

"You are very kind to tell me of her whereabouts. But please, tell me also why you are so angry."

It was all the invitation the woman needed. "The girl has ruined us and if I may speak plainly, 'tis your fault I'd say."

"How..."

"That cult of yours brought the wrath of the gods upon us.

Now we must pay almost 'alf of our yield to the temple each year to make amends."

Helen was stunned. She had never heard of such a thing! The temple received voluntary offerings from the people. Only the king could demand a share.

"Who told you to do this?" Aethra asked.

The woman looked at her suspiciously. "The priest Kalchas. Surely you know 'im, dressed as you are."

"I haven't had the misfortune," Aethra murmured.

"You have been done an injustice," Helen said. "I will make sure that you will no longer have to make compulsory offerings to the temple and will compensate you for your current losses."

The woman looked skeptical. "Aye. So we 'ave the choice of impoverishing ourselves to the gods or being impoverished by their wrath. I must 'et back to work." She stepped from the doorway and stormed away.

"This is bad," Aethra commented needlessly.

"Let's go see Parthenope," Helen said.

Her friend's farm was relatively close and as they turned up the pathway leading to the house, Helen was relieved to see that it was in excellent condition. They had made it halfway up the dirt road when a woman came running from the open door.

"Helen!"

A moment later Helen was wrapped in a warm hug that brought tears to her eyes.

"Is it you?" the woman backed up, pretending uncertainty. "Or do I have to bow and call you queen now?"

"Now not. Not ever. Parthenope you look wonderful."

"And you, of course, are as ravishing as ever. Come inside and meet my husband. When he gets over the shock of you, we can have tea together." The smaller woman linked her arm with Helen's and began to lead her forward. "I'm Parthenope," she said, introducing herself to Aethra.

"Aethra," the priestess responded warmly, silently sizing up the young girl Rhemnesia had invited to her lessons.

"And you are a priestess," Parthenope said, openly studying Aethra. "Helen manages to befriend the most interesting people. She's told you, I'm sure, of Rhemnesia, who tutored us when were young. Your accent is similar."

Aethra was taken aback by the girl's perceptiveness even as she admired Rhemnesia's judgment. "I've heard much about Rhemnesia since coming to Sparta," Aethra said carefully.

"And I wish I could have shared your discussions and told

you more." Parthenope turned her attention back to Helen. "I'm glad to see you well enough to see visitors. On the occasions I came to the palace since your return, your mother said you were too ill for company."

Helen's face hardened. "She had not told me you called."

Parthenope shrugged. "Mothers tend to be foolish. It seems that giving birth alters judgment. Let's hope that does not happen to us."

Tears burned Helen's eyes and Parthenope registered her pain.

"We'll talk about everything later," the woman said, giving Helen's arm a gentle squeeze. "Let's go inside."

The house was simply but beautifully furnished. Wonderfully crafted chairs were strewn around the center room and beautiful wooded vases were artfully arranged by the hearth. Off to one side was an open pit and more chairs around a simple, large table. At the last, a handsome young man sat, carving a block of wood.

"Archelaus I want to meet Princess Helen and priestess Aethra," Parthenope said, as they entered the little home.

"We'll I'd certainly know the princess," he said, rising from his place and giving a small bow that included all three women. "You are more beautiful than they say."

"Stop flirting and clear a place for tea," Parthenope snapped affectionately.

Archelaus rolled his eyes. "Do you see what I put up with," he teased and Helen noticed, pleased, that after his initial reaction to the sight of her, his eyes followed Parthenope everywhere.

"You have a lovely home," Aethra commented as they took their chairs.

"Thank you." Archelaus responded.

"Archelaus does all the woodwork." Parthenope said proudly. "At least in that I was lucky."

"You got better than you deserved, wench."

Parthenope stuck her tongue at him and brought tea in an exquisite wooden set.

"Your work is truly extraordinarily," Helen said.

"Again, thank you," Archelaus responded, beaming.

"Enough," Parthenope said. "Anymore and he'll get foolish. Which leads me to my next question: I presume you visited my mother?"

"Yes," Helen said, gratefully accepting a cup of tea and warming her hands against it. "She said something about the temple demanding offerings."

"And she's a fool for paying them," Archelaus retorted.

"What happened?" Aethra asked.

The good humor died from Parthenope's eyes.

"That stupid priest Kalchas said that I had angered the gods by studying the false laws — something he decided was true of all the girls who used to meet under the tree rather than sit through his boring lessons. As retribution, he demanded that my family pay offerings amounting to one half the yearly crop."

"He can't do that!" Helen said. But it seemed he had done so.

"It began before I married. I told my mother to simply ignore him but she and father were afraid that Artemis would salt their fields or some other nonsense. After I married, he came round here and demanded equal payment from us. I told him he could just go back to his temple and grow old waiting for it."

"Nearly gave him apoplexy," Archelaus interjected, grinning broadly.

"It's madness really, demanding half a crop from small farm holders like us. Apparently several of the maidens who joined us agreed, although most just pay the fine and complain of its effects. I told Kalchas that if his gods are as petty as he is, they should be begging my forgiveness, not the other way around."

Archelaus' grin widened.

Helen remained troubled. "Glaucus has sanctioned such acts?"

"He's not here to say one way or another. A shame. I understand he was a good man. He died on the very day you were abducted. His heart stopped, they say."

"The same day I was abducted," Helen repeated softly.

She had purposely blocked that horrific episode from her mind. Having it recalled to her attention reminded her of the conversation she had with Glaucus earlier that day. "Glaucus had agreed to speak to father about calling Rhemnesia back."

Parthenope pushed her own cup aside. "What?"

"The day I was kidnapped was the beginning of atonement for Kronia. Instead of going off in solitude, I followed Glaucus to the temple to request atonement for Rhemnesia so she could return. He agreed. I don't think he was any happier than I about her exile and even less so about Kalchas' involvement."

"And then Glaucus died," Parthenope said.

Helen looked at her. "Do you think Kalchas had anything to do with his death?"

Parthenope shrugged nonchalantly, but her tense shoulders betrayed her anger. "I would put nothing past that man," she said at last.

Archelaus spoke up. "He did manage to make sure he was the one to tell the king. He did so right after your father learned of your kidnapping so the king was too distracted to pay much attention. Your father told Kalchas to assume responsibility for the temple. Of course, Kalchas readily agreed."

"But he was only an initiate," Helen protested.

"So argued some of the older priests, many of whom do not like Kalchas. The chief priest is elected by a vote of the temple priests and initiates. Kalchas had won the support of some of the younger members but not enough to sway the vote. He cleverly postponed it for several moons. When it was finally cast, he won unanimously."

"How can that be?"

Now it was Archelaus' turn to fake a nonchalant shrug. "It seems that many of those who opposed Kalchas trained with a priest in Mycenae. Rumor is that Kalchas somehow persuaded the Mycenae priest to order the dissenters to support him."

Parthenope looked to Helen. "Mycenae. Isn't that the kingdom your sister rules?"

"The darkness spreads," Aethra grumbled.

Parthenope and Archelaus threw her startled looks.

"There is something I must tell you," Helen said, and proceeded to speak of a vision.

CHAPTER SIX

It took the king five days to interview the men who sought Helen's hand and send a guard to the women's quarters.

"The king requests that the queen, the princess and the priestess Aethra attend him in the receiving chamber," he said, after bowing formally.

Leda dropped her sewing and jumped out of her stool. "We must ready ourselves properly," she declared enthusiastically.

Helen had no desire to ready herself at all but was grateful for any delay. She was pleasantly surprised that her father had included Aethra in his request — she had not thought he had noticed the priestess at all. Perhaps Leda suggested he do so, Helen thought, not willing to pursue the charitable thought further.

The guard cleared an uncomfortable knot from his throat. "The king requested that I wait and accompany you when you're ready."

"The king wants us to hurry," Aethra interpreted.

While the maids dressed her, Helen reminded herself that becoming queen was necessary to her plans. It did little to quiet the unease that spread through her stomach. She focused her mind upon the future, which she was determined to make decidedly different from the present.

Kalchas' arrogance had appalled her. After her visit with Parthenope, she determined to speak with the king and put a stop to his threat.

"Kalchas will surely run to him in protest," Aethra pointed out. "And the king is at least as distracted now as he was on the day of your abduction. He'll probably tell Kalchas to handle things as he sees fit which will, in effect, give royal sanction to the horrors he's perpetuating."

Helen knew Aethra was right and agreed to wait until after her marriage — although it irritated her beyond endurance to allow Kalchas his way for even a single day. Still, once she was married and her father and mother retired to their villa, she could do as she liked. Provided her husband approved.

Perhaps I should have paid more attention to these proceedings. But short of scrying her father's choice, she had no source of information. As he came closer to his decision, the king swore his guards to secrecy. Not even Astyanassa's feminine wiles could persuade the guard who courted her to say anything more.

"Just let it be," she said as the waiting woman fussed with her hair. "Brush oil in it and leave it loose."

The surprised woman clucked her disappointment. "First the girdle, than the hair. Anyone would think you wished to be a peasant, my lady."

Helen ignored her. Since returning to Sparta, she had insisted upon wearing the cord that marked her as Goddess sworn, forgoing the jeweled girdles her station entitled her to. *I am priestess before princess.* It was the only thing that explained the strange circumstances of her life so far and the only thing that kept her interested in the events around her.

She would see who her father chose; if the candidate was too strong willed, she'd plead for her father to reconsider. She had seen the king playing tenderly with the palace children when he thought no one was watching. Apparently, he had a soft heart for younger people. If she did not like his decision, Helen would simply whimper like the child she no longer was. It galled her to have to resort to such foolish behavior to affect a decision that, after all, concerned her above all else. Still, it was probably the best course. The king had paid so little attention to her since she had grown, he probably would still see her as a child if she let him.

Her marriage was not the only challenge she faced. Kalchas had been chosen high priest after intervention from Mycenae. Helen had no doubt that Clytemnestra had somehow been involved — perhaps was still involved. If Kalchas protested Helen's actions, he might seek Clytemnestra's support once more. And this time Clytemnestra could use the threat of harm to Helen's own daughter to exert her influence.

Helen had not told Parthenope about Iphigeneia. Indeed, she had not even told Aethra how her sister had stolen her child. She was too heartsick at the time and too unwilling to relive it afterward. She knew Aethra had suspected something amiss but the priestess said nothing; most likely she feared opening yet another of Helen's unhealed wounds.

Helen had noted that Clytemnestra's husband, Agamemnon, had also been suspicious of his wife. For one brief moment before departing Mycenae, she had found herself alone with the king. He had laid a tentative hand upon her arm.

"I will raise her as the first daughter of my own blood," he said. His compassionate eyes were unbearable. Helen had pulled away from him and fled, not willing to sob before him. Afterward, she regretted her hasty action. He had, after all, sworn to protect her daughter, which was a great deal more than her sister would do. She kept Agamemnon's vow close to her heart and hoped he meant what he said.

"You're not going to wear your hair loose, are you?" Leda's face was a portrait of indignation and envy as she entered the doorway.

"It is not as if my future husband won't see it thus many times," Helen retorted, dismissing the waiting woman and rising.

"But its so unseemly."

Gratefully, Aethra appeared beside Helen's mother. "It will be even more unseemly if we arrive any later than we already are," she interupted.

"You are, of course, right," Leda said, with her manner of agreeing with most every notion Aethra put forth.

The priestess allowed the queen to proceed her and threw Helen a wicked wink. "Come on."

The three women followed the guard through the masses of men who lined the palace hallways. An uncomfortable silence trailed in their wake.

"Let's get this over with," Helen said behind clenched teeth.

The guard ushered them into the receiving room. Helen nodded acknowledgment to her father and started in surprise to see Agamemnon among the three men who attended him.

"King Agamemnon, lord Menelaus, lord Odysseus, I present queen Leda, princess Helen and the priestess Aethra."

Agamemnon was resplendent in his deep blue ceremonial cloak, which exposed his left arm and draped elegantly over his right. A simple pin of the gold for which Mycenae was famous held his garment in place. His curly dark hair and full beard were neatly trimmed. The large dark eyes regarded Helen with the kindness she remembered. Beside him stood lord Menelaus, who was cloaked in a himation of green that hung about him like a bed cover. His face was pleasant — with its strong unshaven jaw, shallow cheeks and green eyes — but not what one would call attractive. His features might have been more appealing if he had let his blonde hair grow. Instead he kept it ridiculously short, which made his embarrassed green eyes seemed to bulge below his high forehead.

Odysseus wore a plain brown tunic, similar to those used for traveling. It looked as if he had not changed since arriving; several stains soiled the tunic front. He did not seem to be a man who cared much for appearances, which was probably just as well. He had a surprisingly large face with laughing eyes that glimmered beneath the permanent squint of a seaman. His sun worn face was marred by the craters left by a constant pelting of water salt, hidden in part by a ridiculous mustache that flapped against his cheeks when he bowed. Helen hoped her father looked elsewhere for a choice.

"Sit down, each of you. We have a problem," her father said without further introduction. They each chose a chair, except for Odysseus who pulled a stool from one corner. It was he who spoke first.

"The men here who have not been chosen will war upon you," he said directly, an amused smile ticking the corners of his mouth.

Tyndareus was taken aback. "You alone did not ask to be interviewed. Did you come here for any reason other than the entertainment value of my predicament?"

Odysseus was undisturbed by the king's angry tone. "Beyond the sea, there is one other thing that runs true in my blood and calls my spirit like a man with a weakness for wine. That thing is intrigue. When I received word of the influx of suitors who humbled themselves before your door, I knew I'd find intrigue enough here to satisfy even my own deep thirst. I can assure you I have not been disappointed."

Tyndareus opened his mouth to protest. Odysseus waved him to silence.

"Intrigue is one thing. War is something else entirely. I have no love for battle or ravishment and have seen enough of both to know that they bring only sorrow and death and long-standing distrust to all sides. Not to mention the restraint such brutality puts upon a humble trader such as myself," he added with a wink.

"You're a thieving pirate and little more," the king responded, with a surprising hint of affection in his voice.

"I am insulted," Odysseus said, with mock sincerity.

Helen was growing impatient. Odysseus had not asked for an interview so it was unlikely the king chose him. Yet Thyndareus was obviously acquainted with the man and liked him. And Agamemnon was there — unfortunately married to her sister and not a candidate — trailed by Menelaus, who looked as if he wished to disappear into his chair.

"Why are you here?" Helen demanded of Odysseus, startling them all. *Curse them anyway*, she thought. *This is my life they are deciding upon.*

Odysseus regarded her for an embarrassingly long moment. "I have loved with sea nymphs bred by the gods for their beauty, my lady, but I may honestly tell you that none compares to your radiance. I have come to set my own eyes upon the woman who can cause such strife among men and to offer you my counsel as to how war can be averted."

"Your offers always come at a price," the king remarked shrewdly. "What is the cost of this one?"

Odysseus gave a full laugh, completely undisturbed by this new insult to his character.

"Being a player in an intrigue such as this — which will be spoken of throughout the land and, I daresay, throughout time — is more than enough for me. But, as you so accurately guessed, there is a favor I seek."

"And that is?" the king prompted.

"The hand of your niece, first born of your brother Icarius."

"Penelope?" Leda asked.

So he is not my father's choice, Helen thought, regarding Menelaus more carefully.

Odysseus was attending Leda's question. "Indeed, my lady. I must confess that when I laid eyes upon her, she worked some spell to capture my humble heart..."

"If she is not spoken for," the king interrupted when it seemed Odysseus would go off on his love song, "I will request that my brother accept your offer and make her your bride."

"My heart rejoices at your generosity, my lord. For though I am humble of birth, I have riches enough from my seafaring to make her a good husband."

"No doubt," Aethra mumbled.

"And now your counsel," the king prompted.

Odysseus fingered his mustache, drawing out the moment. "No man knows your choice. Agamemnon is your son by marriage, Menelaus his brother and I have not requested an interview. They may suspect one of us is the choice but they do not know for certain — which is why I asked to join this conference."

"And so..." the king asked impatiently.

So Menelaus is Agamemnon's brother, Helen thought, curiously pleased.

"Call an assembly of every man present and make each swear upon his sword that he will uphold your choice."

"Do you honestly believe men will keep their word with the prize of Sparta at stake?" Tyndareus asked, incredulous.

"Perhaps not," Odysseus responded, undisturbed, "Which is why you must appeal to that which each man values above even land and beauty. You must appeal to honor. Have each swear to defend the choice with his own life, to raise his sword on behalf of the chosen king against any who tries to unlawfully take palace or princess."

Tyndareus digested the suggestion, a slow smile spreading across his face. "A solution I would have come to myself had I not been so busy with the riffraff out there who call themselves princes," he grunted.

Odysseus bowed his head in ironic tribute.

The king continued. "Brilliant," he declared. "We will take the pledge, make the announcement and escort my gracious guests outside the palace walls by sun rise. This fortress may not be mine to rule much longer but I intend to enjoy the time remaining without being crushed by every highborn who can squeeze himself within my walls."

He rose, indicating his will that they follow.

"He could have at least introduced you to the man you're to share your bed with," Aethra hissed.

Ignoring everyone else around her, Helen made her way to Menelaus and Agamemnon.

Agamemnon moved to greet her. "It is a pleasure to see you again," he said sincerely, bowing over her hand.

Helen had no time for pleasantries. "I'd like to meet my husband," she said, regretting her abruptness. *I do not want Agamemnon to think me rude.*

Agamemnon did not appear to notice her curtness. "Menelaus, come meet the princess."

The man he beckoned walked forward like a puppy.

"I don't know how to court a woman," Menelaus blurted, not meeting Helen's eyes.

The lack of attention was a surprise and a relief. "I don't know how to meet a man," she heard herself say.

Menelaus' laugh was loud. He quieted abruptly at the stern look from his brother.

My father has chosen wisely, Helen thought. *This man will be no bother at all.*

"We must go," Leda said, grabbing Helen's arm and pulling her from the room.

She looked over her shoulder to see Menelaus still staring at her, awestruck, and Agamemnon looking sad and worried.

It took sometime for the men to assemble in the audience chamber. When they had done so, there was hardly room to breath. Helen sat on a raised platform beside her mother and Aethra; her father and Odysseus were to her right. Agamemnon and Menelaus had wisely joined the men who formed the audience.

"Every eligible man in Greece must be here!" Leda exclaimed.

Helen ignored her.

Tyndareus waited for the room to quiet and wondered if anything he did would prevent the cauldron before him from erupting. The room's silence spoke of anticipated disappointment, immanent rage. War.

Tyndareus indicated that Odysseus rise quickly.

"My lords and brothers," Odysseus began. "You see here before you a man known personally to many of you. A man with whom you have shared wine and adventure. A man with whom, I feel compelled to remind you now, shares the sacred hospitality between host and guest with you."

He paused then and Helen followed his stare among the crowd, noting — as he did — which eyes were lowered at the reminder of the sacred oath under which they gathered.

"Is there any man among us who would commit the ultimate blasphemy against man and gods? Who would break the most cherished trust a man can give another man? Who would, in short, betray his honor by drawing steel when hospitality is so generously given? If such a man is among us, I ask that he step forward now and not add cowardice to his dishonor."

Again, his eyes scanned the crowd before him.

"I know many of you, as I have said. Your honor comes as no surprise to me. Nor, I think, will it come as a surprise to you that the princess Helen, the woman who will become reigning queen of Sparta," he paused as if to heighten the drama. "the daughter of king Tyndareus and his beautiful queen, Leda, will not be married to me. And, if you please, do not express your foreknowledge within my hearing."

The crowd relaxed, appreciated the display of humor, and in a single breath tensed tenfold. Among them stood the next king of Sparta. Helen prayed that Odysseus sensed the renewed tension and got on with this before men broke under the strain of waiting.

"Now that you know I am not the chosen one, you are probably anxious to learn who is. I will not delay the king's delivery of this decision any longer than necessary. But a slight delay is necessary. Honor, after all, must come before even love. I ask each of you to tend to his honor now.

"On the sword, pledge to uphold the decision about to be revealed. Pledge further that if any man, at anytime, should not honor the decision made here today, each and every man present shall join in fighting the traitor to the death."

Carefully, Odysseus lifted a ceremonial sword from the wall and presented it to the king. "King Tyndareus, I swear before you and the gods to actively uphold the decision made here today, to support the man chosen as king of Sparta and husband of Helen. I shall honor this pledge while the gods give me breath."

So said, Odysseus looked on the paralyzed crowd with disdain and disappointment. "And here," he said at last, "I thought you wanted to learn of the decision you've all traveled so far from home to receive. Perhaps we should break for a meal and reconvene on the morrow."

"I like this man," Aethra whispered.

Helen, who felt battered by the tension and the blatant attention of the room's guests, shot the priestess an annoyed glance.

"I, for one, do not need to deliberate upon a pledge that my honor commands of me anyway. And I certainly do not wish to wait any longer." A beautiful man pushed his way through the crowd. "Idomeneus of Crete, " he said to Helen before making his pledge.

Astyanassa had not exaggerated about the man's looks.

Thus begun, the procession moved rather quickly to its conclusion. When each man was sworn, the king cleared his throat and turned to the crowd.

"My lords, I ask you to honor your pledge and respect always the claim to my kingdom and my daughter by lord Menelaus, the future king of Sparta."

Helen sought her future husband. All color had drained from the poor man's face. Agamemnon whispered to him and pushed him forward.

"My queen and my wife. I will honor you always, as you have done me on this day," he recited like an obedient child.

Helen nodded, uncertain as to how to respond.

Odysseus saved her the trouble by rising once more. "I think we can all agree that we've strained Sparta's hospitality enough.

I shall be taking my leave at first light and I expect many of you will join me."

He gave the mumbling crowd another of his pointed looks.

"You may return to your rooms," the king informed Helen, Aethra and Leda.

Helen rose gracefully and left the chamber. Agamemnon broke free from the crowd and followed. Aethra, noticing, tactfully detained Leda in the hallway.

"Helen, Iphigeneia is well..." Agamemnon said, as he reached Helen's side.

"Please don't." She turned from his offered kindness.

Agamemnon surprised them both by placing a brotherly arm about her shoulders. "Alright. I understand your pain and will not increase it with words. But there is something I must tell you. It's about Menelaus..."

"Ah, there you are!" Leda's voice bubbled from the hallway as she evaded Aethra's diversion. "Aethra tells me that I have a granddaughter."

Agamemnon's face was a mask of forced sincerity. "Two actually. Clytemnestra just gave birth to our second child. She is still recovering or she would have joined me..."

"Two grandchildren! How wonderful. You must tell me everything."

Helen extricated herself from the conversation and moved toward her rooms, too tired to feel guilty about leaving Agamemnon in the hands of her mother.

Chapter Seven

During the moons that followed, Helen had ample time to regret her father's choice of husband.

"He's become a bit, um, boisterous," Astyanassa remarked.

"He's obnoxiously loud," Aethra corrected.

The servants watched Menelaus from the corners of their eyes. The new king had a tendency of walking quietly along and grabbing hold of some unfortunate individual, screaming about impending fires or some other nonsense. Helen assigned her most trusted and well-compensated guard to follow him everywhere. Then she ignored him as much as possible.

It was not always easy. Interspersed with his fits of madness, Menelaus had times of remarkable lucidity. During those moments, he would speak of more efficient ways of storing the palace foods or a more effective way of organizing guards to secure Sparta's defenses.

During these times, he also decided it was wise to have an heir. He entered Helen's chambers, looking shy and eager. Helen's stomach turned to stone. She flinched as he sat upon the bed and reached out a hand to stroke her hair.

"It is well," he said gently. "I will not hurt you."

Helen wondered if all men lied so to their brides.

The small part of her that was not paralyzed by fear and loathing knew he did his best to be gentle. It was not enough. She tried to push him away, wiggling desperately beneath him. He mistook her movements as a sign of passion and grabbed her tighter. Helen went perfectly still, unable to check the tears that flowed from her eyes. *It is not as bad as last time. It is not...*

Menelaus finished and left the chambers without noticing her distress.

She was grateful that he only came to her a few times. Unfortunately, that was enough to get her with child.

Menelaus was overjoyed

"A baby! A son! I will teach him to fish and hunt and throw a javelin even farther than my brother can!"

He shouted similar pledges to anyone who pretended to listen.

He took the birth of a girl child surprisingly well.

"The next one will be a boy," he said, equitably, and set out to create him soon after Hermione was weaned. Helen endured him, gradually learning to use the techniques that freed her spirit from her body each time he entered her.

She thought he might be right about the gender of their next offspring. The child within her womb sat differently than her previous children. She tried not to think about it. She left her daughter, Hermione, in the charge of Astyanassa, who adored her, and put all thoughts of this second child from her mind.

She told herself she had more important things to do. Tyndareus and Leda had retired to their villa with blessed speed, allowing Helen to assume her role as ruler immediately.

Her first act was to recall Rhemnesia from exile. "We can use her support and knowledge," Helen explained to Aethra and Parthenope.

Parthenope was ecstatic with the anticipated return of her old teacher. Aethra pretended the same at the prospect of meeting the much adored woman, though she knew Rhemnesia would not be returning to Sparta.

"She's gone!" Helen reported when the messenger returned without her mentor. "She vanished about the same time I was returning from Troezen. If only she could have waited a few moons longer!"

Rhemnesia could not have, of course. Aethra had sent to the priestess as soon as she knew she would be leaving Troezen; she needed Rhemnesia to take her place during her absence. Aethra did not say any of this to Helen and, as no one knew Rhemnesia's whereabouts, Helen reluctantly turned her attention to Kalchas and focused upon undermining the compulsory offerings he levied upon the local farmers. His punishment of those maidens who had joined Helen for the lectures was so effective that he placed a similar — if somewhat less costly — levy upon the rest of the populace. A talent of each year's yield — the equivalent of what the palace reserved — was demanded by the temple in return for its intervention with the gods.

Helen was enraged when she learned of this and infuriated

when she found out that a large portion of temple's levies were shipped abroad and exchanged for gold and gems and other valuables. Sparta's people — her people — were slowly becoming impoverished as the temple sat upon a mound of ever growing wealth.

A messenger from her sister arrived, sweetly informing her that Iphigeneia was doing well and, as things stood now, would continue to thrive.

The threat was obvious. Kalchas was working with Clytemnestra toward some end they alone knew. If Helen interfered she would jeopardize her daughter's safety.

She wanted nothing more than to call Kalchas to the palace and demand he cease the offering or be banned from her kingdom; the memory of her daughter's first smile stayed her hand.

"We must undermine Kalchas indirectly," she said to Parthenope and Aethra during one of their daily meetings. "I don't want to provoke him to even harsher action."

Parthenope accepted her decision. If Aethra suspected anything amiss, she did not voice her thoughts; Aethra questioned very little about Helen's decisions since the princess had become queen. The unsure girl Aethra had received at Troezen had become a confident woman, comfortable with giving orders, fully expectant that they would be executed. Aethra was proud of her and, for the most part, comfortable with quietly influencing events behind the scenes.

Helen still listened to her priestess' counsel but Aethra knew that the new queen did not accept her every word as law as she once had. In the matter of Kalchas, Aethra knew Helen would not listen to her at all. She stayed wisely silent, avoiding a confrontation she could not win. Helen's hatred for the priest bordered on madness.

"An evaluation of each crop's yield is certified by the palace magistrate. The magistrate provides his information to the solicitor. This solicitor then visits the household to demand payment. Kalchas, I understand, has each household send an identical payment to the temple. From now on, the magistrate will submit his findings on crop yield to me for review. I will then tell the solicitor to request a talent for the palace and calculate the temple levy at half that amount. For the next five seasons, we will decrease the temple's levy further. Kalchas will be forced to assume that crop yields are declining. By the time he discovers otherwise, the people will be accustomed to paying a lessor fine — with no wrath descending upon them. His threats will have no power over them."

Aethra agreed this was a good plan. She was even more impressed with Helen's thoughts on educating priestesses.

"If we do so openly, Kalchas will find some way of threatening their families. Instead, we will spread the word that I am seeking new waiting women for the palace. Parthenope, contact the maidens with whom we previously met and tell them we are beginning training once more. If they wish to attend or wish their daughters to do so, they should join us at the old meeting place each day. Their families will be compensated by the palace for the equivalent of one day's labor."

"It's risky," Parthenope said. "What if one of the women we contact does not wish to be a priestess and tells Kalchas what we are actually doing?"

Helen shrugged. "Let the man call me a liar then. The people will already know that the palace is responsible for reducing the burden the temple has demanded. His threats of doom will not be as compelling when the people are able to feed their families once more."

Besides, they needed to educate the populace, connecting the people to the natural world of the Great Mother so they would not be at the mercy of Kalchas' demands in the future.

Parthenope and Aethra were less enthusiastic with the next part of her plan. "We must also plan to indoctrinate the men."

"What? How can we possibly involve men?" Parthenope exclaimed.

"In Troezen, the men serve as warrior guards to the Goddess, pledging their lives to keep Her worship alive and Her priestesses safe. Although it has been many seasons since they were called upon for this task," she said, addressing Aethra, "you have said they take their responsibility very seriously. Troezen's wealth is small and offers little enticement to those seeking riches. Nonetheless, that doesn't stop those desperate enough to steal what resources she does offer. Of course, when potential thieves learn that Troezen's men will fight with unusual ferocity to protect their home, these attempts are quelled. Sparta needs guards who will do no less."

Aethra nodded stiffly, remembering a time when she thought to marry Helen to Theseus, uniting the power of the Goddess with the might of a worthy consort.

How powerful they would have been!

She eyed Helen speculatively. "The men of Troezen have not lost their link to the Mother as the men of Sparta have," she said slowly. "Here, the populace believes they need not listen for Her voice. Rather they hear the words of Kalchas and his fellow Olympian priests and think they commune with the Otherworld.

I don't think they will listen to a woman telling them they must work for themselves to hear the voice of their Creator."

"Nor do I," Helen agreed readily. "At least not yet. But perhaps if we can find just one man — powerful enough to command their respect — we can train him and he, in turn, can offer such instruction."

"And where will we find such a man?" Aethra asked. "I cannot send for one of the men from Troezen. The Spartans will not trust a stranger."

"It's too bad Menelaus is mad," Parthenope interjected.

Aethra and Helen looked at her and a single thought was shared between them.

"What? Why are you looking at me like that? I assure you I am not a man!" Parthenope said nervously.

"But your husband is," Aethra pointed out.

Shock, ambition and finally honest consideration washed over Parthenope's pretty face.

"I'll present him with our plan," she said decisively.

"Forget the idea," Archelaus responded.

Parthenope was stunned speechless, so rare an occurrence that her husband laughed aloud.

"Listen, I love you and I adore your spirit and believe in what you're trying to accomplish. And I'm not interested in becoming involved."

"But you're perfect for what we need. You're intelligent and sensitive — you could not make such beautiful woodwork without an understanding of trees. You're strong and powerful and charismatic..."

"While I hate to stop such an accurate inventory of my virtues, I must insist that you save your breath."

"How can you believe in what we're doing and not want to be involved?" Parthenope asked, incredulous at the conviction behind his words.

"By supporting you, believing in you, I *am* involved. I want no more than that. I do not want power over other men. I've seen too often that such authority is used irresponsibly."

"This is not about power..."

"Of course it is. The power of the Goddess over the Olympian gods. The power of Helen over Kalchas."

"It's not that at all!" Parthenope retorted defensively. "The

Olympian priests, such as Kalchas, claim to have the power of the gods to rule the people. They say that they alone can hear Her words — no matter which of their deities they say utter them — and therefore they alone can decide what is best for the people. Such claims have given them control, which they abuse to their own advantage. Look at the compulsory offering they demand. We seek to give power back to each individual, so he or she can once more hear Her words and act accordingly."

"I agree that the offerings are an example of abuse," Archelaus replied. "But the men are accepting it readily enough. No, hear me out. You and I do not listen to Kalchas' demands and are none the worse for it. If others really wanted the power you claim, don't you believe they would do likewise?"

"They cannot. Kalchas has convinced them that the gods will punish them if they do not do as he says. They fear the repercussions he threatens."

"That is exactly my point. It would take great courage to defy Kalchas and none have demonstrated that."

"Because they know no better. Their ignorance chains them. Which is precisely why we must educate them."

"And how will you overcome their fear of Kalchas long enough to get them to listen? You have sent out a call to women — who I frankly believe are more courageous than men when it comes to looking at their own hearts — and still you've gotten only a handful. Meanwhile the hold of the Olympians grows stronger. How long do you think it will be before Helen decides the Olympian threat is strong enough to *demand* women attend your lessons? How long before it is great enough to demand the attendance of men?"

Not very, Parthenope thought glumly. Already, Helen and Aethra were speaking of ways to get more women to join the lesson circle. Some of their proposals included royal orders.

"When you gathered as maidens under the tree," Archelaus continued, "you did so for your own learning. Perhaps when you have successfully overthrown the Olympians, others will do likewise. But they will not do so now. So you must seek to turn the tides of power away from the new gods. To do so, you will have to use power yourselves. Is Helen the same girl you once studied with? Is she still above using her position to gain the outcome in which she believes? I don't say this is wrong. It may even be necessary. But it's not something I wish to participate in directly. Power over my work, my own household and an extraordinarily belligerent wife is enough for me." He gave her his winning smile. "Now come here and kiss me, woman."

She went to him automatically, resting in the comfort of

his arms. She did not want him to change, to become drunk with power — although she was not convinced that had to occur. She also did not want to admit to the changes she was seeing in Helen. The young girl she knew, who learned for the love of understanding, was fast becoming a hard ruler.

"You're too wise, do you know that?" she said into Archelaus' hair.

"How else do you think I won a beautiful priestess like yourself."

Aethra agreed with Parthenope's assessment of her husband.

"He's a very smart man," she said. "And he's right: until the populace is ready to claim their powers, we will have to exert ours to counter Kalchas."

"We can make a start by getting women to join us. But what of the men? How can we train them without a leader?" Parthenope asked.

"Perhaps one will present himself as we follow destiny," Aethra responded, her shoulders rising in a careless shrug that contradicted the concern in her eyes.

Helen, who had remained silent during the exchange, spoke at last. "I think we call upon destiny when we're unable to solve our own dilemmas."

Still, the queen conceded that there was not much else they could do about the men. She turned her focus upon the women, quietly spreading word of the gathering to any who might be interested. As a result, thirty girls and women gathered beneath the tree beyond the palace courtyard. Most were fifteen or sixteen winters. The youngest was twelve, the oldest twenty-five. Half were married and most of these were the wives and daughters of farmers, although several belonged to the merchant class.

All shared the excitement of the journey they embarked upon.

"We cannot train them formally, of course," Aethra explained.

The rigorous, formal training of the priestess began before her birth, when she was chosen for such a destiny by the elder priestesses. To confirm their choice, the child was exposed in a remote area. If the elders were accurate, the animals would leave the child unharmed — perhaps even share their warmth with her — thus beginning her communion with nature. When the sun rose three days hence, the priestesses returned to claim the child. She was given a public name and a private one by which the spirits alone would know her. For the next several winters, her life was that of a cherished daughter: her personal talents were nurtured, and general skills in music, dance and philosophy were perfected. She also learned the secret rituals, one of which she performed at her woman's making, establishing her as a full member of the priestess community.

The chosen girl's acceptance into the temple did not, however, end her trials. She was still required to demonstrate her power over illness, earn recognition from those in her kingdom and neighboring kingdoms and, if so chosen, make a sacred marriage with the man chosen high king to show her loyalty to life and land. Her responsibilities continued to increase until the time of her death.

"Even the temple of Troezen has altered these sacred rituals to accommodate current reality. Most girls don't come to us at birth any longer — except those special few born to priestesses themselves. I understand that the temple at Elysia still follows this training completely, as does the Hittite Empire founded by the Amazons."

Helen was determined to capture the spirit of the ancient training, despite the practical differences. The young maidens undertook solo trips into uninhabited hillsides where they faced the fears that distanced them from the natural world. They learned to make herbal potions to invite the sacred trance and to facilitate seasonal rituals. They grew together, challenging each other, supporting each other.

Each woman was encouraged to identify and cultivate the special talent which she could contribute to the temple community. Parthenope, whose grace was evident in her every gesture, showed incredible ability in the dances that celebrated temple festivals and accompanied sacred trances. Helen surprised them all with talent for medicines — an ability that mirrored Aethra's own. Her advanced knowledge of herbs and plant life, which she gained during her time in Troezen, expanded rapidly. Soon she was making concoctions from willow bark to ease the pain of women in labor and from eucalyptus leaves to ease the cough that often afflicted men during harvest.

During the training sessions, Helen was the inquisitive, perceptive young girl Aethra remembered. She absorbed knowledge with her mind and her heart, balancing intellect and compassion easily. She was maturing into a fine priestess and Aethra was proud. Her pride allowed her to overlook the disturbing distance she felt with the girl during their private meetings.

Perhaps Helen was still recovering from disappointment over her daughter. Hermione had grown to be a big girl of three winters by the time lessons on the ways of the Goddess were underway. Helen had hoped to introduce the child to priestess life early, so she would have a solid foundation in the beliefs of the old religion and continue the work they were undertaking in the future.

It was not to be. Hermione, having been left to Astyanassa's care, was every bit the spoiled princess. She enjoyed the attention lavished upon her by the group of women and resented when they focused upon the lessons. She was unruly in her resentment, climbing into the creek so she'd have to be rescued, breaking sacred chalices, screaming during silences, using the flame of the torch to set fire to a small grove. Aethra was used to disciplining young girls and dedicated her formidable resources to doing so with Hermione.

Spoiled princesses, she soon learned, were a different challenge entirely from the farmer's daughters she was used to. Hermione would blatantly disobey her, refusing to remain at the isolated place Aethra assigned her, screaming unbearably when hit, eating mouthfuls of dirt when deprived of bread. And when all else failed, Hermione would run back to Astyanassa, who cuddled and cosseted the girl, completely undermining Aethra's efforts. By the time Helen and the rest of the women grew tired of Hermione's antics, Aethra was ready to hang the girl from a tree. She wished Helen was as relieved as she was when the child was sent back to the senseless world of sweetmeats and ribbons; the queen's unhappiness was more of a concern to her than she liked to admit. She made what efforts she could to reassure Helen that all would be well. And was failing abysmally.

The priestess would have been surprised to learn how much Helen appreciated her attempts. Yes, Helen's disappointment in Hermione was great, but she realized that she alone was responsible for the spoiled woman Hermione was becoming. Hermione was not Iphigeneia. Helen had not wanted to become attached to her second daughter; it felt too much like a betrayal to her first. She allowed Astyanassa to spoil Hermione and love her to compensate for the distance Helen placed between herself and her child. It was all she had to give her second daughter.

She was determined to reconcile her mistake with her latest pregnancy. As her time approached, Helen adhered rigidly to the ceremonies undergone by an expectant mother. She went to the cool lake for daily ablutions and spent each full moon out-of-doors with her abdomen exposed to the Mother's light. If the babe was a girl, Helen would be the first priestess to have a child reared within their community. And if, as she still suspected, her child was a boy, he would begin his life in celebration of the true Goddess.

When her labor began, she was surrounded by the women of the tree temple, gratefully basking in the warmth of their love and excitement. Rhoeteia, a young woman who showed special skill in women's medicine, acted as midwife. Helen's eyes burned with tears when she remembered the last birth she underwent in such an atmosphere. She pushed the thought of Iphigeneia from her mind and the new life from between her legs.

"It's a boy!" Rhoeteia exclaimed as tiny eyes opened to a collage of beaming female faces. The babe looked about him in wonder for a few moments before throwing back his head and giving a mighty cry.

"Strong enough to begin the temple of men dedicated to the Goddess one day," Parthenope proclaimed.

The women cheered mightily, while the infant's demanding mouth sought Helen's breast and he remained blessedly ignorant of his destiny.

She named him Nicostratus, though most of the women called him Niko. Menelaus was thrilled and demonstrated remarkable gentleness in his child's presence. He spent time patiently encouraging Niko to take his first steps and to roll a deer hide ball up a small hill. Menelaus was also far more gentle toward Helen, escorting her into the audience chamber on the rare occasions when they received visiting nobles and speaking softly when he delivered a personal message.

Thankfully, he no longer sought her bed; he seemed to have lost interest in the preliminaries once his son was born.

Helen was grateful for that. She was also fairly happy when she was participating in the training sessions. Medicine surprised and intrigued her and she never tired of learning how to set a peculiar break of bone or to cleanse a stubborn infection. The appreciation that washed the faces of the townspeople who sought her healing warmed her heart.

The unhappiness Aethra sensed was most prominent at night dark, when Helen lay awake, knowing that something was missing from her life. She chastised herself for her ingratitude. She had work she loved and that, she knew, was making a remarkable difference in the lives of those around her. She was queen of a prosperous kingdom. She was respected for her capable and just rule. She had close friends — even if she did feel a bit distanced from the other women who were thoroughly absorbed by the work of the tree temple.

"As I should be," she told herself sternly.

Still, dissatisfaction chewed at her heart. At day's end, filled with pride in their accomplishments and hope for their futures, the women around her returned to their cozy homes and shared a fire with their husbands and children before going contentedly to their beds. Helen had no such luxury. At the end of her sessions, she had to confer with Aethra about what more could be done to spread the new religion, make sure her husband was tame, attend to the endless details of running the palace and hear petitions from the populace. She envied her fellow priestesses their simpler lives.

From the time of her birth, she was always fighting. Fighting to get her mother's attention. Fighting against her sister. Fighting for the return of Rhemensia. Fighting Theseus. Fighting for the safety of her firstborn. Fighting to create harmony between herself and the man her father chose as her husband. She was always battling for the life that others claimed as their right. She spent many nights wondering how to make her world simpler.

If the answer was presenting itself, she was unable to hear it.

CHAPTER EIGHT

"**T**he wrath of the gods is upon us!"

The women ignored the screams emanating from the palace. King Menelaus was prone to occasional outbursts which often carried to their small grove beyond the women's courtyard. Helen hid a sigh of impatience and hoped Hermus, the guard she had assigned to her husband, would quiet him soon.

"It's upon us! The wrath of the gods is upon us!"

No one present could ignore her husband when he invaded the courtyard. Helen jumped to her feet, outraged that Menelaus entered the women's gardens.

"The gods did not accept our sacrifice! Our people die! Our people die!" He ran to the women, grabbing the arm of one, screaming in the face of another. His eyes were startlingly large, his newly grown hair flew wildly around his face. The women tried, unsuccessfully, to shrink away.

Aethra was the first to lose patience. "Enough man. Speak sensibly and tell us what this is in aid of."

Menelaus did not — quite — sneer at her. "You are a priestess and you do not see the signs. The flesh is decaying from bones. Men, women, children are vomiting until they have only a gooey bile frothing from their lips.

"The gods seek atonement. Atonement, yes. And it is up to me to deliver it. I will sail at once to the graves of Lycus and Chimaereus and observe propitiatory rites. I will cleanse our people."

Helen turned her attention to Hermus. "What is this about?"

The normally complacent guard was agitated. "The people have been plagued. They are dying, quickly and horribly."

Some of the women gasped and turned to run from the court-

146

yard to their families.

"Stop," Aethra commanded, wondering if the authority accorded her would hold in the face of disaster. She gave a small prayer of gratitude when they listened, even as she recognized that their obedience would not last long. She walked to Menelaus, who stood pulling at this hair. "Who told you that this is the wrath of the gods?"

Menelaus appeared to enter one of his unpredictable lucid moments and looked sheepish. "Kalchas," he said, not meeting Aethra's eyes. Madness returned. "I must go to the graves of Lycus and Chimaereus."

He turned and ran to the palace.

"Follow him and if he insists on going to the graves, accompany him," Helen ordered Hermus.

Hermus allowed himself an unprofessional sigh before turning to the palace.

Aethra met Helen's eyes. "Kalchas."

Helen nodded. It was time to confront and silence the trouble-making priest

Two long days passed before Helen discovered the cause of the plague. When she did, she was livid.

In that time, many people died, struck by unbearable stomach pains, endless vomiting, excruciating fevers. Those who passed to the Otherworld were grateful for the peace of death. Families who were struck lost two or three members. Miraculously, other homes were not touched at all. The populace believed the plague contagious and, thanks to Kalchas' loud and frequent proclamations, the revenge of the angered gods.

Helen was determined that the man would speak no longer. He was present, of course, within the crowd that gathered outside the palace walls. It had taken threats and coercion to get so many — including the palace staff — to gather together. Despite her efforts, many others, she knew, remained locked behind the doors of their homes, afraid of contact with those who might be contaminated. Helen was angry but could not honestly blame those who disobeyed her orders.

She herself had seen too many die.

The faces before her were awash with fear, save for the priestesses — including Aethra and Parthenope — who displayed tension. Kalchas assumed a mask of indifference.

Helen decided to skip the words of condolence she had thought to begin with. "We have discovered the source of the plague," she said, throwing her voice to the far corners of the crowd.

"And the wise king Menelaus has gone to the graves of Lycus and Chimaereus to make penance," an initiate beside Kalchas interupted.

Helen kept her face calm. She had not anticipated anyone paying attention to Menelaus' moves; she herself did not. But, of course, many did not know the extent of his madness. They looked to their king as a source of leadership. Helen cursed herself for not seeing the subtle message Menelaus' departure would give and cursed Kalchas for having an initiate point it out.

"The king visited the graves based upon information available at the time," Helen said smoothly, trying to regain the crowds attention. "Since then, we have learned that it is man, and not the gods, who is punishing us."

The crowd was startled and looked at one another suspiciously.

"The gods take many forms," Kalchas replied. "In their wrath, it is not unusual for them to assume the form of man."

"They are angry that we have not given them proper offerings," a man Helen recognized as Parthenope's father screamed.

Others joined in. No doubt this was what Kalchas has told them. The priest must have discovered that she was doctoring the offerings "due" him.

"If we had paid the fines imposed upon us by the temple, we would have starved and been doomed anyway," Archelaus shouted.

A few crowd members murmured their assent, but it was clear that many sided with the priest.

"If the wrath of the gods was indeed upon us, I imagine our punishment would be severe," Helen said with deceptive mildness.

Kalchas looked smug. "The gods would create a plague so deadly that nothing would appease them. Except the penance of a man such as your husband. And, of course, compensation of the offerings due them."

"Kalchas is wise in his assumption," Helen responded, satisfied with the uncertainty that flashed in his eyes. She turned to the crowd. "If, in fact, this was the wrath of the gods, only penance and offerings would appease them."

The crowd looked resigned.

"Which is why we know this is not the wrath of the gods,"

she added.

"There is no doubt that this is the work of the gods," Kalchas said impatiently.

"Let the queen speak, you fiend," rasped an old, careworn woman who stood to the side of the crowd.

Kalchas started and many in the crowd chuckled aloud. The release of tension was palatable.

"Thank you, mother," Helen said warmly, startling Kalchas anew. Helen had never publicly used the respectful name accorded women of age by adherents of the old religion. The knot of peers who surrounded the old woman nodded their approval. Helen looked to Aethra and received a small, satisfied smile.

"We have lost many to this deadly disease," Helen said, returning to a more serious mood. "You may have noticed that some families have been devastated, while others remain untouched. No one at the palace has been affected, nor do I believe, has anyone within the temple."

Kalchas remained wisely silent.

"This is not because, as we originally thought, the disease is contagious," she beckoned a guard forward who carried two stalks of wheat. He handed them to the nearest member of the crowd.

"If you look closely, you will see that one of these stalks has small green mold upon it. The other is perfectly healthy."

The crowd began passing the stalks among them, confirming Helen's words.

"The mold is often caused by heavy rains that compromise the soil during seeding."

A few of the older farmers nodded knowingly. "But we have not had such a rainfall," one protested.

"No, we have not," Helen agreed. "Nor has our soil been contaminated. And yet some stalks have still been afflicted."

Another guard came forward, carrying a pot. "This container holds mud from the bottom of the sea, including several leaves from the plant life found there. When covered and left in the sun, it grows into a green mold. This mold was spread across many of our fields, poisoning the grain we have harvested."

Some members of the crowd understood. Others remained puzzled.

"Which is why whole families have fallen ill," Helen added to explain. "They have eaten the same, poisoned wheat."

Archelaus, who had been briefed beforehand, asked, "How can we stop it?"

"The grain harvested during this season must be burned."

The crowd let loose a collective moan. "We'll starve!" one woman screamed. Others echoed her cry.

"You will not starve!" Helen shouted, shocking them into silence. "As I have stated, neither the palace nor the temple have been affected. Each will provide a portion of its stores to compensate for the loss."

Kalchas sputtered, recovered quickly, sputtered again. "It was the wrath of the gods that brought the plight to begin with! All because the queen and her heathen followers denied them their due."

Helen looked quickly to Aethra. She had hoped to avoid an open conflict between her religion and that of Kalchas. Seeing Aethra's normally calm eyes bulge with outrage warned her that this was no longer possible.

The priestess advanced toward Kalchas. "The true religion of the Great Mother does not demand unnecessary offerings!" she screamed.

Kalchas, displaying intelligence Helen would not have credited to him, took a prudent step backward.

Aethra continued her advance.

"She knows the grain to be Hers and shares it willingly with Her children. She would not send some greedy man to punish the innocents so a temple of lazy priests could grow fat on their labors."

A small group of priestess dispersed throughout the crowd began cheering, joined by the older women who remembered the time of priestess rule. Men who remembered the times of deprivation caused by Kalchas' imposed offerings, joined in. The priest shrank from the mob of angry people.

"We should be looking to the perpetrator. He would be someone who had the most to gain by poisoning the fields," Parthenope's husband shouted, looking directly at the cowered priest. Others followed his gaze, matching his menace.

It was time for Helen's intervention once more. She did not want the crowd to demand Kalchas be brought to justice. Although she was certain the priest was responsible, she had no witnesses. Since she could not hold him guilty without them, a hearing would do little more than erroneously establish his innocence. The people would question once more whether his proclamations were accurate and her gain would be lost.

She raised her voice once more. "You can be sure that the palace will do everything possible to find the unsavory perpetrator." She allowed herself one cold look at Kalchas. "For now, we must focus upon the innocent people who have been afflicted. I have instructed the palace guards to organize a contained burning of the stores affected by the blight. Simultaneously, they will distribute fresh grain from the palace stores as well as the grain they will now collect from the temple."

Kalchas was apoplectic. *You haven't heard all*, Helen thought.

Archelaus, again by pre-arrangement, voiced the question evident among the faces of many of the people. "The queen is most generous in replacing this season's store. But that will not safeguard our futures. We are a prosperous people because we store several seasons worth of grain and can withstand the occasional bad harvest that we experience. How can we possibly re-build our supplies?"

"Henceforth, for the next five seasons, the palace will require only one half of its normal tribute."

An amazed cheer went through the crowd. "And," she continued above the din, "the temple will cease its compulsory offerings for the same duration."

The crowd went wild. They began their day terrified for their future and were now faced with the possibility of greater prosperity than they had previously experienced.

If I cannot punish you publicly, Helen thought, looking to Kalchas' devastated face, *I can at least do this much. Consider it the vengeance of the Mother, whose fruits you poisoned.*

Kalchas dropped his eyes, raising them a moment later to pierce Helen with the force of his hatred.

She returned his gaze unflinchingly.

CHAPTER NINE

***K**alchas is a clever fool,* Clytemnestra thought as she listened to the messenger in the windowless chamber of her private quarters.

"At this time, some fifty families have been affected, many among the merchant class. Panic spreads with word of the plague and people believe Kalchas' proclamations that it is the wrath of the gods, drawn upon us when we withheld just offerings. It is only a matter of time before the people realize that their queen is responsible for cheating the gods and Helen is brought to her knees."

The man had grown from the boy Clytemnestra had sent to spy upon Kalchas' actions. She interupted his practiced monologue.

"What is Helen's reaction to the disaster?"

The man, having lost the rhythm of his message, took a moment to reply. "At the time I left, she had not yet made her reaction known. King Menelaus, however, was very concerned and made a pilgrimage to the graves of Lycus and Chimaereus."

His actions will give credibility to the theory that the gods have been angered, Clytemnestra thought. "You should have waited for Helen's reaction," she said aloud.

The man became contrite. "Kalchas ordered me to leave when I did. I could not disobey him without revealing my loyalty to you."

Which he is already aware of or he would not have sent you when he did, Clytemnestra thought. *Perhaps Kalchas is not as confident of Helen's reaction as he proclaims and doesn't want to risk my learning of his failure. If so, then he did not know of the others in her service who were scattered throughout the Spar-*

tan kingdom. The notion made her generous.

"You have done very well," Clytemnestra said. The man beamed under her praise. "Find the steward and command a meal and bed for yourself. Leave on the morrow and tell Kalchas that I am quite pleased to learn of our victory and await further news of our profits."

The spy bowed with surprising grace and left.

Kalchas had merely accomplished the first phase of her plan. The plague was necessary to undermine Helen's credibility and to turn the people against her. *Serves her right for trying to cheat me of my profits.*

Clytemnestra's partnership with the priest was proving more beneficial than she anticipated. When he had first proposed compulsory offerings from all the Spartans, Clytemnestra thought him foolish. Demanding the fruit of the people's labors would only fuel unrest and resentment, she had thought. She believed her own more subtle means — through which she herself taught classes and heard petitions and received "voluntary" offerings to curry her favor — was far more intelligent. She converted people to the new religion simply by taking an active role herself. It was boring and tedious and at times she thought she'd go mad with the senseless rituals and ceremonies she led. But it served her ends. The people proved quite generous. Of course, Kalchas did not have her power, thank whatever gods there were. His limitations made him dependent. Stores of useless grain piled high within his temple precincts. Clytemnestra offered a boat from her own fleet to be used to trade the foodstuff with Crete and Athens for items of more enduring value. She, of course, received a portion of all the wealth and added it to her personal stores.

Not that she needed more riches. Mycenae had greater wealth than she imagined. Its fields were prosperous, gold was plentiful and the merchants were productive. She enjoyed amassing her own personal fortune, but her real reward was the power she gained over Kalchas' operation — power with which she planned to blanket the entire Spartan kingdom.

With Helen unable to stop the plague and people believing her irreverent actions the cause, the entire Spartan populace would beg for help. Naturally, the queen's sister and the king's brother would be generous. Agamemnon would dispatch his troops to maintain order and Mycenae would send healthy grain and other food stuffs, which would keep the people from starving and, miraculously, end the plague. No one would mind that a token force remained and that Clytemnestra set a steward loyal to her upon the Spartan throne.

The only flaw in her plan was needing to rely upon Agamemnon for the deployment of troops. Her husband was proving increasingly stubborn about using force he deemed unnecessary. During his seasons as Mycenae king, he grew a preference for the rule of law over the force of arms. Worse, the people had grown to respect him as a wise and fair leader.

Clytemnestra was growing very annoyed with her current, complacent husband. *Well, he cannot refuse to disperse troops to aid his brother's kingdom*, she thought. And with Agamemnon gone to supervise the operations, Clytemnestra would be the sole voice of justice in Mycenae. Things would be very different.

She turned her thoughts to more immediate matters. Tonight was moon full and the growing number of women who gathered for her rituals would meet beyond the courtyard. Her efforts in this area were proving quite successful. What had begun as a night of boring rituals had transformed into a meeting during which the women shared their troubles — primarily about their obstinate husbands. Clytemnestra gave careful advice after calling upon the goddess Artemis, supporting the women to rule their households with an authoritative hand. The women left in a blaze of empowerment, which would be bolstered again the following month. Their strength served Clytemnestra well; she had every intention that the men of Mycenae grow accustomed to a woman's strong rule.

She cared not at all that the goddess upon whom she called never spoke to her. Her one vision, beheld long ago during the first woman's ritual, had not been repeated. Since it had not been accurate anyway, she did not mourn the loss. The strong, beautiful man who bent his knee to her in her waking dream turned out to be a belligerent husband who willfully disregarded her advice. If anything, the vision had harmed her. Disappointed that Agamemnon was not the man in her vision — and frustrated with his insistence that he rule her kingdom — Clytemnestra spurned his efforts to court her. After her second child — the boy he craved — she denied him access to her bed. That was a mistake, she realized now. She should have seduced him in earnest, and bent him with the force of his love. But she had felt betrayed by the vision of a man who warmed her blood; she made Agamemnon pay for her dissatisfaction. Her efforts to repair the damage were unsuccessful: Agamemnon was now highly suspicious of her attempts at seduction.

She had no desire to be led astray by visions again. Pretending served her ends far better.

The women who gathered with her did not share her viewpoint. Many would enter a trance upon drinking the sacred herbs and return full of excitement at seeing some incomprehensible sight. Clytemnestra used these incidents to further establish her authority, skillfully interpreting their visions to her advantage.

This was not as easy with Iphigeneia. Helen's daughter was possessed of an extraordinary ability to see in worlds beyond this one. Clytemnestra thought the girl's sight merely the result of an overactive imagination but the women believed in her visions just as they believed her to be Clytemnestra's daughter. At least Iphigeneia's visions confirmed Clytemnestra's own power.

It was one of two reasons Clytemnestra had not killed her. The second was because she needed the power the girl gave her to negotiate with Helen. If Helen refused to award full authority to the steward Clytemnestra planned to place in Sparta, Clytemnestra would threaten to have her sister's daughter flogged to death.

She often thought about doing so anyway. At eleven winters, Iphigeneia was growing to a beauty very much like Helen's own. Her hair was more golden than Helen's and her eyes more gray than blue. But she had her mother's delicate face and the unflattering cloaks Clytemnestra clothed her in could not conceal the ravishing body growing beneath. Clytemnestra hated her almost as much as she hated Helen.

She will be gone before long, just like Agamemnon, Clytemnestra reminded herself. She called her attendants to follow her to the grove.

Iphigeneia was already waiting, along with the mass of women who gathered when the sun had set. They followed her beneath a canopy of trees into the seclusion that she told them fostered power.

When they gathered into a circle, Clytemnestra took a pig from the wife of a farmer and dispassionately cut the wiggling swine's throat. The blood that poured over her fingers and down her forearms was curiously sensual.

"I call upon the goddess Artemis to join us, the vehicles of her power." She threw the sacrificed pig upon a flame which had been lit in the circle's center. "Accept our offering and grant that we may see clearly."

She turned her attention to the smooth slab of stone that served as her altar, and carefully mixed the herbs that induced trance into a large goblet of wine.

"We await your wisdom," she said, raising the cup above her and then passing it to Iphigeneia who, as her supposed daughter, stood to her right. She herself did not partake of the drink, having learned that it distorted her ability to think clearly. The women took her abstinence as another sign of her strong connection to the gods; Clytemnestra needed no assistance to hear Artemis' voice. Iphigeneia took a cautious sip and passed it to the woman beside her, beginning the ritual that would ensure each woman in the circle had partaken of its contents. Some of the women began to sway as the potion entered their blood. *They look like the flute girls who sometimes entertain the palace men*, Clytemnestra thought irreverently. Their heads were thrown back, their arms flayed and their hips spasmed of their own accord. Clytemnestra felt Iphigeneia's generous body brush against her and her amusement faded. She raised her hand to slap the girl for daring to touch her. One look in Iphigeneia's dilated eyes stayed her blow. The girl was swaying violently, tossing her unbound hair about her like dancing flames. Her arms clutched protectively about her chest. Her gray eyes blackened as they looked about her, sobering the other women around the circle. They stopped swaying, their attention completely riveted by the trance-possessed girl.

Clytemnestra needed to take control. "What is it you see, my daughter?" she commanded loudly, keeping fear from her voice.

Iphigeneia did not hear. Her movements became more violent and the women nearest her backed away. They leaped in fright as the girl broke from the circle and ran straight into the fire where the sacrifice was burning. Several women ran forward to pull her from the flames.

"Wait!" Clytemnestra ordered, fascinated by Iphigeneia's dance within the flames. It bothered her not at all that Iphigeneia might be badly burned, her glowing beauty marred. She would pull the girl from the fire before she died; she was still useful after all. But a little singeing would not hurt.

"Look! The flames do not punish her!" a woman cried.

It is true, Clytemnestra thought, astounded to see that the flames licked Iphigeneia hair and limbs and clothes without igniting.

The girl began to scream. "Ah, they burn! They burn!" She jumped from the fire, running about the circle, her dilated eyes looking into the souls of each woman present. "Flesh falling from bones. Stomachs exploding in bile. Redemption brings forth destruction. We will burn. We will burn!"

The terrified women backed away from the screaming girl. Iphigeneia continued her trance, running about the circle, screaming in her unnatural voice. She stopped abruptly before Clytemnestra and her eyes cleared.

"It is you!" she screamed, pointing a condemning figure at Clytemnestra before falling to a senseless heap upon the ground.

"Change the poultice upon her forehead," Clytemnestra snapped at the woman seated beside her. The woman started and moved quickly to obey. Clytemnestra watched her with a critical eye. Finding nothing to complain about, she pushed her chair violently aside and began to pace the room. She was surprised to see dawn enter the window.

Everything had become so confused it seemed impossible that a new day would simply begin.

The women had panicked after Iphigeneia's vision, clinging to each other and looking upon Clytemnestra with real fear in their eyes. Clytemnestra's own fear had momentarily paralyzed her. *She knows! Iphigeneia knows I am to blame for Sparta's plague!*

A long habit of taking charge quickly dissipated Clytemnestra's fright. "We have had a powerful vision from the goddess," she said. "Obviously, she whom we serve has a greater role for me than I anticipated."

That was clever. Let the women believe that Iphigeneia signaled me out to accomplish something important, rather than to reveal my guilt. "I must retire and privately determine the meaning of the message."

The women were glad to end the strange night. Several attendants stepped forward to gently carry Iphigeneia to the palace. Clytemnestra was furious to see awe grow beside fear in the eyes of the women who watched Iphigeneia taken away.

Clytemnestra stormed to the castle and forced a powerful sleeping herb down the unconscious girl's throat, lest she awaken before Clytemnestra decided what to do with her.

I should kill her now, Clytemnestra decided, then immediately dismissed the thought. She still needed Iphigeneia to coerce Helen. And, besides, some of the women might become suspicious if the girl who pointed an accusing finger at her died suddenly. At least, it would make them too fearful to continue drinking the ritual herb for fear of their own deaths.

No, she had to find out what the girl knew and then subtly silence her. But how? How?

A knock at the door interupted her thoughts and gave her an opportunity to release some of her frustration. "I said I was not to be disturbed," she snarled, opening the door to reveal a luckless guard.

The man was annoyingly unmoved by her temper. "King Agamemnon requests queen Clytemnestra join him and his cousin in the audience chamber."

Clytemnestra was livid at the request. "Tell the king that I am otherwise occupied and have no time for his petty councils now." She was gratified to see the man's composure slip slightly at her angry words, though it did not slip far enough to prevent him from continuing.

"The king says it concerns your homeland of Sparta," the guard explained hastily.

Sparta. So the plague had grow so bad that even Agamemnon was receiving word of it. Perhaps Helen had sent a plea for assistance. The thought pleased Clytemnestra immensely. Iphigeneia would have to wait.

"Keep her within this room," she barked to the waiting woman caring for the girl. She looked at her dusty, wrinkled clothing. "Tell the king I will join him shortly."

She pushed past the guard and made her way to her chambers where her attendants were idly doing embroidery. She ordered the women to robe her in a deep red gown that she knew set off her flaming hair and green eyes. Hastily pushing aside their efforts to assist her, she undid her hair from its untidy braid and began brushing through the tangled strands.

"Let me braid it for you, my lady," one of the older women said fearfully.

Clytemnestra, about to hand the woman her comb, stopped herself. "I will wear it unbound," she announced and was pleased by their shocked reactions. *This is what Helen would do*, she thought, wondering why that should matter. Fastening a thin gold band about her forehead, she looked at herself in the bronze mirror, satisfied, and left the room.

The handsome guard who stood before the door of the reception chamber was the same man who had requested her attendance. His eyes widened slightly at the sight of her and she felt a renewed sense of power as the blood rose to his face. He opened the door to announce her presence.

She walked within and again felt a lingering hint of satisfaction as Agamemnon stopped speaking to rise and greet her. She trained him well. *The greatest power is marked by the smallest gestures,* she thought. She turned her attention to the man seated before him who, taking Agamemnon's lead, rose to acknowledge her.

You! Clytemnestra's mind screamed in recognition and for a terrified moment she feared that she had spoken the word aloud. Before her stood the man of her vision, more beautiful than even her dreams had portrayed. With a catlike grace, he bowed elegantly to her and lowered his steel gray eyes to the floor.

"My lady, you do me honor." His voice was a caress of strength and sensuality. Clytemnestra absently murmured the ritual words of greeting and willed her heart to steady itself.

"Queen Clytemnestra, I present my cousin Aegisthus."

Clytemnestra desperately clutched for control. "Let done with formalities, my lord, so we may speak openly of the information brought by our guest." She walked to the chair placed at equal height to her husband's.

A servant immediately scuttled forward with a goblet of wine. She waved him away, not wanting to betray the trembling of her hands.

"As you will, my lady," Aegisthus said, bowing to her again before taking a seat beside her.

Clytemnestra sought desperately to control herself. First Iphigeneia had a condemning vision from some powerful god and then the man from her vision bowed before her. It was almost too much.

Aegisthus' next words threatened to push her beyond the edge of her fading sanity.

"Many have died and few families have been untouched. Yet the plague has been successfully contained. It seems that it was not the wrath of the gods after all but the work of some vicious man. Many of the populace even blame the head priest — Kalchas, I think his name is — for starting the plight."

For one fleeting moment, Clytemnestra was struck by the terror that the gods really did exist and were punishing her for her arrogance. The absurdity of the thought calmed her. "So the plague only raged for a handful of days," she said definitely.

Agamemnon lifted a speculative brow. "How do you know that?"

"I had a vision," she said, waving a dismissive hand in his direction.

Her husband's eyes regarded her skeptically. Aegisthus studied her with interest.

"It is not wise to dismiss the visions of a powerful woman, cousin," Aegisthus said at last.

This is a consort worthy of me, Clytemnestra thought.

She looked at Aegithus' graceful mouth as he continued answering Agamemnon's senseless questions about the state of Sparta's fields and the plague's impact on shipping. Clytemnestra had suffered some temporary setbacks but she was not defeated. In a little time, she would have new plans to replace the old. And Aegisthus would be at her side. Unbidden, the thought of his naked body beneath hers flooded her mind.

Careful, she warned herself. *Twice you have chosen husbands who you believed would serve you and you've been wrong as many times.*

"Enough for now," she said, interrupting the men's talk. "I'm sure your cousin would like to rest and refresh himself."

"That would be most welcome," Aegisthus said formally, although Clytemnestra could see that his need to refresh himself was minimal. He deferred to her nonetheless.

It was a good start. Clytemnestra vowed he would continue to prove himself worthy before she chose him to rule by her side.

She turned to Agamemnon and met his annoyance with a practiced smile. "We shall speak more at the evening meal," she said.

"We shall be dining in the guard's hall," Agamemnon contradicted.

Clytemnestra thought to fight his decision but quickly changed her mind. She'd allow him his authority — until she decided upon the most efficient way to dispose of him.

Chapter Ten

Ashes from the smoldering fires danced in the air, mixing the blighted grain of the land with the remains of those who had died. Grief and loss were elbowed aside by tough-minded people determined to rebuild their farms and their lives. Craftsmen worked through the night to create tools for turning the soil and nobles, robed in their oldest cloaks, distributed large amphorae of wine to ease parched throats.

In no time at all, the combined efforts of the people and the wine turned Sparta's recovery into an ongoing festival. Helen set every one of her kitchen hands to roasting venison and lamb and cattle and baking countless loafs of bread. She and the women of the tree temple served the workers each day, stopping only to lend a hand to harness a plow or tie a fence. The sight of their beautiful queen with loose earth on her clothes and cheekbones inspired the people to work beyond their expectations for themselves.

Kalchas was conspicuously absent from the festivities.

"Perhaps his absence *is* his contribution," Parthenope remarked.

Helen knew the priest's seclusion was temporary. Defeat was bitter wine for a man such as Kalchas and it was only a matter of time before he vomited and needed to fill his belly once more. Kalchas would be back.

So too would Menelaus, Aethra reminded her. After ensuring that the gods of men received no credit for Sparta's recovery, Helen could not risk her unpredictable husband returning to announce that his tributes had stopped the plague. She dispatched her most trusted guards to the port with instructions to deliver Menelaus — quietly — to the palace when he arrived.

By moon full, a guard knocked upon her chambers with news

of his return.

"He saw the blighted fields and at first he thought he had failed. We assured him otherwise but explained that many were still in mourning and that in deference to them, our celebration of his return would be private."

"That's very clever," Helen remarked and the guard blushed. "I will arrange a small feast to make your lie good," she added. "Please make sure Menelaus rests within his rooms until sun fall and we'll celebrate in the dining hall."

"Very good, my queen."

Helen nodded her dismissal but the guard was not finished. He shifted uncomfortably. "The king has brought a guest with him."

Helen looked a question at him.

"It is unclear whether the man is a prince or a shepherd," the man answered.

Helen's brow rose and she hid a smile. *Her face is even more beautiful when relaxed in humor*, the guard thought, admiring the quivering mouth and sparkling eyes.

"Have him put in the guest chamber in the west wing to be safe."

The guard recalled himself. "Very good," he said formally and, with a last, wistful look, turned to go.

Helen decided to inform Aethra of Menelaus' arrival before readying herself for dinner. She walked down the smooth stone hallway to the heavy door of Aethra's chambers. She knocked softly and a moment later the priestess called for her to enter.

When they had first arrived in Sparta, Helen had Aethra's chambers completely refurbished. Chairs of dark, heavy wood were replaced by painted stools of iron, intricately wrought for beauty and lightness. The ornately carved bed was replaced by one of smooth limestone and the deep green drapes gave way to curtains of light blue. Helen proudly created rooms of beauty and simplicity, striving to imitate the exquisite rooms of Aethra's homeland.

Looking about her, she realized the woman would probably be just as comfortable in the stables. Piled upon the floor, the tables and the beautiful wooden stools was a disorganized array of dried flowers and oil jars and manuscript leafs in the strange language Helen did not understand. Aethra poured over one such manuscript at a small table in the room's corner.

"Do you sleep ever?" Helen asked, smiling at her friend.

"My dreams are too fitful for sleep to be productive."

The priestess looked up and forced herself to meet Helen's

smile. It was not very difficult; when the corners of Helen's beautiful mouth curved, it was easy to grow an answering response. Aethra, forgetting her own exquisite looks, wondered if Helen realized the power of her beauty. Even in her everyday cloak of nondescript brown, the curves of her perfect body were evident. The gold in her hastily braided hair more than compensated for her lack of jewels. Aethra's smile became more genuine. Events were going quite well in Sparta; it would be silly to allow a few nightmares to upset Helen. Or herself for that matter.

"Menelaus has made a quiet return," Helen announced.

"Would that his gods see fit to shroud his entire existence in silence," Aethra responded dryly. "I suppose we'll hold a family celebration this night?"

"Yes. I'll have Astyanassa bring the children. He seems to calm a bit in their presence."

"If the preliminaries weren't so distasteful to you, I'd beg you to have a litter more."

"Fortunately, I haven't been called upon for that particular service. I can only hope he doesn't seek my bed as reward for his supposed success," Helen said.

Aethra regretted the worried frown that wrinkled Helen's brow. After the incident with Theseus, the priestess had hoped that Helen would find pleasure with the man she had married. Obviously, doing so with the mad Menelaus was not possible.

"We'll just have to make sure the servants keep his cup continually full. With luck, he'll pass out on his plate."

Helen gave orders to the kitchen hands and arranged for Astyanassa to ready the children before attending her own dressing. Clyemene, her waiting woman, helped her into a blue gown a shade lighter than her eyes and fetched the girdle of lapis that she had worn with it in the past.

"My lady, forgive me. I forgot...," she stammered, as Helen eyed first the jewels, then the priestess cord draped over her bronze mirror.

"It's quite alright, Clyemene. The lapis does go best with this gown."

The woman beamed, eagerly placing the jewels about her waist. She stepped back and eyed Helen appreciatively, though she said nothing for fear her words would knock her queen back off her senses and cause Helen to request the simple braid once more.

"The cord is a symbol only," Helen explained, feeling the unfamiliar weight of the jewels rest upon her hips.

"Of course, my lady," Clyemene said quickly, not understanding at all.

Helen wondered if Aethra would and cringed inwardly as she met the priestess in the corridor. But Aethra did not notice her choice of girdle. Rather, the priestess gave Helen the same harried stare she demonstrated far too often of late. The compliment Helen would have paid her on her exquisite white robe and rosette crown was interupted by the arrival of Astyanassa and her children.

"Well, off to the celebration," the waiting woman said cheerfully.

Aethra's eyes cleared. "Let's celebrate the downfall of a hideous priest," Aethra suggested as they made their way to the dining hall.

Helen smiled but remained silent, uncomfortable at the mention of the Kalchas. She brushed her concern aside and led the women and children to the small gathering. Her eyes moved to Menelaus, who was unbearable in his perceived triumph.

"I saved our people. My people and I saved them!"

Those unfortunate enough to be caught in his dance around the room moved tactfully away at the first opportunity.

"Welcome home, husband," Helen said, pitching her voice to carry above Menelaus' raving. He stopped instantly and moved toward her as if pulled by a string. The room's occupants released a collective sigh of relief and took their seats.

"My queen," Menelaus said, bowing over Helen's outstretched hand. "I have returned from the rites, at which I saved our people!"

"Indeed," Helen responded and quickly propelled Astyanassa forward with the children.

As predicted, Menelaus calmed in their presence, bending over Hermione's small hand and lifting the crawling Niko from the floor. He turned from them to beckon a man forward. "Prince Paris of Illium," he said, leaving Helen to attend their guest while he made his way to his plate.

Helen held out her hand formally to the man her husband called prince.

Heat! The man's touch was lightning that scorched her flesh and seared her soul, leaving her aching with loss when she hastily withdrew. He looked to her and she drowned in the amber flecks that sprinkled his brown eyes.

"Please call me Alexander," he said, his intent stare heating her body once more.

She drowned further in the orbs that stole her breath, held her in the stillness of death.

"Welcome to Sparta," Aethra said, when it was clear that Helen's voice deserted her.

The priestess words — and the nails of her hand which dug subtlety into Helen's arm — recalled Helen to her duties.

"Let us join in the feasting," she said, and led the way to their tables.

She regretted instantly the seating arrangements she had made earlier which placed the women beside the men to compensate for the small crowd. She found herself seated between Alexander and Menelaus. Her husband, thoroughly engrossed in the roast kid before him, ignored them completely.

"What brings you to Sparta," Aethra, seated on the guest's other side, asked politely.

Alexander shifted slightly and his leg brushed against Helen's. She felt her own quiver in response as her mind wondered what it would be like to have those strong legs wrapped about her own.

Her thoughts startled her to reality. *I have been with two men in my life and know how undesirable it is to lie with them,* she told herself. The reminder did little to cool her body's response.

"I was at the grave of Prometheus, where I too was observing the rites," Alexander was explaining politely. "I accidentally killed a man — a friend — at the games."

The guilt and pain in his tone slashed Helen's heart and she blinked away her unexpected tears.

"I had just learned my heritage, you see. Until the games, I was a shepherd's son. And now I am the son of king Priam, son of queen Hecuba. They say I'm prince Paris of Illium."

"How is it you came to be raised as a shepherd?" Aethra persisted, something in her tone alerting Helen to the fact that the priestess was angry.

How can she be angry at such a beautiful, sweet man? A man who had known such sorrow. A man with his eyes...

"Ah, there is much to be said to that," Alexander answered. "It seems a curse had been lain upon me before my birth. A priestess told my mother that the son she bore would bring the doom of Troy. I was to be exposed but apparently my father could not bring himself to kill a royal son." The bitterness in his tone was clearly audible. He took a sip of wine to wash it away. "A shepherd found me and raised me as his own. During the games my mother recognized me as her son — I have a twin sister and our resemblance is marked. The king and queen seemed proud of my victories and suddenly saw me as valuable instead of cursed.

"I observed the rites for the friend I killed and prepared to return to Troy. On the night before my departure I had a dream." He shifted once more and looked directly at Helen, capturing her eyes with his own. She felt a pull through her, within her, as if his gaze had seduced her spirit and merged it with his own. She wanted to stay locked in his eyes forever.

She tore her eyes from his. "I should return the children to their rooms," she said hastily, nearly toppling her chair as she rose.

"I'll see to them," Astyanassa offered reluctantly from her place beside Aethra.

"No. Stay and enjoy the meal. I am tired anyway." She gathered the children quickly and met Aethra's angry stare before leaving the room. Without turning, she knew Alexander's eyes followed her out.

After two days abed, claiming illness that required solitude, Helen recognized what was wrong with her.

Parthenope and Archelaus look upon each other as Alexander and I did, she thought, recalling the envy and confusion she had felt when she saw her friend and her husband.

I desire him. For the first time in my life, I desire a man. The feeling was exquisitely painful. She could not bear to think upon him without seeing him nor imagine seeing him without touching him. So she closeted herself in her rooms, praying earnestly that he depart, despairing that he would.

This is what you've been missing, she told herself as she remembered those long, lonely nights when dissatisfaction and loneliness strangled her. *This is what you've been fighting for, what others have so easily.*

She was no longer alone. Not now. Not with Alexander alive.

Fool, she thought. *You are a married woman and a ruling queen. He is a shepherd and a cursed prince.*

He was a man, she a woman. She knew him from the beginning of time, loved him always, would love him always.

Impossible fanciful thoughts of an unhappy queen! her mind screamed.

He is mine, her heart argued. The love between us is shared with no other. It is the single part of my life that is all mine.

He belongs to Illium and you to Sparta.

On and on and on, her mind and heart spun endless circles, etching a pattern of misery on her soul.

On the third day of her self-imposed isolation, Clymene insisted upon speaking with her.

"Menelaus' grandfather died. He has left for Crete to participate in the funeral games. Prince Paris of Illium, whom he left behind, has requested audience with you."

Surely, the waiting woman could hear her pounding heart. Alexander. She could not see him. She could not stay away.

"Tell him to attend me at sun's peak," she said, hoping Clymene would think her shaking due to her feigned illness.

The sun moved with impossible slowness across the sky as Helen readied herself with icy fingers and a frozen mind. She sat, then, upon a stool, awaiting the appointed time as if for her own death.

"Prince Paris awaits you," Clymene informed her at last.

She moved in a dream, her sandaled feet not feeling the cool stairs that led her to the audience chamber. She pushed herself inside, knowing that if she paused now she would run, screaming, to her rooms.

He stood beside a window, giving her time to memorize the curls of his dark hair, the lines of his broad shoulders, the bend of his wrist where it attached to his sun-bronzed hand.

He sensed her enter and turned, his breath-stealing eyes upon her. Within their depths, she saw reflection of her own inner turmoil, her longing, her completion.

"Helen."

He moved toward her and she extended her hand for him to bow over. He clasped it instead, entwining their fingers while she watched, mesmerized, unable to discern which were his and which were her own.

"Helen," he said again.

And an instinct more knowing than she moved her forward. She felt wonder as her chin rose and lips parted, and ecstasy as he placed his own mouth upon her. Her tongue tasted his lips, his teeth, his tongue, causing an exquisite sensation she had never imagined.

She broke away suddenly then and laughed as never before.

Alexander's beautiful eyes squinted puzzlement which drew more laughter from her disturbed body. She squeezed his hand, erasing his puzzlement and watched, delighted, as laughter sprung from him as well.

Their giggles merged, enveloping them in an impenetrable cocoon. He pulled her to him and their smiles slowly ebbed away, exposing desire. She felt his chest crush hers, his hips blend into her own.

"Helen," he said a third time. And their lips met once more, this time flooding her body with moisture. He eased her gently upon the cool floor, which further heated her body, and lay himself upon her, gently moving his mouth from hers to taste the tender skin of her cheeks and ears and neck.

He stopped abruptly and she thought she would die.

"We cannot," he explained, above the sound of their breathing. "Not here. Not under a roof where I've accepted hospitality."

She looked at his jaw, set in its honorable lines, and loved him and hated him.

"Helen, please listen. I came here after having a dream that was no dream. The goddess Aphrodite has granted you to me and me to you. One to the other. Come with me. Return with me to Illium where we can be together."

She made the mistake of looking away. Reality crashed upon her once more. The goddess Aphrodite. One of the faces the priests had created to weaken the true Goddess. How could she follow such an illusion, give up her temple, her home, her children, for a Goddess created by man?

She looked back to Alexander's pleading eyes. How could she abandon him? He was part of her.

He read her turmoil and could not bear her pain. "Say nothing," he said, placing a silencing finger upon her lips. She longed to take it within her mouth to taste the salt of his flesh, but she dared not, knowing she would leave with him immediately if she did so. "Think upon it," he continued, "You haven't the word of the goddess as I do. You have only what you feel. Think on it for today and tell me in the morning. I will beseech the goddess to speak to you as she has to me."

She smiled at him then, this handsome man who dared make demands of the Goddess' voice. How naive he was! But he believed and he had heard the voice of one aspect of the Goddess. No doubt he could hear Her true call in time. No doubt she could teach him and help him and together — together — they could accomplish what she set out to do...

"Promise me you'll listen for her voice," he said again and she nodded, unable to deny him anything, even if in his ignorance, he did not understand his request.

He stood with the grace of a panther and held out a hand to help her rise. "You know," he said, shyly. "you've not said a single word to me."

She smiled brilliantly again. "I will listen for the voice of the Goddess, Alexander."

He smiled in return and she fled the room before she no

longer could.

With each step that distanced her from Alexander, common sense took hold.

Alexander. Her other half. Her soul's partner. Her consort. He could be priest, friend, partner. Lover. All other considerations of what he might be paled at the thought of being in his arms again. *Think clearly*, her mind admonished her. He believed in the gods of the Olympians but she knew she could change that. And then? Would he stay in Sparta, by her side, as she remained married to her husband? She recalled the stubborn tilt of his jaw (that beautiful, strong face!) and knew he would not. The pull of his homeland was great in him and the need to prove himself to his royal parents was even greater. She could not even offer him the kingship of Sparta to answer his pride. If only she was not married to Menelaus. If only her husband was dead!

The thought stopped her feet and increased the tempo of her heart.

Menelaus dead? In days of old, the consort of the queen was elected by force. Did the Goddess mean for Alexander to challenge Menelaus for her hand? And would Alexander do so? Perhaps. Perhaps when he knew for whom he fought. If only she could teach him. If only she had more time!

Her feet moved once more, with increasing speed, toward the rooms of her priestess.

Aethra was in a foul mood. For three days she had led the sessions at the tree temple, watching Parthenope hide concern over Helen's absence while distracted by her own. The missing queen was a more palatable presence than the Goddess herself. Each of the women present was preoccupied and surly.

The nights were worse. Her rest was stolen by a dream that echoed her former vision: The darkness reached for the light. Only now, instead of emanating from the priests, the darkness was directed by a single man with amber-flecked, brown eyes.

Aethra had seen, as had everyone present, the way Helen and the prince of Illium looked at each other. Indeed, it was hard not to choke upon their desire and longing. Aethra would have ordinarily been pleased for Helen; the girl deserved love. But not with a stranger from the opposite end of Greece! The man was trouble. Aethra would not sleep well until he was far from the palace.

A familiar knock on the door interupted her useless pacing.

"Enter."

Helen opened the door and closed it quickly behind her. Aethra took in the girl's flushed face and swollen lips and felt rage boil within her.

"I need to speak with you," Helen said and walked past Aethra to stare at the countryside. "I have found my consort," she said, her hands twisting upon each other as if wringing the words from her mouth. "I have never felt like this. I know I will be with him forever, have always been with him." She turned abruptly. "Alexander has asked me to go to Illium with him. He cannot stay here without challenging Menelaus and cannot challenge Menelaus until he is properly trained. By leaving with him, I will have time to teach him."

"He has agreed to such training?" Aethra asked, her voice deadly.

Helen lowered her eyes. "He will. Already, he hears the voice of the Goddess."

"Which goddess?" Aethra asked coldly.

"The goddess Aphrodite," Helen said, looking at Aethra beseechingly. "But it is only because he knows no better. When we have taught him the truth..."

The darkness of Aethra's fears enveloped her. "How do you dare!" the priestess hissed, taking a menacing step forward, from which Helen tried to retreat. "You would forsake the destiny laid upon you by the Goddess herself? After She has chosen you? After I have spent the better part of my life caring for you?"

"I am grateful for you care," Helen began carefully.

But Aethra heard her no more than she heard her own words. "I should have married you to Theseus and worried about the wench to whom he was betrothed later. Now look! You wish to leave, to forsake everything we're creating —after all I've done! After I sent Rhemensia to train you. After I risked bringing war upon Troezen by bringing you to the temple. After I forsook my own home to come here. I say you will not defy the voice of the Goddess! You will not leave with this nobody prince from nowhere!"

A nightmare whirled in Helen's brain. Aethra had wanted her to marry Theseus, that horrible brute who dared rape her! Aethra had Helen abducted! Aethra had sent Rhemensia to train her — the woman Helen had thought loved her for herself.

Rage flushed her body, killing the pain that threatened to overtake her.

"How do *you* dare, my priestess?" she snarled, advancing herself. "How dare you play me like some animal you've chosen for a pet? How dare you claim to speak for the Goddess, to do Her work when all you've done is to manipulate me with that brute you call son, with the only woman who had cared for me, who loved me..." The pain was revived with her words, calling unwanted tears to her eyes.

She held them back, freezing them with her loathing. "No more. No more, I say! From now on, the Goddess will speak to me — or not — through the voice of my own heart." She pushed past the priestess violently, uncaring that the delicate woman toppled to the floor, and slammed the heavy door behind her.

*H*elen *continues...*

"The Goddess will speak to me through the voice of my own heart." It did not occur to me to doubt Her existence; I had felt Her power, experienced Her visions too strongly during my years, to deny Her. If anything, Aethra's revelations strengthened my belief, for now I had one woman upon whom to blame the incomprehensible tragedies that had plagued me.

So I listened to my heart, which filled to bursting with thoughts of Alexander, and became even more convinced that he was the consort I needed. I would go with him to Illium — a brief interlude to teach him in Her ways — and return to Sparta so he could challenge Menelaus for the place at my side. Together we would finish the work I had begun on Her behalf.

I had not realized how easily the human ear confuses the fanciful thoughts that support its desires with the true heart's voice.

Still, any doubt I may have felt fled when I told Alexander of my decision. He bowed his dark head to unsuccessfully hide the tears that threatened.

"I will make you my wife and honor you all my days," he said humbly.

"I will make you my husband," I retorted lightly and was rewarded when his tears were replaced by the smile that lit my world.

I left him then to prepare for our leave-taking, for we had to do so in haste, lest Menelaus return and complicate our departure. Within my rooms, I adorned my warmest clothing, carefully tying the cord of the Goddess about my waist once more. A moment of terror seized me as I did so. I had abandoned this powerful symbol when I first laid eyes upon my one true love. Would reclaiming it now clear a vision blurred and show me that my decisions were but folly? But the cord rested comfortably upon me and my choices remained as determined as ever. To this day I wonder why no sign was given to me.

Alexander was taken aback when I greeted him with the cord about my waist, and even further disconcerted when he realized I carried Niko in my arms.

"But he is Menelaus' son," he protested.

"He is my son, born to the Goddess," I corrected.

His eyes strayed to the cord about my waist. "A priestess prophesied doom at my birth," he said carefully.

"This priestess says that your destiny will be great should you display the wisdom and courage to claim it."

How often love and arrogance entwine!

Despite my words, Alexander still looked uncertain but said nothing more as we quietly made our way from the palace and to the port.

Along the way Aethra joined us. We said nothing to each other — indeed my rage was so close to the surface that I knew I could not speak to her without screaming. Nonetheless, I sent a silent prayer of gratitude for her presence.

We stepped aboard the ship I requested, explaining to those we left behind that I was accompanying Alexander to Mycenae, where he would guest with my sister before returning to his homeland. It was only when we quit the harbor that I instructed our rowers otherwise.

"We will travel with the prince to his Illium homeland. Follow his direction."

I was glad to give over the instructions quickly. The surge of the sea I hated worked its waves upon my stomach and I was soon in the grips of familiar sickness.

"My stomach is never placid on the waters either," Alexander had confided, gently wiping my mouth upon a cloth. "During the voyage to Sparta, I spent most of my time bent over the ship's side.

"But the waves are like the sway of love. Let me show you."

And he had, leading me to the small shelter at the ship's center, entering me in rhythm with the water's journey. A constellation of stars exploded behind eyes closed to the light of day and my fear melted in ecstasy as I took him and the flow of the waves inside me.

The water that surrounded us refused to be likewise tamed.

"Get down! Now!" the scream carried on the wind. My arms clutched at my child before I was thrown against the shelter's

wall and felt nothing further.

The stillness woke me some time later.

Nico sat a short distance away from me, his chubby hands playing with the wooden planks that had been torn from the ship. I whimpered in relief and moved at once to gather him in my arms, my battered body screaming protest.

Aethra stirred beside me. "By the Goddess, we're still here?" The priestess did not sound happy about it.

I thought to smile then, appreciative for my deliverance from the sea whose animosity proved as great toward me as mine toward it. Instead, my mouth formed a scream that echoed in the early silence of the storm's aftermath. Beyond me, a piece of crimson cloth lay in the entrance of what was once was the protected shelter.

"Alexander!"

I sought to stand, to run to him and cursed in frustration as my legs refused to hold. I finally crawled to his side.

He lay in the stillness of death, one leg bent at an unnatural angle, his arms reaching inside the shelter, reaching toward me. I threw myself upon him, uncaring of the bruises that protested the impact, uncaring of anything but him.

"Alexander, no! No!"

The body beneath me stirred.

"Helen?"

"Alexander! Alexander! I thought you were dead." I was not ashamed of the pathetic whimper in my voice.

"Dead? I may be. Gods." He tried to sit and fell back, grasping his head in pain.

I moved behind him and lent my weight to his, helping him to rise.

"My head feels worse than the dawn following Choes. And my leg— hand me that plank over there."

When I had done so, he rose, shifting his weight to his uninjured leg and pushing the plank beneath one arm to hold him steady.

"Are you well my love?" he whispered, as if seeing me for the first time.

I nodded, unable to speak.

"Nico, Aethra..." He looked behind me and I thought my heart would explode with the love it was too small to contain. He, who protested priestesses and the presence of my son, now sought after their welfare. "We'd better see how the men fared," he said.

His competence and leadership shrouded me in safety I had

never known. Together we moved to what was left of the ship, stopping but once when Alexander held up a silencing hand. "I thought I heard the music of a festival," he said, shaking his head impatiently.

I knew what he heard, for I too was momentarily caught in distant rumbling and the sound of voices raised in song. I had no time to wonder at its cause as we hobbled to the main of the ship.

"Gods," Alexander swore again.

Men were sprawled along the battered deck, covered in food stuffs and the heavy fabric that once served as a sail, awash in an eerie gold. Alexander bent awkwardly to the one closest us, checking for life. His eyes caught those who stood huddled about what was left of the prow.

He looked at me, puzzled, and more than a trifle annoyed at the men who left the injured for the sight of the world beyond. We moved toward them, a reprimand clearly forming on Alexander's lips.

He held it back as our eyes were captured by the sight that held the others.

"What is this place?" one man whispered.

"They say magic rules in the land of the Pharaohs," another responded.

I could well believe it. Before us lay a land that stole gold for sand. Having set out for Illium, the Goddess had taken us to Egypt.

PART THREE
EGYPT & TROY

CHAPTER ONE

"**I** don't know if it is more beautiful or more terrible than anything I have beheld," Alexander whispered quietly.

His thought echoed Helen's own. Tall reeds swayed synchronically with the distant chanting they had heard earlier. A group of men in flat fishing boats gracefully glided toward their ship. Strong, beautiful faces looked to them in amusement. From one of the boats, a man stood and shouted to them in stilted Greek.

"Stranger, welcome. You be traders, new to this place, yes?"

The man who had muttered about Egypt magic pulled himself upward. "We are in the command of prince Paris of Troy. A cursed storm blew us off course."

"And now reeds papyrus claim you," the man responded good-naturedly. "Well, king Proteus controls water, influences wind. To him you seek hearing."

The strange man gestured to his companions and the boat was surrounded by tiny vessels. "Not much good this," the man said, pulling away a loose plank and hefting himself gracefully aboard. "We leave it here till after festival. It be properly righted then. Come. We'll take care of your wounded and bring you to the king."

The men reverently placed those who would not wake upon their ships to prepare for burial and skillfully lifted the injured onto the flat boats. Helen told her stomach to remain calm — what more did it think to give up? — as a gentle breeze carried them on deep blue water lined with magnificent villas of lime-washed brick and gardens of carefully cultivated flowers. The group issued a collective grasp. To their right, the head of a man stood poised upon the body of a lion, dwarfing everything in view. Helen pulled Niko closer to her breast, not sure if she was offering comfort or seeking it.

"Look there," Aethra said and their attention shifted to a golden boat which carried a tall man and an even taller statue.

"That be king Proteus and the god Ptah," a boatman offered.

Their boat stopped down river from the king and his barge and they were helped to deboard.

"We must wait until Ptah is enshrined," the crew's leader informed them apologetically.

They watched as priests with shaven heads lifted the statue from the king's boat and carried it to a darkened temple. In sight of the crowd, the king made offerings of incense and food. The masses converged upon him in cheerful disarray.

"We best join them or we'll never catch the king."

Helen pressed closer to Alexander as the group from Sparta was consumed by a mob of celebrants. Brown-skinned dancers dressed in exotic feathers beat upon small drums, youth swayed to the songs of their lutes, naked dancing girls somersaulted above the moving crowd. Wrestlers wrestled. Boxers boxed. Charioteers lashed their prancing horses. The mob continued its festivities in total disregard of the strangers among them.

"Ah, and who graces us during this most joyous festival?" king Proteus asked in flawless Greek. Lively eyes looked down at them from a great height, surveying their clothing and their bruises.

Alexander bowed to the king.

"We beg your indulgence for our intrusion. I am Alexander, prince Paris of Illium. We were traveling home when a storm blew us to your lands."

The king extended a hand to the waters around them. "Life and destruction. Two aspects of the same condition. The balance of life reigns supreme even when the will of man..." He turned his attention back to Alexander and noted the prince's confusion. "But now is perhaps not the best time to discuss religion," he said, interrupting himself. "Allow my men to escort you to the palace where your wounds will be attended and you may refresh yourselves properly."

Once more they were ushered forward, led through alleys and carefully paved streets to a magnificent palace of brick and stone. They were greeted by a regal man, dressed in flowing silks of deep red and orange and yellow. Above his severe face rested a large square hat of the same colors.

"On behalf of Proteus, guardian of the Balance of the Two Lands, I bid you and yours welcome. If you will follow me, I will see you to the quarters where you may rest yourselves. Healers and food will be sent shortly."

Helen felt Alexander's hand tighten within hers. "We are most grateful for your hospitality," he said uncertainly.

"This way then." The chamberlain turned and left them to follow.

The main hall was a tribute to beauty and order. Light filtered from carefully placed windows high above them, illuminating intricate wall paintings framed in a band of deep orange. A maze of vibrant flowers offered privacy for those who sought it. Low chairs with legs of ivory and gold were strategically scattered throughout the hall. They were led down a sun-drenched corridor to elegantly furnished rooms.

"Please be comfortable." Without waiting for a reply, the chamberlain bowed slightly and withdrew.

"It would be difficult not to be," Alexander said to his retreating back.

The festival they happened upon was unending. Day followed day followed day and still the dancing continued, ceasing only for exhausted sleep and incredible quantities of food. Each morning they were dressed in clothes of gorgeous white linen and adorned with ridiculously large brown wigs that marked them as guests.

"You must," the chamberlain told Alexander, who shifted uncomfortably under the weight of his massive head piece.

He met Helen's eyes, threw her a mischievous grin and allowed them to drape him in jewelry and paint his body with perfumed oils.

Helen was similarly attended; a swarm of servants insisted on painting her brows and eyelids and lips with heavy pencils.

"Is that my Helen under there?" Alexander teased and groped for her body in confirmation while the attendants tactfully turned away.

She danced with royalty and farmers and soldiers and priests. No longer wife or mother or queen or daughter. She was Helen. Woman. Lover.

"We are free!" she screamed to the applause and shared appreciation of those around her.

Aethra made her way forward, a smile etched across her beautiful face. "You feel it too," she said, addressing Helen for the first time since their departure. "She is so alive in this land. See how they celebrate Her vitality, calling upon Her in every man and woman, animal and plant."

Yes, Helen thought, recognizing Her in the life force that

vibrated around them.

"The queen is honored as priestess, the king as her god," Aethra continued, "And what a wise and strong man she chose. They say this celebration of life is equaled only by that celebrating the king's death. A priestess could learn much by staying here. As could her consort."

Helen locked her eyes with the priestess as if to read the soul that issued such words. "You are wise," she said at last.

"I'm not certain if it's wisdom or cowardice," the priestess responded. "I have been known to confuse the two."

It was all the reference Aethra made to what had transpired between them and, in this land where conflict was superfluous, it was enough. Helen grasped the priestess hands and smiled. "I will speak to Alexander and convince him to extend our stay. He seems as enamored as we." She laughed. "He says this place has a wealth unequal to any he's seen. He says it never ends."

"Well, he has a shepherd's view." Aethra said, the trace of anger in her voice so faint Helen could ignore it. "The wealth here is carefully created. The man, the one with the peculiar hat — the vizier, I think he's called — keeps the king informed of all the supplies used. The stores are managed all year in preparation for this festival." Her tone lightened. "And it seems we're about to partake again of their carefully managed bounty. The king moves to the high table. We should join him for another round of feasting."

Alexander met them at the royal table where they shared oxen and fish basted in honey, lumps of fat in a sweet berry juice and bowls of spiced brown beans. Cups were continuously filled with the strange, fruit-flavored barley beer to ensure a lively celebration.

Alexander drank little.

"We must return home," he said to Helen. "Such wealth is my birthright and I have yet to claim it."

Now was the time to propose remaining. "Why do you need to claim it when it's so freely given?" she asked, clasping his hand lightly. "Alexander, the king here is a generous man and this land has much to teach us. Feel the vitality in the very air and the way in which the people revere the earth and all Her creations. The priestesses here know of healing arts that far surpass my knowledge and you yourself have remarked upon how learned the king is. Why don't we stay for a period and drink of their wisdom?"

His eyes softened as they always did when she spoke to him.

"You speak of a world of Goddesses and learning. Perhaps when I have confirmed my place as a royal son I will have the luxury to do likewise. But for now I must focus upon what is of this world."

"But She is of this world. She is the world. What is the status of royalty compared to a life in Her service?"

Alexander's mouth pulled in bitter lines she had never before seen upon his face. "It is easy for one already royal to say so."

She flinched at the pain of his words and despaired at his ignorance. Well, she had embarked upon this journey to teach him, prepare him to take his place at her side. If he needed to learn that the position he coveted was hollow, then that was what she needed to show him. She regretted the loss of opportunity to learn in this magic place but, she reminded herself, his training was most important.

She smiled and squeezed his fingers between her own. "Alright Alexander. If it will ease your mind to first claim your place in your homeland then that is what we'll do."

He grew a smile to match hers. "I'll talk to the king before the feast is out," he said eagerly.

Helen swallowed a sigh.

"We hate to continue to intrude upon your hospitality," she heard him say to the king as a tray of spiced sweetmeats was passed about. "Perhaps you can loan us some men to make repairs to our ship so we can be on our way."

"At festival — Blah! Men rejoice in time and build in time. Listen to the music," the king said, savoring one of the delicate treats.

A harper, blind to all but a rich inner sight, felt his way to a low stool.

Follow your desire
allow the heart to forget
Dress yourself in garments of fine linen
Increase your beauty
and let not your heart languish
Follow your desire and what is good
Conduct yourself on earth after
the dictates of your heart
Celebrate
but tire not yourself with it
Remember, no man takes his goods with him

and none have returned after going!

Alexander nodded absently at the song and Helen could feel his restlessness grow.

"Do you think we'd be welcomed like this if I wasn't a prince?" he asked her later that night. "Even if I'm a prince who hasn't performed one task to earn the title."

She framed his face with her hands. "You will, Alexander. For now, enjoy this magical place. Fate has brought us here."

She led him to their bed to forget titles and duty. But the relief was short lived. Now that his sight was set on distant shores, Alexander could not enjoy the land upon which his feet walked.

Twenty-four times the sun rose and set in the celebration of the Nile and with each, Alexander's agitation rose. On the twenty-fifth day, when Helen thought he might go mad, she awoke to a disturbing silence.

"It has ended," she whispered, surprised at the depth of her sadness. Her voice woke her lover.

"Listen. There is silence. We're going home." He jumped from the bed. "I must arrange to see the king at once and ask after our ship's repairs."

Helen, unmoving, watched him wash and dress.

"I'll return shortly," he said, making his way to the door. He looked back at her and returned to the bed to place a distracted kiss upon her lips.

This is the journey I must make to bring my consort home, she reminded herself and slowly rose to pack their belongings.

CHAPTER TWO

A watcher had sighted their ship and Troy was prepared for their homecoming. Multitudes turned out on the beach front wearing all manner of finery and making a great deal of noise.

"Prince Paris!"

"Our lost prince has returned!"

"They certainly turn out for a prince," Alexander said, embarrassed and pleased. He turned to Helen. "We are home, my love."

Helen looked into his compelling eyes and smiled, saying nothing.

A contingent of guards helped them to deboard before greeting the members of the foreign crew.

"Sparta, then Egypt..."

"Thought we would never arrive..."

"The gods challenged our journey and we survived," another said proudly. The shared boasting of sailors transcended the differences of homeland and her crew was soon mixing freely with the men from Illium.

She wished she felt as comfortable with the group that approached.

"My son, prince Paris of Illium, has returned," a tall, stately man announced, extricating himself from the royal mob. Formality dispensed, he enveloped Alexander in his bulk and Helen saw tears well in the large gray eyes.

"My son, oh my son." An equally large woman with hair piled high in complicated rings, pushed forward and took Alexander from his father's arms, splattering his face with kisses as if he were still the babe she let go.

Alexander endured her greeting for a moment before gently pulling away and drawing Helen forward. "Father. Mother. Nothing could have detained me from returning to my home. Nothing except a dream and a quest to find my wife to be. I present queen Helen of Sparta."

The crowd buzzed, handing Alexander's announcement to those behind them; the king and queen barricaded themselves in silence. Helen similarly shielded herself, although the thoughts inside her screamed. Alexander's wife? She had not considered that he would propose such a thing so soon. What of the man to whom she was already wed?

"So the queen of Sparta is now to be second wife to the second son of Priam?" A young man moved forward between the king and queen, the line of his jaw pronouncing him their son, his stride proclaiming his right of inclusion.

Alexander took an involuntary step backward. "Hector."

Hector ignored the wariness held in his brother's eyes and turned his own upon Helen.

"Your beauty is even greater than men say. One can only wonder why you would forfeit crown and kingdom to become the second wife to a newly discovered prince — no matter how considerable his charms," he added with a flawless smile to his brother.

Helen did not respond as she strove to digest this second piece of information: Alexander was already wed! And he said nothing of this either. For the first time, she realized how little she really knew the man she chose to be her consort.

"I do not recognize the woman with whom I was raised as wife," Alexander was saying. "Queen Helen is my first love and she will be my first wife."

"I had thought even shepherds were raised to greater honor than that," Hector responded.

"My honor is as great as that of the oldest son of Priam. And I'd say my manners are considerably better."

The two men squared off, animosity crackling between them in shimmering heat.

"Enough," growled Priam.

Hector was first to relent. Charm replaced challenge. "True, father, this is no way to greet my brother," he clamped a friendly hand to Alexander's shoulder.

Alexander, looking bruised, began to murmur something which was interrupted by a high pitched wail from the crowd.

"She is the doom of Troy! Fire, fire trails in her wake. Send her back, send her back!" A young woman pushed herself forward, deep brown hair streaming behind her and Helen saw the eyes of her lover look out from a woman's face, cursing her. She clutched Alexander's hand.

"Enough," Priam shouted again, his voice carrying in anger. "It seems a day for all my offspring to regress to the children they have not been for many seasons." He looked critically at Hector and the mad woman who kept her wild eyes on his and parted her lips to say more.

Aethra, who had stood silently to Helen's side, placed Niko into the hands of an embarrassed guard and approached the girl. "It is Her will," she said firmly, placing gentle hands upon the girl's temples.

The girl's eyes ceased their wild dance and her body relaxed into natural silence. Helen wondered if Aethra referred to the Goddess or Helen herself.

Priam eyed Aethra warily, then decided to turn his attention to Helen. "I will have peace in my kingdom and household. Queen Helen, I bid you welcome to my land and family — if you still wish to become one with us," he added with another look at his family, including his unhappy wife.

"I am honored by the privilege of becoming one with your home," Helen replied quietly. *For a brief while*, she added to herself, using the thought to anchor her as the sands of her world shifted.

Priam, determined to avoid further confrontation, declared that the homecoming ceremony would end with the wedding of Helen to his son. No one contradicted him.

"We had not spoken of marriage," Helen whispered to Alexander as they followed the royal party to the palace.

Alexander's face was pained and bewildered. "I had thought such words were unnecessary between us."

"But I am married already. Would you challenge Menelaus for my hand?"

The proud chin thrust forward. "If necessary, I will do so. But can't you see that this way we can avoid all that?"

How ignorant he was! Thinking to avoid the challenge of the Goddess. Helen beseeched Her to be patient with the chosen consort. Anything more she would say was interupted by a summons by the queen.

"You will follow me," Hecuba ordered.

Alexander gave her a reassuring smile before turning to join the knot of men heading down one of the royal household's many corridors.

I should spite them all and simply follow him. But she knew Alexander would chastise her in his confusion. She met Hecuba's hard eyes and wondered if the queen would apprehend her if she even started to the place she was not invited.

"This way," Hecuba said, turning upon her heel.

The palace of Troy was a confusing labyrinth of corridors and rooms, portions of which were stubbornly replaced each time the Earth Mother shook its foundation. The queen led her to a suite of rooms, turning to eye Helen's travel worn clothing disdainfully. "I'll leave my attendants to help you bathe and change for your wedding," she said curtly.

Her gaze rested upon Aethra and the child. Unspoken questions were evident in the planes of her face. Turning back to Helen, she demanded, "Aren't you already wed?"

Helen flinched before Hecuba's disapproving eyes.

"The man to whom I was wed is mad." The words were drawn from her mouth before she could think. It was true enough, if not informative.

"I'm beginning to wonder if my younger son is as well," Hecuba snapped.

"Oh, mother, let her alone." A small, beautiful woman in the dress of a princess moved forward.

"Even your husband had the good sense to question Paris' judgment," Hecuba said.

"And the grace to apologize for his rudeness," the woman retorted.

Hecuba returned her attention to Helen. "Well, it seems you have one friend here at least," she turned and left the room.

"Stubborn thing," the young woman swore affectionately. "Don't mind the queen. She was probably looking forward to being first in her lost son's heart for a while. The gods know she fought me long enough when I married Hector. I'm Andromache. And I suggest we get moving. It won't do to have the bride late for her own wedding."

In a whirl of efficiency, Andromache arranged for Nico to be cared for, Helen's women to be given fresh clothing and Helen herself to be bathed and adorned in a gown of light silk.

"There is not a woman in Troy who won't be sorry you ever touched down here," Andromache declared when Helen was ready.

Aethra saved Helen a reply. "Yet you seem undisturbed."

Andromache considered the priestess. "I make my own decisions about people," she said, with a shrug of indifference that contrasted vividly with the passion of her eyes. "Come, let's get this ceremony over with. We're to escort you out to the temple, which will serve as the home from which Paris will take you.

Hecuba tried to argue that we should send you back to Sparta to make the ceremony authentic. Priam, fortunately, has better sense."

A growing part of Helen wished that they would, indeed, send her back to Sparta. The events that whirled about her carried her in a direction she was uncertain that she wanted to go. She was as powerless to protest as she was to brake free from the throng of women who began to surround her including, to her surprise, Hecuba.

"A queen must sometimes do what a woman would not," Hecuba explained. "At least that is how we're reared in Troy."

The temple was a short distance from the palace. An efficient mob of servants had laid out a feasting table for the women to enjoy.

Helen knew if she tasted anything she would vomit.

"You shouldn't let the queen's remarks spoil your appetite or you might find yourself a great deal thinner before long," Andromache advised, mistaking the reasons for Helen's abstinence.

The women joked and bantered and ate with the relish due a happy celebration, gleefully oblivious to the disapproval emanating from their queen and the tension that choked their guest. An eternity passed before the men's procession approached.

"Surround your bride," Andromache ordered, rolling her eyes in exasperation when the queen remained stubbornly seated. Fortunately, the women around her did as their princess demanded, carried forward by a tradition stronger than the queen's refusal to participate. They circled Helen in a mock effort to shield her from her abductor. Alexander pushed through them with blessed speed and carried Helen to the carriage that would lead them to his father's palace.

"Isn't it magnificent," he whispered as they moved forward amidst the procession of nobles and villagers and flute-playing girls who lit their way with torches, while minstrels played the hymeneal chant.

"Alexander...," she began, not certain what she would say.

"I give this all to you," he interupted, the eyes she loved glowing in torch light.

What does matter really that we are wed by the customs of his homeland? The bond will only strengthen the tie between us. And soon we will resume our places in Sparta.

"I will always cherish this moment," Alexander told her as the chariot came to a halt and he lifted her across the threshold.

How could she deny him his pleasure?

"I have to sit with the men," he said, setting her down before a mob of women. "I leave you in the loving hands of my mother." He bowed gracefully and left the two women to stare at each other.

"Well, there's no help for it," the queen said at last.

Helen was grateful to be placed between Aethra and Andromache.

"Are all these people part of Priam's immediate household?" Aethra asked.

"Most of them," Andromache answered. "We're an unruly group."

Helen decided to allow curiosity to replace her confusion and scanned the crowd around her. Her eyes met those of the woman who had cursed her upon her arrival. "Who is the strange girl who King Priam claimed as his own?"

"Cassandra. She's Paris' twin and a priestess of Apollo."

"She is so pretty. Is she mad?"

"Oh, she's not mad," Andromache responded, "Most of the time, she's quite lucid. It's only when the god possesses her that she cries out like that."

"Like at Delphi. It is what becomes of a woman when the voice of the Goddess that grips her is controlled by an Olympian god," Aethra said softly.

"Perhaps," Andromache said. "It is said that she is indeed cursed by the god Apollo — though I can't imagine what for. She's quite a sweet thing, actually. Listen," she continued, drawing their attention to the men seated at the hall's opposite side. "My husband's about to speak. Although I doubt it's to toast your happiness," she added to Helen.

"Father, I must once more plead with you to end this farce for the good of Troy," Hector stated. His carefully controlled voice betrayed his rage.

"Well, I'm glad it is but once more that you feel compelled to do so," Priam responded. "You've said your peace. Now be silent."

"Can't you see this is just the excuse king Agamemnon and the Achaians need for war. No doubt they have plotted long to overtake our rich land — and bypass the tariffs for sailing our waters."

Helen started, thinking of her former husband's brother. She could not imagine Agamemnon greedy for riches.

"The tariffs are mine by right," Priam snapped, "won by my forefathers who dared come to this land. The Achaians know they haven't the strength to conquer us — they're too busy fighting themselves."

"And if they do attack us, will you abide by your fate and return to your homeland," Hecuba demanded of Helen.

"Oh come, mother," Andromache interjected. "It was your son after all who brought her here and asked her hand in marriage — a proposal I'm sure she's regretting with each passing moment of this squabbling. See here, even Cassandra and her god have seen fit to remain silent and not torment the poor girl on her wedding day."

Helen looked to Andromache's right and saw the pretty girl sitting in quiet, her eyes fixed in longing upon Aethra.

Alexander rose and faced his brother. "You yourself said Cassandra is mad," he said tactlessly. "Better to listen to my brother Polydamas, who also has the voice of the gods and has showed me nothing but kindness since I arrived."

A delicate young man rose from his seat. "Our fate was sealed when you entered these walls with the queen," Polydamas spoke softly. "There is little we can do now to avoid it."

Helen felt Aethra start beside her and looked at her questioningly.

"Later," the priestess murmured, her brow knit in a disquieting furrow.

"I'll never understand why the gods saw fit to give me two doomsaying children," the king said peevishly. "We will deal with what the gods give us and not quibble over possibilities."

Hector murmured something too quietly for Helen to hear. Hecuba's face was like stone.

"Great geese the kitchen supplied us with this evening," Priam said, cutting off further discussion.

The celebrants gratefully washed away the tension and the conventions that separated men and women in the abundant flow of wine.

Alexander joined Helen with a lanky man whose eyes shifted constantly, reminding her unpleasantly of Kalchas. "My lady can confirm what I say," Alexander slurred. "I was telling him of the splendor of Egypt," he added to his wife.

Helen ignored his companion's overly eager stare, "The land was magnificent. I believe it was the happiest time of my life," she said rebelliously.

"We will strive to overshadow even that happiness," the man drawled.

"My foster brother, Deiphobus," Alexander introduced, his breath clouded with drink. He dropped down beside her. "Are you well my darling?"

"Tired," she said, some surprising part of her still unwilling to spoil his homecoming.

Deiphobus watched her intently, as if relishing her ill-concealed misery. Helen did her best to ignore him.

"I'd say it's time we retired and sought a more quiet celebration," Alexander was saying to her now.

He signaled and the crowd gathered to guide them to their rooms, offering a drunken rendition of the marriage chamber song.

When they arrived, Alexander bowed gracefully and closed the door behind them. "I thought they'd follow us in here," he said and closed the distance between them. "My princess. My wife. My love. We shall never be parted."

She clutched his promise to her heart as she did his body to her own.

My consort. I will teach him well.

CHAPTER THREE

Helen barely saw him. At first light Alexander departed to meet with the men, leaving her to join the women — an occurrence more tortuous than his absence.

"I had heard that the queens of other lands disdain doing the embroidery necessary to clothe their households," Hecuba said with predictable bite. "I am pleased to learn otherwise. At least this debacle will result in less work for the rest of us."

Helen worked the bone needle through the coarse wool garment in her hands, trying not to envision using it to puncture the Trojan queen's heart.

"Come mother," Andromache said, "It seems to me that we've much to learn for our guests."

"Hmph," the queen replied, but nonetheless looked covetously at the perfect blue cloth upon which Aethra worked. "You are a priestess and clearly well trained in herb lore. I'd like to know how you set the dye so fine." Her voice softened, as it always did upon speaking to the priestess.

"It's not difficult really. Only a matter of letting the liquid sit smoothly when drying. Helen and I will be glad to show it to you."

Aethra gave Helen a pointed look, which she ignored. This was worse than when she first returned to Sparta and had to endure the endless needlework sessions with her mother.

At least then I was in my own household, able to come and go as I pleased. Here, she was denied even that much and it took all of her meditative practices to stay patiently seated and not stand and declare her intention to return home.

"How unusual for a queen to be so versed in herb lore," Hecuba mumbled.

"Helen is priestess in her own right," Aethra responded.

Helen felt Hecuba's critical eyes upon her. "It's unfortunate that my daughter Cassandra despises you so. Perhaps she, at least, would have something to talk to you about."

Helen looked forward to the evening meals, when she could at least catch sight of Alexander. She was very grateful for the Illium custom that directed men and women to take their meals together. Although the women sat to one side of the hall and the men to the other, she felt better for being in the same room as Alexander.

She looked to him now, seated as always beside his brother Deiphobus. Her eyes narrowed. Her initial dislike for Alexander's sibling had intensified with each night she saw them together. It was almost as if the man was forcing the tight lines of his miserable face upon the smooth features of her lover's, claiming Alexander's relaxed strength for his own.

I must contrive to loosen Deiphobus' hold upon him.

As if reading her mind, Deiphobus caught her eye and raised his goblet in ironic salute. Helen suppressed a shudder, dropping her eyes before seeing Deiphobus' hideous smile bespeak the satisfying warmth that flushed his body.

Deiphobus felt best when others were miserable.

As the first of Priam's illegitimately born sons, Deiphobus had suffered until his features twisted in a pattern of permanent discontent. From the moment his low-born mother pushed him into the world, he was at a disadvantage, overshadowed by Hector, the darling of his father's heart.

Brilliant, strong, beautiful Hector.

Secretly, Deiphobus knew himself superior in every way. Secretly, he wished Hector dead with every fiber of his being.

Unfortunately, his hearty, protected brother was not accommodating his desires. Deiphobus was forced to content himself with undermining Hector's popularity.

It was easier when they were younger. Then, Deiphobus had only to whisper untrue words to gentle Polydamas and Hector's attention would be distracted for moons at a time, keeping him from his circle of admirers and throwing his followers into a spasm of resentment.

"Hector says you'll never be a real man," Deiphobus had told young Polydamas, sending the delicate boy into a wave of tears that was followed by a stubborn silence whenever Hector approached.

It had taken a puzzled Hector over two moons to make amends.

This tactic had served Deiphobus well. Until Polydamas grew old enough to confront Hector directly.

Hector responded by connecting his fist with Deiphobus' already large nose in full view of a pack of palace spectators. Thereafter, Deiphobus' attempts to create dissension became much more difficult. He continued to seize the limited opportunities available to him, waiting patiently for the moment he could wage a full and open war against his brother.

The moment came with the unexpected arrival of another of Priam's sons. With the admittance of Paris into the Trojan palace, Deiphobus was no longer the least popular man in attendance. He was certain he could use this to his advantage.

No doubt the beautiful princess was jealous of the influence he exerted over her dainty beloved. Deiphobus' smile deepened as he thought how little Helen could do about her disapproval. He leaned over to murmur near Alexander's ear. "Look, a guard has entered to confer with Hector. I wonder how Hector will discredit you this time. He has always been unbearably jealous of his more capable brothers."

Deiphobus hid his delight at Alexander's scowl and sat back to enjoy the imminent entertainment.

He was not disappointed. A moment later Hector rose, waving the guard away with an agitated hand.

"Father, before all those present, I must speak."

Priam, who was busy gnawing at the wing of a chicken, looked to his oldest son and nodded.

"The messenger you allowed me to send has just returned with word that troops are amassing at Aulis, not far from Mycenae. They say king Menelaus is among them."

Priam put the fowl down regretfully and looked to Helen. She met his eyes and suspected — rightly — that he had agreed to let the messenger be sent in an attempt to quiet his son's constant ravings about the threat of war. He was not pleased that his plan backfired.

"My lady," he began, addressing her directly. "What do you say of this threat?"

The hall quieted as everyone ceased their conversations to await her reply. Helen forced her voice to carry above the uncomfortable silence.

"I have met King Agamemnon on but a few occasions. My impression is that he is a just and wise ruler — not one to enter war lightly. And I do not believe Menelaus capable of rallying the troops required for an attack on Troy," she forced herself to say, feeling guilty for betraying her late husband.

Ironic that I should feel guilty now and not when I left. She dismissed the thought, reminding herself that she had only done what she must.

"With all respect, lady," Hector said, his lean body crackling in intensity, "You impressions do not seem to count for much in light of what we have learned."

Helen's eye caught Deiphobus leaning to speak to Alexander and she was dismayed to see her husband rise an instant later.

"You insult my wife," he screamed. "And I take offense."

Hector sneered. "It is I who take offense to plunging my country into war for the deeds of one dishonorable shepherd!"

Alexander's face turned an unbecoming shade of purple. "Coward! I believe you fear the test of might. Father, if a threat does present itself, allow me to lead the troops against those that my brother fears will overcome our own."

A general murmur ran through those present, though it was unclear how many agreed with Alexander and how many were appalled by his arrogance.

There was no doubt as to what Andromache's loud hiss indicated, nor with whom Hecuba's sympathies lay.

"I'm beginning to doubt that child to be of my body," the queen snarled.

Priam, equally angry, stood at last. "Enough!" he bellowed. "Hector, if it is as you say and the men of Greece rally troops against us then I am certain we can meet the oncoming threat. I will lead the troops and I expect you to serve at my command with the courage and skill I have bred in you bones."

He threw Alexander a withering look and regained his seat. "I will hear no more of this until possibilities become reality," he said, letting his eyes rake the room.

Hector, somewhat mollified, took his seat. Alexander, clearly furious, did the same, while Deiphobus handed him a goblet and tried to soothe him with insidious whispers.

Everyone pretended to eat for the time remaining, blessedly giving up before long.

"I suppose it would be too much to ask that you talk some sense into him," Hecuba said when Helen rose to join Alexander and return to their rooms.

Helen glared at her, her anger equaling Alexander's own as they walked the stairs to their chamber.

She took a calming breath as the door closed behind them.

"Alexander..."

Her words were interupted as Alexander threw a sandal to the corner of the room, startling her.

"I should have expected as much," he said, rummaging through the room's drawers and discarding items Helen had not seen before. He moved to his sack of arrows, plucking several and cracking them across his knee with the force of his anger. "My dear brother won't even allow me to lead the archers, although he's deigned to allow me to stand among them. He says I'm untried; I know it's because he doesn't trust me. And even now, when he's proven himself the coward that he is, my father grants him a place to which he is unworthy — merely because he was first born."

"This is a fate you cannot fight," Helen said soothingly, approaching him. "Why do you fight him when you cannot win? A greater destiny awaits you."

"This is my destiny!" he screamed, turning on her. "It was almost denied me upon my birth. I will not let it occur a second time. I am of royal blood. I will be accepted as such and not bow to a lessor man's rule."

"There is greater power than that accorded royalty," Helen said, feeling her skin burn. How could she say so after so recently chaffing under Hecuba's authority?

"Do not speak to me of goddesses and priests. If I do not have royal power, I want no other."

The words rang like an oath in the air between them and panic flooded Helen's body. *He means not what he says*, she whispered to She who hears, begging Her to be deaf to words spoken in anger.

"Alexander..."

"My name is Paris," he said coldly. He gathered his broken arrows and piles of discarded linens and left the room, slamming the door behind him.

"He knows not what he says," Helen repeated again to the silence. *When no war occurs and he realizes that he will be but another Trojan prince, he will look to claim his true place at my side. I must prepare for that time, be ready to seize the opportunity. It will come sooner if there is no war.*

If. She heard herself think the word and wondered. It was as she told Priam: She did not believe Agamemnon would wage war. Nor was Menelaus capable.

Unbidden, a vision of Clytemnestra flooded her mind.

"She cannot..."

But Helen knew her sister could and would support destruction in her name.

Must I *fight this darkness as well?* She collapsed onto the bed, awaiting an answer she was not certain she wanted.

CHAPTER FOUR

*H*_{*elen took Menelaus' final hold on sanity with her,*} Clytemnestra thought, observing the wild man before her.

"Gold, jewels, my son, my wife...," he paused, listened to his own words. "My WIFE!" He fell to the floor.

Clytemnestra looked to her husband; Agamemnon looked acutely embarrassed.

"What is it you want done?" the king asked, quietly.

Menelaus threw back his head. "Revenge! The gods demand revenge!"

A shiver ran through the room; even Clytemnestra was impressed by the power of Menelaus' mania.

"Men did swear oath to avenge any encroachment on Menelaus' right as husband," she reminded Agamemnon.

Menelaus, hearing, jumped up from his place on the floor.

"All the land is sworn to vengeance. The gods demand it. The gods demand it!" He moved to a corner — for which Clytemnestra was sincerely grateful — and muttered to himself.

"And Illium is a rich land — all the more wealthy for the tariffs she imposes upon us for simple trade," Clytemnestra said loudly enough for Aegisthus to hear.

His nod of approval was a welcome caress.

Agamemnon, however, looked through her, without acknowledging her in any way. *I loved her once*, he thought, *or would have if she had let me.* Something was broken deep inside his wife's heart, something he did not understand but had wanted desperately to heal. Beneath her facade of strength and cunning, there was a vulnerability to which Agamemnon could not help but respond. Or perhaps he fancied this was so. His attempts to win her heart had only decreased her trust in him and increased her hostility. Her responses were like a plague that spread to his own heart until he found himself equally distrusting. He had not liked his wife for some time, no matter how he willed it otherwise. *A broken sword cannot be mended.* He forced his thoughts back to the matter at hand.

War, he reminded himself. The sharing of bread, the sharpening of weapons, blood cascading through veins to remind of the glory of life.

Agamemnon's blood was sluggish.

War proved the strength of a man and granted him glory. War propelled Agamemnon from the common life of a common prince onto the pinnacle of valor.

He remembered.

Battle upon battle. The excitement of pitting his endurance against that of another man, of waiting for a lowered shield, for the vulnerability that would allow him to pierce heart or lung, to spill the ropy insides of a belly.

He remembered. As he remembered his fear — a fear that he would admit to no other — that the battles would fade with his conquest of Mycenae. He had observed strength grow in men, as a child grows in a woman, becoming separate from the flesh of the creator, nourished by the fears and beliefs of those around them.

No one fought him any longer. No one would risk the certain death they believed they would find.

Agamemnon had feared his reputation would suck his true strength from his breast. Perhaps he was right to fear this.

In the time since the battles ceased, Agamemnon had found new challenges — running a complex and powerful holding, pitting his wit against a wife who had her own in abundance. And new pleasures — his son, who would one day grow to a man, his daughter, whose eyes mirrored the slant of his own.

Iphigenia.

The child of his heart, if not of his blood. Beautiful, graceful Iphigenia. The daughter of a woman he could have possessed once, but knew he never would. Even if he were not married to Helen's sister, Agamemnon would not have pursued Helen for the same reason that other men had: He did not want her to think him unable to see beyond her beauty. Too many had not been able to see beyond his strength.

Too many could not now. He met the eyes of his wife and saw amber specks within depths of green spark red.

Strength. The gods demanded he be worthy sire to the image he birthed. He wondered if he would ever be more than his reputation demanded.

"I'll sound a call to all those who swore allegiance to the king of Sparta," he heard himself say. "You men, attend me in my chamber. Aegisthus, I request that you guard the kingdom in my absence."

Aegisthus bowed his head in supplication.

Clytemnestra bowed hers to hide her glee.

Agamemnon walked to his chamber, head held high, a man confident in his decision. *One decision*, he thought. *A single decision can change the fate of men.*

Clytemnestra did not bother finishing her dinner; her stomach was too wild for digestion. She retired to her rooms, dismissed her servants and threw herself upon her bed. Her body wriggled in anticipation.

Agamemnon gone. Aegisthus here. Whatever gods there were showed her favor. *Aegisthus must prove himself worthy*, she reminded herself, stilling the roar of blood to her brain. *He must prove himself capable.*

She tested him at her side during the two winters Agamemnon summoned his troops. Together, they chose the animals for sacrifice, apportioned grains for the palace stores, settled disputes among the servants. His presence was necessary by the king's decree; her authority was assured by her voice of command.

The unconsummated heat grew between them.

"Agamemnon requests signs from the goddess for the upcoming war," she lied, reminding Aegisthus of her power. "I will retire this day with my daughter and the palace women to prepare for the ritual."

She did not miss the flame that ignited behind his eyes at the mention of Iphigenia.

"Leave me," she commanded harshly.

Iphigenia sat among the women and children in the sewing room, a rose amidst weeds, reminding Clytemnestra that the girl was not a child of her blood. Beside her sat Clytemnestra's own Electra, handsome rather than beautiful, her shoulders bent in perpetual defeat. Behind them, the baby Orestes played, an innocuous boy whose presence was forgotten until one stepped on him.

No one would forget Iphigenia. Aegisthus did not forget Iphigenia.

Her end is upon her, Clytemnestra decided. She dispatched a messenger to summon Kalchas.

❧

"The wind is against them," Clytemnestra explained to the travel stained priest some days later. "After more than two seasons of preparation, of petty arguments among craftsman hoping for glory through elements of destruction, and of land ignored and corn trampled then lamented as supplies grow low, they are still here."

"That is the way of it sometimes," a weary Kalchas responded, wondering indifferently why Clytemnestra roused him from his quiet temple.

Helen's victory over him had affected him deeply — the farmers still looked upon him with suspicion, while the nobles had all but ceased to grace him with offerings. His dreams of glory were dying fast and his ambition was leaving with their passing.

Clytemnestra ignored the apathy that spilled from the once industrious priest. "I have had another vision," she said, resorting to the tactic that had stirred Kalchas so much in the past.

A familiar light kindled in the man's eyes and, though it was not as bright as Clytemnestra hoped, she was determined to make the most of it.

"I was quite surprised at the prominent role you played within it," she added, repeating the words that had served her before. "You are to travel with Agamemnon to Illium and once there..."

"Illium? Illium is the stronghold of Apollo," Kalchas interupted, eyes gleaming as he awoke from his trance of indifference and entered a stupor of fanaticism.

Clytemnestra remembered why the priest's passions unnerved her. Every time she thought she knew all the dark corridors of Kalchas' puny mind, another would open before her. What difference did it make which god held prominence in Troy?

"I believe he does," she said quickly, anxious to return to her original plan. "But before you can set eyes upon his temple, the army must leave."

"Apollo tests me," Kalchas muttered.

Clytemnestra hid an impatient sigh and continued. "As I said, the troops have been stranded here overlong. The north wind refuses to blow, denying them the assistance necessary to sail."

This time, she was less successful at covering her impatience. For moons, she had been sending Agamemnon messages, suggesting that he row his way to Illium. The response was always the same: He would not tire his men unnecessarily before a major war. Clytemnestra raved each time she received his response — even doing so in front of Aegisthus, with whom she had carefully cultivated a mask of omnipotence. Her slip before her soon-to-be lover had proved surprisingly beneficial.

"Fret not, my queen," he had soothed, his dreamy eyes driving her wild with distraction. "I have spoken with the farmers, who read weather even better than sailors. The wind will pick up before the moon wanes."

He had smiled at her then. Before Iphigenia had entered the hall and captivated his attention.

Clytemnestra thought to execute him right there. Her forbearance was about to pay off.

"The goddess has shown me the reason that her winds do not cooperate," she said, reclaiming Kalchas' attention once more. "The fault lies with Agamemnon."

Kalchas looked up from whatever thought entangled him. "Agamemnon?"

"Yes," Clytemnestra responded with a confidence that did not allow further questions. "He has offended the goddess; the only way to appease her is to sacrifice she whom he holds most dear: Iphigenia must burn!"

Kalchas gave her his full attention at last. "Iphigenia? Why shouldn't Agamemnon be sacrificed?"

Clytemnestra wanted to throw one of the palace's many priceless vases at the man's head. *Because Aegisthus looks too favorably upon Iphigenia. Because if Agamemnon is killed now, one of the many warriors camped beyond the walls will take over Mycenae. Because Agamemnon is needed to destroy Helen.*

"Because the goddess wills it," she responded firmly.

Kalchas let out a nasty whistle. "Agamemnon must have done something very hideous to incur the sacrifice of his daughter. How exactly did he offend the goddess?"

"She chose not to reveal that to me," Clytemnestra snapped. Why couldn't the man just accept what she said without asking these endless questions? She decided to turn the knife of her words in what she knew to be his weakest point. "I'm sure you understand how visions are — an inspired priest like yourself. The gods reveal only what they believe we need to know."

Kalchas scowled petulantly.

"The goddess indicated that you would discover the reason for her anger. Before you joined the troops headed for the Apollon temple in Illium," she added.

Kalchas leaned forward, his eager gleam ignited once more. "Tell me what I should do?"

Much better, Clytemnestra thought, satisfied.

"You have a very important role," she said slowly, heightening his anticipation. "You must let the men know that the lack of wind is their leader's fault. Let them know that the goddess has demanded Iphigenia's sacrifice in retribution."

"Why don't you tell them yourself?" Kalchas asked with the shrewdness Clytemnestra remembered.

"I? I am a mere woman," she answered innocently. "The men will not listen to me."

Kalchas, though clearly skeptical, moved to more practical matters. "And why would they believe me, a foreign priest? Surely if Agamemnon is as irreverent as you say, he will deny the truth of the prophecy and fight to save his daughter's life. Why would the warriors believe me over their war leader?"

"That is an excellent question," Clytemnestra said, as if she had not already considered it herself. "We must make sure Agamemnon does not learn of Iphigenia's sacrifice until it's too late."

"I sincerely hope your goddess provided guidance as to how we are to accomplish that."

"Of course," Clytemnestra retorted. "It seems that the lack of wind is causing the scalps of a great many warriors to itch. None is more affected than the great Achilles. Apparently, the man already blames Agamemnon for the army's inaction. He has ensconced himself within his tent and grows more surly with every moon. You will tell Agamemnon that the warrior demands Iphigenia as his bride if he is to continue with the army."

Kalchas' eyes lit with approval. "Agamemnon will not risk losing Achilles. The warrior's men fight with the strength of armies twice their size. And if Achilles defects, it will not be long before others do likewise, leaving Agamemnon in a bad situation indeed."

"Exactly. Tell Agamemnon that he has angered the goddess and she demands his daughter be given in marriage to Artemis' favored hero. I'll have Iphigenia delivered to the camp with all ceremony. Once there, you will reveal the true reason for her presence and we'll sacrifice her upon the pyre."

"I hope the goddess is quick about granting the north wind.

Agamemnon will kill us both — and none will gainsay it — if there is no effect."

He'll kill you, not I, dear Kalchas. He'll believe I am as ignorant of Iphigenia's sacrifice as he is. If Aegisthus' information was accurate, she could count upon the wind blowing at moon full. If not — well the men would continue to wait and Iphigenia would be gone. Agamemnon would indeed kill Kalchas but though the priest had proven useful, he was not by any means irreplaceable.

"Trust her," Clytemnestra said aloud.

Kalchas bowed his head in deference. "I am her tool."

Kalchas had not realized that being a tool of the goddess meant getting so dirty. In the three days since he joined the Greek camp, he had experienced nothing but the unexpected hardships of an army preparing for battle. The tent Clytemnestra provided him was luxurious, of course (as was fitting for a man of his station) but with so many men in one place, the earth had been trampled to a very affectionate dust. He wondered if he'd ever get his official robes — not to mention his matted hair — clean again.

Nor did he make much progress toward his goal. Agamemnon was indeed irreverent — that much was clear from the man's indifference to Kalchas' own arrival. Still, the priest had yet to find a single, specific incident of blasphemy with which to condemn the leader. The frustration was as maddening as the prospect of spending another day traipsing about the crowded camp site, seeking information. It was only the prospect of joining the Apollon temple that kept his feet moving.

Apollo. At last Kalchas would serve a male god. At last he would be revered as he ought to be — not scorned by the goddesses whose narrow-mindedness did not allow them to see past his gender and use him as the truly exceptional vehicle he knew himself to be.

At last, he'd have visions.

Kalchas was so consumed by his lustful thoughts that he nearly bumped into the warriors who would offer his deliverance.

"...and a fine hunter he is too. They say he brought down a white stag all by himself."

Kalchas stopped abruptly, turning to face the foot soldier with startling intensity. "What is it you said?"

The man stepped back form the fanatical light in the priest's eyes. "I was saying that my lord Agamemnon is a superb hunter," the soldier responded defensively. "Brought down a white stag all by himself."

"A white stag! A white stag, you say?"

The two warriors exchanged wary looks, each moving hand to sword for comfort.

"The white stag is sacred to the goddess Artemis," Kalchas exclaimed, oblivious to the unease of his audience. "The commander has angered the goddess!" His feet led him in a very unattractive prance. "I must confer with the gods," he announced, striving to compose himself and failing utterly.

The soldiers watched his retreating back. "Warriors and priests don't mix," one said at last.

Several days later, Agamemnon sat within his tent, brooding upon the same conclusion. He was mightily sick of this whole war — and suspected his feelings would only intensify when it actually began. Once, he would have craved the command that fate handed him. Now, he wanted only to leave the chaos that surrounded him and return to the order of his kingdom.

He was heartily tired of forestalling the impatience of the warriors about him, halting the inevitable minor skirmishes that broke out among them, managing the dearth of food stuffs, ignoring the increasing discomfort of camp life.

He was particularly fed up with hearing of the condemnation of the gods.

"You have angered the goddess by killing a stag under her protection," the priest Kalchas declared. Loudly. Men gathered to listen. "In retribution, you must marry your favorite daughter to the goddess' favored warlord Achilles."

The priest was a fungus.

"I will not," Agamemnon said to the air that surrounded him. Agamemnon cared less for the goddess' taste in warriors than her taste in priests. Achilles' madness made Menelaus look sane. What priest would demand he marry his beautiful child to such an animal?

"Danaus, attend me."

The man who waited outside his tent came instantly. Too old to fight, too loyal to be left behind, Danaus sought to achieve the impossible: He managed supplies, keeping the warriors fed, the fires kindled and bathing water available. The man's sore lack of success did not blind Agamemnon to his efforts.

"I need you to travel to the palace and deliver a message." Agamemnon saw surprise flick in his servant's eyes; the king also knew that such a task would be better on the shoulders of a younger guard.

"There is no one else I trust," Agamemnon said simply.

The man gave a slight nod, all that was needed to indicate his honor to be chosen for the task.

Honor. Was Agamemnon saving his own by ignoring the desperate attempt of a priest hungry for power or betraying it by ignoring the will of the gods?

How could he know?

"As you know, Kalchas claims words with the goddess Artemis. He says the goddess informed him that I killed a white boar that had been under her protection. Her vengeance is withholding the north wind, preventing our departure. How I could have killed anything under the protection of a goddess the man could not say," Agamemnon added and rose to pace his anger. "Kalchas further claims that only the marriage of Iphigenia will appease the angered lady."

Iphigenia. *The madman will never have my daughter*, Agamemnon swore.

"I will not sacrifice my daughter to that beast. If this decree of the goddess is other than folly, she can take out her rage upon me personally and leave my daughter alone. Go to the palace and tell my wife that the wedding is not to take place."

Danaus' eyes did not blink within his crinkled face. "I will go at once, my lord."

Honor. Agamemnon turned to a bowl of wine and proceeded to slowly drain the night in its contents.

The sound of his brother's voice was an unwanted interruption.

"You have no honor!" Menelaus raged, savoring the words, feeling bravado rise within him.

The comforting effects of the wine burned away. "What have you done with Danaus?" Agamemnon demanded.

"Do other men know what manner of commander they have chosen? Do they know they chose a man who would as soon commit them to doom as lead them to victory?" Menelaus addressed himself to the fire that roared in his brother's brazier, the flames that rose in kinship with his spirit, contained despite the desire to destroy.

"What have you done with Danaus?" Agamemnon repeated.

But Agamemnon's voice sang from a distant place, far on the horizon of the reality the gods granted Menelaus alone. Mere men could not bridge the distance to the place where Menelaus lived. The fire could, kindling his spirit, capturing the rage of his loneliness and the grandeur of his isolation.

I must contain myself despite my desire to destroy. "He has died the death worthy of a trader," Menelaus declared to the impostor who claimed brotherhood with him.

Agamemnon advanced upon him and smashed a fist against his face. "How do you dare murder a loyal man, a man of honor!" He lifted his fist again, wanting to deny what had happened by force.

I must contain myself, Menelaus' reminded himself. "A man loyal to a traitor is no man at all," he responded calmly, unafraid. "The gods have decreed that Iphigenia be sacrificed to Achilles. It will be so."

He turned and left the tent of the man called his brother, carrying the power of the fire within him. *Someday I will unleash the fire,* he promised himself.

Iphigenia was a statue upon which women heaped beautiful silk and ribbons and gold. The laughing banter that usually accompanied the readying of a bride-to-be died on her attendants' lips. Their princess had spoken three words since they began dressing her and those only when the queen demanded to know where she had spent the night past.

"In the grove."

The words washed an icy silence over the queen's rage.

"Beautiful enough for the gods," Rhytia exclaimed, willing gaiety into her solemn charge.

"Let us hope," Iphigenia responded with a sad smile. The women surrounded her and walked her down the palace stairs where the queen awaited them.

"Come," Clytemnestra ordered, leading them from the palace.

"This is unlike any wedding ceremony I've ever attended," an older waiting woman remarked.

At the far entrance, Aegisthus awaited them. Clytemnestra's breath caught at his splendor. Adorned in a long ceremonial robe of crimson, his long dark hair fanned about his shoulders. Aegisthus. A man who appreciated her womanhood, who matched it with his manhood.

"My lady." He addressed her with an elegant bow. Clytemnestra was pleased and relieved that he had spoken to her alone. She even allowed him the sparkle in his eyes as they rested upon the bride. Iphigenia would soon be beyond his grasp, beyond the grasp of any man.

The thought gave Clytemnestra a sensual shiver.

She boarded Aegisthus' chariot, relishing in the heat that grew between them as their bodies rocked in harmony with the vehicle's sway. All too soon, they arrived at her husband's camp.

"My lady," Agamemnon said, looking past Clytemnestra to the chariot that held Iphigenia. Something in his eyes hardened dangerously. "I will speak with you and my daughter, my queen."

Clytemnestra read the resistance in Agamemnon's posture and saw the nervous shuffle of Kalchas, who stood directly beside him.

"Of course," Clytemnestra said, sweetly. "Let's get the festivities underway and you will speak with us all you wish."

"I will speak to you before they begin," Agamemnon corrected.

Clytemnestra threw Kalchas an urgent look. "Would you deny the goddess her due now that she is so close to receiving it?" the priest screamed loudly.

"We have been here long enough!" a warrior from the surrounding crowd added.

"Agamemnon would bring the goddess' curse upon us all," another agreed.

Clytemnestra felt the knot of warriors close about them dangerously.

"Surely this can wait," she said.

"It cannot," Agamemnon insisted and Clytemnestra heard a chorus of swords being released from the belts that contained them.

This was not as I planned, she thought, casting Kalchas a second urgent glance. But the priest was too busy shaking in fear.

Clytemnestra licked her lips nervously. "My husband..."

"Wait." The beautiful voice cut through the crowd and Iphigenia stepped from her chariot, gliding to the center of the circle. Clytemnestra heard the men gasp at her beauty and felt overwhelming resentment at Iphigenia's power even as she realized that the girl had stayed the threat around them. "Father," Iphigenia said softly. "I know you've had no part in what is about to transpire." She laid a delicate hand upon his cheek, bringing moisture to the great warrior's eyes.

"I will not allow it," he croaked.

"You must," Iphigenia said simply. "They will kill you if you don't."

Acceptance and denial warred in Agamemnon's eyes.

"All will be well," Iphigenia said, looking to him intently before turning her attention to Kalchas. "I believe I am to go with you," she said calmly.

Kalchas fidgeted. "Ah, yes. That's right, my lady. You will come with me and I will ready you for the, ah, wedding."

"The wedding," Iphigenia repeated, smiling softly. "Yes, of course." She gave her father one last look and made her way to Kalchas.

"I do this in willingness for my father," she said to those around her, then turned, locking eyes with the woman who raised her. "Good bye Clytemnestra."

Clytemnestra stared into depthless gray orbs, seeing accusation, acceptance, knowing.

Knowing.

Iphigenia knew!

Clytemnestra swayed, breaking the deadly contact between herself and her sister's daughter. She did not feel Aegisthus' supporting arm, did not hear the awed murmurs that followed Iphigenia's progress to the camp's far end.

Iphigenia knew of the sacrifice.

"Clytemnestra, we must stop this," Agamemnon said, moving to her side.

Iphigenia knew Clytemnestra planned her death.

"Come to my tent. We must think of something." Agamemnon took hold of her arm and pulled her to his quarters, sitting her rigid body upon a chair. "We can't allow this. I can see how upset you are but we must think, take action, before it's too late."

It is already too late. Iphigenia knows and has cursed me for it.

"Here, have some wine. It will settle your wits."

Clytemnestra ignored the cup within her hands, focusing instead upon the faint, familiar scent of incense that wafted through the tent's walls.

It is done.

"Clytemnestra, listen to me," Agamemnon said, before the smell reached his senses as well. "What is that? Something is burning." Forgetting her altogether, Agamemnon ran from the tent.

Clytemnestra rose slowly, entranced, and followed.

Iphigenia knew.

A rush of men gathered at the camp's far end, standing about a great pyre, lit against the gentler light of the sun passing from the world. Behind her, Clytemnestra knew the full moon rose proudly, adding her light to the night.

A night of power. The incense of sacrifice.

Iphigenia knew.

Her feet took her forward. She did not hear Aegisthus call her name, did not feel him touch her as she stumbled, trying to steady her. She watched the useless priest lead a lone figure whose silk gown and garlanded hair streamed proudly behind her. She watched as the priest raised a glittering knife, illuminated by the light of night. She heard Agamemnon's bellow of outrage and pain.

Clytemnestra did not know when her own screaming began.

Her voice carried impossibly over the raging fire, chanting priests, an army of men, and echoed to the lone figure.

Iphigenia heard. The knife was raised and her eyes sought Clytemnestra's as she grew with the glamour of the goddess, grew beyond the grasp of the priest, who fell from his ladder, grew until an awed hush fell upon the magnitude of men who comprised the army.

Grew until the flames consumed her.

Clytemnestra did not hear the shouts that accompanied the vision, did not waste time listening to men speculate and then argue over what they had witnessed. She picked herself up and marched forward through crowds of men, through the heat of the dying fire.

"I will kill you myself!" Agamemnon raged, his anger giving him a sloppy hold upon Kalchas' neck. The priest's face turned an unattractive shade of green as the air was wrung from his body.

"You will not kill him!" a voice screamed as several very large men surrounded Kalchas, extricating the gasping priest from Agamemnon's hands. Achilles stepped forward.

"You!" Agamemnon accused. "You are responsible for this!" He threw himself at the warrior, only to be stopped by a swarm of men.

"The gods demanded this sacrifice for your blasphemy," Achilles shouted as Agamemnon struggled against the hands that held him. "The priest has deemed it so and he was right. Feel the wind about you."

Clytemnestra's dulled senses stirred as she felt the wind swirl about her.

Iphigenia.

"You will pay for this," Agamemnon snarled at the warrior

before him.

"It is you who were required to pay," Achilles retorted. "Our wait is now ended."

Clytemnestra regained a hold upon her slipping sanity. *It has worked,* she told herself, *my plan has succeeded.* She turned her back on the pyre and her husband.

This night, I claim my consort, she said to the moon before her.

CHAPTER FIVE

"**T**he waiting is driving me mad!" Helen exclaimed.

Aethra was not her first choice of confidants, for though the priestess had not spoken of Helen's decision to follow Alexander to Troy since their ill-fated talk in Sparta, she felt the priestess' lingering disapproval. Still, since their arrival, she had developed no ties to others. Hecuba kept close watch upon her throughout the day, ensuring her hands were busy with the endless sewing and weaving of the large household. The queen was determined that Helen lament her decision to visit this land; much of Hecuba's time, it appeared to Helen, was spent in search of an opportunity to chastise her guest with her sarcastic barbs. The few times Helen attempted to converse with Andromache resulted in Hecuba's sudden, pressing need for her daughter-by-marriage to run some errand or other. Helen quit her efforts to connect with the princess for fear Andromache would resent her offered friendship.

Helen would not admit that Alexander seemed to likewise resent her. She still saw him at the evening meals, attended by all of Priam's household. But more and more frequently he would attend the men's councils late into the night, arriving too tired or too irritated to speak to her. Only during increasingly rare occasions, when his eyes would meet hers across their separate meal tables, did she remember why she was in this strange and uncomfortable land at all. At those times, he would invariably enter their chambers much earlier than usual, taking her within his arms and renewing the connection between them.

"How simple it is for me to forget what is really important," he said one night, when the scent of their love wafted around them like a shield against the intrigues of the world.

"Perhaps we could leave this place," she said eagerly, "and

discover what is important outside the distractions of this court."

His jaw had assumed that stubborn tilt she had grown to abhor. "This court is my home. I will go nowhere until that is recognized."

"I recognize it," she said softly.

He had patted her arm absently. "Thank you, my love, but Hector does not. He would have me do as you suggest, leave permanently and never challenge his self-appointed place as my father's favorite. He has always been greedy for attention."

The remark startled Helen; until a few seasons ago, Alexander had never met Hector. How could he possibly know that Hector had "always been" anything? She forbore asking him, fearing that she knew the answer: his step brother Deiphobus, whom she disliked as much as she had upon first acquaintance, had told him so.

Alexander would not be nearly as stubborn about leaving if it were not for Deiphobus' influence. The man was the real enemy to her plans, she decided. But how could she break his hold over Alexander when it was he, not she, with whom her lover spent his days?

"I don't even know what I am waiting for any longer," she continued, realizing that Aethra eyed her intently.

"Perhaps it is She who is waiting for you," the priestess said gently, raising a delicate hand to stay Helen's protests. "Since we have entered this land, the moon has waxed to full on many occasions. Did you celebrate the rites? Nor have you continued your own practices. It is almost as if, instead of training Alexander to your ways, he is training you to his — whatever those may be."

"I have had no choice," Helen flared defensively. "You see how Hecuba keeps me busy day after day. She treats us like servants brought for her use!"

"You've behaved no differently than a servant, so why should she treat you otherwise?"

"And would you have me defy her openly — refuse to complete one of the endless cloaks or shifts she sets into my hands — and have her disparage me more than she already does?"

"It seems to me that the foreign queen's opinion of you is of even less importance than the royal household's opinion of Alexander," Aethra retorted.

Helen felt shame color her cheeks. Was she no better than Alexander, seeking meaningless approval? She did not even have Deiphobus' dubious influence upon which to blame her own behavior.

"I am not suggesting open defiance," Aethra continued. "But you always have choice. It would be wise to make more constructive use of that freedom than defying a queen who will probably never grant you acceptance."

"I suppose a more constructive course has suggested itself to you," Helen said sharply.

Aethra was unperturbed. "As a matter of fact, it has. Arrange a meeting with Cassandra."

"Hah! I should arrange a meeting with the girl who sees only doom from my presence? Better I would invite Hecuba to flog me for my misdeed in arriving here!"

"While I'm sure the queen would welcome that opportunity, it is not a course I would recommend," Aethra responded, her own anger becoming visible. "Cassandra has the ear of the Goddess and has no reason to love the male gods who have apparently cursed her for the honor. In connecting with her, we may continue the work begun in Sparta and I presume she knows of others who are sympathetic to her plight."

The suggestion was not without merit. Cassandra *was* in a position to help them continue their work. Maybe if they spread word of the Goddess throughout Troy, Alexander would be more apt to listen to Her words. And Cassandra might be no small ally in convincing Alexander — or Priam, if it came to that — that the prince's destiny lay elsewhere. And, anyway, it was better than focusing all of her attention upon Hecuba.

"What you say makes sense," Helen said, willing her tone to be conciliatory. "But I don't know if the queen will permit me to meet with the princess and I certainly do not think she will grant me the privacy to do so alone."

"True enough. But she will listen to Andromache, who has already agreed to speak with her sister-by-marriage and request a meeting. Andromache suggested we tell the queen that Cassandra requested the meeting to discuss herb lore and the rituals of other lands. Hecuba, as we have seen, cares for little outside the running of her household and her precious sons. It is unlikely she will wish to attend such a meeting."

The last was certainly true. Hecuba's days were consumed by the tasks of managing the palace. Besides needlework, she supervised the staff in arranging the evening meals and the servants in accommodating the royal guests who frequented Troy's ports. She received a daily report of the general activities in the kingdom, though her interest focused primarily upon the actions of her sons. In the moons Helen had been in Sparta, Hecuba had not ventured beyond the palace walls. Helen began to wonder if she ever did.

She controlled her anger at Aethra for speaking to Andromache before consulting her. At least the priestess was doing something. "Your plan is a good one. Let's see if such a meeting can be arranged."

Andromache scheduled one a few days later. She suggested they gather in the gardens after the noon meal.

"I know how much you priestesses like the outdoors." she said, much to Helen and Aethra's surprise. "My mother was queen and priestess." she explained. "I can't say I have much use for religion myself but I was certainly exposed to it."

"Thank you for your understanding and your assistance," Helen said, heartfelt.

Andromache shrugged. "I love my mother-by-marriage but even I realize how deadly prolonged contact with her lethal tongue can be."

Helen could only nod agreement to that and be grateful when, as they took their leave following the noon meal, Hecuba declined to join them. "Just make sure my daughter does not become too agitated," she ordered, her eyes holding fast to Helen's. Helen only nodded, not wanting to risk words that might prompt Hecuba's presence at their gathering.

"There was not much chance of that," Andromache said when Helen voiced her concern. The princess led them down one the palace's many stairways to the garden located below the women's quarters. "Cassandra is a bit of an embarrassment to the queen — she tends to avoid her daughter as best she may."

Helen remembered her own mother's distance and wondered if she and Cassandra's similar experiences might somehow forge a bond between them. Her hope dwindled as they exited the palace walls and entered the gardens. Extending beyond the doors was a path of smooth stones, which curved lazily about a riot of fruit trees, safflowers, roses and carefully tended sage grass. Helen heard the regular flow of water which indicated a fountain nearby. As Andromache led she and Aethra along the winding path, Helen inhaled deeply, feeling life flow back to her veins under the open sky.

Her enjoyment came to an abrupt halt as they rounded the dense trees and came upon Cassandra.

"I am told you wished to speak with me," the girl said, rising from the stone bench upon which she sat. Her blue priestess robe flowed about her lithe frame, catching in the slight breeze and making her seem more apparition than woman. Hair of the same dark black as Alexander's hung in a thick braid down her back and the features of Helen's lover, softened with feminine beauty, etched the plains of her face. Helen hoped that she never saw the barely contained hatred that shined from Cassandra's amber flecked eyes in the similar ones of her lover.

"Helen and Aethra are priestesses as you are," Andromache offered.

Cassandra's eyes never left Helen's. "I suppose you follow the goddess Aphrodite as my brother seems to," she said disdainfully.

"I do not recognize the Olympian gods created by the priests. I follow the voice of She who rules all," Helen responded. "As I understand you do," she added, deciding to take the offensive with this angry young woman.

"It seems Her guidance serves you as well as it does me," the girl said sharply.

"Perhaps neither of you listens very well," Aethra said sweetly.

Helen and Cassandra turned upon her in unison.

"I do listen to Her word. Aye, and I'm cursed with speaking it as well. It is others who will not hear," Cassandra said sharply.

"And I as well. It is another who turns deaf ears to my plea," Helen said, her own voice quite angry.

Aethra smiled innocently and Helen realized what she had done: by insulting them both she rallied them to a common defense upon which to build an alliance.

The strategy was clear to Cassandra and Andromache as well. "Well done," the latter cried, clapping her hands in mock applause.

"If you are as crafty a priestess as you just demonstrated, there may be much I can learn from you," Cassandra said begrudgingly.

"And we from you," Aethra replied sincerely. "But first. I would know how it is that you came to serve an Olympian god when Her voice is so strong within you."

"Would that I had another option," Cassandra murmured. "Let's move to the cluster of benches behind those trees where we can see the approach of any servants sent to tend the gardens. There's enough gossip twisted from my words — I don't intend to provoke more, if I can help it."

Cassandra turned and led them to the indicated spot, not meeting their eyes as she sat and began her story without preamble.

"My earliest memory is of visiting the temple with my mother to make a harvest offering. In those days, the queen was far more active in religious affairs than she is now. Maybe she feels she's sacrificed her daughter to Apollo and has no need to do more. Or maybe she simply prefers to avoid me altogether," she added.

"I can't see that the temple has served her in such a way as to warrant additional involvement," Andromache interjected. "First, they say a son of her womb must be exposed, then they condemn one of her daughters to the ridicule you have endured. Those actions would not garner my gratitude."

Cassandra's eyes softened as they looked upon Andromache. "Always you defend her, though I know you find her as irascible as anyone who spends time in her presence. She has lost much, but so has she gained — particularly in you as a loyal daughter."

Andromache shrugged off the complement. "I came to her more tomboy than maiden. At first she was appalled, but time — and our joint interest in Hector — have created a bond between us. I think I remind her of the sons she let go."

"How not? Your heart is as much of a warrior's as theirs. But for whatever reason, Hecuba has taken solace in your presence, even as she has scorned mine." Once again Cassandra's eyes moved beyond them to a place where her memories resided. "I remember how great the temple was, as I climbed the steps that were almost too big for my little legs to span. The quiet that echoed off the walls was so unlike the noise of the palace. I thought I wanted to stay there forever. I wandered about, led by curiosity, as my mother conducted her business with the priest. My steps led me to the altar where a statue in the likeness of Apollo stood. I gazed upon it, unmoved by the workmanship and about to move on to more interesting sights, when the image began to change."

Her lips shut over what she was clearly reluctant to speak. The three women who were her audience remained silent, wondering if she would continue. After several moments she did, her voice the barest of whispers.

"Before my eyes, the statue blurred as if it were made of cotton instead of stone. The harsh plains of Apollo's face softened into the likeness of a woman whom I could not see clearly, though I knew she was incredibly beautiful. I heard a voice but it was inside me rather than without. 'My truth is your own,' She said, 'Guard it well.'

"I turned to see if anyone else was within the room. Of course, no one was. When I turned back to the statue, it had returned to its true form once more. I continued to stare at it unblinking, willing the lady to return. I don't know how long I stood like that — long enough for my eyes to water — before my mother came to claim me, the priest trailing in her wake. I interupted whatever reprimand she was about to give me for my wandering, telling her excitedly what I had seen. Needless to say, she did not share my enthusiasm. Nor did the priest, who said that fanciful children should not be allowed to blaspheme the gods with lies.

"When I insisted that I was not lying, the priest said something about imprudence and my mother slapped my mouth, taking me home and sending me to my rooms without the evening meal.

"I smartly decided not to speak of my experience again, though I wondered about it endlessly and listened diligently for the voice to speak inside me once more. It was several seasons before She did," Her lips stretched in an ironic smile. "She told me that the beer my mother was harvesting would be spoiled. I, of course, reported this right away, believing everyone would be as excited as I about learning such useful information. I was wrong. My mother was skeptical and more than a trifle annoyed. Still, I must give her credit for making the appropriate inquiries. But when she learned the truth of what I said, she accussed me of going to the cellar and ruining it myself, which I of course had not. Things got worse from there. I would hear all manner of messages and report them and then be punished. I suppose I should have stopped saying what I knew but I felt as if the voice — Her voice — demanded I speak. Her command was far more important than any punishment I received. The servants and waiting women who had witnessed my behavior began whispering to themselves behind their hands. Eventually Hecuba became fed up both with my lies — as she deemed them — and her staff's gossip. She sent me to the temple of Apollo to enter his service."

"Why didn't she send you to the house of maidens?" Andromache asked. "That would seem much more appropriate." She felt Helen's and Aethra's questioning eyes upon her and forestalled Cassandra's response to explain. "The temple of maidens is a house where royal and noble daughters are fostered. They learn the rituals of the land, as well as the means to manage a household, while they await marriage. They don't follow a particular god or goddess and the education is more practical than religious. Cassandra's sister Polyxena is there. I would have thought Hecuba would have sent you there as well," she said, returning her attention to Cassandra.

"I think Hecuba would have liked to but feared I'd continue my uncanny behavior in front of the noble daughters. The last thing she wanted was to have the girls return to their families, and speak of the queen's peculiar offspring.

"I went to the Apollon temple readily enough, hoping to see

the figure I had encountered when I was younger and join with those who I assumed heard a similar voice.

"I quickly learned how wrong I was in my assumption. Though I learned many interesting things in the temple, I did not meet others who shared my experience. Oh, the head priest Chryses claimed to hear the voice of Apollo and attributed many of the temple's rituals to his word. As the rituals are rather simple rites, I wondered why the god would bother speaking of them. Still, as moons passed, I listened with the others and thought perhaps my mother was right and the voice I thought I heard was a fancy of my imagination. Throughout my priestess training I did not hear it. Only when I was about to be initiated did She speak once more, as if She knew what was to come and wanted to assure my obedience before I pledged myself to Apollo.

"Her words prompted me to speak out at a convocation for the spring sowing. Chryses was preparing to bless the fields and the other priests and priestesses were in attendance. As you can well imagine, most everyone in Troy was present at so important an event.

"As Chryses raised his hand to begin the sowing of the seed, the voice rang through me one more. 'Forgo this event for, on the morrow, the earth will shake all that has been laid.' I spoke what I heard aloud, my voice somehow carrying above the din of those gathered and cutting through Chryses' prayers.

"The people looked to each other uncertainly. Chryses was clearly angry. 'How is it you know this?' he demanded.

"'A voice has spoken to me,' I answered honestly. People moved away from me, some from respect for the god, some with fear.

"'I am the high priest of the god,' Chryses said. 'He speaks to me above all and I say no such prophecy will pass.' With that he dropped the first seed into the soil and beckoned the wary populace to do likewise. 'You shall never contradict me like that again,' he shouted at me when we returned to the temple. I was confined to my rooms for the remainder of that day and most of the next.

When nothing I had said came to pass, Chryses called me before him. 'As you can see, the earth lays still, accepting the seed we gave it. Now what have you to say of your voice?'

"'The words I spoke are true,' I said simply, for I knew it was so.

"'Well, make certain that the next time you are spoken to, you keep any messages to yourself. I will not have you publicly defy me.'

"I bowed my head and said nothing, knowing I could not do

as he asked even if I wanted to. This proved true later that evening. As I prepared for bed, I knew that the earth was no longer solid beneath my feet. Once more the voice rose within me and I ran from the temple proclaiming Her words. 'It has begun. The earth will quake!' I screamed, running through the streets. 'Quit your fires and leave your dwellings lest the very roofs that offer you shelter fall upon you.'

"Of course I caused all kinds of mayhem as people ran from their homes. Chryses rose from his bed and he stood at the top of the temple stairs, screaming for the people to ignore me. 'The god does not speak through her but to me and I say...'

"Whatever he would have said was left unspoken as a great rumbling shook the ground beneath us. People began screaming as stones crumbled about them, knocking them aside. Mercifully perhaps, I was knocked down by a brick and my consciousness taken from me. When I awoke, dawn was stealing across the sky and debris of the night's destruction was everywhere. I rose slowly and walked beyond the people to the fields, seeing, as I knew I would, the work of the sowing laid to waste.

"I don't know what I expected when I returned to the temple. Redemption perhaps that my words were proven so true. That is not what I received. Instead, Chryses called a general assembly at which he told everyone that my words of ill omen were false and only belief in them made them come to pass. I was astounded. How could he say my words had no power but then claim I had the power to make the very earth shake if I was convincing enough! He said the god Apollo told him this and said I was a challenge laid upon the people of Troy to hear only the words of truth uttered by the priest."

"Anyone with sense could see that he feared your power and wanted to secure his own," Aethra said disdainfully.

"I have not found many to have much sense when dealing with circumstances they don't understand," Cassandra said sadly. "But whether or not the priest chooses to believe me, nor anyone else for that matter, my words are true. Just as they were when I said Alexander's return and your presence will bring Troy's doom," she added, her face angry once more as she turned toward Helen.

"In coming here, I listened to the voice of my own heart," Helen responded carefully. "It has never been my intention to stay here — nor that Alexander should for that matter. I would like nothing better than to return with him to my homeland."

"They why haven't you done so?"

"Why, indeed?" Andromache asked. "I've wondered myself. Surely Hecuba's hospitality is not too pleasant to forego."

"Indeed it is not," Helen responded. "But Alexander does not realize that his destiny is at my side and until he does so, I am unable to depart."

"How do you suppose to make him see that? From what I've seen of my brother, he cannot see past his own pride," Cassandra remarked.

Helen ignored the dig that was more true than she wanted to admit. "That is what I am hoping you will help me to learn," she said boldly.

Cassandra eyed her carefully. "Well, in this our goals are the same, at least," she said at last. "What is it you'd have me do?"

What indeed?

"A plan of action has alluded us," Aethra interjected smoothly. "As I'm sure you've experienced, the voice of the Goddess is sometimes silent. Perhaps working together we can hear Her more clearly."

Cassandra nodded dubiously.

"I have just become superfluous," Andromache said, rising. "All this talk of gods makes me sleepy. I leave you to do what you need to and know you'll forgive me for not participating." With that, she turned and made her way back to the palace.

"How I envy her ignorance," Cassandra said with a small smile.

"Like all else," Aethra responded. "Her ignorance is a blessing and a curse. But there are more times than not when I look upon the likes of her and see only the blessing."

"Well, since we are cursed as we are, how do you propose we proceed?"

Knowing no more than either Helen or Cassandra, Aethra suggested they begin daily training sessions such as they had conducted in Sparta. "It cannot hurt and perhaps something more concrete will result from it."

Unlike in Sparta, they could not summon others to join them; doing so would arose the suspicions as well as the resistance of the queen.

Cassandra, however, agreed to speak with one of the women in the temple. "She's one of the few who believes me over the priest and she is terribly bored within the temple. I'm sure she'd welcome an opportunity to join us."

And so they planned to meet after the next day's noon meal. Hecuba, told once more that the meeting concerned herb lore and dye techniques, seemed accepting enough when Aethra informed her that they needed to meet for some days to impart the knowledge they held. The queen's only response, predictably, was to look upon Helen with obvious doubt that one such as she had any knowledge worth sharing.

Helen shrugged off Hecuba's torment with greater ease that usual. She looked forward to continuing the sessions begun in Sparta and did not care what Hecuba said as long as the queen did not prevent her from doing so. Andromache agreed to stay behind — clearly no hardship for one with as little interest in their work as she displayed — and agreed to make sure Hecuba did not decide to join them.

After a morning of weaving the coarser wool that would make cloaks for the upcoming winter, Helen forced herself to eat the food set before her, hiding impatience as the queen drew out the meal.

When she thought she could wait no more, Aethra rose. "My queen, I am sure you will forgive us for departing. Your daughter Cassandra awaits and I know not how long she has before she must return to the temple."

Begrudgingly, Hecuba nodded her dismissal. Helen saw Andromache bury a smile beneath her hand.

"I thought that meal would last forever," Helen growled as she and Aethra made their way down the stairway Andromache showed them the previous day.

"She is a stubborn thing, isn't she? But at least she's not unreasonable. She could just as easily have changed her mind about allowing us to depart."

"I suppose," Helen responded, unable to muster gratitude for anything the queen did.

"Come on," Aethra said, excitement growing from her. "We have more important tasks at hand."

They entered the gardens and followed the winding path to the cluster of benches they had previously occupied. Cassandra awaited them, the girl she mentioned seated at her side.

"This is Nomia," Cassandra said with her characteristic abruptness.

The young woman who nodded in their direction could not be more than fifteen winters. The eyes that looked upon them were of light blue, set within a round, remarkably pale face. Even her blonde hair was more white than yellow. It was as if some force had drained the color from her body.

"I am the priestess Aethra, Queen of Troezen. This is priestess Helen, queen of Sparta."

The girl cast a wary glance at Cassandra, who nodded her reassurance.

"It is a pleasure to meet you," she said at last, then stared fixedly at the hands wringing in her lap.

Aethra raised a dubious brow, which Helen's thoughts echoed. The girl obviously adored Cassandra and would follow her in all things. Still, one needed to stand upon one's own strength when facing the Goddess, in which case Nomia seemed a poor choice indeed for joining them. Helen felt Cassandra watching her closely and knew she could say nothing of her concerns without alienating the strange princess.

"Shall we begin?" she asked instead.

Nomia looked up anxiously, seeking Cassandra's assurance once more. Cassandra looked to Helen, nodding.

As senior priestess — and the one least likely to trigger Cassandra's hostility — Aethra led them in an opening ritual to purify their minds and prepare for the word of the Goddess.

"Great Mother, we call upon you to show us the way to realize the destiny Your hand has set upon us. Be here now. Guide us so we may make Your truth known."

So said, she led them into the trance state where they might more readily hear Her voice. Helen felt her breathing slow and her body take on the familiar lightness that accompanied such states. The feeling of longed for connection stole over her and she felt tears warm her cheeks. Time without measure passed as she stayed within that place of comfort until her cramping body demanded her return. She opened her eyes to see those around her doing likewise, an unspoken command calling each back to normal awareness.

"I have not felt such peace since I looked upon the vision of the woman who obscured Apollo's statue so many years ago," Cassandra whispered, her face softened by a smile of contentment and a glow that enveloped each of them.

Even Nomia smiled openly, seeming more solid than she had when Helen had first looked upon her.

"I did not hear any specific message," Aethra said, recalling their purpose, "and I presume none of you have either." The three women shook their heads in agreement. "Still, She is upon us. We should continue to meet and see what unfolds."

Each agreed once more, Nomia nodding with a vigor that brought welcome smiles to the faces of the others.

"Until tomorrow then."

Aethra and Helen made their way to the palace, while Nomia and Cassandra returned to the temple.

Over the next days, they became comfortable in their familiar routine. After noon, they would meet and induce the trance that drew them closer to the Goddess and to each other, although a hoped for vision was not forthcoming.

It wasn't until the moon waxed near full that a subtle shift occurred.

"I feel we have reason for haste," Nomia said, articulately a vague feeling each of them experienced.

"Yes," Cassandra agreed, "though I don't know what we need to hasten to."

"We have asked the Goddess to guide us," Aethra said slowly. "It may be that She calls upon us to use our wits to discover the first step in our plan."

"Lovely," Cassandra complained. "Always Her voice comes upon me when I wish it would not. Now I seek Her actively and She leaves me to my own resources."

"She would not do so if She did not think those sufficient," Aethra admonished.

"Let's start with what we know," Helen said quickly before the volatile Cassandra could respond. "You, Cassandra, have foreseen that Alexander and my presence is the doom of Troy. I have seen Alexander as consort to me, presumably in Sparta. It seems clear that our goal is to get both Alexander and I to return there."

"Agreed," Cassandra said. "So why is it that you have not gone?"

Helen was pleased that the angry tone with which Cassandra had once asked this had mellowed to honest inquiry. "Alexander will not leave until he is accepted by his family," she responded.

"I doubt that," Nomia said with surprising boldness. "If all he wished for was his family's acceptance, he should be well content. Hecuba and Priam have already formally acknowledged him."

"As their son, yes. But not as a worthy member of their family. I think he seeks Hector's respect."

"Just as soon await the sun to set in the Black sea," Cassandra grumbled.

"So it would seem," Helen agreed. "My attempts to persuade Alexander that his worth is not contingent upon the thoughts of his brother have been completely unsuccessful. I think that Deiphobus is to blame," she said quickly. "Alexander was far more reasonable before he was swayed by his half-brother's influence."

"Deiphobus is a fool and known as such by all the court. It is Paris' own fault if he is swayed by such a one."

Helen bit her lip and would not meet Cassandra's eyes. She wanted — needed — to hold Deiphobus responsible for Alexander's behavior. She could not believe her chosen lover was acting from his pride alone. *Cassandra does not hear Alexander's words each night or she would realize the threat Deiphobus poses,* she told herself firmly.

"Whether the result of Deiphobus' prompting or some inner flaw of his own, it is clear that Alexander will not leave until his family — namely Hector — publicly acknowledges his worth," Aethra summarized practically. "I think our attention should focus upon how to get Hector to do so."

"That will be a challenge," Cassandra said. "Hector believes only in the power of force and Paris is clearly untried in battle — I'd prefer we did not give my twin the chance to prove his strength by engaging Troy in a war with Sparta."

"And yet Alexander — Paris, as he's called here — must face the battle of arms Hector requires." Aethra said, continuing when she saw Cassandra's and Nomia's puzzled looks. "In order to win the right of consort, Alexander must challenge Menelaus in a dual to the death, while swearing to set his own life aside for the good of the land. This ancient rite has not been exercised for many a season — and certainly not since the coming of the Olympians. Yet it is in my mind that the Goddess demands such a demonstration of honor in Her name to raise the power necessary to diminish that of the man-made gods. I believe this is why she set Alexander in Helen's path."

While the others nodded, Helen sat in startled silence. She had thought Aethra disapproved of her decision to claim Alexander as consort — had even doubted her own motives for chosing her lover as time had passed. But the priestess' words made sense and gave her much needed confidence. The destiny that influenced her choices rang strong within her once more.

Which did not, of course, provide any further enlightenment as to how to make it come to pass.

"Does Paris know he is to challenge Menelaus?" Cassandra asked.

Helen shook her head. "I felt it necessary to train him to Her ways first so he would truly understand what was before him."

"A luxury best saved for when you're on a boat returning to Sparta," Cassandra said dryly.

"That may be, but I'm still left with the challenge of getting him aboard a departing ship at all," Helen retorted.

"*We're* left with that challenge," Nomia interjected with a pointed look at both Helen and Cassandra.

Aethra smiled warmly in Nomia's direction. "It seems to me that we need attack this problem on several fronts. If Hector's information proves accurate and troops are amassing to descend upon Troy, Alexander must be convinced that his worth is best proved in challenging Menelaus to single combat. We must also convince Hector to believe the same. And finally, we must convince Agamemnon and Sparta's other allies — as well as Troy — not to retaliate whatever the outcome of the challenge."

"The first is my responsibility," Helen said, not wanting to focus on the outcome of a challenge between Menelaus and Alexander. How could Alexander not win after all their planning? "Convincing him will be that much easier if Hector voices his approval of such a challenge, preferably publicly. I still worry about what Deiphobus might do to interfere..."

"Deiphobus has never been able to undermine Hector. Even if Paris is malleable to my half-brother's ways, Hector is not. With Hector in agreement, I don't think Deiphobus will be much of a concern," Cassandra said.

"Our biggest issue will be keeping the other kingdoms from retaliating," Aethra added before Helen could protest further.

"I think we can ensure that Troy will not," Nomia said unexpectedly.

Cassandra studied her. "Chryseis?" she asked.

Nomia nodded.

"Chryseis is, obviously, Chryses' daughter," Cassandra explained. "Although Chryses scorns my words publicly, he apparently takes heed of my beliefs privately. Of course he would not deign to ask me what I may know himself. Instead he has his daughter speak to Nomia, whom he knows to be my confidant."

"In the past, I've been very careful to avoid her all too obvious manipulations," Nomia said, distaste evident on her tongue. "But perhaps now I could carefully report Cassandra's 'knowing' that all of Troy will be doomed if this war is to come upon us."

"No doubt Chryses will claim such knowledge came to him from Apollo. But it will at least get him to spread the message we seek to be spread. I don't think Priam wants war anymore than we do. A command from the gods will give him the excuse he needs to refrain from entering one."

Aethra nodded. "That leaves us with Sparta's allies — namely Agamemnon. If he will agree to maintain peace, I am sure the other cities will do likewise."

Once more, the face of Clytemnestra came unbidden to Helen's mind.

"I believe that Agamemnon will avoid war," she said carefully. "But I don't trust Clytemnestra will if she decides her interests will be best served by conflict."

Aethra looked at the declining sun. "I believe Agamemnon is a reasonable man, as well. If anyone can forestall your sister, I think he can. Besides, if Troy agrees to remain neutral in the challenge, it provides Agamemnon with a reason to do likewise. I think we must focus upon what we can do right now and deal with any obstructions as they arise — one of which could be Hecuba if we don't get back shortly."

They all agreed. "Tonight, then, Helen will begin speaking to Paris. I will talk to Andromache and recruit her to work on Hector and Cassandra and Nomia will arrange for Chryses to have the information he needs to support our cause."

"I'll take Nomia back to the temple and then return for the evening meal," Cassandra said. "That way Nomia can tell Chryseis that I have heard the king's reluctance to war. Chryses will be further inclined to support our goals if he thinks he can win royal favor."

Aethra nodded. "Until tonight then. Her blessing be upon our efforts."

CHAPTER SIX

The women had cause to wonder if the Goddess forsook them utterly when a messenger arrived shortly after the evening meal began.

"King Priam, lord of Troy, the lords Odysseus and Menelaus wish conference with you."

Helen's heart skipped several beats. She looked to Aethra, whose tense features brought no comfort. Nor did Cassandra's angry shake of head.

Priam looked decidedly uncomfortable as well. "Tell the gentleman that I will gladly offer them a taste of Troy's famed hospitality the next time they grace our land's ports."

The herald cleared his throat uncomfortably. "They are here now, sire."

Priam's hands grabbed dangerously at his table. "How is it these men arrived without our notice?"

"They entered quietly, my lord, with a ship devoid of identifying colors. Our men assumed they were a small trading vessel."

"Have them shown in," Priam said. "And tell the man on watch that he best be sure I receive no other surprises."

The herald nodded and opened the door to admit the waiting guests.

Priam rose as they entered the room. Menelaus' eyes darted widely around the crowded hall, passing over Helen in his frantic search for her.

He is worse, she thought, feeling nothing but pity for the man who fathered her children. He started toward the women's tables, restrained by Odysseus' gripping hand upon his arm.

"My dear king Priam, it is an honor to see you again,"

Odysseus bellowed in a voice that resonated throughout the hall.

"I can hope that I have reason to be equally pleased to see you again, old friend," Priam responded, his features cautious. "For now, I bid you and your fellow traveler peace and welcome and invite you to join us."

Menelaus opened his mouth to protest.

"We will gladly partake of your sacred hospitality," Odysseus responded before Menelaus could draw breath. He pushed the protesting man to the table indicated by the king.

Odysseus moved to the women's tables.

"Queen Hecuba, if my good friend had not married you already, I would have taken no other as my wife. You grow more beautiful with each passing moment." He bent graciously over the queen's hand.

"And you more outrageous than ever," she responded, with a pleased chuckle. "If you had married me, you would not have been safe to pursue all manner of female form as you currently do."

Odysseus' eyes widened and he threw back his head in a hearty laugh.

"I fear you are right, my dear woman. Though your king here isn't much better," he winked in Priam's direction and the king blushed. "The rumors beyond the seas number your prodigy in the hundreds."

Odysseus turned his attention to those nearest the king.

"Hector, you grow more regal with each year. Nothing like a good woman to make a man," he added, winking at Andromache. His curious gaze fell next upon Alexander, who returned his stare defiantly. "Why, you are indeed as pretty as your sister," Odysseus said and Helen saw Alexander flush several shades of angry red. Odysseus gave him no time to respond. "Cassandra," he said, gently. "My heart grows ever more sorrowful each time I think that the god has claimed you before I could."

"With the number of women to whom you say so, it is no wonder you haven't died of a broken heart long since," Cassandra answered, admirably hiding the tension she surely felt at Odysseus' presence.

"And queen Helen," he said, moving to where she sat, "it is a pleasure to see again the woman who helped me secure the only wife on this gods-created earth who will put up with me."

Menelaus, seeing Helen for the first time, started from his place. Once more, he was prevented from approaching by Odysseus' deft interference.

Helen attempted to smile warmly at Odysseus, certain the strain showed on her aching features. "And how does Penelope?"

"Alive and well and with her hands full between our son and a pirate that cannot stay home for more than a single moon."

"Nor remain silent for more than a moment," Hecuba interrupted, not at all pleased that Helen was shown such courtesy. "Do sit down Odysseus, before we all die of hunger."

"It is my fate always to be ordered about by women," he responded, raising eyes dramatically toward the ceiling and assuming his seat. "But I shall not argue with a home-cooked meal. There was a great shortage of good food on the journey from Aulis."

Once again Menelaus looked as if to speak.

"The reason for our journey will be discussed after we partake of our host's gracious hospitality." Odysseus raised his goblet in Priam's direction and gave Menelaus a silencing glance. The other man scowled and began to pick at the food placed before him.

Odysseus went on to regale them with comical tales of his journey as if his was no more than a social visit. Even Priam put aside his caution, laughing heartily at Odysseus' outrageous stories until the meal was completed and the servants poured additional wine for the hall's guests.

"So now we may speak of the true purpose of our little visit," Menelaus said, rising aggressively.

"Though some would say the fine food and finer company of the house of Priam is reason enough," Odysseus added.

Menelaus ignored him. "King Priam of Troy. I demand that you return to me my wife, whom your thieving son kidnapped when under my hospitality."

Priam regarded him squarely. "Kidnapped? I had not been aware that your wife had been kidnapped."

"Do not mince words with me!" Menelaus screamed. "Your scion son stole her against her will and mine. I demand her return."

Priam assumed the relaxed posture of an experienced leader. "Again, you apprise me of a situation about which I had no knowledge. It is my understanding that the woman you claim to be your wife came here of her own free will. If I am indeed mistaken, do forgive me. Queen Helen, perhaps you can clear up this misunderstanding. Do you wish to return to your husband?"

Helen wished she was elsewhere. She shook her head and stared at her hands, avoiding the many eyes she knew were upon her.

"You see," Priam concluded, "Queen Helen is here of her own free will."

"She is not!" Menelaus shouted "That son of your has beaten her into submission."

Alexander rose, "I have no need to beat any woman, Menelaus. I am sorry that we left without taking proper leave of you. But you were gone and we did as the goddess prompted us."

Helen felt her lips twist in an ironic smile. If only Alexander recognized which Goddess had done the prompting; if he had, this unfortunate meeting would not be occurring.

"I care not for your apologies nor your goddess. Return my wife to me at once or I shall burn us all," he ran to the wall and grabbed a torch from its holder, staring fixedly at the flames. *The fire. The fire will cleanse all, will provide redemption. I will burn them all, scorching their remains. The fire will free me.*

Not yet, not yet, whispered the voice that sometimes spoke in his brain. He listened like an obedient child.

Priam gave a signal and four guards quickly unarmed the surprisingly unresisting man. "You have heard from your wife's own lips that she has no wish to return to you. Leave here at once and do not presume upon my hospitality again."

Strength returned to Menelaus' spine. "Oh, I will presume on your hospitality again," he sneered. "My brother's army lays in wait beyond the cove. We will claim my wife and all that you call yours, Priam!"

"How nice it must be to have a man to fight your battles for you," Priam retorted disdainfully.

Menelaus face contorted in wrath and he fled from the room.

"See that he is escorted back to his ship and does not wreak havoc on my city," Priam ordered to his guards. He turned his attention to Odysseus, who spread his hands helplessly.

"I had hoped that seeing his wife — my pardon — ex-wife, contented with another man would have sparked his pride and we could prevent war," Odysseus explained. "I should have known that madmen do not respond as the rest of us."

"I still don't understand how you became involved with him at all," Priam snapped, "And I certainly do not understand how it is that you traveled with the Achaians," he added, using the insulting term the Trojans had to identify all the Greeks upon the mainland.

Odysseus ignored the bite.

"I had no choice. Ah, I see you are skeptical. But what would you do if the choice was between warring against a friend — no matter how deeply you honor the relationship — and killing your own first born son?"

"You speak in riddles," Priam responded, annoyed.

"As the fair Helen can attest, I and all the men present at her betrothal vowed to protect the right of Menelaus to her hand and her kingdom."

Cassandra started and turned to Helen sharply. Helen looked down once more. *The oath! How could I have forgotten the oath?*

"This agreement," continued Odysseus, "which I am now sorry to say was my own suggestion, was meant to avert war. But the gods will have their will and it seems war was pre-ordained; this same agreement renders men honor-bound to fight any man who laid claim to Helen over the right of her then chosen husband — which means we're honor bound to fight Troy." He fingered his mustache thoughtfully. "It seems this war is indeed fated. This was my second attempt to avoid it. When Agamemnon called we oath-bound men, I had my dear wife send word to the house of Mycenae that I had lost my wits. I presumed Agamemnon would have more than enough madmen under his command and not wish to serve with another," he explained.

"Menelaus would indeed seem more than enough," Hecuba interjected.

"Alas, my queen, I underestimated the king of Mycenae. He came to my peaceful home to see for himself the truth of my wife's tale. I, of course, made a great show of madness, harnessing oxen to plow and proceeding to sow in an area clearly ready for harvest. A fine mess I made too, although, it was no doubt a great show."

Priam was not amused.

"But our good lord Agamemnon has too much experience in madness. He tested me by grabbing hold of my first born son and throwing him before the oxen. Scared ten years off the toddler's life, and as many off my own. I had a choice: run down my child or give up my farce and swerve away. You can imagine which I chose."

"I understand, my friend," Priam said at last. "It would seem the men of Mycenae are all mad."

"Oh, Agamemnon is far from mad — for which you will be grateful in the days ahead. Crafty, yes, and determined. But truth be told, I suspect he has no more mind to warring than I. It is he who suggested that I meet with you and Menelaus to see if some agreement could be made."

"Are you saying there is still an opportunity for peace?"

"Alas, no. It seems clear that the gods are demanding blood and we mere mortals, having done all to avert bloodshed, must now bow to their will."

Helen looked up then, meeting Aethra's eyes, then Cassandra's, heartened by the determination she saw in each. *The gods may desire war but the Goddess does not. It is Her will that will prevail.*

Helen's confidence in their ability to realize the will of the Goddess waned remarkably as the moon waxed toward full.

"This situation is impossible!" Cassandra raved, pacing back and forth, throwing tufts of grass with her sandaled feet.

Helen envied Cassandra's energy; her own had been depleted many days before.

"At least you convinced Hecuba that it was necessary for us to continue our meetings," Aethra said, trying to soothe the irritated princess.

There is that, Helen thought. Nearly a moon had passed since the arrival of the Greeks to Troy's shores and the women had last met within the sanctuary of the gardens. Helen's every waking moment had been spent stitching cloaks for the Trojan army, bolstering the palace stores against possible siege and making sure the soldiers who filled the palace were adequately housed and fed. Hecuba would not hear of them continuing their lessons in 'herb lore' during such a crisis. Indeed, it seemed to Helen that the queen wanted to occupy Helen's spare moments with this task or that; Hecuba saw Helen as the sole cause of the threat that surrounded them and she did not hesitate to work her like the lowest slave in reparation.

"I did accomplish that much," Cassandra said, mollified. "And it was worth seeing Hecuba so disconcerted," she added.

Helen agreed with her. She and Aethra could think of no way to resume their meetings and even the clever Andromache had been at a loss of suggestions.

Apparently, Cassandra had become as fed up with their lack of communication as Helen and Aethra were and stormed into the women's quarters, demanding that she be allowed to resume her afternoon sessions once more.

"My dear child," Hecuba admonished in the condescending tone reserved for speech with her daughter. "Do you not realize that we prepare for war?"

"Do you not remember that I was the one to warn of such in

the first place?" Cassandra retorted with white heat. "Who better than I knows the dangers we now face? We need the help of powers beyond us and these two — whatever else they might be — are priestesses. Would you deny them joining me to do what is necessary to stop this war?"

"Whatever else they might be includes being the cause of the danger that awaits us," Hecuba snapped, her cold eyes turning to Helen. "How do I know that you have not engaged my poor simpleton daughter to plot further treachery?" she demanded.

"The treachery to which you refer," Cassandra answered, drawing her mother's attention once more, "was brought upon us by your own son, about whom you did not heed warning. And I assure you that my wits are in better working order than yours if you believe that the power of an army alone will halt the danger we face!"

"Child, I think you are too excited."

"Indeed, you will learn how excited I can be when I scream to the populace that their queen scorns the assistance of the gods."

Hecuba blanched and Helen knew Cassandra's threat found its target. Hecuba might not concern herself with the gods but she was quite aware of public opinion.

"Alright then, go," the queen said with ill-natured defeat. "But if I learn that this is one of your tricks," she added to Helen. "I'll hang you from the battlements myself."

Helen remained wisely silent, folding the work beneath her hands and hastily following Aethra and Cassandra from the room.

"Having gained this much, we must use our time wisely," Aethra said, bringing them to the issue at hand. "From what I can see, the arrival of the Greek forces does nothing to alter our basic plan. In fact, with the presence Agamemnon and anyone else who might seek retaliation upon Alexander's challenge of Menelaus, we are in a better position to ensure that there will be no reprisals."

"*If* Paris challenges Menelaus." Cassandra responded. "Did you see Hector's eyes alight when Priam named him battle commander? I don't think he will readily give up the chance for the glory that he now thinks awaits him."

"There are other influences that may stay Hector's hand. Know you of the prophecy read at his birth? As I understand it from Andromache, it is said that his death will come at the hands of one who now sits in the Greek camp."

"Achilles," Cassandra said, nodding. "Immediately after his birth, Hector was brought to the temple. A priestess — the same one who stated that Paris would be Troy's downfall — stated that Achilles would be the hand of his death, should the two meet in battle."

"It would seem the woman is graced with the power of the oracle," Aethra said with professional interest. "Is there anyway we can petition her to join us?"

Cassandra shook her head, "She fled the temple shortly after Chryses was appointed high priest. I would imagine that he appreciated her gifts no more than he does my own but, as she was not the daughter of his king, he could rid himself of her more easily."

"The man is consistent in his dislikes."

"Agreed. But he is proving somewhat useful. As we planned, Nomia has been telling his daughter of her fears that Troy will indeed perish should we engage in battle. I overheard Chryses tell some nobles that the people needed to increase their offerings for Apollo's protection to avert the threat which will surely mean our ruin."

"So he'll profit from taking up our cause. Despicable but I suppose it will ensure his continued cooperation."

"And now that you've reminded me, I'll have Nomia tell Chryseis of the warning for Hector, stating of course that I thought Chryses issued it himself. If we're lucky, he'll take the credit and even petition an audience with the king to reiterate the danger to his heir, should war break out."

"Good. Andromache has also agreed to remind Hector," Aethra added, her face lighting with unexpected mischief. "She's as much of a warrior as her chosen husband but enough of a woman to dread losing the father of her child."

Cassandra nodded and turned her attention to Helen. "You've been awful quiet. Have you had an opportunity to speak with Paris?"

"I have seen him but a handful of times since the Greeks have landed," she said carefully. "He has taken to sleeping in the men's quarters after the evening council," she added reluctantly.

"I'm sure they all have," Cassandra said, surprising Helen with a comforting pat upon her hand. "Yours is perhaps the greatest task of all. You must connive for him to return to your bed so you can convince him of his need to challenge Menelaus singularly."

"I did mention this to him," Helen said carefully, embarrassed by Cassandra's concern. "He did not seem overly eager. He was far too concerned with his place in Hector's army. I suspect that he will come to agree to fight Menelaus alone if Hector urges him to do so."

"Then we'll have to make sure Hector does. In the mean time, do what you can to get Alexander alone."

Helen nodded, relieved that they moved on to speaking of other things. She did not want to tell them what Alexander *had* said during one of their few nights together. She feared her own disappointment would show too greatly.

"Do you realize that if Hector should die in this war, I will be heir to the kingdom," Alexander had snapped when she asked him to challenge Menelaus.

His words appalled her. "You speak treason."

"I speak common sense," he retorted. "Don't you know that Hector plans for my death to conveniently occur in the skirmish."

"Alexander, how could you possibly believe such a thing? Who put these crazy thoughts into your head?"

His flush of embarrassment was answer enough. "I know what I know," he said stubbornly.

She wanted to scream at him then, to accuse him of killing the man she had fallen in love with and replacing him with this prideful, ignorant puppet. For the first time since her arrival to Troy, she wanted to claim her son and depart. Only her growing suspicion that another child grew within her kept her from doing so. She was not ready to share any of this with the two women beside her, who would surely despise her for not having the courage to leave when doing so would clearly stem the danger they now faced.

Things will be different once Alexander challenges Menelaus, she told herself stubbornly. *Then Alexander will become the consort I've chosen once more.*

"Helen, have you gone into a trance?" Aethra asked, mercifully interrupting her thoughts. "We must return to the palace."

"I'll join you again this time tomorrow," Cassandra said, rising and smoothing the folds of her simple cloak. "I can't bring Nomia again. With the threat of the Greeks beyond our walls, most people are sticking close to home. Her presence beside me will only cause suspicion and maybe even alert Chryses to the fact that we're up to something."

"That's probably best," Aethra agreed.

The women took leave of each other.

"Will you tell me what ails you?" Aethra asked Helen as two walked back to the palace.

"I just want us to succeed," Helen answered evasively, not wanting to share her doubts nor news of her pregnancy just yet.

But the fates forced her to do the latter far sooner than she would have liked.

"Does my son know that you carry his child?" Hecuba asked her later that afternoon.

Helen cursed herself for showing her surprise and was careful to avoid Aethra's eyes. "It is too soon to know for sure," she said steadily.

"Blah, I know a breeding woman when I see her," Hecuba grumbled.

"A child!" Andromache exclaimed, "What an unfortunate time to bring new life into the world."

"We must make an offering to the gods that the lady delivers a strong boy for Troy," declared one of Hecuba's vapid lady companions. Helen thought her name was Briseis.

Hecuba threw the woman a searing look.

Briseis remained completely oblivious to her queen's displeasure. "We should make a visit to the temple of Apollo so he will bless your son with strength and courage," she continued to Helen. "Today would be none too soon."

"Helen cannot go out of doors," Hecuba replied, not bothering to contain her annoyance. "No doubt her very presence would send that mad husband of hers into a frenzy of attack that would make us the worse for it."

Helen refrained from reminding Hecuba that it was her son — not Menelaus — to whom she was now married.

"Well, we'll go for her then," Briseis persisted.

The queen took a calming breath. "Take some others with you, and sacrifice to Apollo in her name if you're so insistent on going." She met Helen's eyes briefly and resumed her weaving.

CHAPTER SEVEN

Boredom among men is a dangerous thing. Agamemnon surveyed his army, huge beyond his ever imagining, and cursed the day his parents conceived their second child. He recognized the strong step of Odysseus behind him.

"They want action," Agamemnon declared.

"The desire for action is what got us into this mess in the first place," Odysseus observed.

Agamemnon turned and studied his companion, the last man he thought he would ever trust, one of a handful he actually did.

Either war brought out the best in people or it had scrambled his brains.

"You're right, of course," Odysseus remarked as casually as if they were discussing a petty point of governance. "Enough action to raise morale."

"And not enough to expose our rather sizable weaknesses," Agamemnon finished.

Odysseus laughed and Agamemnon wondered — not for the first time — if anything ever bothered this man.

"You know, I never thought you and I would..."

"Nor did I," Odysseus answered.

Their camaraderie was interupted by the bellowing war cries the echoed further along the camp.

"It would seem the men have taken matters into their own hands," Odysseus remarked mildly.

Agamemnon felt the muscles in his jaw tighten and he moved toward the melee. The sound of victory muffled the cries of the wounded as he approached, soldiers parting before his increasingly angry steps. Agamemnon did not acknowledge those he passed as he continued his march forward, beyond the Achaian camp that had grown outside the Trojan walls, beyond the piti- ful gardens in which inept warriors tried to farm much-needed crops from the land, until he reached the outskirts of Trojan territory once more.

The site before him was not as well fortified as the rest of Troy. It enclosed only the sparse wood huts of the occasional Trojan farmer whose crops yielded only that necessary to sup- port his wife and children.

Agamemnon's mouth curled in distaste. Only a barbarian would attack such a place. With a rough hand, he grabbed hold of the first outfitted warrior he found, distaste giving way to anger as he realized he held the arm of a Myrmidon. "What has happened here?" he demanded, his voice silencing those who had been lost to celebration.

The man he held pulled aggressively in an effort to lose Agamemnon's grip and scowled dangerously when he could not do so.

Achilles appeared from the throng, stepping forward to an- swer Agamemnon's inquiry. "We have begun the war we have set out to have," he sneered.

His Myrmidon allies hit spears to shields in approval.

Agamemnon shoved the man within his grip aside and closed the gap between himself and the warrior he hated.

I should kill you now, he thought, feeling loathing fire through his spine. Achilles met Agamemnon's smoldering eyes and squared his large form in challenge.

"Murderer!" Agamemnon hissed the accusation without thinking, knowing that he reviewed again the horror of seeing the young woman he called daughter burn upon a pyre. A ratio- nal voice within told him that Achilles alone was not respon- sible for Iphigeneia's death. He paid it no heed. Pain too great to endure was shielded by anger in need of a target. The mad bar- barian who stood before him was a perfect outlet for his rage.

"I am a warrior," Achilles growled.

"You are that and no more!" Agamemnon roared. "You do not command these forces. I do. And I say we do not war on those too helpless to defend themselves!"

"I'd say you do not wish to war at all," Achilles screamed in return, with surprising perceptiveness.

Predictably, his Myrmidon allies murmured their assent. Agamemnon ignored them, wishing he could do the same with the similar sentiments voiced by those who followed from his own camp.

I should quit this madness now and let Achilles take charge — he's better suited for it.

"You'd rather make us into farmers while the fields here remain open for our taking," Achilles continued.

And if the madman was in charge, everyone present would suffer more than they can imagine, while additional innocent people would be slain. I cannot — I will not allow that to happen.

Pride did for Agamemnon what passion could not. "How many baskets did you take before the Trojans beat you back — ten, twenty even. That will not even feed your own troops for a single day. Would you deprive innocents the right to feed their families for an entire season to fill your belly for a single night?"

"They are the enemy," Achilles responded implacably. "And we took more than food." The warrior reached back into the crowd and shoved two women forward. "These can help with the sewing and the harvesting," he declared.

The younger of the two was dressed in a fine cloth of blue linen that fell to her sandaled feet. Her blonde hair flew unbound about her face. She regained her balance and thrust a quivering chin defiantly forward. Her older companion, more elaborately dressed, fell to her knees wailing.

"And you think these two will care for the whole Greek army?" Agamemnon shouted, his fury renewed.

"There are more where they came from," Achilles responded casually.

Agamemnon's sword was in hand, the point at Achilles' throat, before any could move to prevent him.

"There will be no more food taken nor innocent women kidnapped without orders from me. Is that understood?"

Achilles eyes gleamed wildly but he did not flinch beneath Agamemnon's gaze.

Defy me. Give me reason to kill you where you stand, Agamemnon thought, willing Achilles to accept his silent challenge.

"As you will, commander," Achilles said at last.

With regret, Agamemnon sheathed his sword.

"As a token of my fealty," Achilles dared to go on, "take the young one for your services."

"And the other?" Agamemnon asked.

"The other is mine," he said, yanking the older woman to her feet. "I think she'll prove a worthy seamstress."

The woman wailed monstrously. "Be silent," Achilles commanded with surprising mildness.

Agamemnon knew he could push Achilles no further without earning a Myrmidon knife in his back for his trouble. "If any harm comes to her, you will answer to me," he said. He ignored Achilles' mocking bow, turned on his heel and beckoned the younger girl to follow.

He felt tension leave those around him, blowing away like summer fog. Agamemnon did not share their release. He walked without meeting the many eyes that turned to him, keeping his thoughts and his lingering anger carefully hidden.

At least I have forestalled any further attacks on the helpless. It was small solace. The men were growing increasingly restless and it would be all too soon before they turned to him for action. The indisputable knowledge that the Trojan fortifications could not be breached would not hold for long against hunger and blood thirst. It would not even stay the hands of the army's more honorable leaders: Nestor, king for three ages; Diomedes of the great war cries; Aias of Salamis, with his twelve ships full of lusty followers and his deadly spear; Thersites, slight of build and ferocious in speech. Even if these great leaders had no more wish to fight than he — as he suspected was true for Odysseus and Nestor — they would do so; the oath they swore forced them to fight or forsake their honor. They would expect him to fight similarly. *But my honor transcends this oath and I will not fulfill it by needlessly wasting their lives and those of our chosen enemy,* he vowed.

The guard outside his tent saluted smartly at his arrival. Agamemnon ignored him, instead pushing back the flap to allow the girl who followed him entrance. She planted her feet to defy him.

"You will be safe in here. I cannot guarantee the same beyond this tent," he whispered.

Startled, the girl looked about her, meeting the lustful eyes of those who roamed the camp and decided to take her chances on Agamemnon's promise.

He gestured that she move to his private quarters, sectioned at the rear of the tent. Her eyes darted about her frantically as she saw his bed pallet within. "I tell you I shall not harm you," he said again, impatience coating his words.

With a look that clearly indicated her disbelief, the girl made her way forward, inching around his bedding.

"I'll have a second pallet brought in here," Agamemnon continued, inwardly flinching against the speculation he knew that action would bring. "Are you hungry? Our food supplies are sparse but I can have some brought to you."

The girl shook her head, some of the stubbornness she displayed earlier returning.

Agamemnon sighed, wondering what god he had angered to bring this additional headache into his life.

CHAPTER EIGHT

The clash of armor and screaming of men echoed through the stone walls of the Trojan palace. As one, the women ran from their sewing room and into the main courtyard, where streams of townspeople were pouring through the gates.

Hecuba grabbed the nearest of the guards.

"What has happened?" she demanded.

The guard did not even look up. "You'll be safe in here, my lady. Just keep moving to the inner courtyard. The guardsmen have it under control."

Hecuba's frustration rang in her command. "Answer your queen," she said, startling the guardsman into looking into her face.

"The Achaians are raiding," he blurted. "They have stolen two of your waiting women — and with respect, lady, I don't know why you let them outdoors. The forces of Troy, led by the gallant Hector, have contained the enemy but they managed to burn a bit of the lower country and confiscate supplies before we could beat them back."

Hecuba's look inevitably turned to Helen, who braced herself for the violence of the queen's words. "You really don't mean to create the chaos that surrounds your every move, do you?"

Helen felt blood rise to her cheeks and focused upon the pattern of eels laid into the floor.

The queen turned her attention to the chaos around her. "You there, take the knot of people around you and be seated in the far corner of the courtyard." The group ceased their wailing and moved as directed, responding reasonably now that orders were issued.

"Come on." Andromache grabbed Helen's arm and pressed

her into the service of passing wine among the townspeople. "Wine will keep them occupied and focus what wits they have," the princess explained.

It did. The panicked crowd eventually regrouped into little knots who shared drink and exaggerated tales of sorrow and inconvenience.

The gates reopened to the thunder of hooves and the clanging of armor.

"Make way for the protectors of Troy!" the guardsman screamed, sounding ridiculously pompous.

Hector burst into the room. "The Achaians have retreated to their camp!" he announced, reawakening chaos.

"Perhaps he'd like to calm this mob down a second time," Andromache screamed at Helen's side.

The remaining men filed in, removing their heavy gear as they did so, sharing tales of the fighting. Alexander walked apart, the hated Deiphobus at his side.

I will speak with you this night, Helen vowed silently. *Even if I must drug your wine to do so.*

No such measure was necessary. The men, having tasted the first bite of war, wanted to be admired and cosseted by their women folk. Alexander was silent until he and Helen entered their rooms.

"They're blaming me, you know, saying that the attack would not have occurred if the queen's women had not sought blessing for my child." The words slurred from a tongue heavy with wine.

Helen felt her blood heat dangerously.

"Deiphobus says he overheard Hector complaining that the loss of the waiting woman was already too great a price to pay for my return to Troy."

Deiphobus. The name filled Helen's heart with a hatred once reserved for the priest Kalchas. "If Hector did indeed say so, which I cannot but doubt, I'd say he was right," she said coldly.

Her words shocked Alexander sober. "How can you possibly say so?" he wailed.

"How can I not? Perhaps the man to whom I pledged my love had greater worth but not the man before me now. I don't even know who you are anymore Alexander. Or maybe I know all too well and have denied it. You have shown yourself to be nothing more than a selfish, prideful child, a pawn to the game that the vile Deiphobus is playing!"

"Deiphobus is my friend and my brother. Do I need remind you that he is the only one who welcomed me to this court?"

"Such welcoming as his you could surely do without!"

She was sure her voice carried beyond the stone walls of their chambers and could not bring herself to care. Anger and disappointment too long denied lashed out of her, seeking its due. It carried her to her dressing table, where she began packing her belongings.

"What are you doing?" he demanded, coming to her and grabbing her arms.

She turned upon him viciously. "Don't ever lay rough hands upon me again!" she snarled. "In fact, you will touch me no more. I'm leaving this awful place. I'm leaving you and I hope you and Deiphobus enjoy yourselves — certainly there has never been a pair more deserving of each other's company."

"Helen, please, put that down. Be reasonable." His own anger could not hide his fear.

Helen took perverse satisfaction in hearing it. "Reasonable? And what would you say is reasonable? Remaining here, forgotten, while you go off on some insane campaign to prove your manhood and probably die in the attempt? No, Alexander. No more." She turned her back to him, continuing her packing.

"Helen, please, you are my love and my life. Can't you see that I am doing this for you? So that I can be worthy of you?"

She wanted to lash out at him once more, to further release her anger. But she had been taught to listen for truth and could not deny that Alexander's words contained such; some part of him honestly believed his actions were for her benefit.

She turned slowly to look into the eyes that once captivated her so. "As I have tried to explain to you, it is not me to whom you must prove yourself but rather the Goddess I serve. Wait. I know you know little of the Great Mother and maybe it is my fault for not teaching you further. But it is She — not one of the man-made gods — who has drawn us together. It is She who has determined the course necessary for us to remain together."

"I hear your words as I have before," Alexander said, hopeful now that she spoke to him reasonably. "I can only say that for me, it was the goddess Aphrodite who portended our union and asked no more than that I pay her homage with our love."

"Your goddess is an image born of your own mind," Helen said sadly, turning to continue packing once more.

"Wait," he said, reaching for her then stopping himself. "In time I may learn to revere the Goddess of whom you speak. Please don't leave me. I will do whatever it is you or She asks of me."

He moved in front of her and Helen felt her heart melt at the earnest expression on his face. *I love you still*, she thought desperately.

She wanted nothing more than to reach for him, to proclaim she would never leave his side. Instead, she let her lingering anger harden her features. "Will you? Will you honestly face the test She has set upon you? Even without fully understanding its nature?"

"Yes," he responded eagerly. "I will do anything to remain with you."

Helen took a breath. "Then, Alexander, you are charged with challenging Menelaus to single combat in which you will fight to the death. If you should succeed," she continued, her voice faltering slightly, "you will rule Sparta at my side in Her name. Are you agreed?"

Alexander licked his lips nervously. "You set upon me no easy task. I don't know that Hector will forgo his own opportunity for glory by allowing me a chance at my own."

"She will take care of Hector," Helen responded. "I only ask that you challenge Menelaus when the opportunity arises."

"And if I so promise, you will not leave?" he asked. At Helen's nod he continued. "I swear by all I hold dear that I will challenge Menelaus to single combat when the opportunity arises."

Helen studied his beloved face, the honor in the lines of his beautiful features, and smiled at last. "Now come and hug your wife and your new son," she commanded with feigned severity.

Alexander beamed and gathered her in his arms, holding her tenderly. She murmured a silent prayer of thanks over his broad shoulder and sunk into the oblivion of love.

CHAPTER NINE

The kidnapping was not enough and for the first time in his gods-forsaken journey, Agamemnon wished the Trojans would attack so he could slaughter someone. He took to remaining in his tent with greater frequency, knowing his men thought him well occupied with his captive. *How they would sneer to learn I sleep upon the ground like the lowliest of soldiers and spend my time virtually begging the girl to partake of the food I save for her.* He kicked the table before him, heartily cursing all women to Hades. His tantrum was interupted by the entrance of a guard.

"What is it?" he demanded.

"My lord, I'm sorry to disturb you so soon after your victory." The man's eyes sparkled as he sought the bedding chamber. Agamemnon vowed that this ignoramus would stand on the front lines during the next confrontation.

"You would not have disturbed me if it was not urgent," Agamemnon prompted.

"Ah yes, my lord." The man blushed and resumed his soldering. "There is a priest of the Trojans who demands word with you."

"Demands?"

"Quite loudly, my lord."

"Priests tend to be that."

"My lord?"

Agamemnon followed the guard to the edge of the camp where a tall blond man stood in pretend dignity at the center of the Achaian commanders. The long robe brought back unpleasant memories.

"Lord Agamemnon," the priest bellowed as the leader neared, loud as the messenger claimed.

246

"Indeed," Agamemnon replied carefully.

The priest carried himself with the appearance of his kind. His audacity prepared Agamemnon to deny whatever he asked. But the man was not interested in making a request.

"You have angered the great god of Apollo by taking his priestess. I demand that you return her to me at once."

Agamemnon heard the murmuring of the men behind him at the name of the god.

"The Trojans are mighty cowards to send a priest as their lackey," Agamemnon remarked because he was expected to and because the men would approve.

"I was sent by the gods alone," the priest answered and Agamemnon focused upon the bulging pulse in the man's neck.

"We are honored that the gods take such interest in our affairs," Agamemnon responded calmly, wishing their priests did not do likewise.

"The gods take interest in all matters where justice is required and vengeance may be necessary," the priest answered. "You have taken my daughter. In the name of Apollo, I demand you return her to me or face his wrath!"

Of all the women in Troy, Achilles' men had to steal the daughter of a priest. The gods, Agamemnon decided, had an annoyingly ironic sense of humor. His men looked at him expectantly. How easy it would be to return the girl and be done with it. But he knew that, in doing so, he would lose their respect and, perhaps, their obedience. Thoughts of their flocking to the orders of the blood thirsty Achilles shivered his spine.

"I fear Apollo's wrath no more than your own. Return to your temple while I still allow you to do so."

"A curse upon your house and your men!" the priest wailed, turning and stalking off.

Agamemnon remembered why he hated priests.

"See that I am not disturbed again by trifles," he ordered and stormed back to his own tent and the young woman who caused this mess.

CHAPTER TEN

"**H**e's deranged!" Cassandra declared once the guards present in ever increasing numbers were banished to the far walls of the garden by the three women. "Personally, I would find the loss of Chryseis a small one, except for her role in our plan. Now we have no one to feed Chryses information. Nor do I think he'll listen."

"When would he have time?" Aethra asked rhetorically. "All day he paces the battlement walls like some crazed god raining his colorful curses upon the Greeks."

"If only his curses were idle," Cassandra murmured.

Helen and Aethra looked at the young princess sharply.

"I'm sure word will arrive at the palace soon enough. It seems a plague has fallen upon the Achaian camp." Uncertainty and the beginnings of fear were clearly visible on Cassandra's usually closed features. "Could it be that the male gods have a power of which we are not aware?"

Aethra leaned back on the patch of grass she always chose to sit upon during their noon meetings.

"The power to work our will in the world was granted to us since the beginning of time," Aethra said carefully. "When we call upon Her, we focus that power. It is possible that the priests have learned to do likewise with the male gods."

"Or at least pretend they can," Helen retorted, her mind remembering another time, another priest who had sought to fabricate power in the name of the gods. "The Achaian supplies must be quite scarce by now. Is it possible they are purchasing food stuffs from the Trojan merchants?"

"Not just possible, but likely," Cassandra responded. "There are always those merchants whose loyalty is to their own riches rather than their homeland. In fact, they are the ones who spread information about the Achaian activities to those outside the palace — it's how I heard of the plague before Priam's official messenger informed the palace."

"Then it's possible the plague is more the product of Chryses' mind than his god," Helen responded curtly, looking to Aethra for confirmation.

Aethra nodded. "He may have employed the same means Kalchas did to coerce those he could not otherwise threaten."

"You'll have to explain this to me," Cassandra demanded.

"There was a priest in Sparta who was more greedy for his own prestige and wealth than for the spirits of his people," Helen explained. "He saw our work on behalf of the Goddess as a threat to his authority. To forestall us, he insisted that the families of those who attended our sessions make a compulsory offering to the temple, lest the wrath of Artemis — the Olympian who has gained hold in Sparta — destroy their labors. The people were so cowered that they did so. Kalchas was so pleased with his success that he expanded his compulsory offerings to all." Helen's lips curled over her anger as she went on to explain her efforts to thwart his activities and his subsequent retaliation. "I wanted nothing more than to hang him from the castle walls but without solid proof as to his hand in the actions, bringing him to justice would only falsely indicate his innocence," she concluded.

"Well, we might be able to attain proof on Chryses, though I doubt Priam will try him for causing the death of Trojan enemies. Late at night, when Chryses finally does return to the temple, he performs some ritual in one of the offering rooms. By morning, the noxious smell that permeates the halls is so great that the older priestesses have taken to fanning the area with their bed coverlets."

"That would seem to prove Chryses' hand in this so-called plague," Aethra agreed. "But as you said, such proof is meaningless. If anything, his actions will be seen as assistance against the Achaian enemy."

"I don't understand why Agamemnon doesn't just return the girl and be done with it. Her charms aren't all that enticing, especially compared to your sister's. I understand Clytemnestra is stunning enough in her own way, even if she doesn't share your spectacular looks."

"And I don't understand what the women were doing in that place to begin with," Aethra interupted before Helen could answer. "Isn't there a more direct route between the palace and temple?"

"That is an interesting point. The path they were using is

the one I myself have been taking — it's longer but less conspicuous than the paved one. Chryseis must have known of it also. Which means she either followed me here or found her own way to the palace. Either poses some interesting questions."

"None of which are relevant now that she's gone," Helen pointed out. Her mind was beginning to drown in all the intrigue.

"True enough," Cassandra conceded. "But what is relevant is that we've lost whatever influence Chryses could gain us by advocating that we avoid war with the Achaians. He is saying — quite loudly — that it is our divine duty to destroy every last one of them. I wouldn't be surprised if he seeks audience with Priam to declare more of the same."

"Chryses is not the only one adversely affected by the incident," Aethra added. "According to Andromache, Hector is flushed with pride at his first victory in pushing the Greeks back to their camp. From her words, he speaks of nothing beyond leading the army to the next battle. Suggesting a single combat between Menelaus and Alexander is out of the question for the time being."

"If Alexander would even agree to the challenge," Cassandra said. "I take it you've had no more success than we in forwarding our plan," she added to Helen.

Helen smiled in contradiction. "In fact, I have. Alexander has agreed to the challenge and is only awaiting the proper moment to propose it."

Her smile broadened as she thought upon how solicitous he had been since she threatened to leave. Even on nights when the men met in council, Alexander visited with her in their chambers. His voice sang once more with the gentle quality that had captured her heart, even when they discussed the challenges he faced with Hector and the other men of Priam's household. Deiphobus' name was rarely mentioned, for which she was extremely grateful. They even found time to discuss their future and the life they desired for their child. She had begun to subtly relay the destiny the Goddess had shown to her and to hint that they would return to rule together in Sparta. If he didn't commit to this plan — yet — at least he no longer argued with her. She was confident that, in time, he would be properly trained for his role at her side.

Her hand moved to her still flat belly, hoping that all was resolved before the life within left the safety of her womb. She felt a pang of guilt for the other child whom she dedicated to the Goddess. It had been many moons since she spent any time with Niko. Shortly after the Greeks set camp beyond the Trojan walls, he and the other youth participated in the men's councils, refilling wine goblets and helping to polish weapons in anticipation for their later life as warriors. She had seen him briefly a few days ago when her healer skills were called upon to assist those injured in the skirmish. She was astounded at the growth that had taken place in his small body. He was at a stage when each day brought more changes than adults could tolerate in a season. She had gone to him, wanting to fold him in her arms. The pride in his eyes had kept her from doing so. She wondered if he had inherited it from her or from Menelaus or if the men that surrounded him passed it on like a disease.

"Well that's something," Cassandra was saying, "although one could certainly wish Alexander had found opportunity to offer challenge before the priest went mad and bloodlust descended upon Hector."

"For the time being," Aethra said, "we'll have to celebrate Helen's accomplishment and wait to see how this other nonsense plays itself out."

Reluctantly, Cassandra agreed.

She did not have to wait long.

Helen sat at her customary place in the feasting hall that night, between Andromache and Aethra. Hecuba sat silently at Andromache's left, while the chair to Aethra's left — formerly occupied by Briseis — remained conspicuously vacant.

"When this treachery has ceased, she will return to us," Hecuba said with the angry look Helen had grown accustomed to.

The fresh fowl that had been baked for the meal was all but wasted on the diners, whose attention was absorbed by argument.

"I say that priest is doing us a favor by pacing the cliffs and demoralizing the men in Agamemnon's camp," Hector said, contemplating his wine.

Deiphobus, noting that his despised brother was the center of attention once more, leaned to whisper his grievance in Paris' ear. "Hector would rather let a priest fight than dirty his own hands," he whispered to Alexander, putting a second goblet of wine in his brother's hands.

"We don't need priests to do our fighting for us," Alexander said, loudly. His eyes moved inadvertently to Helen's face and his angry features softened. "I will challenge Menelaus to single combat and end any further fighting."

He smiled into Helen's eyes, a gesture she reciprocated.

Deiphobus choked on his wine. He followed Paris' gaze to Helen and scowled. She offered him her most brilliant smile.

Hector turned several interesting shades of red. "I will decide how we conduct this war."

"Your husband's timing is deplorable," Andromache remarked lightly.

"You're about to learn how true that is," said a second voice.

Helen turned as Cassandra sunk into their chair reserved for Briseis.

"I do hope you don't mind that I join you this evening," she added sweetly to Hecuba, who had raised a disapproving brow.

"Hmph," Hecuba replied, returning her attention to the men.

"Gracious as usual," Cassandra murmured.

"So what news has brought you here?" Andromache prompted, her attention caught by the entrance of the king's messenger.

"You're about to find out," Cassandra said unnecessarily.

The man who entered the hall saluted smartly before the royal table and waited impatiently for permission to speak. Priam noted the man's agitation and hid a sigh before signaling Hector to begin the questioning. Hector stood proudly and nodded toward the guard.

"The arrows of Apollo have struck justice on the Achaian camp," the man blurted.

Hector raised an eyebrow in a comical imitation of his father. "Go on."

The guard composed himself to begin an explanation that, in his haste, he had forgotten to prepare.

"The priest — Chryses — shot the arrows of Apollo into the Achaian camp and began a plague on the men. Even now, they burn their corpses and isolate some of their forces. They have begged the priest to return."

"Now is the perfect time for attack," Deiphobus grumbled, still nursing his grievance against Paris for not repeating his words alone.

"And bring the plague upon our own people through contact?" Hector responded sarcastically. He returned his attention to the guard without awaiting Deiphobus' reply. "Has it affected any of the commanders — Agamemnon, Achilles, Odysseus?"

"No, the leaders have apparently moved to an unaffected area of the camp."

Hector pretended to be disappointed. "Too bad. Well, command the priest to the palace and we shall go to meet the Achaians together."

"The priest is already here, my lord," the messenger informed them.

This time it was Priam who raised his brow. The guard looked to Priam and back to Hector.

"Well, he, uh demanded — requested to speak with you."

"Let's not keep him waiting then," Priam said.

The guard bowed again and left to show the priest in.

"Now this should be interesting," Aethra remarked, sitting straighter in her chair.

The door opened once more, admitting a startling tall man who moved aggressively toward the high table.

"My lords," he began without hesitation, "The wrath of Apollo has spoken. I will now have the return of my daughter in his name."

"The wrath of Apollo indeed," Aethra hissed beneath the awkward silence that accompanied his pronouncement.

Priam looked to Hector, who shrugged his ignorance.

"Good sir," Priam said patiently, "with respect to yourself and your god, who is your daughter?"

"My daughter? My daughter is the reason for the wrath. Agamemnon stole her and refused her return. Now I — I mean the god — shall refuse mercy."

"He is all you said and more," Aethra whispered to Cassandra, who nodded glumly.

"And how — or should I say why — are you refusing mercy?" Priam asked, an edge creeping into his voice.

"He has spoiled a virgin of Apollo. There is no mercy." The priest retorted stubbornly.

"You are saying you will not negotiate for your daughter?" Hector asked.

"I will command that he take her to wife and pay a bride price or else the wrath will continue tenfold."

"Agamemnon — as you may know — already has a wife," Priam interjected.

"Then he will put her aside."

"Clytemnestra will love this one," Helen whispered.

"And should he refuse?" Priam asked with deceptive gentleness.

The priest waved his arms frantically. "Then the plague shall continue, eating the flesh of man away to nothing, destruction reigning free."

Priam's patience ended. "And contained beyond our walls?

My experience with destruction would indicate that it seldom remains confined once unleashed."

"Then it shall reign until justice is served," the priest replied.

"It will continue until it touches the first of my subjects," Priam responded coldly.

"You question the will of the god?"

"No. Only of his vessel should that vessel command the destruction of the very kingdom that houses him — at my pleasure, I remind you."

"Good response that," Andromache observed.

Hecuba turned sharply, waving her to silence. Andromache issued an unrepentant shrug.

"The god is imperious to threats," the priest responded, jutting his large jaw.

"Nor do I threaten the gods. But I shall not hesitate to threaten a man who likewise threatens my lands and my people. Surely, the god would not protest if another was elevated to your high station — with all the princely gifts and sacrifices that a king can command."

The priest opened and closed his mouth several times.

"You will allow Agamemnon to make reasonable — and I do mean reasonable — amends and then call upon your god to cease the threat to our very walls."

Before the priest could respond, Priam rose from his table and proceeded to leave the hall, his sons and guards following. The priest had the option of following or remaining behind with the women. His eyes scanned the room's occupants, meeting the cold stares offered him by Andromache, Helen, Aethra and Cassandra. Chryses wisely turned and made his way to the king.

"At least we need not worry about the priest's influence any longer," Cassandra said as he disappeared through the doorway.

Helen, who knew more than she would like about the ways of priests, said nothing.

CHAPTER ELEVEN

Chryses was very much on Kalchas' mind. The sight of the unusually large man storming the battlements — with the posture of a proud war horse, his silk cloak bellowing behind him, his golden hair grabbing the rays of the sun — was imprinted upon Kalchas' brain.

Of course the man is the chosen of Apollo, Kalchas thought covetously. *Chryses is grand beyond reason.*

No doubt Chryses had visions.

A great longing filled Kalchas' heart. He thought to forsake his position as chief priest among the Greek forces and throw himself at Chryses' powerful feet, begging for acceptance. Only the fear that he would be denied by one of such obvious greatness kept him from doing so. He needed to prove his worth to a man whose own was obviously so high. The plague that had struck the Achaian field had only confirmed Kalchas' understanding of Chryses' power. Kalchas' awe temporarily blinded him to the sign the god offered him.

Temporarily.

As he walked through the camp — careful to avoid those struck with the deadly disease — his mind cleared and what should have been obvious from the first asserted itself. The plague, though perhaps sanctioned by the gods, was the work of man. As Kalchas studied the men around him, he realized that the seeming randomness of the plague was closely linked to the foodstuffs eaten.

The priest had orchestrated a plague similar to Kalchas' own.

With the certainty of a man convinced of the profundity of his every thought, Kalchas knew that this was the sign he awaited, sent to indicate the god's willingness to consider his service.

A sign and an opportunity.

Kalchas was determined to seize it, to prove himself as worthy as the god suspected. How?

He moved across the camp, careful to avoid the wearisome requests to pray over the contaminated. The Apollan priest was not present this evening, as if to punish the men further with the absence of his divine presence. *I must make myself known to him*, Kalchas fretted.

He could not simply tell the priest that he knew of the clever mind that orchestrated the plague. He doubted that Chryses would appreciate Kalchas' discovery of his treachery any more than Kalchas did when that far too beautiful and overly presumptuous princess and her cackle of heathen priestesses discovered his. No, direct confrontation was not the answer. He would have to be far more subtle to impress the likes of Chryses.

He had considered telling Agamemnon that he knew the plague's source but dismissed the idea immediately. Agamemnon ordered Kalchas' tent to be placed at a considerable distance from his own and the commander called for silence when a single word passed from Kalchas' lips. In one thing, at least, Kalchas and Clytemnestra were agreed: the commander had no imagination. He still begrudged the sacrifice of his daughter despite the motivation it provided to the Greeks. What was the life of one useless girl child compared to glory for an entire land?

Besides, Agamemnon would probably take credit for the information himself, depriving Kalchas of his opportunity to demonstrate his own cleverness.

Perhaps he should tell no one at all. Yes, that was it. He would announce that he had a vision (a vision!) that showed him how to stop the plague. Then he would sneak into the tent he knew held the foodstuffs, destroying the offending meal. Of course, the tent was well guarded but Kalchas knew all sorts of simple concoctions that, when slipped in a man's wine, would disarm him utterly.

His pace quickened with enthusiasm. A vision, yes. Surely that would enhance his prestige in the Apollon's eyes. He would not reveal the man's secret; better to keep such knowledge between equals.

He stopped abruptly as a thought of utter brilliance developed in his mind: He would say that the god told him that Agamemnon must return the priest's daughter to end the plague. He was dazzled by his own cunning. Surely the hand of the god was present in his brain.

Chryses would know that Kalchas knew his secret and kept it. And that Kalchas was responsible for orchestrating the return of Chryses' beloved daughter.

But would that be enough to convince the Apollon priest to accept a member of the enemy camp into his temple? Worry started Kalchas' feet once more. No, the risk was too great that he would be denied. Entering the Trojan temple, Kalchas thought, would only come when he and the priest were not in opposing camps. Which meant a truce must be called between the Trojans and the Achaians. Grand thought that. But how was he to arrange a truce when belligerent Agamemnon would not begin the war?

An obnoxious man, dressed in the simple armor of a warrior without rank, pulled on Kalchas' arm. "Dear priest, please come pray over the head of my sword brother. He has been struck."

"Can't you see I'm contemplating more important matters," Kalchas snapped, pulling his arm free and pushing past the man, who stood unmoving with shock.

A war, yes. A war that would rid the world of useless soldiers like that one. And useless commanders like Agamemnon. Kalchas had fretted over how to fulfill Clytemnestra's order that her husband not return, especially when season after season passed and the only time the leader lifted his sword was to polish it. Kalchas had no desire to kill the man himself but he also did not want to risk being on the wrong side of Clytemnestra. *The woman has visions*, Kalchas acknowledged reluctantly. *It is probably better not to offend her.* War would rid him of Agamemnon; if the man did not fall to an enemy sword, than certainly a knife in the back would be easy enough to arrange in the chaos of fighting.

If only he could get the fighting to begin. Again the god supplied inspiration. Visions. What if Agamemnon had a vision? What if Zeus himself, king of all gods, demanded Agamemnon attack? Surely not even one as irreverent as Agamemnon would deny an order from a god.

And perhaps a little help from the wine Kalchas would use on those guarding the food tent would facilitate the coming of such an apparition.

Kalchas began to whistle, oblivious to the dark stares he garnered from the members of the bleak camp.

I must plan very carefully, he cautioned himself. *The gods may provide inspiration but it is up to man to use it wisely. I must first make my vision for halting the plague known — and make sure Agamemnon heeds my words.*

He looked up to find himself surrounded by the uncanny, large men who swarmed Achilles' tent like ants.

"We sit here fighting disease when we should be fighting men!" shrilled a voice within the tent.

Kalchas moved closer but could not make out the words of the man who responded — Patro?, no Patroclus — the small young man who accompanied Achilles everywhere.

"Agamemnon is a coward and a fool!" Achilles roared in response to whatever his friend had uttered.

Another piece of Kalchas' plan fell into place and he walked confidently toward the giant who guarded Achilles' tent. The man drew his spear.

"I am here to see your commander," Kalchas announced, ignoring the threat the large man posed to his modest person by reminding himself of his special favor with forces unseen.

"And who'd you be?"

Kalchas told himself to be patient with a man who possessed more muscles than brains. He locked his knees and strengthened his voice. "Kalchas, high priest of the gods," he announced.

The man eyed him skeptically; Kalchas vowed to curse the man at the first opportunity.

"Is my lord expecting you?"

The curse would extend to the man's family.

"A man such as Achilles always expects the word of the gods. And he will be mightily displeased at being denied their voice."

The man hesitated for an annoyingly long moment while Kalchas suffered his scrutiny.

"Wait here."

Achilles appeared from his tent and Kalchas' legs turned to water. *The gods test you*, he reminded himself as Achilles approached close enough for the warrior's hot breath to suffocate him.

"What do you want?"

"A word," Kalchas choked. He cleared his throat and waited.

"I'm listening, but be quick about it."

Kalchas thought maybe he would forget the whole thing. *What if Achilles laughs at me, or worse, strikes me down in one of his mad fits. Surely, I am too important to risk to such a fate.* The image of the great Apollon priest, walking defiantly across the battlements, filled him with renewed confidence. "The gods have given me the solution to this curse of Apollo," he said proudly.

Achilles was unimpressed.

"Such a solution will allow you to get on with the important business of warring," he continued, allowing a very satisfying pedantic note to enter his voice.

A dangerous glint fired Achilles eyes. "Go on."

"The solution from the gods must be announced among all the great leaders," Kalchas hastily explained. "I call upon you, Achilles, as the first to gather and hear his word!"

"Meaning you have not yet called upon Agamemnon?" said a voice behind Achilles. Patroclus stepped from the larger man's shadow.

"The god led me to seek out Achilles first," Kalchas replied quickly.

"How convenient," Patroclus murmured.

"Let's go to Agamemnon's tent then and get on with this," Achilles ordered.

The priest protected himself with an armor of dignity and walked proudly to the tent of Agamemnon, delighting in the group he felt gather behind him, the multitudes who would, at last, recognize his considerable talents. He stopped before Agamemnon's tent, stealing strength from the bodies surrounding him.

"The high priest Kalchas and great warrior Achilles seek counsel with lord Agamemnon in the name of Zeus."

The guard outside the leader's tent wavered. Kalchas was prohibited from entering the king's domain. The war leaders, however, could not be turned away. He turned to the tent to inform his commander. Let Agamemnon decide.

The king did, emerging from his tent and attacking Kalchas with his eyes. "What is it?"

Kalchas forced his voice to ring loudly to the masses. "The great god Apollo has brought me a dream to end his curse," he announced and drew confidence from the awed murmur that greeted his words.

Agamemnon was unmoved.

"And no doubt you have gathered us here to hear his wisdom," Agamemnon snapped. "Mind you, there are no more innocent children to sacrifice so don't even suggest it."

"I suggest as the god prompts me," Kalchas said with bruised dignity.

"Get on with it," Agamemnon demanded.

Kalchas turned to face the crowd, lowering his voice to force his audience to lean forward to catch his words.

"Our dear lord Achilles, beloved of Apollo, has bidden me to address you, to relay a prophesy from the gods." Kalchas did himself the favor of not meeting Achilles' eyes. "I will speak as the god has spoken to me. And yet I must admit to fear," bad opening that, "not that the god will not protect me," he added hastily, "but rather that my word will bring repercussions from a powerful man whom I may anger."

When it was clear he would say no more, Achilles, not known for his patience, spoke up. "Speak man, and all here will vow to protect you from whomever it is you fear."

Kalchas winced — unwise to have admitted fear. He watched the crowd's reaction and, sensing impatience grow to a level that would not serve him, continued. "Here the words of the great god Apollo: It is not that the gods have rejected our rituals of protection that we suffer this ghastly fate."

"Of course not," Agamemnon muttered.

"Rather, it is because the king Agamemnon, called commander, insulted a priest of the god by refusing to return his daughter. Apollo, to whom the priest swore allegiance, has chosen to rage war upon us with his weapon of disease. He will not cease this plague until we have returned the daughter to her father."

Kalchas stared at the men, willing himself not to smile as the angry eyes turned upon Agamemnon. *I do more than Clytemnestra a favor when I rid the world of Agamemnon*, Kalchas thought smugly. He turned to face the commander and cursed himself for his involuntary step backward. Rage poured from Agamemnon's eyes.

"Does the god always advise you to take women away from me?" Agamemnon bellowed, advancing upon the priest with his intended malice clearly etched across his strong features.

Kalchas' courage deserted him. His knees bent of their own volition, his body sank into the protective earth below him. He was, fortunately, ignored.

Achilles own considerable rage ignited. "Once before you tried to stay the hands of the gods. Do not do so again. Hand over the hapless girl and let's get on with the fighting!"

Agamemnon whirled in fury to confront the voice that issued one too many demands upon him. Priests. Madmen. Women. War. Plague. Famine. And Agamemnon was at the center of it, held captive by strength he no longer prized and the intelligence that beat through his body with every thud of his heart. *Would you leave the army in the hands of madmen like Achilles?* his honor asked him. *No*, he vowed, *but nor will I allow this man to best me ever again.*

The liberation of stupidity cursed through him.

"I'll give back the girl, yes," he raged. "It is not for me to defy the gods — if they in fact decreed her return." He cast a murderous look at Kalchas. "But I will take your woman, you insane slug who calls himself warrior."

Achilles placed his hand upon his sword at the same time Agamemnon reached for his own. *At least and at last, we shall end this*, Agamemnon thought, glaring hatred at the madman, allowing himself to blame Achilles for all the turmoil within himself.

He watched as the young Patroclus ran beside his foe and cast a restraining arm upon him. Achilles almost threw him off before recognizing who touched him. Agamemnon was annoyed to see tenderness replace anger, intelligence overcome the madness in Achilles eyes.

The gods help us if anything should ever befall Patroclus, he could not help thinking and considered having the man shadowed during battles.

At last, Achilles turned to him. "Take her if you can," he sneered.

Agamemnon shot him a look of contempt before signaling to two men in the crowd. "Tathybios, Eurybates, bring the woman Briseis from lord Achilles tent to my own."

Achilles rage burned anew at the order.

"See if I shall give up my prizes and continue to fight for you then!" Achilles raged.

"Your absence gives me one less thing to worry about," Agamemnon snapped.

The mad warrior turned, his sandals kicking dirt about him, and stormed off. His stone-faced Myrmidon warriors sized up those beside Agamemnon with distaste before turning to follow. Patroclus met Agamemnon's eyes and gave a sad shake of his head before doing likewise.

"Bad piece of business that," Odysseus said softly behind Agamemnon.

Agamemnon ignored him. "Beckon the Apollon priest and let's get this charade done with." His attention fell to Kalchas. "And if this does not work, know that our next step shall be to offer the god one of his humble servants for sacrifice."

CHAPTER TWELVE

"**T**he men are this moment facing the Achaians. Why is it we sit here sewing and weaving when that foul-faced priest gets to see everything?" Andromache moaned, attacking the garment before her with her bone needle.

"It is a woman's fate," Hecuba said patiently, carefully working the cloth beneath her own hands. "And don't call the priest foul-faced. It's disrespectful."

"Why is naming a man what he is disrespectful simply because he has a title?" Andromache retorted querulously.

Aethra met Helen's eyes, rolling her own and hiding a smile. Watching Hecuba and Andromache's good-natured bantering was one of the few high points of the tedious afternoons.

Especially since it keeps the queen's tongue from my direction, Helen added to herself.

"My dear child," Hecuba said, dropping her work to her lap and lifting aggrieved hands in Andromache's direction. "Why are you so contentious this day?"

"Because here we sit, senselessly weaving and sewing what could wait a whole season, while our army faces the Achaians for the first time."

Hecuba smiled in the indulgent way reserved for her daughter-by-marriage. "I know you'd rather be on the front lines yourself. Sometimes I wonder if you're more warrior than Hector — perhaps there's Amazon blood in your veins somewhere."

"For all the good it does me sitting in this room," Andromache grumbled.

"Alright child, out with it!" Hecuba said at last.

"We could go to the battlements of the high castle and watch the confrontation for ourselves instead of waiting for that useless messenger to supply information second hand."

"And be ready targets for any Achaian archer who decides to pick us off?" Hecuba asked.

"Hector has the walls so lined with guards and archers that the Achaians would be hard pressed to pick us out from amongst them. Besides if they get close enough to the palace to do that kind of harm, we're probably doomed anyway."

"You are so morose," Hecuba complained. "But I suppose watching the men's battle is better than battling with you all afternoon — which I'm sure I'd have to do if we stay." She neatly folded the cloth upon which she worked. "You women can stay or go as you please."

Andromache threw Helen and Aethra a victorious smile and the women hurried to fold their linens before Hecuba had a change of her perverse mind. Many of the younger women did likewise, while the elder ones sat more comfortably on their stools.

"Come on then," Hecuba said, rising to lead the excited group to their selected viewing place.

As Andromache stated, the watching wall of Troy's palace was lined with guards and archers. They had to shoulder their way forward, pushing aside guards who were not pleased at forfeiting their own view.

"Prince Hector will not be happy about this, my lady," one remarked.

"Then he'll have to take it up with his wife," Hecuba responded sweetly.

"Which would probably be as useless as my gainsaying my own dear lady," the man grumbled.

From where they stood, the women could see the faces of the men who lined up outside the palace gateway. "Too bad we can't hear them as well," Andromache said. "It seems as if Hector is getting the best of one of the Achaian commanders — do you know which it is Helen?"

"Agamemnon," Helen supplied, recognizing the familiar face of her sister's husband. She wished she could speak with him and wondered, suddenly, if he hated her for dragging him to Troy's walls.

"Hector certainly does appear pleased with himself," Aethra noted as the Trojan prince turned to address his men with a grand sweep of his hands.

"I don't think he's ever been happier," Andromache acknowledged. "At least not since they pushed back the Achaians from the lower land. Fighting suits him." She took a step back from the wall to speak with Helen and Aethra privately. "It is not a role he's going to relinquish lightly," she whispered behind her hand. "Rumor has it that Achilles has quit the war for good. If that is so, I think Hector will welcome the chance to try his hand in battle."

"Lovely," Aethra responded.

"It is what he was raised to be," Andromache replied defensively. "Anyway, if you're still intent on having Paris challenge Menelaus to single combat, I think you're going to have to proceed without Hector's consent," she added to Helen.

Helen said nothing. Alexander still attended her each night and showed his willingness to keep his promise to her. Without Hector's support, however, it was going to be very complicated to arrange a single combat.

"Another complication," Aethra grumbled, as if reading Helen's thoughts.

"Well, at least you don't have to worry about the priest any longer," Andromache said optimistically.

Aethra's grumble became a growl. "We must always worry about the priests."

"Did you come here to watch or to gossip," Hecuba snapped, turning toward them.

Andromache shrugged and the women pressed forward to see the Trojans offer a great ox in sacrifice. They watched as smoke billowed from the site.

"We should teach these men something of herb lore," Aethra choked, placing her hand over her nose and mouth to block the stench of the burning animal. It offered little relief.

The distribution of sacrificed meat and other elaborate rituals looked to go on and on. "This is boring," one of the younger waiting women complained.

"It is the way of war. Everyone is all excited at the onset, as if some elaborate games were arranged for their benefit. When they find out how tedious it really is, they grow bored and complacent and eventually it becomes no more than an ordinary event in everyday life," Aethra said, offering Helen a pointed look.

She's right of course. I'll have to speak with Alexander soon before he, too, becomes accustomed to this war. Helen ignored the fear that rose within her at the prospect of her lover's battle. What if he lost? What if Menelaus killed him? *The Goddess will protect Her own,* she told herself forcefully, determined not to worry about that which would not, could not, come to be.

The sun moved lower in the sky and still the elaborate sacrifices went on below.

"This will go on all night," Hecuba complained. "I'm going to arrange a meal for the guards on duty and have ours sent to our rooms. I trust you've seen enough," she added to Andromache.

"Yes mother," Andromache responded complacently. "Maybe when the plague lifts on the Achaian camp there will be more to see."

Hecuba rolled her eyes skyward before turning on her heel.

"She's right," Andromache said to the others. "There's nothing more to be learned here and nothing we can do in any event — at least not for now."

No, not for now. Not until I convince my husband to challenge the man to whom my father wed me, Helen thought.

CHAPTER THIRTEEN

At least I'm not burdened with sharing a tent with that woman Briseis any longer, Agamemnon thought.

When he had first ordered Briseis taken from Achilles' tent, Agamemnon had not thought past his own anger and the small satisfaction to be derived from thwarting the madman.

Agamemnon had not been prepared for the reality of Briseis herself.

The disheveled woman had looked fearfully about his tent, eyeing him as if certain he would ravish her at any moment. None of his reassurance to the contrary had any effect and she started the wailing that she had perfected since joining the camp, demonstrating a tenacity of lung that would have been impressive if it weren't so irritating.

Agamemnon had cause to wonder if the Trojans planned Briseis' capture to drive him mad.

It didn't take long before he had a new tent erected and the screaming woman placed within its muffling walls, threatening the guard he stationed outside it with the point of his sword should any harm approach her.

"I can't guarantee the men won't relieve her of her tongue if she continues," the guard complained unhappily.

Fortunately, the seclusion had silenced her ample voice and Agamemnon was able to reclaim his tent once more. *Not that it matters much*, he thought as he spent another night seated at his small command table contemplating shadows.

Agamemnon hated this war. He hated madmen and priests and women and swords and tents and stale food and bugs and heat.

Agamemnon could not sleep for hatred.

He hated sleepless nights.

Not even the wine sent by the healer, who must have noticed the black circles growing under his eyes, seemed to have any effect. In fact, the heavy spiced stuff seemed only to muddle his brain further, forcing him to remain awake and chase his own thoughts. It seemed to have a similar effect on his vision — or perhaps the blurring of sight had resulted from too many nights without rest. *Even the shadows appear different tonight.*

"Agamemnon!" the call startled him and he forced his disobedient eyes to focus upon the source of its issue. Before him, he could make out the waving lines of a shadow detaching itself from the others.

"Agamemnon," the voice demanded a second time. "How can you sleep when the city of the Trojans is wide open to you?"

Agamemnon tried to rise but his legs proved as unreliable as his eyes.

"Who are you?" he slurred, with a feeble attempt to grasp for the sword at his side.

"Do not presume to place demands upon me," the shadow retorted, "Agamemnon, so favored among men, so disappointing to the gods."

Agamemnon started. The gods. He willed his eyes to focus once more so that he might learn the identity of the shadow. He was rewarded by a skull-cracking pain.

"I am the messenger of Zeus," the voice intoned.

Where those really stars that danced about the shadow's head, trailing exploded lightning?

"You have earned the disapproval of the greatest Olympian. Your actions are those of a coward. I will give you this chance to redeem yourself. Rise. The city of Troy is open to you. Fight. Win. Return home victorious.

"Believe!"

Agamemnon sat for an eternity, staring at shadows, now blessedly silent. His eyes had cleared. His limbs returned to his control. His head still ached in reminder.

Did he dream?

Believe!

The remembered words echoed in his head, threatening to explode his skull should he ignore them. The god Zeus was angry with him.

Agamemnon remembered a time when he believed in the gods, a time of innocence, when he called upon them like good luck charms, a time when they didn't demand that he sacrifice everything he loved.

The god of his night vision demanded victory.

Agamemnon dressed swiftly and left his tent, colliding with the guard counting paces outside it.

"My lord?" the guard said, recovering himself with remarkable speed.

"Gather the commanders immediately. I have received, ah, information that I need them to hear."

The guard looked in awe upon a commander who received information during the night's stillness and saluted proudly before turning to his errand.

Agamemnon grabbed his scepter from inside his tent and awaited the arrival of his men, pulling his faith tightly about him like a cloak against doubt.

Doubt came first in the form of his brother.

"Are you mad to summon the council in the middle of the night?"

Agamemnon threw faith like a blade aimed at the back of Menelaus eyes. His brother quieted.

Nestor and Odysseus approached, walking as if fully rested, ready for the day despite the late hour. The sight of them filled Agamemnon's confidence to overflowing.

Thersites of the endless speech marched forward like poison.

Lastly, Achilles approached, proud and wary. *He probably believes this conference to do with him.*

Agamemnon ignored the angry warrior, as well as the minor kings and high-ranking officers that were forming an ever widening circle. He did not see the dark form of a priest slip into a distant place.

He looked into Nestor's eyes and, clutching the specter, he began. "Fellow fighters. We have traveled far. We have experienced much. Most of it has been hardship. Much of it has been loss. The gods test us," he added softly and felt the attention of his startled listeners reach out to him. He continued more forcefully. "We have reached a critical time, a juncture when the call of home is stronger than the call of victory."

From the corner of his eye he watched his brother gulp air to speak and Odysseus pound him on the back to ensure continued silence.

"I too have felt the call of our own lands, our own people, our own women. But this night, Zeus has sent me a message that has let the call of victory ring loudly once more. He bade us, one and all, to arm. The fall of Troy is at hand!" The last he bellowed, passionate in his certainty.

A muted hush greeted him, shaking his faith. Thersites scowled and grabbed the scepter from Agamemnon's hand.

"My fellow fighters," he began and for once noticed that men placed their attention elsewhere when he rose to speak. "I do believe our commander has gone mad." he announced quickly.

The rumble began, starting from the outer circle, growing in intensity as it moved within.

"Enough of this war..."

"Not even for a woman who is my own..."

"Why fight for a man who cannot hold his wife..."

Many others who had counted upon the loot of victory protested passionately. "Are we to have gained nothing but the skills of farmers?"

"Who but a coward would skirt a fight?"

"I did not come all this way and wait all this time to return home like a dog kicked by its master."

Even spirits cannot overcome the stubbornness of man, Agamemnon thought and snatched the scepter from a disgustingly pleased Thersites.

"The gods promise us victory and you decide that now is the time to flee?" he roared. "Who more than I has stayed our hand from a battle that I have thought useless? I tell you now that the gods call upon us to demonstrate our valor and honor the pledge made so long ago in Sparta!"

"The gods showed their will when they gave us the plague," a voice from the back shouted, ignoring custom and speaking out of turn.

"I've lost more men to disease than to the skirmish," another echoed.

"And the gods showed us how to end that awful plight. I listened, even when my pride would have prevented me from doing so!" Agamemnon responded.

Some of the men agreed, beginning to use fists when words alone did not convince the dissenters of their opinions.

A dark figure in the back of the circle pulled his cowl closer to hide the smile that snaked across his face.

"May I?" Nestor's kind eyes met Agamemnon's, his usual good humor shadowing his request. Gratefully, Agamemnon released his scepter.

"If any man said to me that a god sent him word of victory over the Trojans, I would say he was delirious," Nestor began.

The men stopped their squabbling, giving the speaker the attention earned by an elder.

"Any man, that is, except Agamemnon," Nestor added mildly.

Achilles snapped the scepter from Nestor's hand. "And why is it that the god came to you now?" he demanded, turning his rage upon Agamemnon. "Is it that you want us to capture more women for you? Is Briseis not enough? Do you want everything else I own, all glory I will bring myself?"

Nestor did not wait for Achilles' megalomania to explode. "May I?" he asked a second time. Achilles looked at him, puzzled. Nestor indicated the scepter in his hand and Achilles, startled to see it there, handed it meekly over.

"The gods have spoken," Nestor declared. "Let any man who flees now forfeit his honor and their protection."

The army stopped and even those who argued most fiercely for departing looked uneasy. Thersites, furious, moved once more to take his turn at speech. He was blocked by the huge form of Odysseus. "I believe it would be wise for you to continue to enjoy your power of silence," the war leader commented mildly.

Thersites choked on the words he swallowed and stepped back.

"I want all men armed for battle," Agamemnon ordered after respectfully reclaiming his scepter. "On the morrow, Troy will be ours."

A spark ran threw the crowd but did not ignite into the flame he had hoped. "What more can they want if not a message from the gods?" Agamemnon muttered.

"I have marked that men only welcome divine interference when it matches their own will," Odysseus said casually and walked away.

At the fringes of the crowd, Kalchas turned, and began to run to his tent, baffling even the most stalwart fighter when he leapt for joy.

As Hecuba predicted, the sacrifices went on through the evening meal and it wasn't until late in the night that Alexander returned to Helen's quarters.

"I would follow your Goddess if only to avoid interactions with the likes of that man Chryses," he said with a tired smile.

Helen hardened herself against the exhaustion that

slumped his body. "Then that will have to be enough," she said. "You must challenge Menelaus the next time the two forces meet."

His puzzled frown broke her heart. "You know I have promised to do so, my love. But Hector would scare appreciate my offer if made this evening. You should have seen him when Agamemnon handed over the priest's daughter. He strutted about today's events like a prized stallion."

"It may be that we can no longer await Hector's permission," she said coldly. "With each interaction with Troy's enemies, Hector's pride swells. He may not give you the chance to make such a challenge for fear it will compromise his own importance."

"Why, now you sound just like Deiphobus," Alexander said bitterly.

Helen cringed, forcing herself to go on. "Nonetheless in Her name I command you to issue challenge when next the forces meet."

Alexander hung his head, remembering again the awful time she threatened to leave him. "So be it, my lady."

And so it was that he met her eyes meaningfully when all had gathered for the meal the following evening.

Once again, the king's herald appeared, the very embodiment of agitation.

Priam looked up from his eating reluctantly, causing several alarmed eyebrows to be raised, before impatiently gesturing Hector to handle the unwelcome interruption.

Let them believe what they will, the king thought, annoyed that another perfectly good dinner would now be spoiled.

Since the time the Achaians camped beyond the walls of his city, the king fought a war within his body, urging it to swell with life as it prepared for a heroic death. He willed flabby muscles to harden, blood to flow with greater speed, his heart to beat a stronger rhythm, his spirit to soar with the prospect of glory so late in life.

But his body continued to crave soft food; his spirit sang only for warming hearth fires.

Before the Achaians attacked, Priam surrendered.

It's Hector's time anyway. I did not spend all these years raising him to manhood so I could continue to coddle him like a child.

Hector rose, determined to make his father proud. "Speak."

The messenger released words that had grown too hot for his mouth to hold. "My lord, the Achaians have organized a sizable army. Our men have reported flames of sacrifice. The enemy is on the march toward Troy!"

Hector looked to his father once more before speaking; Priam's gaze was held by his plate. "Men, arm yourselves to do battle with the Achaians."

The hall erupted as men ran for the weapons that had received a permanent location in the feasting hall. The women made various exclamations of alarm.

Alexander met Helen's eyes and nodded.

I am doing what is requested of me. Guard him to victory. She forced herself to meet his gaze squarely, ignoring her own panic.

Priam, surveying the confusion around him, leaned over to his wife.

"I'm sorry to ruin your dinner, my dear."

He rose slowly and followed the men from the hall.

Hecuba stared at her husband, her own panic plainly visible. As she watched his receding back, the lens of the past closed and she viewed him with the eyes of the present.

He is old, she thought, forcing herself to look objectively at his folded skin, his thin legs, his careful movements.

My husband is old.

I am old, her mind informed her relentlessly.

It had been some time since she gazed within her mirror; the device had ceased being her friend long ago. But her mind's eye conjured the image she had seen last, the strands of hair that fell in dull wisps about her face, the body worn by time and child bearing, the skin that had grown too loose for shrunken bones.

No, she rebelled. *I will not yet release my life and I will not let Priam do so either.*

Strength returned with her decision.

"Well, women, we can sit here and pretend to finish our meal or go to the wall to cheer our men to victory. I, for one, intend the latter." She rose and exited the hall, not waiting to see if any followed.

"This is certainly a night of surprises," Andromache remarked.

Aethra nodded before noting the frozen grip of Helen's hands upon her goblet. "Come," the priestess said gently. "It is time."

Together, Aethra and Andromache ushered her to the group of women who gathered around Hecuba to watch the Achaian march and await the appearance of the Trojan forces.

"Quite an impressive line," Andromache commented, pressing forward to see the enemy approach.

Hecuba turned to her and scowled.

A hand clasped Helen's arm. "What are we to do now?"

The question was asked by Cassandra, whose dust covered cloak testified to the speed with which she had made her way to the palace.

"Pray for Her assistance," Helen answered.

On the plain directly outside the city stood a steep hill which men called the Hill of the Thricket but their gods christened the burial mound of dancing Myrina. The women watched as the Trojans gathered around the site in an impressively short time.

"It is time," Aethra intoned soberly. This time, the women had no difficulty hearing the words shouted above the roar of the marching men.

"Men of Mycenae, you fight this war for my actions!"

Helen watched Alexander step forward and noted how Deiphobus successfully held Hector from intervening. A loud silence descended at her lover's words. "I understand your honor has bound you to fight and I respect your right to uphold the pledges you've made. Still, there is a better way to end this dispute, one that will decide this matter without unnecessary bloodshed to either side." He paused as if drawing breath. "I, Paris of Troy, second son of Priam, challenge Menelaus, King of Sparta, to single combat for the hand of Queen Helen. May this conflict be decided by the victor."

Hecuba's eyes narrowed and she turned to Helen. "Perhaps he's not as complete a fool as I thought."

Helen ignored her, willing her mind to the stillness necessary to call upon the Goddess. Her eyes noted the uneasy silence that spread through the camp, watched as Hector moved forward to protest. Agamemnon and Priam closed about him, silencing his words. As if in a dream, she watched Hector thrust his reluctant spear to the ground with dramatic flair and men cleared an area for Alexander and Menelaus to meet.

Helen's spirit watched dispassionately as her husband moved to the area that had been cleared. *Help him,* she pleaded. *He is ignorant but nonetheless bows to Your will.*

She felt Cassandra and Aethra move to her side, holding her swaying body. *Be with him now, he fights in Your name.*

Spears and swords engaged and Alexander dodged the rage of her former husband.

He is Your servant.

The spirit within her shifted, growing more powerful as if every slash of steel against skin, every drop of blood shed, strengthened her. She watched as Menelaus' recklessness caused him to throw away both his weapons.

He is your tool.

A moment later Menelaus charged forward to overcome her husband with the bulk of his body and the violence of his spirit.

Help him.

Menelaus' determination was more than adequate to collapse Alexander beneath his weight, then raise his prey a moment later, dragging Helen's lover by the helm. A great cloud of dust obscured the women's view as Menelaus twirled Alexander in great, swooping arches.

He is Your servant.

The helm came lose in Menelaus' hand. He ran several paces before realizing the loss of weight behind him and looked in disbelief at the broken chin strap dangling from his hand. His rage grew beyond control. He flung the useless helm at his camp and his pulsing body at the stumbling Alexander. Helen could feel the crush of Alexander's bones, as if they were her own. Her body convulsed with pain. *I call upon You to help him.*

From the base of her spine, power rose, replacing the pain she was enduring with a new, unfamiliar agony. A force not her own moved her to the wall, forcing her to climb to its narrow edge.

"What in this world is she doing!" Hecuba exclaimed, backing away fearfully.

"Do not touch her," Aethra ordered.

Helen was oblivious to them all. The power that controlled her pulled at her gown, ripping it from her breast and torso, exposing the ripeness that held a growing child.

"Men of Mycenae and of Troy," screamed a voice not her own. "Do you know for whom you fight?"

Fog rose from the distant sea, swallowing the surrounding mountains and camps of tents and whining livestock, obscuring everything except Helen and the body that stopped men's breath, stole their ability to move, held their eyes transfixed. Helen beat a heavy fist upon her chest. "Your ignorance is your defeat. Think well upon how you serve Me."

Her scream echoed to the world's end before the power within grew too great to contain within her fragile body. It left her with an immediacy that seared her blood and turned her bones to dust.

What is Your will then? Helen's brain cried, as her body fell in an unconscious heap upon the cold stone of the wall.

Chapter Fourteen

Blood quenched the land between two rivers and men piled the bodies of their comrades on a funeral pyre, trying not to feel the loss of death and the shame of being alive.

Behind him, men stabbed him with their anger and their grief. He accepted both. He was their leader.

Before him, the remains of comrades and friends fed the blazing fire, rising smoke adding new patterns to the darkened sky. The repugnant stench of death carried through the night air.

Hector wondered numbly about the forces of life housed within the bodies turning to ash. The priests said they went to Hades. But Hector knew they were in the air about him, swirling independent circles about the clouds of ash.

Perhaps it was the spirits of those long dead who had appeared upon the battlements where the women stood, plunging men into war.

Some said they saw the beauty of Aphrodite, urging them to fight for love. Others — including priests on both sides — said they saw Apollo demanding victory. Still others claimed that Zeus himself had appeared, demanding to be honored.

Hector was no longer certain what he saw. He knew only that his fantasies of glory and expectations of prestige were awash in blood.

"Commander, they have found the body of Prince Paris," a guard informed him, clearing his throat uncomfortably. "He rests quietly within his room, nursing his injuries."

The small bones of Hector's back moved closer together, becoming an unbreakable rod of determination.

Paris. Whatever had befallen the forces of Mycenae and

Troy, Paris was its cause.

Paris was the reason for the fire before him.

Paris, who had fled the combat and trailed carnage in his dust.

Paris, who had stole Hector's dreams.

Hector turned a hardened face to the men still living and led them to the palace.

"What happened?"

Helen opened her eyes slowly, wincing at the pain that fired her battered body. Her vision focused upon the familiar surroundings of her room, gradually resting upon the face of Aethra.

"Apparently we did not know Her will as well as we thought," the priestess responded, unusual vulnerability present in her eyes. "Here, drink this. It will help strengthen your blood."

The priestess lifted Helen's head and held a foul smelling goblet to her lips. "Drink. It will not hurt your babe."

Helen forced herself to swallow several offending drops. The liquid burned her throat and hit her stomach like a fist, before strengthening her limbs as promised. With strength came memory.

"Alexander!" she cried, panicked.

"Sit back. I gave you a healing remedy, not a miracle cure. Alexander's resting quietly in my quarters. Andromache and Cassandra are attending him. He's got a few cracked bones and a great many bruises but otherwise he's fine. The women will inform us if he awakes."

Helen sunk back again, relieved. "And Menelaus lives as well?" she asked, not needing a response. "What did happen, Aethra?"

The priestess shrugged. "She came through you — for all the good it did. Apparently Cassandra and I were the only two to recognize Her. The men in the camps claimed to have seen this god or that, each hearing a different message. I suspect the words echoed what their hearts desire most," she added bitterly.

"But why?" Helen persisted. "She did not support Alexander's victory nor did She side with Menelaus. She didn't even assure Her own message was heard."

"Perhaps Her words were meant for our ears alone. I certainly felt the sting of ignorance She warned against. Maybe She is departing from the world after all."

Alarm moved Helen forward. "You don't believe that!"

Aethra responded with another tense shrug. "I don't know what to believe. I know She is real — at least within my own heart — and I've certainly felt Her power. Yet She does not place a decisive hand in the affairs before us. Maybe She has decided it is for each to seek Her or not as he wills."

"No simple task when She abandons us."

Aethra looked to the hands upon her lap, stretching the silence between them. "I would tell you something so you might understand my actions, even if I can't explain Hers," the priestess said at last, not meeting Helen's eyes.

"When I was a young girl in my father's house, I used to watch the priestesses of our land with awe and a great deal of envy. Never did it occur to me that these esteemed women sacrificed so much for the power they gained. Day and night, I spoke of nothing but serving Her — to the point where my father, a very pious man, threatened to have me gagged if I did not stop my blabbering.

"I did not care. I knew my destiny and the impatience of youth hurried me toward it. On the night I finally caught up with fate, I was awakened from sleep in my father's palace. The voice of the Goddess awoke me and said I was to go to the tomb of Sphaerus and pour libations. It did not occur to me to question Her words," Aethra added, "though I realize now it may just as easily have been the voice of one of my father's chamber women who beckoned me.

"I waded in the waters of the mainland until I reached the island of Sphaeria. I began to perform the ritual, when I suddenly saw a man emerging from the water I had just crossed."

Her smile broadened. "I suppose I should have been alarmed, but I was not. Moonlight reflected from his golden hair and from the water droplets that clung to his beautiful, muscled body. His eyes were the gray of the truth and when he said I was meant to love him, I did not question.

"I was quite foolish really. My fantasies of the Goddess and my budding interest in men combined to chase intelligent thought from my head.

"Our union was ecstatic, a joining with each other and the earth below us and the stars above. A man and a woman. Coming together to become more than either." Aethra looked to Helen then, noting understanding in the other's eyes.

"When I awoke the next morning, he was gone and I — as I later learned — was pregnant. Nine moons after, I gave birth to a son, a beautiful boy who would grow into a heroic man, a child of the Goddess." She continued, shaking her head with the disbelief that still held her. "It wasn't until many years later that I learned my lover was not a god but a king. A man. A man with a wife. And without an heir, save for the one he fathered upon me. Many nights I spoke to the stars, seeking answers. Should I go to him or should I stay? When fear overcame my desire, I told myself that our night together was colored by the longing of a romantic young girl. When the urge to go sucked at my bones like the waves of a swirling tide, I told myself that I was being irresponsible to the obligations I had assumed in my homeland.

"I was faced with one of those choices that thereafter determines the road of life, stranded at the fork that would magically disappear once I took a single step in one direction or the other. There would be no going back.

"For many moons, I stayed at the crossroads of my decision. I would perform my duties as priestess, resentful that they pulled me from my thoughts of love. I would think of love and be resentful of its power to make me negligent in my duties. My indecision became an impossible attempt to live in two worlds that could not coexist. To remain indecisive I had to die, inside, where death is most deadly.

"Looking back, I believe Theseus suffered from my indecisiveness as much as I. When I was not preoccupied, I set myself to the task of rearing him to priestess ways. I believed I needed his support should I decide to return with him to his father. And if I did not return, I wanted him to institute Her rule when he assumed the role of king.

"I knew, of course, that I would show him the way to lift the rock from the sword and sandals — the trick the Attican king devised to ensure his populace that he did indeed have a son.

"'My son will know how to do this,' his father had said when he explained his plan to me. 'Or you will figure it out for him.' He smiled then, that intelligent, beautiful smile that I loved from the moment I saw him. He had a great gift, that king, for when he bestowed that smile upon me I felt I was beautiful and intelligent as well.

"When I remembered that smile, I thought for sure I would return to him when Theseus set forth." Her expression turned suddenly serious. "And then the dreams began, horrible night visions that stole my sleep. Night upon night, I was paralyzed by the horror of great darkness cast upon our land by the hands of the priests who created gods more to their understanding — and their liking. The only light to be found illumined from Sparta. It was then that I knew I must stay in Troezen and do what I could to support that light.

"I sent Rhemensia to your homeland, where she assumed

the role of waiting woman to the queen to best discover the unusual woman I knew would champion the light. When no such was found, she observed the birth of every child within the kingdom. Still no one appeared to justify my belief. I think even Rhemensia — the most ardent supporter of my prophesy — grew skeptical.

"And then the queen gave birth, casting forth four babes at once from the small confines of her womb. The tales told about her birth captured Rhemnesia's attention. But it was the sight of one child in particular — the most beautiful, radiant being she had even seen — that interested her most. When she first set eyes upon you, she knew you to be the woman we sought.

"She set out to befriend you — a task which Leda made horribly easy — and to teach you Her ways." The priestess turned her eyes upon Helen once more. "Doubt it not that she loved you well, even though her mission began as duty to the Goddess. I saw her tears behind the indifferent words of the messenger she sent to me and her anger at your treatment at the hands of Leda and Clytemnestra."

The priestess' eyes narrowed as she watched tears flow silently down Helen's sculptured cheeks. She had the compassion to allow Helen release, looking beyond the woman as she continued.

"We had thought to wait until you were old enough and then bring you to Troezen to complete your training. I had not anticipated that Rhemensia would be exiled from Sparta, nor," she cringed, "that Theseus had become so hateful. I had thought to marry him to you, to restore Her ways over vast and powerful kingdoms. Perhaps there is no greater blindness than that which seizes a mother who looks upon her children," she added bitterly.

"When I learned what he had done to you, I knew he was no longer my son." She lowered her eyes to Helen once more. "I felt She was handing down Her strictest justice for my finding in you the daughter I longed for with all my heart. I think that is why I was so angered when you thought to make Alexander your consort — I felt you chose him over me. When I could think more clearly, I saw that you were right to do as you did. Choosing a consort in the old ways would do much to restore Her rule."

"If only She saw it that way," Helen interupted bitterly.

"Indeed. But She has not. Or perhaps Her power is weakening as men's beliefs are channeled to the new gods." She ignored Helen's alarmed look and continued. "Note you that She did appear and Her actions did save your chosen consort's life. And yet each one who saw Her confused Her with their own de-

sires. In the face of such confusion, I don't blame Her for retreating from this world."

*Retreating? But why would She, whose power is so great,
need to retreat? Why didn't She simply impose Herself upon the
minds and hearts of men?*

"I do not know why She does not insist upon being known,"
Aethra said, as if Helen had voiced the questions aloud. "In all
the years I have dedicated myself to Her ways, it is I who have
searched for Her. She has never come to me unbidden. I can
only assume that this, too, is Her will. How else would we grow
if not through the search for Her?

"It is this I believe. As I believe my own search is not ended.
I must return to Troezen."

"No!" the refusal left Helen's lips, even as she realized that
some part of her knew Aethra's decision when she had opened
her eyes. *I cannot live through this on my own.*

"This is not my journey any longer," Aethra was explaining. "I am uncertain where my road will lead but I, as you, must
continue down my path."

"Take me with you," Helen whispered, begged, forgetting
Alexander, the babe within her womb, Menelaus — none of these
seemed important compared to the loss of Aethra.

"Is that where She calls you to go as well?" Aethra asked,
her tone that of the high priestess Helen resented and loved.

"I don't know where She calls me," Helen responded evasively.

"Then it would seem you best stay until you do," Aethra
said decisively, before leaning to give Helen a sacred blessing.
"We shall meet again — in this world or the next. Remember,
She has been with you always, through me and sometimes despite me. She will not abandon you. Nor have I."

"You cannot leave. They will not allow it."

"They cannot stop me," Aethra responded simply. "But I
must go now, under the cover of confusion that still blinds them."

"Cassandra. Andromache. You cannot not leave without
saying good-bye," Helen's voice sounded childish. She did not
care.

"There is no time, child. I must go."

Through her tears, Helen saw Aethra's pain cascade from
her own eyes. *She feels it too,* Helen thought. *I can use her vulnerability, her pain, to make her stay.* "May Her blessing follow
you on your journey and always," she forced herself to say, returning the priestess' blessing.

Aethra smiled a watery smile before grabbing a small pack

hidden beyond the bed and melting from the room like fog.

She's gone. Gone.

The words filled Helen's mind, leaving room for no other thought, crowding her heart so she did not feel the pain. She focused upon them, allowing herself to disappear within their simplicity.

Gone.

She did not know how long she sat before Cassandra and Andromache burst into her room, interrupting her reverie.

"He's awake," Cassandra blurted.

"With impeccable timing as usual," Andromache added. "It seems Hector and his forces have returned. The guards we set outside Aethra's rooms wanted nothing more than to join the returning warriors. I told them they'd have more to fear from my bludgeoning fists than from the entire Trojan army if they left."

"Where's Aethra?" Cassandra demanded, looking about the room.

Gone.

"Andromache, why don't you go and see what state Hector is in," Helen forced herself to say. "Cassandra, help me dress. I must see Alexander."

Without hesitation the two women did her bidding.

"We saw Her," Cassandra said, dragging Helen from the bed when it was clear the woman could not rise on her own. "Andromache and I saw Her. One moment you stood there and the next you were someone else entirely. Those fools did not recognize Her. They say they saw their own gods telling them whatever their ignorance wanted to hear. Even Hecuba did not recognize Her, for all that she stood right beside you. The queen claims to have seen a blazing light that told her youth would be restored to Priam once more. Blah. Where's Aethra? We need someone to explain this?"

Helen slipped into the cloak Cassandra held for her, leaning heavily on the other girl's arm. She had not wanted to tell Andromache of Aethra's departure, fearing the warrior woman would do something rash to stop the priestess' flight. Now she found that she was no more anxious to tell Cassandra.

"The experience has drained me utterly," she said, stalling.

"So I can see," Cassandra responded, slipping an arm about Helen's waist. "You're as weak as a newborn. I'm sure Aethra has some potion to strengthen you. Where is she?"

Helen looked directly into Cassandra's eyes. "She's gone.

Her own journey has called her back to Troezen."

A handful of emotions played across Cassandra's delicate features — pain, anger, betrayal. Helen saw her own experience reflected on the face of another.

"She could have at least waited. There are safer ways out of the palace than the ones she knows," Cassandra snapped, settling on anger.

Helen understood the pain behind Cassandra's hostility. "She wanted nothing more than to wait and say good bye to you personally," she said gently. "You have grown quite important to her."

Cassandra bowed her head and Helen thought — hoped — the girl would weep to release her pain. Footsteps bounding up the stairs beyond the door kept her from doing so.

"Hector is demanding that Paris be brought to the dining hall," Andromache explained, running into the room. "He has sent several men to carry Paris down if it is shown he can't walk himself. From the look in Hector's eyes, he would not mind if your husband was flung down the stairs."

"What should we do?" Cassandra asked. She and Andromache looked to Helen expectantly.

They think that because the Goddess inhabited my body that She's granted me some special wisdom, Helen thought. *They're going to be terribly disappointed.*

"I must see Alexander," she said and stifled the embarrassment that rose to her cheeks as Andromache immediately joined Cassandra to usher her into his room.

"I'm going as fast as I can, man," Alexander was saying to one of the several guards Hector had sent to deliver him.

Helen swayed as she looked upon his face, which swelled in a meadow of colorful bruises.

He saw her there and his voice softened. "It looks worse than it is," he said, his swollen lips moving to form a ghost of his previous smile. "My ribs are bruised and they say I broke a toe. Nothing a few days rest won't heal."

"Alexander," she moved unsteadily between the guards that surrounded their bed, dropping to her knees beside him.

"I was ordered to bring him down immediately," one of the men said, squaring his jaw.

"Stand back and give him a moment to speak with his wife," Andromache snapped. "Do you think he's going to vanish if you wait a few moments?"

The slight narrowing of the man's eyes indicated that that was exactly what he thought.

"Just do what she says," grumbled one of the guard's Andromache had set at Alexander's door. "I'm sure Prince Hector will understand the needs of a demanding wife."

Reluctantly, the man waved his comrades back, giving Helen and Alexander a handspan of privacy.

"I saw Her," Alexander whispered urgently, wincing as he grasped Helen's hand. "She told me to run and to renounce my ignorance. The glory I seek will be mine!"

It seems each person did indeed interpret Her vision to speak to the desires of his heart. Helen could guess what Alexander's interpretation was by the unnatural gleam in his eye.

"My love," she began carefully. "You do realize that She saved you for the greater glory of serving Her at my side."

"And how better to do that than to prove myself triumphant in this war. She has meant for me to rise above the common fighters — including the esteemed Hector — not to challenge but one man alone."

Despair reminded Helen of her own exhaustion. How could she make him see clearly?

"Enough," the man charged with escorting Alexander ordered. "Prince Hector will not thank me for delaying here any longer. Nor will it bode well for you," he added with a threatening look in Alexander's direction.

"I have no desire to stay abed any longer." Alexander responded, wincing again as he forced himself to rise. "We have a war to win."

The guard's eyebrows rose almost as much as Andromache's.

"We might as well follow and discover what new complication has arisen in Her plan," the princess said.

She joined Cassandra in helping Helen rise and together the three made their way to the dining hall.

"We'd best take our places," Cassandra advised wisely as they entered the hall.

Hector stood before his chair, failing to control the anger that shook him. Alexander sat at his own seat, his hands clutching sore ribs.

"What have you to say for yourself, coward?"

Alexander looked annoyingly puzzled and Hector wondered if his brother's escape had cost him the few wits he possessed.

"The Goddess saved me," Alexander answered at last.

Hector's control vanished. He overthrew his chair and advanced upon his brother. "The goddess saved you? You? You are not worth a single man butchered this day by the sword of Diomedes or any of the Achaians whose blood heated in the flame of his rage. You? Our men were slaughtered by the hundreds! But the goddess saved you? The same goddess who brought your ill-fated carcass to this land in the first place?" Hector's punching hand closed, ready to deliver the force of his rage in a way more eloquent than his tongue was able.

"It was not Aphrodite who saved me but the Great Mother who rules all," Alexander said stubbornly. "She saved me to win this war."

Audible gasps, mingled with outrage and agreement, stirred from the crowd of men at Hector's back. Helen cringed. *How can these ignorant warriors possibly believe that She will support them in their senseless carnage. The world is being turned upside down by shortsighted men. No wonder the Goddess has chosen to retreat from it!*

A beautiful man with sun-kissed hair and eyes the color of summer grass rose to stand at Hector's side. "Whether it was the Goddess or a demon from Hades, it seems clear that you are to lead us to victory," he said to Hector, placing a warning hand upon his arm.

"That's Aeneas," Andromache whispered. "Son of Anchises. It is said that he was beckoned here by the goddess Aphrodite to fight beside the Trojans. It's claimed that her hand will save him from harm no matter what the war's outcome."

"Well at least she didn't scramble his brains as she did my brother's," Cassandra added, eyeing him in such a way that Helen knew it was not the man's brains that captured the princess' attention.

Hector shrugged off Aeneas hand with considerably less force than Helen expected. "You'd best pray that your goddess continues to protect you," he growled at Alexander. "We and the Achaians have set a truce to honor the brave men who died. Once completed, we will undoubtedly continue the warfare that should have ended this day. I expect you to be at the fore of battle." He turned and reclaimed his seat, waiting for his hands to cease trembling before lifting the wine goblet to his lips.

"Now what?" Andromache asked. "It doesn't seem that any of our men share the wisdom of ending this war."

"Then we'll just have to appeal to someone wiser," Helen growled.

Her own anger had grown so great that she did not remember to mind that Cassandra and Andromache had turned to her for direction once more.

CHAPTER FIFTEEN

*A*s *if I need to hear the mating patterns of two farm animals*, Clytemnestra thought.

"And so you see, my lady, my neighbor begets his calves for free and charges me for repairs to his fence, though the simplest man among us knows a bull left alone like that will charge a cow in season."

And even the simplest farmer could have settled this dispute before it became a third generation fight that led to the death of two sons, Clytemnestra thought in frustration.

The owner of the bull stood with killing eyes upon his neighbor.

"A bull allowed to run riot will cause as much damage to your family and neighbors as this dispute has threatened to do," Clytemnestra said coolly. "From this season forth, you shall see that the animal is pastured to the far side of the land whenever the heifer is ready to mate. In the interim, I hold you responsible for the broken fence."

The man looked annoyed while his neighbor allowed himself a smug grin.

Clytemnestra turned her attention to him and proceeded to alleviate his satisfaction. "For generations, your cow has been sired at no cost and what would appear to be very little inconvenience. For the next two seasons, your cow will continue to be sired by your neighbor's bull — which will attend her by entering through a gate — and the calves will be awarded to him.

"Beginning three seasons from now, the animals will be allowed to peaceably mate and the offspring shall be awarded to each of your households in turn. I expect your households will get along as well as your animals from this day forth."

The men looked at each other and Clytemnestra noted the spark of animosity that flew between them.

"Hear me now," she continued, "If anything should happen to either the bull or the cow designated for the coupling, all your animals will be forfeit to the palace."

The men grumbled their assent.

"And may the goddess bless each of you in this agreement," she added by way of dismissal.

The men's querulous faces gave way to awe at the mention of the goddess. They saw what they wished to see. *Simple acts have the most power.*

Clytemnestra raised a finger to signal the guard to escort the farmers from her hall.

As tedious as these daily petitions were, they provided Clytemnestra with an easy way to establish her rule among the populace and strengthen the connection between herself and the goddess in their minds. By now, most of them knew of her equitable solutions — indeed, it felt as if most of them had been through her doors in the past several seasons.

She sighed and prepared herself for the next — and gratefully last — public meeting of the day.

Her gown dragged softly on the floor as she made her way to the training grounds. She stood for a moment and drank the sight of her lover. Aegithus' dark hair clung to his shapely skull, his muscles glistened in the afternoon sun. Across from him stood a gangly boy, intent on causing harm to that beautiful body with a wooden practice sword. Aegisthus met him blow for blow and went down suddenly, startling the boy completely.

"My lord?" the child asked timidly, all blinking eyes and concern.

Aegisthus waited until the child drew closer and suddenly sprang on him. The flat of his blade connected with the boy's side and sent him halfway across the courtyard.

"Never let up on an enemy until you are certain that he is dead or disabled. Never. The fight is not over, the war not won, until then."

The boy looked at his instructor, admiration burning away the constellation of lights that swirled before his eyes.

Aegisthus turned his attention to Clytemnestra. "My lady, as you can see, your men are advancing in their weaponry," he said, his voice carrying through the noise of the training ground.

Her men.

"Indeed, they are," she acknowledged and proceeded to skirt the edges of the practice skirmishes, calling personalized complements to the youth and guardsmen.

No matter that they were but half-trained boys. They had no family connections to the existing guard and standing army; when the time came, they would follow her command unburdened by the hesitation they would have felt if they were fighting kinsmen.

She left the practice field, satisfied, and retired to her chambers for a much deserved bath and massage. Her mind turned to the new moon festival scheduled for the evening, a time to further cement the loyalty of the women.

A time to extract loyalty from her daughter.

Electra shared her father's complete lack of understanding for the goddess' blessing. It showed. No vision would come through the girl, no matter which herbs Clytemnestra gave her to swallow.

All things will smooth over in time, she reminded herself and shifted her attention from her troublesome child to the other participants.

Over thirty maidens would lend their strength to hers during this powerful ritual. She had selected them carefully — common daughters of retired guardsman and craftsman from throughout the country. Young enough to be malleable; old enough to delight in their chosen place as the queen's attendants and to boast of their status and power to their families and neighbors. Like the guardsman currently under training, they too would be reared to her rule, loyal to her sovereignty. When Agamemnon died in this blessed war over her sister, her people would pass the line of rule to her. And if by some curse of fate Agamemnon remained alive, her populace would not sit idly by when the king who abandoned them returned and attempted to assume leadership. Perhaps when she was proclaimed ruler she would birth a daughter by Aegisthus — a daughter who would be the successor that Electra was not.

Electra moved quietly among the rooms, seeing ghosts in every corner. Her father. Her sister. Loyal guardsmen who fought a distant war.

The ghosts were comforting.

"Electra, it's time for your lesson. Come in here. Orestes is too fidgety today for me to come to you."

Orestes was fidgety everyday but Electra came as Rhytia requested.

Her brother saw her approach from behind the makeshift fence Rhytia had erected to keep him from running riot through the room. Electra smiled and realized that it must have been a long time since she had done so; her face felt strange at the unfamiliar movement.

"Ectra! Ectra!"

"Yes, come here little monkey so I may see how fidgety you are." She lifted him above the fence and allowed his chubby hands to twine about her neck. The touch brought tears she did not understand; she turned quickly, hoping Rhytia would not see.

Rhytia did see, as she saw everything her charges experienced.

"Well, bring him here, child. Perhaps he will sleep on your lap. No, no sit on the floor here before my chair and I will brush your hair and tell you a tale before your lessons."

Like a puppy separated too soon from her bitch, Rhytia thought as the child pretended indifference and sat herself before the woman.

"No, Orestes, you must sit quietly," Electra said, repositioning the baby on her lap.

Rhytia's heart broke at the girl's tone, that of an adult trapped in the body of a child not quite eleven winters.

"Our last story led us to the creation of Mount Olympus and the admission of Prometheus and Epimetheus to the realm of the immortals."

"A reward for remaining neutral in the battle between Zeus and the Titans," Electra interjected.

Rhytia kept her combing steady, wondering if the girl would be similarly rewarded for remaining indifferent to the silent battle raging between her parents. She returned to her story. "Despite his acceptance among the gods, Prometheus secretly held the mortals from whom he ascended closest to his heart. When Zeus took his place as king of Olympus, men and gods no longer ate and drank together. Zeus decreed that the gods were supreme over man and that man should make sacrifices to the gods. He placed Prometheus as the mediator of the sacrifice between god and man. Now Prometheus, still partial to man and angry at Zeus' arrogant behavior, took an ox and cut it up. He then offered Zeus a choice of two portions — the first contained distastefully displayed meat, the second contained bones, which Prometheus artfully smothered in fat. Zeus, of course, chose the deceptively appetizing fare. Upon realizing the deception, he became furious at man even though the choice of offering was his own. He raged for nights on end and finally decided to withhold fire from mankind."

"Fire," Electra said, considering. "Why not food or water?"

Rhytia patted Electra's head in approval. *Always thinking. Would that her mother would prize the girl's intelligence instead of scorning her for her disinterest in the goddess Clytemnestra herself revered.* "Without fire," she explained, "men cannot forge tools or bake crafts. Man cannot develop, cannot grow. What cannot grow, dies.

"Prometheus could not bare to see the extinction of his beloved mortals so he went to the island of Lemos, where the god Hephaestus kept his forges. He stole a brand of holy fire, which he enclosed in a hollow stalk and secretly carried back to man.

"Zeus, of course, was in a rage when he learned of this. He heaped all sorts of evil on the lands of men. He sent floods and earthquakes, plagues and famine. Prometheus combated each and every catastrophe. Perhaps Zeus became bored with inflicting suffering. Or perhaps he realized that, while mankind was worried over the devastation he wrought, they could not sacrifice to him. Instead of continuing to punish mankind, he chose to punish Prometheus alone. He arranged for other gods to capture Prometheus and to chain him upon the rock of Mount Caucus. He then set a winged monster with teeth so sharp they've never been seen before or since to devour Prometheus' liver. Each day the monster fed upon Prometheus' organ. Each night what it ate grew again so that the torture was unending."

"So he saved mankind and suffered for it," Electra stated and Rhytia's heart ached at the cynicism in the young girl.

"Sometimes it hurts to stand alone for what you believe." The platitude sounded trite even to Rhytia's ears.

Electra turned and gave her the bored, polite look children offer well meaning adults.

"Well, let's get to the tallies then," Rhytia said, lifting the sleeping baby from Electra's lap.

"Yes, we must get on with it so I can prepare for another of mother's endless ceremonies."

Rhytia stayed wisely quiet.

Electra knew the goddess did not exist.

A goddess would not care for the chanting of ignorant peasant women. She would not concern herself with one little kingdom when she had to supervise the growth of crops, the fall of rain, the rise and set of sun and moon.

A goddess would not allow a girl of ten winters to out smart one of her most ardent disciples, as Electra did with Clytemnestra.

Electra added hazel and laurel to the wine brewing at the counter. No one questioned the lonely, lost girl who assisted in the preparation of the sacred wine. They all presumed Electra was following her mother's command. She added a strong dose of fennel to cover the smell of hazel lest anyone discover she rendered the sight-inducing potion useless.

She learned herbology from an unsuspecting kitchen woman who thought to amuse a solitary child. But Electra used her learning well; she would no longer allow her consciousness to be stolen, her voice used by a being that was inside her but not of her. She braced herself on the first night she drank the doctored portion, fearing her efforts wasted, feeling the joy of deliverance when she did not slip into darkness. Other women in the circle continued to chant ridiculously with her mother. She watched and listened, pretending trance, present for the first time.

And she understood.

Her mother fabricated the goddess to deprive her father of his land. To set herself up as ruler. To wield power over the ignorant women who populated her circle.

If there was a goddess, her mother would know Electra only pretended to be drugged. And Clytemnestra would know how carefully Electra plotted to thwart her plans.

CHAPTER SIXTEEN

"**I** haven't seen any sign that Agamemnon is half so reasonable," Cassandra complained as she paced the path she had worn in the women's gardens.

Andromache and Hecuba had been as disappointed as the princess by Aethra's sudden departure, though the latter had hid it far better.

"What more could be expected of foreigners?" Hecuba had snapped.

But in her upset, the queen had forgotten to forbid Helen her daily meetings with Cassandra.

"Agamemnon tried to stop this war at its beginning, you may remember," Helen said to Cassandra now. "It was only Menelaus' unreasonableness that rendered his attempt impossible."

"Agamemnon also refused to return Chryseis to Chryses, even when the plague threatened to wipe out his forces," Cassandra pointed out.

"Chryses is an arrogant fool. Anyone would sense would hesitate to answer the demands of that one," Helen said patiently.

Cassandra stopped her annoying pacing to consider. "Good point," she conceded before resuming both her trudging and her cantankerous tone. "But that still does not mean you can talk to him. There's no way you can slip through the enemy lines." She raised a hand to interrupt Helen's argument. "We cannot count upon the Goddess' assistance just because we will it so. The Lady is very unpredictable in Her timing and may not oblige us by turning you into a soldier at the appropriate moment."

"Then we'll just have to take care of that ourselves," Helen snapped, willing herself, unsuccessfully, not to be baited by Cassandra's querulous nature.

Cassandra looked at her skeptically. "It would take a mighty heavy set of armor to hide those curves of yours. And even if we did, your beautiful face would shine through. You'd be recognized in a moment and then where would we be?"

"No worse off than we are now," Helen mumbled.

"But no better either," Cassandra retorted. "No, you should not be the one to go. I should."

"I can't ask you to do that," Helen protested.

"Oh don't argue. It's my homeland that's at stake, remember? I can slip among the Achaians far more easily than you and have Agamemnon meet you in one of the secret rooms of the temple." Her chin took on the stubborn line Helen had seen far too often in Alexander.

"Why would Agamemnon follow you anywhere, let alone into the Trojan camp?"

"If he's as reasonable as you say, he'll see the sense of it," Cassandra drawled. "I'll take one of your rings just to be safe."

"There's no way to be safe behind enemy lines. You're the daughter of the king they're fighting. You'd be in more danger than I."

"If they know anything about me at all, they'll know how unlikely it is that my parents will ransom me," Cassandra responded dryly. "Besides, I won't take any unnecessary chances. I'll stay here the next several nights and watch the Achaian camp from the battlements to see if Agamemnon has a regular bed time routine that we can exploit. I'll just wander around in my nightdress, claiming I can't sleep. The guards all think I'm crazy anyway. I'll also scout the area to determine the best point of entry — something you certainly cannot do. And we'll pick our time carefully, a time when the fighting is not too great so the guards on each side are not as vigilant."

"I still don't like it," Helen said. "But I suspect I'll have as much luck changing your mind as I have changing the mind of that stubborn brother of yours."

"Less," Cassandra said, smiling sweetly.

Helen had thought that, once decided, they could implement their plan immediately. She should have anticipated the wait — it seemed all she had done since arriving in Illium.

"I have noted that Agamemnon often goes to a large rock some distance from his tent when the rest of the leaders retire for sleep," Cassandra whispered as they joined the women for another afternoon spent watching the men from the palace walls. "And I think I've found a good way to pass the walls and reach him. Now it's only a matter of finding the right time."

"Stop whispering so we can hear what's happening," Hecuba snapped.

Since the famed day when the Goddess appeared, the men of both sides joined in minor skirmishes designed to test the other's strength without engaging in full battle. This day promised to be no different and Cassandra shrugged as she and Helen pressed closer to the wall to discover what held Hecuba's interest.

"Doesn't Priam look strong — and so young. It won't be long before he takes command of the troops once more," Hecuba exclaimed as she had every day since the great light had appeared beside her and told her it would be so.

"I think the visitation by your Goddess rattled her wits," Andromache observed, her attention drawn by the unusual scene below. "What is happening down there?"

The women shook their heads to indicate their ignorance. From where they stood, it appeared as if the war leaders on both sides were doing the same.

Two men from opposite sides were engaged in a senseless attempt to give each other armor. From helms to sandals, the two stripped and swapped garments in answer to whatever bizarre challenge they had posed.

"We'd best meet with Agamemnon soon. Otherwise the men may begin to battle in earnest out of sheer boredom," Cassandra whispered. "Be ready tomorrow night," she added, slipping from the throngs of women to make her way back to the temple.

Helen could not sleep for trepidation of what the morrow would bring. Her stomach roiled with discomfort and even Alexander's nightly visit did not soothe her.

"You do not look well," he noted, eyeing her critically.

"I'm just tired," she answered evasively. "Perhaps you should rejoin the men."

He kissed her hand and she hid her relief as she watched him go.

What would he think if he knew I was going to confer with his enemy before the moon rises again? she wondered, ignoring the thought as pain shot through her belly once more.

By first light, the pain was worse, intensifying to a cramp that she could no longer confuse with fear. Her anguished cry rang through the halls, bringing the women rushing to her cham-

ber.

"Get Cassandra," she implored, her teeth clenched against a second, painful spasm.

"It is unseemly for a maiden and a princess to attend a birth," Hecuba said primly.

"It's unseemly to argue with a woman in this horrid state," snapped Andromache, whose dark complexion turned whiter than the snow topping the mountains of Sparta. "I'll fetch her from the temple," she added to Helen before running from the room.

Helen focused inward, easily able to ignore Hecuba's disapproving clucking and the bustle of the many women drawn to the scene. It seemed the moon had moved a full cycle before Andromache returned, pulling a disheveled Cassandra at her side.

"Well, this is an interesting time for a birth," Cassandra remarked. She did not sound pleased.

"Make it stop," Helen begged as yet again pain sliced at her abdomen.

Cassandra's surprisingly competent hands felt Helen's body. "Only you can do that," the priestess responded. "Come now, you've been through this before," she added gently.

Helen screamed anew. "This is different," she groaned. "Worse, this is worse."

Cassandra felt her abdomen thoughtfully.

"I see," she turned her attention to one of the waiting women. "Help her walk. It will go quicker."

But Helen couldn't stand and Cassandra at last agreed to let her stay where she was.

"I need Alexander," Helen moaned. "He must see his son."

Cassandra lost her patience. "No wonder this is so hard. Stop whimpering and pay attention."

Helen growled at her and used her anger to push harder, harder, until she felt the child squeezed into life, until she should have felt release.

"Keep pushing," Cassandra ordered.

She did, unable to stop, unable to claim her child.

A second scream wailed through the air.

"Twins," Cassandra said, holding the babes like prizes of war.

"You should take something to prevent this from happening again," Andromache whispered. "Oh, don't look so shocked — even we common women know a thing or two about herb lore

— if only those remedies we need most. I've given my lord an heir and I'd rather face a whole army of enemy swords than go through that again," she added defensively.

"Everyone must leave now," Cassandra ordered, saving Helen a response. "She must rest."

"Twins," Hecuba muttered. "From my experience, they bring nothing but trouble."

"Yes, yes mother. I'm perfectly aware of your thoughts on this matter. Now please leave," Cassandra snapped.

"Hmph. Ordered about by my own daughter after she acts like a common midwife."

"Yes, it is indeed horrible mother," Andromache said, tossing Cassandra a wink as she led the queen beyond the room's doors.

"Well," Cassandra said, when the last woman took her leave. "It seems our plans are on hold once more."

"Not for long," Helen said, shifting the weight of the babes to make herself more comfortable.

"Don't be silly. Those darling sons of yours tore you pretty badly. You need time to recover."

"I'll recover soon enough," Helen responded stubbornly, her determination to end the war increasing as new life drank from her breasts.

CHAPTER SEVENTEEN

In less time than Cassandra thought prudent, Helen walked down a neglected stairwell, carefully shielding her sole source of light. She felt her way through the maze of corridors, hoping she followed Cassandra's directions exactly.

"The south stairwell will lead you to a street directly below the temple," Cassandra had said, after showing her how to work the lock that opened the concealed doorway along a little used corridor.

Helen no longer cared where the passage led her as long as her destination had fresh air. She pushed against the door, certain that the entire castle heard its protesting wail, and gratefully found herself on the street described. She extinguished the torch and thrust it in the doorway to keep the door ajar and allow her reentry.

She told herself to remember to ask for a new torch before she left the temple, pushed the hood of her robe about her head and walked toward her destination.

Tonight, she thought, *tonight it will end.*

The strongest herbs do not cover the smell of a dead man's burning flesh.

If Zeus has in fact shown himself to me, he's clearly forsaken me again, Agamemnon thought and cringed as yet another man's skeleton popped in the flames.

He walked away from the funeral pyre, seeking solitude on the beach. His men would not question him; anything he did would be seen as the brave act of a warrior king. Such was the blessing of the commander.

And when the sun made its final descent in the sky, each man would lament his dead friends and blame their warrior king. Such was the curse of a commander.

As the others retired, he moved to the solitary rock beyond his tent, seeking answers in the stars. Beyond him, he heard waves gently crash in arrival against the shore, sounding strangely like a female voice calling his name.

"Lord Agamemnon," the voice persisted.

He turned, expecting to see an image from his own mind to confirm that he was indeed mad. The small girl in simple priestess robes was too real for even his deplorably active imagination.

"Come quickly," the girl hissed. "Princess Helen awaits you in the temple of Apollo. She would meet with you secretly."

Agamemnon's warrior eyes scanned the space beyond the girl, seeking enemies lurking in the shadows.

"There's no one else here," the girl snapped. "At least not yet. And if men do arrive, I'd say it is my head — not yours — that they'll be after. Here," she thrust forward a hand containing a ring of gold fitted about a stone of amber. "She said you'd recognize it as her sister wears its duplicate."

Agamemnon reached for the ring tentatively, still expecting sabotage.

"It won't bite you," the girl went on relentlessly. "Now are you coming or not?"

An unlikely trap, Agamemnon thought. *Women are far more polite when they ensnare you in some scheme.*

"Let's go," he said decisively.

The girl produced a worn cloak with a heavy hood. "Put this on," she commanded. "If you're seen within the Trojan walls, it will be both our heads."

If all Trojan women are like this one, we'd do best to surrender now, Agamemnon thought, donning the garment and following the girl along a shadowy path to the temple.

"Helen said you were honorable. Do not use your knowledge of this path to attack innocent people," she admonished.

"I doubt not that you would lay an ambush to deter me if ever I should try," Agamemnon retorted. "May I ask with whom I have the pleasure of traveling?"

The girl stopped to face him. "Cassandra, daughter of Priam and former priestess of Apollo."

Of course. The mad one, Agamemnon thought, resigned now

to whatever treachery awaited him.

"Only one as crazy as I would lead my people's enemy behind these walls," Cassandra said sarcastically, reading his thoughts from the lines of his face.

"And only one as crazy as I would follow," Agamemnon responded.

The girl nodded in dubious approval and led him to what appeared to be a back garden of the temple. "Wait here, while I check the halls," she ordered, throwing back her cloak to reveal surprisingly beautiful features. She was gone before Agamemnon could protest and reappeared before his concerns about a trap could return.

"This way," she whispered.

He followed her down the stone hallway, barely lit by a single torch set upon the right wall.

"In here," she said, pulling back a curtain that revealed an even darker room. Agamemnon barely made out the figure on the far bench as his eyes adjusted to the dim light.

"I'll lead him back when you're done and wait in the hall to make sure no one happens this way until then," Cassandra said. "Just be quick," she admonished before slipping away and drawing the curtain once more.

The shadowy figure rose and approached him slowly. "Agamemnon," the beautiful voice acknowledged, as the even more lovely features became clear.

"Helen. Sister," Agamemnon responded, choking back pain as he saw the girl he called daughter in the face of the woman before him.

"I'm glad you've come," Helen said warmly, hoping he did not sense her discomfort.

Agamemnon had aged a hundred winters in the scant dozen since she saw him last. Lines of worry were etched upon his face, the dark hair that escaped his hood was liberally decorated with gray. Only his eyes remained the same, deep brown globes of wisdom and strength and compassion.

"I almost believed this would be a trick," he said and tenderly embraced his former sister-by-marriage. "Do you know how dangerous this is?"

"As well as you," she responded and ushered him to the room's bench. "I would not be doing this if it wasn't necessary." Her eyes turned serious. "You wonder why I've requested you here," Helen said, unable to hide her nervousness any longer.

Agamemnon nodded.

"I need you to end this war."

Agamemnon stared at her for several heart beats and then, for the first time in many seasons, felt a smile caress his lips. *I need you to end this war she said*, with the same stubborn assurance he had so treasured in Iphigeneia.

"Do not laugh at me," she bristled, mistaking his response. "I have done everything I can to stop it from within the Trojan palace — even to setting Alexander's life against Menelaus' to avert unnecessary bloodshed. That did not work and Hector is too stubborn to listen. So now I appeal to you."

"I wondered why Alexander challenged Menelaus, despite Hector's obvious disapproval," Agamemnon said slowly. "Did you plan the rest of what happened that day as well."

Helen looked down at her hands. "I did not. The rest was at the will of the Goddess. Did you see Her?" She looked up with an earnestness that puzzled Agamemnon.

For many days after the fateful event, Agamemnon had listened to men argue about what they had seen until he doubted his own vision. He had thought he saw the face of Iphigeneia, beckoning him with words he could not hear clearly.

"I don't know what I saw," he said truthfully. "I don't seem to have much talent for hearing the gods accurately," he added thinking of his dream of Zeus.

"Well, you're certainly not alone in that," Helen said dejectedly.

"Nor are you alone in wanting to end this war. I would do what I could to leave this place and not return but the men are intent on victory — particularly after the visions they had."

"Why is everything always so confused?" Helen asked peevishly, then shrugged, noting Agamemnon's puzzlement.

"I will continue to do what I can here," she said at last. "I only ask that you do the same on your side."

"You have my word on it," Agamemnon responded seriously, wondering what, if anything, he was capable of doing. "I won't even ask if you'd consider returning to Menelaus," he added, "I only wish I could have warned you of his madness before the marriage was held."

"There are times when I've considered returning," Helen said slowly. "It's no joy to be in a palace where the queen hates me, the household blames me for the destruction of their peace and the man I love has so little time for me. I rarely even see my son and do not doubt the two I have just birthed will be taken away soon enough. I don't seem very good at holding onto my children," she added with a bitter smile.

Agamemnon flinched and dropped his eyes. "Nor did I prove

effective in protecting the one you gave to my hands," he said.

Helen's heart beat loudly. "Tell me," she whispered.

"I don't know what happened," he said. His discomfort made him brutally honest. "One moment I was told that Iphigeneia was to marry Achilles, the next she was being sacrificed upon a pyre in the name of some goddess. It all happened too quickly for me to do anything." His voice cracked in grief and anger. "I think that priest Kalchas planned it all and tricked Clytemnestra and I thoroughly."

Helen sucked in a menacing breath.

Kalchas. Of course, Kalchas and Clytemnestra. Even when Helen was gone, they sought to punish her by taking the life of her beloved daughter.

"Helen, do you know the man?"

"Yes," she said shortly. *And I know he was not alone in planning my daughter's murder*, she added to herself. In the face of Agamemnon's anguish, she could not bring herself to tell him that his wife was a murderess.

But someday, someday, I shall, she promised herself. *Clytemnestra does not deserve this man.*

She walked back to the bench and knelt beside him. "It is not your fault," she said softly.

He smiled weakly. "Perhaps someday I'll believe that."

"Are Castor and Polydeuces with you?" Helen asked tersely, needing to quiet the emotions they shared.

Agamemnon's eyes softened further with pain.

"They are dead," he whispered. "I'm so sorry, Helen. They died even before this war began. They attempted to kidnap two women — Phoebe and Hilaera, I think were their names — and were killed by the men to whom the women were promised."

Phoebe.

"It seems my entire family is made stupid by love," she said ruefully.

He looked pained once more and Helen regretted her sarcasm. "We'll have time to mourn the past well enough," Helen said, placing a comforting hand on his. "For now, we must do what we can to prevent further pain."

"Yes," Agamemnon agreed, squaring his shoulders once more. "Let us pray that the gods give us a choice."

She always does, Helen thought, willing herself to believe it.

Agamemnon followed Cassandra in silence, renewing his determination to end this senseless debacle.

The sounds of swords crashing upon shields interupted his reverie.

"What is it?"

"Hector," the princess hissed. "I'm beginning to think She's abandoned us altogether."

Before Agamemnon could ask what she meant, Cassandra grabbed his arm, urging him to run the remaining way. "Go now. I must see what stupidity my brother has started this time."

She shoved him toward the wall and vanished.

The camp he entered was abustle in confusion.

"Lord Agamemnon!" a guard called, after Agamemnon hastily discarded his disguising cloak. "The Trojans! The Trojans attack now!"

"So much for choice," Agamemnon muttered.

His men stopped thinking of the recent dead in a rush to keep themselves alive. Swords slashed, spears jabbed, bodies oozed blood. And when at last the Trojans pulled back, well after the moon had fled to the sky's highest point of shelter, the men were too exhausted to think at all.

"We're doomed," Agamemnon said, to no one in particular.

Diomedes chose to take the comment to himself.

"Now that we sacrificed men for you and the pathetic man you call brother, now you want to leave in defeat! I will not and I say any man with honor shall not!"

A weak assent followed his words.

"The men crave their homes and their wives. If there are any gods, I'd say they've forsaken us," Agamemnon said. "It is only our own stupidity that keeps us here. We can choose to leave at any time." *Our choice*, he thought.

"My wife is here," Menelaus cried plaintively.

"Your wife calls another man husband," Diomedes retorted inconsistently.

"We are honor-bound to complete this fight," Aias pointed out. "The gods will chase our shades all over Hades if we leave."

"If there are any gods, they have forsaken us," Agamemnon repeated.

"You, you who were visited by Zeus say so?" Diomedes demanded.

"Zeus — if it was he — promised a victory that has been denied us. We fulfilled our side of the bargain, he did not. I see no need to answer to an unfair god."

"But what of the vision?" a voice yelled from the back of the crowd.

The question brought renewed debate, just as Kalchas planned.

Nestor watched the men squabble like children, saw the touch of madness shimmer in Menelaus' eyes. He stood, age serving as his scepter, and the bickering ceased.

"Agamemnon, I share your despair, even as I share Diomedes desire for triumph. With the wisdom of my years, I advise this: Let us put our thoughts of action aside for the moment and eat."

With solemn command, he sat down on his tripod once more.

Agamemnon, Menelaus and Diomedes looked to him with the empty stares of cattle. The men around them, however, were quick to grasp his wisdom.

"Bring sheep," said several.

"And that bread the women from Lesbos baked."

"And wine," added Aias.

Men found strength to assist in preparation of the feast.

"Hector's watchmen will take us for men deranged." Agamemnon muttered to Odysseus.

"They'll think we're confident. And confidence in one often encourages insecurity in another. Let them wonder and worry."

When the men had a great deal of food down them and an even greater amount of wine, Nestor stood once more and commanded silence.

"Perhaps he'll now advise us to get a good night's slumber," Agamemnon grumbled.

"The enemy fires rage close to our ships," Nestor began. "Here is the night that will either break our army or bring us triumph."

The men listened hard.

"Agamemnon, Zeus has given you his scepter and I see no reason why he would forsake it now, except one: your pride over the girl Briseis. We need Achilles back to win this war. Make amends with Achilles and let's get on with this." For the second time Nestor sat down.

And again Agamemnon stared at him, this time in anger he had not realized he had the energy to feel.

"Steady," whispered Odysseus for his ears alone.

Agamemnon whirled around, feeling more confident attacking his younger friend than attacking his older one.

"Think it through," Odysseus added. He turned before Agamemnon could speak and walked away with his characteristic uncaring shrug.

Agamemnon bit down on his tongue and felt drops of blood heat his inner mouth. The taste calmed his anger. *Pride has cost me dearly once during this war*, he reminded himself.

Choose.

What did he have to lose? If Achilles reentered the war, they'd beat back the Trojans. If not, which was more likely, surely the men would see the wisdom of leaving.

Perhaps the gods were presenting him with another chance to end this war. Perhaps the choice was his once more.

He rose and addressed Nestor.

"My dear friend, your advice is, as always, the wisest counsel. I will make good to Achilles. This night I will grant him apology and, to demonstrate my good intention, I shall offer him gifts of splendor: seven unfired tripods, ten talents weight of gold, twenty shining cauldrons and twelve strong horses."

Men murmured their assent and whispered of his honor and generosity. Nestor alone withheld his approval.

"And, of course, I will return Briseis to him." Agamemnon added reluctantly.

The old man nodded. "It is probably best that you send messengers with your offer," he suggested.

Agamemnon agreed. "Odysseus will go, taking Aias and Phoenix." He addressed Phoenix. "He is more apt to listen to his foster father." *And you can perhaps control the madman*, he added to himself.

The older man nodded and sighed as if Agamemnon had spoke the last aloud.

The trio submitted to ritual before departing, allowing water to be poured over their hands to signify the purity of their intentions, listening to their fellow soldiers call upon Zeus to grant them favor once more and to reward them for their commander's humility. When they were finally permitted to leave, those left behind called for more wine to continue the celebration.

Achilles was also celebrating, sharing his cup with his good friend Patroclus while playing quietly upon a lyre with a bridge of silver.

Odysseus saw him first. "I did not know your foster son is a musician," he remarked to Phoenix.

"His head does not hold two thoughts at once. When he is at war, there is no music. With music, there is no war."

"Well, perhaps with music in his brain, he can listen to reason," Odysseus suggested and ignored Phoenix's dubious look of response.

The men approached quietly as Achilles continued to play, accompanying his melody with a chorus of sagas that rang painfully into the night.

"Are we to wait all night for this entertainment to end?" Aias hissed. Achilles presence during the war made him nervous but that anxiety was nothing compared with seeing the giant man seated leisurely upon his purple coverlets, playing to his lover. The sight made the small hairs on Aias' arms absolutely straighten.

Odysseus nodded to Phoenix and the men approached. Achilles let off mid-word.

"Ah, welcome, my earthly father and my friends of fate." The warrior rose and embraced his foster father, then Odysseus. He moved to greet Aias who, at a warning look from Odysseus, willed himself to stand in stillness and not squirm away from the touch.

"Patroclus, bring wine for our dear guests," Achilles continued. He turned, releasing a grateful Aias, and placed a sheep thickly covered with lard on a roasting stick. He carried the meat to the fire, ignoring his guests. Patroclus returned with watered wine and Achilles joined them once more, letting his meat fall carelessly back into the flame.

"Be welcome to the tent of Achilles," Patroclus said, patiently passing a goblet among them before attending the fire and turning the meat Achilles had left forgotten there.

Achilles beckoned his guests to be seated on his surprisingly luxurious and comfortable couches. Odysseus and Aias looked to Phoenix.

The older man cleared his throat. "My son, you are a great host, but our matter is quite urgent and keeps us from giving your hospitality its due." He leaned forward as a man does when he wants to show the sincerity of his plea.

"My dear father on earth, it would appear that you have been over urgent for a prolonged time. Perhaps the relaxation of good company will ease your heart," Achilles reached behind him toward his forgotten lyre.

Odysseus and Aias moved involuntary hands to stop him; Phoenix's look of warning stayed their efforts.

"There is wisdom in your words, son, but now is not the time for rest. The Trojans are camped just beyond our defense ditch. They will storm the ships if we do not act at once."

"Ah." Achilles eyes held sympathy — and little more.

Odysseus decided it was his turn to intervene. "We need the greatest of our heroes. Each man in our camp recognizes this, including Agamemnon himself, who has bid us to beg your help in his name."

"I can't imagine the great commander begging anyone," Achilles interrupted shrewdly.

Odysseus told himself not to be unnerved by the madman's burst of lucidity. "Oh, but he has, and he bid us further to offer you the return of the woman over whom this rift began, as well as the most kingly of gifts."

Achilles studied the three of them, feeling their desperation begin to choke him. "You are my guests and therefore I will answer you honestly and with consideration for the urgency of your situation. Not a single moon ago, I would have embraced your offer. But I have had time — the thing that forces wisdom upon even the most reluctant of men — and I have seen this: there are more important treasures for me in this world than the satisfying lust of battle. The soft sound of my lyre, the ocean rocking me to slumber, the dear companionship of true friends." He tossed Patroclus a soft smile. "It seems to me that this life offers the same riches to those who fight and those who are weak. The weak appreciate them more."

He continued his thoughts in the privacy afforded by his wine cup.

Phoenix watched him with resignation, Odysseus with amused admiration.

Aias was enraged. "What has gotten into the thing lodged in your skull? It is far more honorable to die in battle than live quietly as dishonor prevails. Help us now and win for yourself the glory the gods accorded you." He was on his feet, for once taller than the man to whom he spoke.

But Achilles did not accept the challenge posed by Aias' aggressive stand. "It seems this war is a perfect demonstration that few men know a just cause when they see one, though many will seek any excuse to kill others and call it glory."

Aias' face betrayed killing anger.

"We respect your words," Odysseus said, rising smoothly and placing himself between Aias and Achilles. "But we also must bid you to reconsider. Should the Trojans storm our ramparts, they will also storm your own ships. In fact, knowing Hector, they will probably seek your ships first."

"If they do, my men are readied to row homeward. I suggest yours be prepared to do the same."

Aias drew the breath of a man about to speak rashly; Odysseus elbowed his diaphragm.

"Again, my lord," Odysseus continued. "I ask you to reconsider while my companions and I return to our weapons."

"Well, you must do as you see fit," Achilles answered amicably. "But you will stay and rest, won't you father? A man of your years should not be so entangled in these senseless games."

It seemed unwise to refuse the offer; Phoenix gave a shrug of acquiesce and Odysseus grabbed Aias' elbow and pushed him toward the outskirts of the camp. Achilles, who had already forgotten their visit, called for a fleece bed for his father.

"You let that madman toy with us!" Aias hissed when they were well out of earshot.

"Achilles is no use to our army in this state. He'll snap out of it soon enough," Odysseus replied.

"With Hector's army screaming victory on the perimeter of our camp, we haven't the luxury of waiting on one man's mental state!" Aias screamed.

Odysseus ignored his wrath. "It is not the Trojan taste of victory which is our problem. Rather, the problem is our own feelings of defeat."

Aias looked at him uncomprehendingly.

When they re-entered the camp, they found the men they left behind still drinking. Agamemnon, who barely sipped from his cup, was the first to note their return.

"He refused," Agamemnon guessed.

"Yes," Odysseus answered.

Diomedes leapt to his feet. "You offered him too much," he screamed, turning on Agamemnon. "You ignited his pride and now we shall never win him back."

"Sit down, you fool," Nestor shouted and shoved the advancing Diomedes down to the ground with surprising strength. "I trust Achilles didn't slay his own father for the insult," he added to Odysseus.

"No, we should all be spending this night as Phoenix is," Odysseus answered and turned to face the men before him. "Achilles did say one thing that you should hear: He said he would never answer a plea for help from men who did not even attempt to confront the ill-fate upon them without him."

The men stood in stunned silence for less than a heart's beat.

"What does he mean?"

"How dare he..."

"Does he think he's a god?"

"We don't need that boastful lout!"

"What are you talking about?" Aias demanded, adding his voice to a chorus of others.

"Shut up and agree with me," Odysseus whispered. He raised his voice to address the angered crowd. "At least the madman still has some wits in working order — more than can be said for many of you." As intended, his insult got their attention. "What have we done except drink ourselves into a stupor?"

A gratifying silence met his words and he pursued his advantage. "Think men. We have the advantage. That ditch so many of you scorned to dig is now our ally. To cross it, the Trojans must abandon their horses and their chariots." He fingered his mustache and effected a sneer. "The Trojans associate horses with manhood. Let's take advantage of this to unman them further."

He looked past their puzzled stares to Agamemnon.

"A horse raid," the commander interpreted, sensing choice slip from his fingers once more.

The men pounded their approval on the backs of their fellows.

Diomedes eyes glowed. "We'll steal their horses," he agreed, enchanted.

"Odysseus will steal their horses," Agamemnon corrected, needing to regain some semblance of control.

"And I," shouted Diomedes, glory in his eyes.

Odysseus looked dubious. "A horse raid on an enemy camp demands a quiet foot and a silent tongue."

"I can be silent as I must," Diomedes protested.

"War can bring out the best in any man," Odysseus commented.

He moved to Agamemnon's side and the two walked out of ear shot. Agamemnon turned shrewd eyes upon his fellow leader. "What did Achilles really say?"

"He says he enjoys the comforts of peace over the glory of war," Odysseus answered honestly.

Agamemnon eyed him skeptically. "If I believed you I would demand that you report his words to the men and force them to see the fruitlessness of staying here. As it is, the tale you told sounds closer to the truth."

Odysseus shrugged. "Lies usually do." He departed once more, a silent Diomedes at his side.

"If you utter one word, I will slice your tongue from your

brainless head and feed it to my hounds," he had warned Diomedes.

His companion locked the threatened body part behind his teeth and followed Odysseus into the enemy's camp.

Hector's first thought was to strangle the man whose frantic cries shattered his dreams of victory.

"All of the horses held by the Phrygians have been stolen and many of the men have been slain!"

His second thought was to burn every Achaian still alive.

Horses. Precious, beautiful horses. A man could lie or ignore an oath or lose courage at the exact moment when he was to guard your back. A horse never lost his courage, remaining loyal, determined to save the life of his rider even at the expense of his own.

The horses had been kidnapped.

Hector had suffered too many losses. His dreams for glory faded with each passing day. His men had grown restless. Paris had grown more obnoxious. Worse, many seemed to sympathize with his brother, especially since that ill-fated day when Paris escaped sure death at Menelaus' hands. Hector could stand no more. The surprise attack on the Achaians was just what his men needed, just what he needed. He had not counted on the Achaians' cunning.

Hector dressed himself hastily and turned his face to the sun slowly rising a fuzzy red over the eastern sky. The dawn of victory, the red of blood.

It will be so, he vowed. *No more losses.*

He led the charge forward, trying to feel comfortable racing forward on two legs instead of four, as he balanced his spear and threw it with all his strength at a Achaian charging him. The move cost him his balance. It cost his opponent his life; the spearhead passed through the enemy's neck and tore at his brains.

For my losses, Hector whispered.

The Trojans behind him focused on the gore dripping from the dead Achaian. The sight ignited their courage.

They swarmed the enemy, reveling in their new-found ability to fight on foot. They fought in retaliation for the boredom the Achaians caused them. The humiliation the Achaians dealt them.

The horses the Achaians captured, Hector reminded himself, slaying men within reach, pushing others into the ditch of their own creation to be impaled by the spears artfully placed within. He saw his men follow his example, then waver as the enemy retreated beyond the ditch, leaving the deadly hole between them and victory.

"You there, grab the shields and batter these spears aside. And you, lead your men around where it's not quite as deep," he commanded.

The men, renewed by a possible solution to their dilemma, hastened to follow his orders.

Hector held his breath as a young warrior raised his spear to Agamemnon. "He was to be mine!" Hector screamed, frantic to be heard over the deafening din of battle. Some god acknowledged his claim; the warrior's spear soared wide of its mark, grazing the commander's arm. Agamemnon screamed in pain and outrage before slaughtering his attacker and vaulting onto the chariot ready to carry him from the fray.

As if I don't have enough men to kill, Hector chastised himself belatedly and thrust his spear through the hide shield of a new attacker, spewing guts on the earth.

The sun illuminated the slick red of the beach and Hector felt the rosy glow of victory within his grasp. He allowed the gods to use him, to move him forward with strength and stealth, confident that they would replace the energy he spent tenfold.

He was invincible.

He was in no mood to listen to omens.

"My lord, the men at the far side have stopped their fight."

Hector whirled on Polydamas, keeping one eye to the enemy to track any advance.

"The entire force?" he screamed. He saw his gentle brother flinch and fought to bring his volume under control. "What is wrong with them?"

"A bird sign appeared to them."

Hector gave off tracking his enemy.

"An eagle, flying majestically across the sky, held a serpent in his claws. The serpent writhed in death throes and suddenly struck at the bird's chest. The eagle screamed a death wail and dropped its prey."

Hector was incredulous. "The men had time to see all this?"

"Only the fall of the serpent, my lord. But I witnessed the flight of the eagle and read the message of Zeus."

"And the message is?" Hector prepared to hear his victory message from the gods.

"Hector, my brother, we must leave off fighting the Achaians. The eagle died from the prey it thought it captured. We shall also if we believe ourselves victorious on this day."

Hector did not attempt to hide his astonishment. "You are suggesting we retreat?"

"Zeus himself suggests we retreat."

"Did you tell the men this?" Hector asked softly.

"And not tell the commander first? My brother, you insult me!"

"It is you who insult me by misreading the message of the gods! Tell the men the sign confirms the obvious: On this day, we shall rid ourselves of the Achaians forever!"

"My lord..."

"Go now! And get yourself out of the way of the fighting."

Hector left him no time for response. With a cry, he and his spear vanished into the fray.

Polydamas turned and walked slowly to the far end of the fighting. *I cannot lie. I will not lie.* The phrase kept time with his heart and his step and too quickly took him to the men who continued a half-hearted attempt at fighting.

"Well, what of it?" Damasos demanded of him.

Polydamas commanded his voice to be strong and ring with truth.

"Your great commander urges you to continue your fighting," he bellowed, wishing his brother had decided to give the order himself.

"And what of the omen?" Damasos persisted.

"Your commander promises victory this day over the Achaians," Polydamas continued.

Damasos fought in many battles and read the signs as any seasoned warrior could. He regarded Polydamas, marking how the man would not meet his eyes. "So it's like that, is it?" he said at last. "Well men, let us continue to feed the Mother with Achaian blood."

With a great cry, he turned and entered the battle. But even Polydamas could read the hesitation in his approach.

CHAPTER EIGHTEEN

"**H**ector could not have picked a worse time for attack," Cassandra murmured as the women watched the carnage below.

"What are you talking about?" Andromache demanded. "He's winning."

The sky blazed in flames of red and orange and brown, interupted by clouds of black that exuded a perfume of burning timber, fried livestock and seared flesh. Unable to hold the remains of all those who had died, the air rained ashes over men frozen in horror and disbelief and fear.

The Trojans advanced. The Trojans torched Achaian ships. The Trojans were winning.

Achaians not dead or screaming in hot pain watched, too numb to admit defeat, too terrified to rally for an unlikely victory.

"There will be no winners in this war," Helen said sadly.

Her companions did not share her resignation.

⚜

Leagues away, one man stood with a weary sadness etched on a face housing a newly quieted spirit, and agreed. "Such a waste of life," Achilles whispered.

"We cannot just stand here and allow this to happen!" Patroclus screamed, wincing as a second ship exploded in flames and agonized screams.

"But we can, Patroclus. Each man can make his own decision and each man must live with the consequences. Our fellow soldiers face the fate of their choosing."

Patroclus was a quiet man, known for his patience and his wisdom. He recognized both in Achilles, applauded each and could share neither.

"I cannot do as you do, Achilles. I cannot stand here and watch men — friends — die without hope."

"And how can one man give another hope, Patroclus? Nay, it is not possible. Stay where you are."

"It is possible," Patroclus insisted, placing an urgent hand on his friend's exceptionally large arm. "There are men who embody the hope of others, who ignite it as fully as the Trojans have ignited our ships. You are one such man, Achilles. You can give our men hope and the strength that is derived from it."

Achilles wavered, feeling Patroclus' distress speak to him, wanting to calm his friend's anguish. He looked once more at the flames, at men running, at men screaming, at men fighting.

The monster inside him raised its head in interest. Blood. War. Pain. Death. It hungered for his action, threatened to take over his body once more, to eat at his flesh, to use him as a tool for destruction."

"No!"

Patroclus' heart leaped, causing his body to do likewise.

Achilles turned urgent eyes on his friend. "I cannot. Battle lust has burned a pattern in my brain. If I enter this war, I will not stop at offering hope, at lending strength. I will not stop until either I or every Trojan still living is slaughtered.

"You think my calmed spirit is a gift from the gods, a gift that has transformed me from war leader to a man of peace. I tell you this is not so. I tell you that the battle beast is within me still, threatening to destroy my peace and my life. I cannot reenter this battle."

Patroclus nodded in silent understanding. The Achaians needed Achilles and Achilles would not fight. Patroclus needed to fight and the Achaians did not need him.

How like the gods to create such a puzzle, Patroclus thought, knowing the gods did so for a reason, to test the strength of men, to confer wisdom and creativity. If Patroclus was Achilles...

"Allow me to wear your armor then." The words tumbled from the heart of wisdom to Patroclus' throat, bypassing the mind that would surely puncture his plan with logic. "Allow me to enter the battle in your likeness. The men will rally behind your image."

Achilles resisted, seeing the monster peek out from behind Patroclus' eyes. But the monster within his friend was tamed somehow and would not consume with the ferociousness of Achilles' own. Achilles knew Patroclus' heart would break from inaction, crushing him as surely as uncontrolled battle lust.

Achilles, man of peace, saw that Patroclus wanted war no more than himself. Patroclus wanted to stop death.

"Go then. And when you have forestalled death, return to me and together we will make our way to our home and our new life."

"What are we to do now?" Cassandra demanded, as more cries reached the battlements where the women stood.

Helen forced herself to answer with the calm assurance she knew Aethra would affect.

"We wait to see what opportunity presents itself," she said aloud.

Armor and battle fury overtook him, surprising Patroclus with its power. Around him, the newly roused Myrmidons swarmed the overconfident Trojans, cutting down men stupid enough to get in their way. Patroclus led charge after charge, taking advantage of the speed his small body afforded him despite the heavy armor that encumbered him. He found himself retreating less frequently, using his speed to lead him to the enemy. The Trojans thought him Achilles and began to draw back in horror.

Patroclus, small little friend of a madman, cut them down.

Glory injected Patroclus with strength.

Strength gave him the illusion of immortality.

He no longer saw men; he attacked demons who tested his strength, his cunning, his power. He slashed and speared and felt gloriously alive as blood bathed his arms and splashed freckles on his face, as guts oozed between his fingers.

He barely felt the sharp bite of the javelin on his neck, the burning spear thrust under the too large armor. Death seeped slowly into his brain and his mortal mind recognized Hector's face before it faded in silent gray.

CHAPTER NINETEEN

"**T**his is not Achilles!" Hector howled, a great bellow that carried to where the women stood.

"I hope this isn't the opportunity to which you referred," Cassandra snapped, not bothering to whisper.

Helen forced herself to quiet, listening for a sign from her Goddess.

Nothing. Nothing since that day when She had appeared. She did not meet Cassandra's eyes, looking instead at the spectacle below them.

"What difference does it make?" Alexander demanded, pushing past his brother, greedy arms extended in readiness to tear the beautiful armor from its corpse.

Hector grabbed his arm, staring intently at his brother's face, unwilling to face the man he murdered. He had fought savagely, ripped the guts of a man said to be his doom, stabbed at fate to puncture its power.

And he had killed a man no larger than a child. A man of gentleness and wisdom. Patroclus. The only man capable of quieting Achilles.

Alexander tried to pull free.

"Achilles' death I would proudly claim," Hector said with forced calm, tightening his restraint on his brother's arm. "This man died attempting to save his people, knowing he could not possibly survive. He is a hero, no matter what side he fought on. Let his corpse be returned to his fellows, with his armor about him."

Alexander looked at him in disbelief. When the sun rose, they were winning, burning the ships that threatened Alexander's future, burning the blemishes of the past. Since he escaped the challenge against Menelaus, men who had previously eyed him with distaste began to shun him completely. He, more than anyone, needed victory against the Achaians. Only then would men see him as a prince who granted them glory instead of an outcast shepherd who caused their friends to die.

Only then would he receive the respect denied him life long.

Prince Paris of Illium.

"You are mad!" he screamed, pulling forcefully away from his brother, the obstacle between him and glory. "Do you see this armor — it's gold and bronze and some other substance that not even the sharpest spear will pierce. We shall take it and give it to our craftsman to copy."

When today's glory is over, our people will rest confident in their invincibility in the future.

Prince Paris of Illium. Protector of his people's future.

Hector was short-headed.

"The man died an honorable death," Hector insisted, nearly trampling the corpse in an effort to stand between it and his brother. "His armor shall be returned with him."

Alexander stood above the corpse, unwilling to give ground.

Deiphobus, standing some distance away, watched his brothers while stabbing his opponents with special glee. The fraternal battle ended too soon.

The Myrmidons advanced and the only armor the brothers considered was their own. Hector let his shield fight their spears and inched slowly backward, waiting for a knot of his comrades to surround him.

Aeneas was the first to arrive. "Nasty fighters these," the tall man said and casually thrust his spear through three men in rapid succession.

"But men nonetheless," Hector replied, trying to match his tone.

Men like Patroclus.

"Aeneas, pull back and let these men take over."

Aeneas did not question. They fell back together

"I killed Patroclus, " Hector said, forcing himself to meet his friend's eyes. "An honorable man deserves an honorable funeral. I want to return him to his comrades in full armor."

Aeneas' eyes focused somewhere in the distance.

"Well then, we'll have to retrieve it first."

Hector followed his gaze and saw a pack of men shedding the armor from the corpse, while the Achaians tried desperately to recover the body; Alexander was at the center.

"The gods of Hades take him," Hector swore, calling for his recaptured horse. "We must stop this."

He swung himself upon his mount and pushed through the fray, heedlessly striking any who presumed to stop him. Aeneas thundered behind.

The Achaians saw them advance and doubled their efforts to reclaim the now naked corpse before them. Hector, horrified, watched as two sides tugged the small man's body between them.

"Leave off!" he screamed, cutting the throat of an enemy determined to stop him.

Alexander paused long enough to give his brother a contemptuous look and returned his attention to the dead man whose head he was determined to have.

"I said leave off!" Hector bellowed again.

The men around Alexander stopped and looked uncertainly from one brother to another.

Hector swung from his horse and stood inches from Alexander. "If you continue, I will kill you where you stand."

Deiphobus decided his intervention was necessary. "Hector's always been jealous of glory. Now he denies you yours," he hissed into Alexander's ear.

Alexander's eyes smoldered resentment as he jumped at his brother.

The Achaians took advantage of their struggle to recover Patroclus' body.

Deiphobus shook his head as Aeneas came to Hector's rescue and pulled Alexander from his body. Hector afforded his brother a single, searing look. "If you ever attack me again, I will kill you." He turned his attention to the Trojans awaiting his words and the Achaians awaiting the continuation of the fight. "It is sun down. We will return to the camps and allow the Achaians to honor their man as we will honor our own fallen comrades."

Hector turned and remounted, leaving the men of each side to stare uneasily at each other.

"Well, I certainly can do with some wine," said one man into the awkward silence.

A man from the opposite side agreed, startling each.

CHAPTER TWENTY

Tension filled the bellies of the men in the dining hall, soon stealing the appetites of the women as well. Even Priam, who demonstrated a surprising tenacity for keeping his stomach operational, picked at the scrawny wings of fowl, eyeing them critically, before replacing them upon his plate.

Servants rushed about in stressful attempts to keep wine goblets full. Despite the large quantities of liquid consumed, their masters remained stubbornly sober.

It was into this room that the unfortunate herald entered, choking with discomfort of his own.

"What is it?" Hector barked.

The man bowed gracefully, for the forms must be followed, and began his announcement. "My lord, there is a, um, well, a person to see you."

"A *person*?"

The herald raised his chin in a futile attempt to maintain his dignity. "Yes, my lord. A lady. I mean a warrior."

"I have no time for trifles," Hector warned. "Show it in. But know you are under my greatest displeasure."

The man nodded, swallowing past the injustice in his throat, and turned to open the door. "My lord. The person."

Hector rose to greet a being who was clearly female and certainly unlike any he had ever encountered. She strode into the room with an arrogance reserved for men, her bare, sun-tanned legs rippling as she moved, igniting competitive envy in every soldier present. Bulging calf muscles strained the laces of her sandals. Her strong thighs were outlined by a short tunic covered by crimson spirals. Atop her narrow skull was a helmet adorned with fanciful feathered crests that floated down her back. Upon her right hip was a sheath that did not conceal the curved ax within; upon her left hung a similarly curved — and equally menacing — short sword.

She and those who attended her surveyed the room. Their heavy browed, narrow eyes came to rest upon Helen and the group bowed their heads in acknowledgment, before doing so to every other female seated, including a flustered Hecuba.

Their leader's gaze turned to an annoyed Hector, giving him the briefest of nods. "I am queen Penthesilea and these are the members of my cavalry."

The six women flanking her offered similar, insulting nods.

Hector rose, forced politeness along every line of his taunt body. "I am prince Hector, heir to Troy, commander of the Trojan forces. What service do you seek?"

"Rather ask what service we offer. We have come to join your battle against the Greeks."

A surprised murmur, laced with a man's nervous laughter, spread through the hall.

"We are honored by your offer," Hector said in a tone that indicated he was anything but. "However, it is not customary for us to include women within the ranks of our fighters."

"Nor is it customary for us to fight beside men. Necessity changes customs," the woman added with a surprisingly elegant shrug.

"One custom that cannot change is to allow those who pass through the enemy camp into our forces," Hector snapped.

"Obviously, a wise strategy," Penthesilea said mildly. "We have not done so, but instead followed the north path, successfully avoiding the Greeks."

"The north path offers nothing but a treacherous journey," Hector responded skeptically.

Again, the queen shrugged. "Still, it is no match for our mounts," she responded, causing a new cascade of whispers to ripple through those gathered.

"Why is it you wish to join us?" Hector demanded.

"We share a common cause," Penthesilea asserted, with a subtle, startling glance in Helen's direction.

"Your offer is most gracious," Hector began.

"Oh, let them fight. The Amazons have already proven their prowess on this very soil during our ancestors' time and we're not in such a great state that we can deny what service is offered." Priam's peevish voice echoed off the hall's walls, startling his audience and apparently awakening his appetite. He looked upon his meal with renewed favor.

"We are planning to return to camp this evening but invite you to remain within the palace walls to rest after your journey. You may report to me tomorrow," Hector said, quickly regaining the authority that had been momentarily wrested from him.

The woman's nod was sardonic. "We are hardened against the need for such soft luxuries. But I will not gainsay a night of Trojan hospitality."

Hector gestured to a steward, who led the women from the hall. As the doors closed behind them, stunned exclamations left the lips of those left behind, excepting Hecuba, who looked adoringly at her husband and uttered a very satisfied "I knew it."

❧

Helen sat in the cushioned chair to one side of her chamber, waiting, although she knew it unlikely that Alexander would join her this night.

Always waiting. Her numbed brain knew her wait was at last coming to an end. The fighting on both sides had intensified; it was only a matter of time before one force annihilated the other.

"We have failed," she said into the empty space. "What would You have me do now?"

No voice echoed in the chambers of her heart. Instead, a strong scratch played at her door.

Unthinking, Helen rose to answer, wondering who would call upon her at this time. The sight of the Amazon queen surprised her.

"I would speak to you," Penthesilea said directly.

Regaining her composure, Helen opened the large door to allow the queen entrance. Penthesilea looked about her surroundings with a warrior's seasoned eye, noting the silk curtains and heavy fleece coverlets with a distasteful wrinkling of her long nose. She returned her attention to Helen. "I bring word from Aethra, queen of Troezen. She wishes you to know she is well."

Helen's numbed brain began to warm. *Aethra...*

"I see I have struck you with speechlessness. Let us sit and I will tell you all while you regain your composure."

The queen ushered Helen back to the seat she had just vacated, procuring a second chair of wood for herself, lifting it from the corner as if it were no heavier than a pile of feathers. "As I am sure you know, I am of a race that has dedicated our lives to the worship of the Goddess. Many, many seasons before there were kings and queens and cities, we roamed the earth, worshipping Her amid the trees, upon the soil, at the streams and great rivers. I've often wondered what such a peaceful life of devotion was like and even deluded myself into believing I might someday experience it. It has not been meant to be. Since birth, I have been raised to the necessity of fighting for our way of life against bandits who would take our womanhood. The fighting has grown so great that we've scarce had time for birthing new warriors into our ranks. Death is surpassing life and after wandering our plains, searching for the bands that once were and are no longer, I decided to make our way to Troezen, where the Goddess still rules and our way of life might be restored.

"This decision, as you may well guess, was not a popular one. The members of my band were also reared to the freedom of the plains and the power of the sword. The notion of soft living does not sit well with us. But the thought of extinction weighed heavily upon me. I did not want our band to be slain by nameless bandits and forgotten. So we made our way, however reluctantly, to Troezen. It was then that we found Aethra. Or I should say she found us."

A wide, full-toothed smile spread across Penthesilea's face, a smile filled with remembrance and admiration. "You could say she appeared in our path, so suddenly our horses near ran her down. We have, of necessity, grown very wary of strangers and your priestess cast a strange sight indeed, ragged and tattered as she was from the journey. Yet, despite this, the woman managed to look like the very Goddess herself, alight with a power even the horses deemed worthy of respect. When we questioned her and learned who she was, she told us of her history and your plight. It became evident that we would do ourselves greater benefit to come here and fight for the right of the Goddess rather than skulk in Troezen."

A shrill laugh escaped Helen's lips, showing the visiting queen the extent of her tension. "I fear you and I and perhaps Cassandra are the only ones to view this war so," she said with ill-concealed bitterness.

Penthesilea shrugged. "That is enough."

At Helen's skeptical glance, she continued. "Already, the priests tell lies of my people — even claiming that we never were. I fear that all too soon we will be no more. No matter what the outcome, our participation in this war will at least ensure that we do not drown in obscurity."

She smiled again, this time with hard determination.

CHAPTER TWENTY-ONE

"**T**he Trojan commanders have returned to their camp."

Agamemnon felt the uneasy looks of the leaders who surrounded him and hid a sigh. He had successfully convinced them to await telling Achilles of the death of his friend until Hector's return, calling upon their honor in a way that twisted the word past recognition. *At least I have ensured that the madman will not slay leaderless troops in his rage.* The thought did not offer much comfort. He could delay no longer.

Silently, he rose, feeling the men about him do likewise. Limping, injured, the great Achaian heroes arrived at Achilles' tent. Agamemnon faced the questioning man squarely.

"My lord, I bring you news that grieves my heart to utter. Brave Patroclus, leader of men, is dead," he said formally.

Achilles eyes locked upon his face, awash with the emotions that crashed upon him. Disbelief. Pain. Grief. Rage.

For a brief moment, Agamemnon thought Achilles would unleash his pain at him alone and almost welcomed the predicted onslaught. Instead, Achilles threw back his head and wailed, a single, unending sound that pierced the eardrums and paralyzed the mind.

The Trojans in their camp shivered and men rubbed the small hairs on their arms.

The Achaian soldiers heard and thanked the gods. Surely, their hero would now lead them to victory.

At that moment, their hero's beefy hands tore clumps of hair from his head.

"We have recovered his body," Agamemnon said softly.

Above the torment of his agony, Achilles heard the whisper. "Where? Where is he?" Achilles advanced upon Agamemnon.

The commander did not move. "He is being brought by the guards. But I warn you, the corpse is naked of armor and badly damaged. After killing him, Hector fought to retain his body as a prize of war," he said reluctantly.

"Hector!" Achilles' scream rang once more over the camps of two armies, carrying the promise of pain.

Hector forced a wall of stone around his fear. *This is the battle I awaited,* he reminded himself.

Agamemnon stepped back, allowing a litter to come forward with Patroclus' body.

Achilles' rage melted in mourning. "Why? I told you to come back. You were supposed to come back to me. You promised."

The men averted their eyes as Achilles kissed the corpse and continued his whimpering.

"Call for the healer. I want him to tend his body."

The men stood uneasy at the request; healers were for the living.

"Get the healer. Now!" Agamemnon ordered, willing to placate a madman, striving to contain Achilles' killing rage.

But the madman was not thinking of killing, his eyes were held by the unseeing ones of his friend.

"Let's leave him to attend Patroclus," Odysseus suggested. "We need to discuss strategy and prepare for the moment when he decides to fight."

Agamemnon turned to two of his own guards. "Stay here. Bring me word at the slightest change in his disposition."

"Yes, as if we'll know when a crazy man becomes crazier," the guard whispered to his companion when the commander turned his back.

"This is the victory the soothsayers predicted," Nestor said as he walked beside Agamemnon.

Agamemnon stared ahead. "If I have learned but one lesson in the past ten seasons, it is this: fate is fickle. Events predicted do not always come to pass."

"You have gained wisdom during this time," Nestor remarked.

"Yes," Agamemnon said sadly, "And I've learned that while wisdom makes a man sound smarter, it rarely makes his actions more intelligent."

"Why else do you think we elders sit back and advise?"

They returned to the command tent to find a frightened knot of warriors attempting to look brave.

"Achilles will reenter the war," Agamemnon said, curtly.

"We will await his return to battle. In the time between, let's begin our feast of victory."

Victory. The word had no meaning.

Boars and sheep backs were taken from the diminishing stores and the cooks did their best to garnish the meal with vegetables and seaweed to make it appear that there was food in plenty. Wine was passed about and men used it to wash away the smell of charred bodies and burnt ships and dried blood.

The horrors of the day faded and men eased back against the earth and allowed healing sleep to wash over them.

Agamemnon sat awake and alone and contemplated thrusting a dagger through Achilles' heart and ordering a retreat as he listened to the men whimpering dreamer's screams.

Agamemnon did not need to close his eyes to see men die again, to see skin covered in blood and bitten by flames. His memory provided him with a picture of the past as accurately as it provided him with a vision of the future.

Achilles would reenter the war.

The carnage would continue.

They would win.

And the glory would be his.

Poets would chant his name, speak of his strength and valor. And leave him alone to count the price. *The men will not thank me for denying them their victory*, he told himself, envious of their ability to ignore the cost of winning. Would they be forever haunted by the sights of mutilated bodies and the memory of strangers advancing upon them, intent on their death?

Agamemnon wished he could ask them.

His guardsman galloped expertly around the sleeping bodies and halted before him.

"My lord, Achilles has prepared for battle."

Agamemnon stood, slowly.

"Wake the men. Call the priests and arrange for a funeral pyre for Patroclus while the soldiers arm themselves."

The guardsman shifted uncomfortably. "My lord, Achilles will not send Patroclus to the Otherworld until he can sacrifice Hector's body beside him. He has enlisted several Myrmidons to keep the flies away."

The food that had set so well in Agamemnon's belly shifted uncomfortably.

The taste of victory, his disgusted brain informed him.

The battle was terrible. Men who saw their death reflected in yesterday's sun slashed and speared with giddy relief over their unexpected second chance at life. They killed in gratitude, with joy, heedless of form or pageantry.

They murdered heroes and cowards. They killed in the new style demonstrated by their new war leader.

The monster raged within Achilles' brain, pumping his un-stoppable legs forward, moving his untiring sword arm to butcher the enemy.

Death was not enough; the monster compelled torture.

Achilles sliced his victims to inflict the greatest pain, ig-noring an exposed heart to slash at ropes of guts, opting to sever limbs when a downed enemy craved one final thrust.

Death was a gift his victims earned with suffering.

As Patroclus had suffered.

As Achilles suffered.

"I cannot watch any longer," Aeneas screamed to Hector as he ran his short sword through the neck of a stocky Myrmidon.

"Achilles is mine," Hector growled in reply, warning him off with the voice of a commander.

Aeneas was not intimidated. "Let's stop him now and ar-gue about the glory of it later."

He did not await a reply and ran straight toward Achilles, who was delighting in carving the liver from a fallen foe. The grotesque warrior looked toward the golden man stupid enough to charge him head on. His eyes glowed madness and a small hint of recognition, his mouth stretched in primal glee.

Aeneas stepped to one side, waving his arms, taunting Achil-les with the easy target of a Trojan hero. Achilles left the man he tortured to die in satisfying slowness and stood to meet this more interesting opponent. Aeneas continued circling, teasing, until the dying man lie between him and the madman. Achilles did not wonder why Aeneas stopped. He willed strength to his spear arm, imagining it tear through his opponent's offending body. Aeneas waited until Achilles spear was cast, wondering briefly how the man moved under his burdensome armor, and fell to the ground, avoiding the projectile at the final moment.

"I grant you a merciful death," he whispered to the man below him whose mouth moved in silent agony. He plunged his sword into the man's heart. Achilles howled outrage at Aeneas and his presumptuous mercy. He advanced as Aeneas scrambled to regain his footing.

"They say your destiny calls for you to survive this war," he screamed, trying to catch Aeneas as the warrior circled from his grasp once more.

"I defy destiny," Aeneas yelled before falling gracelessly into a sandy hole created by the impression of a dead man who had occupied it.

Achilles gave a loud scream and raised his sword. Aeneas closed his eyes and whispered a silent apology to the goddess whose plan he thwarted.

Apparently, his goddess was unwilling to be denied. A wall of Trojans surrounded him, striving not to step on him as they pushed the Achaian warrior back.

"Call the healer!"

Aeneas recognized Hector's voice beside him and forced his wits to settle. "No need for a healer."

"There will be if you sit here like a dead man."

"I thought I was."

"You should be," Hector answered, helping his friend. "Achilles had posed his sword perfectly to slice you in two. His own men backed into him while fighting their opponents. He turned his rage upon them long enough to allow us to circle you."

"I don't envy those sorry Myrmidons."

"They no longer have use of their heads. And since you do, start using it. Stay away from Achilles."

"We have to stop him, Hector," Aeneas said seriously.

"I have to stop him," Hector responded.

Aeneas looked past him. "I say now would be a good time."

Hector followed Aeneas' gaze. "What is that madman doing?"

The madman was running a large knot of Trojan warriors into the Xanthos river, delighting in the red puddles that bubbled on the crest of the waves as his sword penetrated wet flesh. He pushed them further into the water's depths, cutting at flaying limbs and bobbing heads, offering a choice of deaths, letting them die as warriors or as sacrifices to Poseidon.

Sacrifices. Sacrifices denied Patroclus.

As suddenly as he began the slaughter, Achilles threw his sword to the sand and grabbed men unfortunate enough to remain alive, throwing them in a stunned pile upon the beach front. "Move back to shore! Back to shore! A sacrifice to Patroclus!"

He forced his captors to stand, to move forward in the direction of his camp.

"Now is the time to attack, " Hector declared. "He will be focused on controlling the hostages. He will be vulnerable."

But his hostages were not presenting a problem. Defeat lived behind the glazed eyes and the warriors went where led, immune to the threat of death.

Only one had the energy to turn, the will to seek out the eyes of another.

Polydamas' eyes turned to meet those of his brother. Hector forgot the charge and victory and war, forgot glory and honor and battle.

Polydamas.

Your men will be trapped before they can return home.

His men. His troops. His brother.

Trapped by his unwillingness to listen to the voice of the gods when he thought victory was within his reach.

The gods hated pride.

His pride had deprived men of victory, had deprived men of life.

His pride was about to cost Polydamas his life.

"No!" his primal scream rang through the masses, a futile attempt to deny the death of his brother. And his role in it.

Your men will be trapped before they can return home.

Aeneas grabbed his arm and screamed into his ear.

"Hector, you must lead the charge."

But Aeneas was wrong. He must restore the balance.

He turned to Aeneas with maddened hope. "Get the men to the gates."

"Hector..."

"Now!"

Aeneas looked at the determined eyes and unyielding jaw and clenched fists and stopped protesting.

"Come on men! Trojans! To the gates." He moved from group to group, rallying men who had longed for retreat for so many movements of the sun that they hesitated briefly when given orders to do so.

But only briefly.

Thousands of feet thundered to the safety of the Trojan city.

Achilles felt the ground vibrate beneath him and turned to see a mass of exposed enemy backs.

"Cowards! You will fight in honor of Patroclus!"

Honor was meaningless in the face of certain death; the Trojans continued their escape.

Achilles grabbed the first large Achaian his eyes fell upon. "Watch them," he ordered, indicating his hostages. "If a single one escapes, my sword will drink your blood."

He let loose a loud and unintelligible war cry and raced to the fleeing enemy, thrashing his sword at the backs of Trojan knees and the backs of Trojan necks.

"Gods, we've given him an advantage." Aeneas remarked, horrified as Trojan after Trojan fell to Achilles sword.

Hector stepped forward.

"Achilles. Would you like to hear Patroclus' last sounds?"

The Achaian war hero stopped mid-swing.

"Would you like to hear how he whimpered under the point of my spear?"

Aeneas ran to Hector's side. "Have you gone mad? This way now, lose yourself in that knot of men there."

"Enough men have already died because of my folly. I will not allow anymore to do so."

"Hector, please..."

Hector measured the vast distance between his men and safety.

"Aeneas, go now! Get the men to safety. Promise me you will get them to safety."

He fled in the direction opposite his running men. "Come Achilles, let me share Patroclus' last sounds with you."

The warrior was crazed from the taunting and insane that this brave warrior, this murderer of his dear friend, his only love, would utter such words and then turn to run.

And Hector did run, over sand that impeded his progress, around gates that surrounded his Trojan city, through enemy fighters too wise to strike him and deprive Achilles of his prey. He ran a step for each life his pride had lost. He ran a step for each life he could now save. He ran despite pain that pierced his side and fire that burned his lungs.

He ran until every Trojan was safely within the walls of Troy. Then he stopped and calmly turned to meet his fate.

Achilles was enraged. His armor grew heavier with each forward step, his heart beat faster as his enemy refused to face him fairly.

Patroclus' murderer. A coward. And then Hector stopped running and stood before him, strong and tall and alive.

Achilles thrust his sword in the exposed artery beneath Hector's helm and Trojan champion fell to the ground. Achilles stood for some moments above the man he had so easily killed.

Dead. A swift merciful death. An undeserved heroic death.

"Get up! Get up and fight, you coward!"

The monster in Achilles did not allow regret, only anger, red thick anger that grew as the corpse below him remained still, remained immune to the countless tortures Achilles had planned for it.

Achilles roared his outrage and tore the armor from the dead leader.

"You coward! I will expose your flesh and feed it to the dogs!"

His Myrmidon troops moved cautiously to his side.

"Bring my chariot," he ordered and a half dozen men fled to obey.

"You will suffer. I will beat your bloodless flesh until your spirit finds no rest in the Otherworld."

He set himself to cutting perfect holes in the tender skin of the dead man's heels. The blood flowed slowly. His warriors began to quietly inch away.

"Give me the leather about your waist!"

The unfortunate man next to him hesitated a moment before replying and Achilles used his dagger to cut it from his body. The man's lungs inflated with outrage; his companion knocked his ribs before he uttered his first dooming word.

Neither man stayed to watch Achilles tie the leather band in the hastily made holes of the dead warrior's feet and bind the corpse to his chariot.

Chapter Twenty-Two

"**L**et me through. I'll kill the madman myself!"

Andromache broke free from the group of women and ran down the palace stairs, punching at soldiers who blocked her way, elbowing men as they sought to rest in the safety of palace walls, clawing at the stupid few who attempted to hold her back.

Helen ran with the rest of the women, striving to offer comfort where none could be accepted.

"Andromache. Andromache! Listen to me!" It was Aeneas who caught Andromache, finally. He wrapped strong arms around her, pinning her arms to her sides, resisting her attempts to flee. "Listen to me," he repeated, his beautiful voice harsh with pain. His anguish spoke to her own, pushing her into the incapacitating abyss of loss.

She sagged against him as Helen pushed herself forward to help the princess crumple softly to the hard, stone floor.

"He led a hero's life," Aeneas explained, as if the words meant anything to any of them. "He died a hero's death. His spirit does not care what happens to his flesh."

Andromache heard the truth in Aeneas' words and met it with the truth of her own heart. "I care," she responded

Deiphobus pushed himself arrogantly forward and Helen's arms moved about her friend protectively. "Andromache's right," the detested man said. "We must regain the body. My honor demands that I lead the charge!" *This is my moment, the moment I awaited lifelong,* he thought. Deiphobus. Leader of Troy.

Helen saw Aeneas' features tense over his anger. "Your greed for power demands you lead the charge," he responded softly. "The men must rest. There will be no fighting until we can offer meaningful battle."

Deiphobus's face turned an unflattering shade of red. "I am now Priam's first born son," he said, conveniently forgetting Alexander. "I will decide when we are ready to fight and I say we charge now." He looked behind him, searching for allies among faces too stunned to pay him heed, remembering Alexander at last. Deiphobus reached back to pull his brother forward.

"He's right," Alexander said, fatigue slurring his words. "Honor demands we fight now."

Aeneas stared at Alexander, before returning his attention to Deiphobus. *Oh Hector*, his heart cried, *you were wrong to sacrifice yourself. We need you alive.*

He tucked his anguish inside and faced the men who would undo the temporary safety his friend's death created. "The two men least qualified to determine the course of honor strive blindly to do so," he said with deceptive softness. "Hector died so his men could live. I will not have you contradict his act of bravery."

Deiphobus face contorted in an ugly sneer.

"I will not have a mere guest dictate the moves of the Trojan army." He turned to the crowd of men who formed to watch the exchange. "We will charge now. Arm yourselves once more and be ready to move forward."

The men looked to each other uneasily.

"You will go now I say!" Deiphobus insisted, angry at their hesitation. No one had hesitated at Hector's command. No one would hesitate at his. "Now!"

"They will stay where they are." A voice not heard in several moons bellowed through the hall. Priam stepped forward, carried by the strength of the past. "The men will rest and regroup."

His eyes turned soft as they rested upon Andromache. "Our men are encumbered by fatigue," he explained. "We must rest. I personally pledge that Hector's body be returned or my own life be forfeit."

She stared at him with eyes that had died with the passing of her husband.

"The men are indeed tired," a rough voice cried out. "But he who died bade us to rest during this battle. We will recover him now."

Helen turned with the others, seeking the source of the proclamation that brooked no argument. She too gasped at the cold majesty of Penthesilea and her women, donned in their intimidating armor, deadly blades at their sides.

The tired warriors sat straighter at the sight of them, their spines answering the pride that radiated from the warrior women.

"You face no ordinary foe," Priam informed them carefully.

"Nor shall Achilles," Penthesilea responded, a chilling smile stretching her lips.

Priam studied her closely, a leader assessing the potential of his troops. Penthesilea and her leaders returned his stare, unblinking.

"Go. And may the gods assist you," he responded at last.

"It is the Goddess who will do so," Penthesilea responded, her gaze seeking Helen's. She marched her women through the crowd of warriors.

"We must watch them in their victory," Andromache cried, hope bringing new strength to her limbs. She freed herself from Helen's arms and ran into the castle. A group of men followed the women to the wall where they had watched the war since its inception.

"Look, the Achaian army does not move to strike them," Andromache exclaimed, a frantic light dancing in the orbs of her eyes.

Helen moved to her side, feeling the press of bodies around her.

"She's right," Aeneas said. "It's as if they fear that a horde of goddesses have descended upon them."

Below, Penthesilea and her little band walked forward in the formation of an arrowhead, unchallenged by the stunned Achaians. Only Achilles moved in their presence, continuing the endless circles of his chariot as he dragged Hector's body along.

"If he had any sense, Hector would have used these fighters earlier," Deiphobus muttered, his bitter scowl intensifying when everyone present ignored him completely.

With the Achaians still frozen in disbelief, Penthesilea gave a calm signal to her women. In unison, the Amazon warriors unslung their bows and cocked their arrows.

"Now," the queen ordered.

A hail of deadly projectiles rained upon Achilles. Still, the Achaians did not move. Achilles' armor easily deflected the weapons flung at him. The clank of their ineffective crash against the heavy metal that coated him was joined by the madman's loud laughter. "Is this the best the Trojans can do?" he screamed, lashing his horses to greater fury.

Again, Penthesilea gave a silent signal. This time, her women unsheathed their curved blades and, with unreal swiftness, flanked Achilles chariot.

Again the madman laughed, stopping abruptly as several of the women slashed the reins from his hands and several others worked at the ties to Hector's body.

"No!" he screamed, jumping from his chariot to battle them.

Still, the Achaians stayed as motionless as the Trojans who watched from the palace walls.

"They are succeeding," Andromache whispered.

The Myrmidons who stood silently in the Achaian lines awoke to the same realization. Instantly, they joined their leader, fending off the avenging women.

"They're holding," said a familiar voice and Helen turned to see that Cassandra had joined the fray. She had no time to acknowledge the princess as the scene below captured her attention once more.

The Amazons were indeed holding against the Myrmidon onslaught, calmly scything down the large warriors with their unusual blades. Helen felt hope soar within her. *They're winning. In the name of the Goddess, they're winning!*

Her joy was quickly extinguished as the superior numbers of the Myrmidons began to turn the tide of victory. One by one, the Amazons were swarmed by the ruthless men, cut down by the weight of those too numerous to fight against.

"No!"

Helen did not know if the protest was her own or Andromache's. She continued to watch as the six Amazon warriors fell, leaving only Penthesilea to fight in earnest against Achilles. The match was even, as the warrior queen pitted her swiftness against Achilles' strength, the length of her curved blade against Achilles' dagger.

"She's winning!" a surprised warrior exclaimed.

Once more, the confidant proclamation was followed by disappointment. A sole Myrmidon stole behind the proud queen and nearly severed her head from her body.

No!

Achilles waved the warrior away, standing triumphantly above the body of his slain foe. He knelt to strip his enemy of armor.

"It's a woman!" he screamed.

Horror filled the hearts of those at the wall, shared by those in the camp below, as Achilles hiked up his armor and threw himself upon the corpse, entering her in a maddened frenzy.

No!

Andromache sunk to the floor, pulling Helen beside her.

Helen put her arms about the stunned princess once more, neither knowing nor caring if she did so to give comfort or receive it.

Cassandra moved beside her. "What does it mean?" she whispered, her pupils dilated with the horror she had witnessed.

What did it mean? The champion of the Goddess slain, violated by a madman.

Helen looked to Cassandra, the hot tears that flowed down her cheeks the only answer she could offer.

Priam moved to where the women sat, focusing upon Andromache's unmoving form. "We will return him to you," he promised.

His compassion roused the defeated princess. She brought her hand to his cheek and choked back the tears that threatened to drown her.

"My husband learned honor from his father," she said before rising and proudly walking through the hardened warriors who could not find the courage to meet her eyes. They parted to allow her passage.

Priam turned his attention to his sons.

"Achilles is at the height of madness. He is an impossible threat to us and of absolutely no use to the Achaians. Let our men rest and let the Achaian commanders talk sense into the man."

Slowly, the group began to disperse. Helen rose and sought Alexander, longing for the small comfort his arms could provide. But her husband did not look to her. Instead, he moved with the others, stunned with defeat, to await the actions of the Achaian commanders.

The Achaian leaders refused to approach Achilles.

"We cannot allow this to continue!" Agamemnon screamed and from the corner of his eye he saw Achilles whip his horses in a maddened frenzy, dragging the corpse of Hector behind his chariot.

"You would risk his anger again?" Aias yelled back.

"You are honor-bound to lead the Achaians to victory," Deiphobus added. "Without Achilles we cannot win."

Agamemnon looked upon his fellow commanders in disbelief. "Honor that condones such a barbaric act is perverted beyond meaning."

But his men would not stop Achilles and he was powerless to do so alone.

He turned his back on them and walked to his tent with disgust chewing his stomach.

"They want to win."

Agamemnon stopped to face the one man who dared interrupt his silence.

"The cost of winning is too great, Nestor."

"The cost of winning is too great for you."

"It is too great for any thinking man!" Agamemnon cried. "I've watched men die, horribly, from disease and fire and enemy swords. I've watched madmen proclaimed heroes and intelligent men goaded by being called cowards. Women have been slain. Crops trampled. Homes abandoned. All for the supposed glory of winning. It is not worth it, I say!"

Nestor's eyes were annoyingly calm. "It's difficult to be a wise man in a world of fools." He turned and headed back to the campsite.

In the opposing camp, Priam listened as lesser men argued the best way to charge Achilles' chariot.

"We must surround him with our own chariots."

"We must overpower him by foot."

"The archers should slay his horses."

On and on and on, men suggested plans rejected by everyone else. And still his son's body was dragged through the sand at the mercy of a madman. He ignored the stiffness of his bones and stood. "I will go to Achilles and petition the release of my son."

Silence, cold, icy, seared the breath of men around him, depriving them of speech.

It was shattered by a single, painful wail from a woman who pushed through the crowd.

"No! Not you!" Hecuba threw herself at her husband's feet, grasping at his ankles, holding him back.

The kindness and love of a husband momentarily appeared in Priam's eyes before parting for the stubborn strength of a king. "Woman, would you have me send our men to die a death I would not risk myself?"

"No, of course not," Hecuba answered quickly, the simple intensity of remembered youth lifting the complex lines of age from her face for one brief moment.

Priam smiled and gently caressed her head, before removing her hands from his legs.

"I will take a talent of gold and the finest tunics my kingdom possesses."

"You will reward him for the humiliation of my brother," Deiphobus sneered, moving before the king, unhappy to find his aging patriarch capable of holding the reins of leadership once again.

"I will negotiate fairly for my son's honor." Priam's contempt clearly indicated that he'd be less likely to do so for the son before him.

Deiphobus vied again to recapture the leadership that seemed forever beyond his grasp. "We will follow you secretly and kill Achilles when his attention is focused upon you," he yelled, heartened to hear several men who had no desire to face Achilles' sword again murmur their assent.

Priam's face flushed with rage. "You would kill a man unprepared! I knew I raised a son without honor. I had not realized I had also raised a coward."

Deiphobus' rage mirrored his father's. "It is not only I who say we should go thus. All the sons of your blood agree. Tell him, Alexander." He stepped backward to grab his brother by the arm. "Tell him."

But, for once, Alexander did not echo the sentiment of his ambitious brother. He seemed unable to utter anything at all. Helen wanted to cheer aloud and sob uncontrollably. *Why did it take such incomprehensible horror to break Deiphobus' hold upon him?*

"Have you gone mute?" Deiphobus screamed. "Tell him you agree with me."

Priam did not await any response Alexander might have offered. "Enough!" he bellowed. "I will leave now with my body servant. If you so much as attempt to follow me, my guards will cut you down before your second step."

A shocked breath ran through the crowd, shared by Deiphobus. *My own father would kill me. My own father!*

He lashed his confusion and embarrassment upon Alexander. "Why didn't you say anything? Why didn't you answer?"

Alexander did not answer still, his eyes fixed upon the strong back of his father. He watched long beyond the moment his father left, then walked, wrapped in a cocoon of silence, to the knot of people who waited tensely for Priam's return.

Helen edged quietly to his side. "I'm glad that you agreed with Priam," she offered.

He patted her hand absently. His eyes continued to stare inward at some place beyond her reach.

Deiphobus was as uncomfortable with Alexander's withdrawal as Helen was. Someday, when Deiphobus' power was confirmed, this son of Priam would be a threat. Someday Deiphobus would have to dispose of Alexander to eliminate the danger he posed. Someday. But not this day. Priam was still very much in control. Deiphobus still needed Alexander's support.

He moved to Alexander's side. "You were right to allow Priam the right to negotiate for his son," he whispered, the lie coming easily. "But when he returns, we must regain command. Our father is too old for such a position."

Deiphobus ignored Helen's threatening glare but shrank from the knowing one that looked at him from Alexander's eyes. "Our father is a man of honor," Alexander said quietly.

Deiphobus went off in search of more trustworthy supporters.

"Your father is a man of honor," Helen agreed quickly, seeing an opening to Alexander's heart, feeling the door close a moment before she entered.

Alexander did not respond.

Alexander did not hear; the thunder of his internal shame deafened him to the voices of those around him.

My brother was an honorable man. My father is an honorable man. And I?

His family's honor was cold water on the flame of his greed for glory. His mind walked amid the ashes of his life, seeing with a clarity denied him by the fire of his ambition.

He was a man who stripped the armor of an honorable foe. A man who used every opportunity to undermine the leadership of his rightful commander.

A man who plunged his family into a bitter war. A man who broke the sacred oath of hospitality to win a woman of surpassing beauty and unsurpassed rank.

Did he ever love Helen?"

On and on and on his actions circled his mind, offering ugly images. He surrendered to them, accepted the shame that was his due.

He ignored the wine that the other men used to wash away the time until Priam's return, ignored the nervous conversation around him.

He did not share the relief that washed over the hall's occupants when Priam, at last, returned. He felt Helen rise with
the rest as the king entered and felt her regain her seat when he
did not stir. He felt her fear that he was no longer concerned
with her, no longer caring for her plans and schemes and demands.

Did she ever really love him?

The women swarmed around Hector's body, washing it tenderly, readying it for mourning. Andromache stood aside, immo-
bilized by the cold, battered skin that no longer held the spirit
of her lover.

Alexander reached beyond himself and rose, heedless of
Helen's steps behind him, unaware of the angry hiss that rang
from those who had just begun to taste the first drops of grief.
"Your husband was a man of unequaled honor."

He did not await Andromache's startled response. He turned
to his rooms to prepare for his final battle.

It was not long coming.

"We must strike now, men," Deiphobus proclaimed throughout the funeral games, pleased to see that the return of Hector's
body drained the last of his father's leadership. "Achilles capitu-
lated and in doing so has been weakened."

The men nodded absently. Their obvious apathy did not
reach Deiphobus. His people were listening to him. His people
bowed to his leadership. That was all that mattered.

Even the great Aeneas agreed with him. "We lost the greatest of champions. In his name, for his family and the families of
each man present, we will defeat our enemy," Aeneas proclaimed
at the end of the games.

Deiphobus pushed his way to Aeneas' side to share the roar
of genuine approval issued by the crowd. The men regrouped for
battle and Deiphobus watched Alexander descend the stairs to
join the ranks of the archers. He began to approach his brother,
halting abruptly when he saw an unpredictable light shine from
Alexander's eyes. Deiphobus shrugged; he no longer needed
Alexander.

For Alexander, Deiphobus no longer existed. All his energy
was focused upon the small drop of honor he had found within
himself, the honor he carried carefully forward as he joined the
line of archers, as he eyed Achilles, seeking his chosen opponent's
vulnerability.

He fingered his arrows carefully, drawing the one he had
saved from the time when his life was simpler. Then, he was but
a shepherd, sharing a hut with the young girl he had grown to

love. How often had he hunted for their meal, content with his role as provider for his uncomplicated love? How often had he teased the same young girl for her unending care of him, for the love that had her experiment with herbs and simples until she discovered the poison which would heighten his chances of survival against the large game he hunted?

Ironic, that his path toward glory led him to his beginnings.

Achilles came within sighting distance and Alexander read the ecstasy in the warrior's eyes as he slashed and speared his Trojan enemies.

Alexander wondered if Achilles would read death in his.

Heavy armor covered Achilles skin, a barrier to his destruction. Only his feet remained exposed, carrying him forward in the light sandals that he had donned in his haste to see the blood of more enemy warriors.

Time stopped, allowing Alexander to slowly retrieve his poisoned arrow, to position it within his bow, to let it fly in a perfect arch to Achilles' heel.

The warrior brushed it away carelessly and continued his fighting. Alexander ceased his, watching patiently as the poison took effect. Achilles' free hand reached down to scratch the irritated site. He dropped his sword all together when the poisoned fire crept mercilessly through his blood, burning away life in its wake.

His howl of agony tore through the stomachs of those around him.

"We killed him!" men around Alexander cried, victory urging them to greater victory, to more savage fighting.

Alexander alone did not resume the fighting, standing with eyes fixed upon his fallen foe, his mouth stretched in a strangely satisfied smile.

He did hear the charge of the man who jabbed the sword into his exposed side.

CHAPTER TWENTY-THREE

So *this is where you were*, Helen thought.

Her eyes did not leave the corpse laid out before her. His dark curls fell in grimy disarray about his face, giving the illusion of familiarity. But that which was Alexander was no longer before her. He, the man she had loved, was shrouded in a permanent silence.

Helen wrapped herself in a similar silence, one that couldn't be penetrated by the condolences offered by some around her nor the angry shouts of others.

Cassandra had approached her, Helen knew, standing beside her and offering words Helen could not hear and comfort Helen could not feel.

What blessed relief not to be a part of this world any longer, she thought, pulling further into the stillness of her heart. If only those around her would cease their arguing and leave her to succumb utterly to the numbing peace.

But they would not. The arguments grew louder and she would have been irritated. If she had felt anything at all.

"We'll hold funeral games in his honor," Aeneas proclaimed.

"He had no honor!" Deiphobus screamed, conveniently forgetting his camaraderie with the dead man in an effort to contradict the increasing authority of this live one.

Do you hear how your brother betrays you, she asked the corpse. *Do you believe I did?*

"We will have a wedding," Deiphobus announced loudly, pleased that Priam did not even raise his head to protest.

Aeneas moved between Deiphobus and the women. "A wedding between whom?"

Helen heard his question, wondering what difference it

made. *Only let them leave me to the silence.*

Deiphobus would not be opposed by anyone any longer, particularly a nobody from nowhere like Aeneas. When Hector died, Deiphobus considered taking Andromache as his wife just as he took Hector's leadership. One look at Andromache's hard eyes was enough to make him reconsider his decision. But Helen's eyes were not dark with fury. Helen's eyes were a deep, subservient blue. Helen's spirit was already broken.

And Helen's body...

"I will wed queen Helen of Sparta."

Helen heard the crunch of bone as Aeneas' fist made a surprising connection with Deiphobus' jaw.

"You will not!" he shouted, "You've schemed for power you do not deserve and trampled upon the memory of men you are not fit to wait upon! No more. You will not wed Alexander's widow."

Alexander would have liked to hear that, Helen thought.

Deiphobus tried to rise several times from his undignified place on the floor, but Aeneas took all the space above him.

"I will. Ask Helen if she would object!" he screamed at last, further battering the wall Helen surrounded herself within.

"Enough," she said aloud, her voice as dead as her husband. "I will do as he asks."

She ignored Aeneas' puzzlement, Cassandra's stricken face. *How interesting that they still care about events around them.* Helen herself knew that nothing mattered any longer. *Only let there be silence.*

The wedding did not take long at all. *I can retire now.* Without word to Deiphobus, she left when it was concluded, her legs carrying her up the stairs to her rooms.

"You will sleep in my chambers," Deiphobus demanded, catching her and pulling her forward.

What did it matter?

Deiphobus speared her with his manhood, trying to gain entrance into the world in which he had no part.

"Let her sleep," Cassandra commanded, forcing a potion down Helen's throat, believing slumber would heal her condition.

"Wake up," Deiphobus demanded, believing Helen would respond to him if she left her peaceful slumber.

What her new husband could not obtain with his manhood, he sought with his fists.

"You are mine now!" he raged, pummeling her face again

and again and again.

She did not lift her hands in her own defense. It did not matter that he beat her. It did not matter that he stopped.

Her world had no room for red blood or brown potions or clear tears. Nor did she wonder about love and consorts and God-desses. *What games we play to make ourselves believe life has meaning*, she marveled, retreating further into the comforting gray that covered the past, denied the present, was uncaring of the future.

She slept and was safe. She ignored the body snoring next to her and the throbbing of her bruises and the thunder beneath her bed, which threatened her silence again and again and again.

❧

"And again!" Odysseus ordered, commanding his men to thrust the wooden weapon against the walls of Troy.

"It's not working," Agamemnon remarked casually as the walls of Troy repelled the wooden form once more.

"It will work." Odysseus responded, equally casual.

It was not working. The silence was not holding against the thunder and Helen whimpered, pleading for its return.

"It's not working, I say," Agamemnon repeated, urging Odysseus back from the crowd of men who pushed forward.

"It will," Odysseus insisted, picking Agamemnon's restrain-ing arm from his hand. "It must. We have no other choice."

Choice. Agamemnon moved to stop Odysseus once more. The earth beneath him buckled unexpectedly, throwing him back-ward.

The ground beneath her threw her from the bed. She sat on the cold, billowing floor, dazed and angry at the quaking earth and ready to jump under the next pillar that threatened to crash in deadly force to the ground.

"Mother!"

The walls of Troy crashed to the ground with deadly force. "Pull back. Pull back until they crumble," Odysseus ordered as men tried to obey and control their movements on the rebelling ground.

"Now!"

Agamemnon watched as the Achaians rushed the walls of Troy, opening the wooden contraption to allow the men inside to rush over the obstructing debris.

"Apollo welcomes me!" a voice screamed and Agamemnon watched an entranced Kalchas run toward the walls. Kalchas did not notice the commander. His sight was fixed inward on a vision of triumph. He saw — actually saw, as if it already happened — himself within the temple of Apollo, claiming his place to a roar of accolades. His vision filled further and he heard trumpets and saw the rays of the sun shining about his magnificence. He screamed again, an inarticulate howl of joy, before a particularly large stone broke free from the wall and hurled itself at his head, leaving him in eternal silence.

Agamemnon rose slowly to join those storming Troy's crumpled battlements. He had no choice.

"Mother, hurry. The Earth Mother has betrayed us and the Achaians are storming Troy." Nico's voice oscillated with the quaking ground.

How ironic that the Goddess would demonstrate her rage now, Helen thought, swaying with the buckling floor.

"Helen, stay here and help me lift this damn rock off my arm," Deiphobus growled.

"Mother!"

"Helen!"

She stayed where she was, drinking the wrath of the Goddess.

"Mother. Come on! Now!" Nico grabbed her arm and yanked her to her feet, forcing her to follow him through the collapsing palace. He halted abruptly.

"What is that?" He changed direction and pulled her further into the palace.

"You can't leave me!" The death wail penetrated Helen's comforting isolation, reaching into her, matching grief with grief. She felt agony burst within her own heart.

Her son pulled her shaking body to the source of the cry and they found Hecuba lying in debris, her night shift torn to show the bloody slashes she received in her attempt to shield her husband's corpse. She turned wild eyes on the two approaching her.

"He won't get up!"

Helen dropped beside the queen and wiped the fallen stones from Priam's face before gently closing his eyes.

"Mother, we must go," Helen said gently, her voice catching in the sobs she had yet to utter.

Hecuba slapped her away. Helen pulled harder.

"He has earned his rest. Yours is not yet," Nico said quietly and took the queen's other arm.

My child of the Goddess, Helen thought, wondering if it mattered.

"One of the queen's legs is broken," Nico continued, addressing her. "You need to get help," he added, the beginnings of impatience edging his voice.

Help.

Helen stood and made her unsteady way down the endless corridors, trying to cry out with a throat that lost its practice at speaking.

"You meant to escape me," challenged a voice behind her. She started and fell on the uncertain floor.

"I must help my son," Helen stammered.

Deiphobus jerked her roughly to her feet. "He does not matter. He's not my son. Or did you wish to return to that man you abandoned now that the Achaians have stormed our walls?"

Deiphobus towered over her. The ground let loose once more and he fell atop her, pinning her under his weight. "It's your fault!" he screamed, lifting himself enough to hit her, letting his fist attack her face and arms and chest. "I attain everything I want and it falls into ruin! It's your doing. Don't you think I know how you cursed me!"

Darkness hovered just beyond her grasp, tantalizing her with its peace. *One more blow,* she promised herself, *one more blow and the pain that is entering my heart will no longer threaten me.*

Deiphobus's hand went limp and he fell on her in a flood of warm blood.

Beyond him stood Menelaus, sword poised to give her the peace she had been denied.

One more blow.

Menelaus sheathed the sword and pushed the dead body of Deiphobus off her. "Come." He grabbed her hand and pulled her from the room.

She pulled away. "I must help my son."

Menelaus stopped, but he did not look at her. Instead he stood mesmerized by the scene revealed beyond the crumpled wall. *Fire. Fire spread everywhere, swallowing Troy, growing from the homes and people and livestock that fed it.*

"Fire," Menelaus whispered, awestruck. "The fire unleashed will consume all." He felt something in his hand and looked down to find the hand of another. "Helen!" he acknowledged, startled by her presence.

Helen stared warily into his quiet eyes. "I must help our son."

"Our son," Menelaus repeated and his face warmed in a sad smile. "Of course. Show me where he is."

The floor beneath them remained still, as Helen led her husband to their son.

CHAPTER TWENTY-FOUR

The men were heavily laden with the prizes taken from the Trojans and anxious to return home. *At least there is that*, Agamemnon thought. *At least we can return home and begin again.*

He looked at the silent, still form of Cassandra, who waited numbly to board his ship, and wondered if it was possible to start over after all.

"We will wait until all the Trojan injured are tended and the fires are contained," he announced to the surprise of all except Odysseus and Nestor.

Menelaus moved forward from his place between Helen and Nico. "My men and I will depart now," he said simply. "I have already sacrificed more than my due to the fires."

Agamemnon looked into the calmed eyes of his brother and felt his own burn in response.

"Indeed you have," he said at last, clasping Menelaus' shoulder affectionately.

Helen pushed past them to the place where Cassandra stood. "He will take good care of you," she offered lamely.

Cassandra looked to her with unseeing eyes. "Andromache is dead, crushed by the debris. My sister, Polyxena, was burned as an offering to Achilles. Hecuba has been claimed by Odysseus. And I," her eyes focused upon Helen's at last, "I hear Her words still. They tell me my end is near and I am as powerless to change that as I was to prevent the destruction of Troy. She has abandoned us."

The princess' icy calm chilled Helen's spine. "Agamemnon will take care of you," Helen insisted.

Cassandra's bruised face twisted in a sad smile. "She is

346

gone. There is no one to care for us any longer."

Helen saw the defeat she felt reflected in Cassandra and could not bear the pain. She pressed the young woman's hand. "We must find Her again," she said, then fled before Cassandra could witness the despairing tears that washed her cheeks.

She found herself face to face with Agamemnon. His eyes held grief and relief and anger and apathy and dejection. Hers, she knew, held the dying light of the same.

"We did not win," she said.

Agamemnon bowed his head. "We did not win," he agreed.

She turned and made her way to Menelaus' ship.

CHAPTER TWENTY-FIVE

"**I**t's simply not possible," Clytemnestra repeated to herself, then swore for wasting the precious time.

Rumors confirmed each other with annoying regularity.

Troy had fallen.

Agamemnon was alive and returning to reclaim his place of power.

Her place of power.

She would not allow it. Not again. Not now.

She had rid herself of Helen, rid herself of Iphigenia, married Electra off to an obscure peasant, fostered Orestes out to a distant uncle, killed those servants loyal to Agamemnon, burned the subjects she suspected of treason.

The kingdom was hers, earned by right and through her power.

She would remain the ruler.

She would marry Aegisthus at last and birth children loyal to her alone and raise an army to conquer neighboring lands and drench the world in a red sacrifice to her rule.

It was her kingdom.

It was her right.

It was her power.

CHAPTER TWENTY-SIX

He won.

Violent storms with walls of water and relentless winds and deafening rain had tested his strength and he had won. The men said Poseidon's wrath had descended. Agamemnon knew better. Whatever gods there were had provided the opportunity for him to test his resolve.

The struggle had been fierce. What had once been a fleet of ships carrying the heroes, the injured and the stunned, was now a few boats that reassured themselves of each other's presence through meaningless conversation shouted over the sides of battered decks, and by constant glances over sagging shoulders.

Agamemnon felt the presence of those who were missing and hoped each was making his way safely home.

As Agamemnon was.

The sounds of swords clashing would be replaced by the laughter of children. Wails of death would be replaced with the soft conversation of a quiet life. The hungry would feast. The spilling of blood would be substituted by an outpour of love.

Agamemnon felt an intense need to balance the horrors he had lived.

He would reunite with his children, become reacquainted with his wife, learn more of his people.

He would fight for peace with the strength of his mind, for justice with the valor of his heart.

He would win.

"Land, land on the horizon!"

Rowers and cooks and deck hands and captains crowded the prows, squinting into the sun, searching for the place where the endless waters gave way.

Searching for home.

"Aye — it is there!" a man screamed, pointing uselessly, as if his companions could sight the speck on the horizon down the length of his hand.

Many tried, crowding behind him, closing one eye and looking down his arm.

"Aye, the more fools we! She won't come to us. Let's get rowing!" he ordered, shaking them off.

Men raced to their places, energized by the knowledge that their destination was in reach, determined to arrive in the shortest time possible.

Cassandra made her way to the prow they vacated.

"You will be welcome in my kingdom," Agamemnon said to the silent, still girl beside him.

He had taken Cassandra as Odysseus had taken Hecuba, vowing to honor her as she had been honored in her homeland, promising himself that he would repay her for the trust she demonstrated when she let him confer with Helen in her temple.

She stared toward her new home, dead eyes rekindled with a spark of life. "Blood! Blood will be sacrificed to the hearth!" She raised her hands above her and repeated her warning, swaying in the grip of mania.

Her scream caused one of the men to fall overboard.

The men who remained at the ship's prow backed uneasily away.

Agamemnon decided he liked her better silent. "My wife is going to love you," he murmured, forgetting his resolve to look at Clytemnestra with new eyes.

The rowers doubled their efforts to reach their homeland and the distance it would offer between them and the Trojan priestess.

"You would think more people would come to greet us," a rower mumbled when the water gave way to shallows in reward of the efforts.

Agamemnon agreed, some instinct deep inside him growing uneasy as he inhaled the strange scent that surrounded his home. His eyes rested upon a single woman who moved arrogantly forward as he deboarded.

"Welcome to Mycenae," she said, handing him a cup of strangely spiced wine.

"My queen. It is indeed good to be home."

Something deadly sparked in Clytemnestra's eyes. "Many of our people are preparing for a feast in your honor," she said before he could ask. "I thought you and your men would like to bathe and rest before you joined them."

She distributed a smile of calculated sincerity.

Agamemnon was relieved to be greeted by the small group. Perhaps his wife longed for the same simplicity he craved. He saw her attendants passing cups among his men; only Cassandra refused to drink. "I see Aegisthus is not with you," he commented, diverting the deadly stare his wife was bestowing upon the Trojan priestess.

"He is within the palace," Clytemnestra responded curtly.

"I am anxious to thank him for holding my kingdom safe in my absence."

Again, Clytemnestra's eyes sparked. "Let's prepare your bath then," she responded coldly and turned toward the palace, leaving Agamemnon and his men to follow.

I have much to do to create harmony within my own home before I spread it throughout the kingdom, Agamemnon sighed.

I cannot wait to warm my hands on your blood, Clytemnestra thought.

She led the men to her home and ordered servants to attend them.

She attended Agamemnon and his mistress herself. "This woman will come with me," she said, indicating that Agamemnon should retire to his own chambers.

Loathing hung heavy in the air between the two women.

"I will make myself ready to greet you properly," he said, with a placating bow to his wife. "Go with her," he added to Cassandra. "You will be safe and I will join you shortly."

Indeed you will join her shortly, Clytemnestra thought. She watched her husband enter his chambers, making sure the warriors she had chosen guarded the door he entered.

She turned her attention to the priestess. "You are unexpected," she said with a smile of calculated sweetness.

"And you, exactly as I foresaw," Cassandra responded.

Clytemnestra's smile faded and she pushed the woman forward.

For many moons, Agamemnon was surrounded by water, longing to be free of its captivity. He now sunk within it, allowing its warmth to bathe his muscles and joints and skin.

This is peace, he thought, forgetting the harsh stares of his wife, overlooking the tension that hung in his palace, the lack of ceremony that greeted his victorious return.

A larger victory awaits me, he reminded himself and inhaled sweet visions of raising his children and courting his wife and establishing peace and justice in his kingdom.

He would fight for harmony. He would win. This was his choice.

His body relaxed, falling deeper into dreams enhanced by the drugged wine that coursed through his blood.

Victory.

He did not feel the sack that suffocated his breath.

I will win.

Nor the sword that severed his life, spilling his blood down the side of the marble tub, across the tiled floor, toward the small fire that warmed the room.

"Blood on the hearth," Clytemnestra said aloud. "On my hearth."

She turned her attention to the bound princess beside her. "I believe he wanted you to join him."

She lifted a sword with the force of her hatred and severed Cassandra's head.

CHAPTER TWENTY-SEVEN

"**M**adness," Menelaus said. "Madness and hatred. Would that it were possible to understand the plans of the gods."

Would that it were possible indeed. Helen wanted to die, to end at last the life she was tired of trying to understand. And yet here she was, aboard a ship once more, her dulled senses immune, for once, to the motion of the waters, her mind too exhausted to retreat to the comforting numbness into which she had slipped so many times before.

"What is it father?"

Helen watched Nico join Menelaus at the ship's prow. Father, he had said, as if there was only Menelaus, had only ever been Menelaus, at his side.

Husband, she had called him, as if there had only been Menelaus at hers. She had uttered the word after their harrowing journey through uncertain winds and tumultuous waves. After her husband saved their lives, urging men into gales intent on their destruction and waters that promised certain death.

After he patiently chewed their limited portion of meat and fed it to her from his fingers when it was clear she had neither desire nor motivation to feed herself. After he taught her son to build a small net with which to catch the sea creatures that darted through the shallows.

Father, Nico called him.

And tears of human pain and human joy welled in Menelaus' eyes.

"Why?" she had asked him, her first words in many moons, not knowing if her question related to the chaos of their existence or the simplicity of his loving gestures.

He had shrugged the shrug of a proud and self-depreciating man. "I am your husband."

"You are my husband," she repeated, anchoring herself on the only reality available to her.

"We must put ashore and offer my brother what assistance we may," he said now, directing his men forward.

Helen surprised them both by rising and joining him. "What is it?" She looked before her and saw the fires that flamed on Mycenae, heard the screams that carried across the sea.

"Is it war, father?"

Menelaus hesitated before answering, privy to a knowledge that eluded Helen and her son. "Let's wait and see."

No one could tell them.

Women ran screaming, men marched without direction, children played in hushed voices which were their only acknowledgment that danger threatened their existence.

Menelaus grabbed at anyone within reach as they made their way to the Mycenae palace.

"The queen is dead!" a woman howled.

"Right to avenge the king," a man muttered.

"The poor, poor boy," an older woman cried.

None of it made sense. Mycenae was blanketed in the confusion of war yet no invading troops could be found.

Clytemnestra would never allow herself to die, Helen thought. Legs that had grown unaccustomed to walking quickened to keep pace with her husband.

The chaos inside the palace took a different form from that without. Servants stood, stunned, unable to move, unwilling to answer questions. Menelaus gave up asking. They moved further and further within the massive fortress.

"What is that?" Nico heard it first, an unnatural laughter that stabbed the nerves and the stomach.

Menelaus paused for a moment to listen and flinched. "Let's go."

She sat in the middle of a stone floor. Her worn clothes were torn, blood stained her hands, clotted her hair.

Menelaus motioned Helen and Nico to remain where they were and slowly, gently, sat himself before the rocking, laughing girl, taking the bloody hands in his own. His touch set off a shrieking sound that sent Helen and Nico jumping backward; Menelaus stayed patiently where he was. The shrieking stopped.

"She's dead and her goddess with her," the girl said, punctuating her announcement with her unnatural laugh.

"Where is Agamemnon?" Menelaus asked softly.

The girl slumped into herself and began whimpering. "Father, father..."

A look of recognition crossed Menelaus' face. "Electra?"

"She killed him, you know," the girl informed him, malice giving rise to clarity. "She and that lover of hers. But Orestes avenged him. We have had our revenge."

A fanatical light flickered in her eyes.

Menelaus gently dropped her hands and rose; she resumed her rocking motion. "There is nothing to be done here," he explained, approaching his family. "The gods have chosen to act here. We can only await the conclusion of their drama." He took Helen's hand.

"Let's go home."

PART FOUR
HOME

CHAPTER TWENTY-EIGHT

*H*elen *continues...*

Home. How easy it is to mutilate a word until its meaning is obscured beyond recognition. Many times I tried to make Sparta my home, the place where I understood who I was, the place that reflected my nature. As many times I failed. And yet it was to Sparta that I returned, spending more and more time in a bed chamber that no longer offered rest, with a heart overwhelmed by questions.

The populace to whom we returned was as confused as I. For too long they, like our neighboring cities, were run by those who were not their rightful rulers. Uncertainty laced the corners of the eyes that met us; suddenly the familiar had become strange and though the people were relieved by our return, they demonstrated a wariness that had been previously absent. Perhaps the wariness was shared by all Greeks and was responsible for the many battles between former peaceful allies that occurred after Troy's destruction.

Or perhaps too many men had grown accustomed to life with battle and were afraid to relinquish it.

In these battles, Sparta fared far better than most — a state most certainly attributable to Menelaus. Not only did their rightful ruler return, but in Menelaus the people found a strong, competent leader. For the remaining seasons of his life, Menelaus ruled with a steady hand, leaving Niko with a strong legacy to follow. Even my daughter Hermione found solace in his presence, though she and I could not do so in each other. Our lives were too different — hers a simple one of ribbons and trinkets, mine a confusing montage of Goddesses and love and betrayal. It did not surprise me when she married a local noble, shortly after Menelaus' death. The palace offered her no more than it did me.

I have taken to wandering the countryside, seeking respite and answers. Often, my feet lead me to the monument that holds Menelaus' body. The people erected it, with glorious pillars and slabs of limestone. Great white steps usher one to a central fire kept mysteriously lit. The locals say that the flames are tended by Menelaus' spirit, bridging even his descent to the Otherworld, demonstrating his enduring love.

Maybe they're right. I've come to realize how little I know about love.

Perhaps what Menelaus and I shared was that elusive emotion, weighted by loyalty and duty. I wonder then what I felt for Alexander. When I call upon his memory, my body is once more infused with the welcome passion so familiar to me in his presence. It is tainted by guilt and betrayal. But not by loss.

That particular anguish is reserved for the Goddess.

It was worse during my first seasons back in Sparta. Then, my emptiness would fill with impotent rage, roaring through my heart like a tenacious sea squall. I would fling the coverlets from me and storm through the palace, as mad as Menelaus formerly was, searching for...something. I knew not what and that was more frustrating than anything else.

Menelaus was very patient with me in the way that only those personally familiar with madness can be. It was he who suggested that I contact Aethra. Maybe she would have the answers that would offer me some peace.

When I learned that she had died, peacefully in slumber, my rage died also. Perhaps Aethra did have answers but now she could not share them with me.

The emptiness that I've grown almost comfortable with began to steal upon me then. It was not so complete as now, however. That did not happen until I visited Parthenope's home.

It was much as I remembered, though age had tattered its edges. The mud plaster had given way at some places, diligently replaced by new, which looked like an intruder to the original structure.

Even the warmth and joy that had formerly emanated from the place seemed battered by time.

So too did Archelaus.

"She died several seasons ago," he explained, the lines that licked the corners of his eyes crumpled in unhealed pain. "She insisted upon giving birth a third time, even though she almost died with the birth of our second daughter. 'We must raise children to the Goddess,' she said."

Tears flowed freely from his eyes, though my emptiness did not allow me such release.

"She died needlessly then," I said callously, unable to give solace and regretting the pain I knew I caused him.

But Archelaus did not turn upon me, did not shout or rave as I expected he would. Instead, his eyes were painfully compassionate.

"She did not. Success simply did not look the way you had thought."

I forced a smile, unwilling to hurt him further, and wondered what entity blessed men with such naiveté.

I cannot even regret not sharing Archelaus' beliefs. The emptiness is too great for that, too all encompassing. Soon, it must be soon, I will pass myself, though I'm no longer confident the Goddess will await me on the other side of death. She has abandoned this world. Whose to say She didn't just as readily abandon the next?

I awoke this morning with an urge to walk the palace grounds once more and the sun has risen as I aimlessly ponder why this would be so. Perhaps some stubborn part of me still believes the answers I seek are nestled in the walls of Sparta, the place I have returned to again and again throughout my journey.

I will rise and follow this impulse, if only to quiet it and be free once more to lay within my chambers and await my end.

The robe I wear is old and ragged but I have long since ceased to care about appearances. The palace staff no longer takes an interest in me. Those who have always been here grant me the respect of privacy, while those who have come since Niko's reign watch me surreptitiously, no doubt wondering how the wraith who prowls the halls can possibly have caused the destruction the priests claim.

Since Hermione's departure, few walk the women's corridors anyway. I step beyond my room and walk down the gratefully dim hall to what was once the weaving room. The light is fiercer here, as the windows are free of curtains. There are no shadows hiding the ghosts of the past, though my memory offers glimpses of Leda and Clytemnestra, Rhemnesia and Aethra.

I move on, allowing my feet to carry me where they will, past the rooms I stayed in during my woman's making, past the chambers where Alexander first spoke his words of love. The cold stone of the stairway is curiously pleasant under my bare feet and I descend to the doorway that leads to the women's gardens.

Outside the light is even brighter and it takes my eyes a few moments to adjust. When they do so, I look dispassionately on the flower beds that have been allowed to run riot and the cracked stone ways where unchecked weeds have pushed their way through. When Niko takes a wife, she'll probably order the flora tamed and the stones replaced; she will be young enough to believe that the world can be ordered to her wishes.

I walk beyond the main courtyard, uncaring of the chaos. The earth is warm under my feet and in the distance I see the tree that sheltered my innocence. Here there are shadows and as I approach, I see the ghosts of women who gathered in the past. How real they look, though they are far younger than the ones I remember. Leading them is a young Parthenope, her features obscured by youth.

She nods to me respectfully and her followers do the same.

"Won't you join us?"

The voice is different than I remember. I want to shake my head, awaken the past to the reality of the present. Unrequited longing causes me to sit instead, silently taking my place among them.

"Close your eyes and open your heart so that She may enter," the girl who is and is not Parthenope intones.

I obey mindlessly, wondering if this, then, is my death.

I hear, as I once did, the sound of the birds nesting in the branches above and the gentle flow of the river beside us. I hear the breathing of the ghosts seated next to me.

Concentrate upon the one-song, I remind myself, as if it still matters.

The sounds become muted and a state of half-forgotten trance is upon me.

So cruel to torture my final hours with memory of the bliss I had known!

You have abandoned us, my quieted mind screams. Where have You gone?

The silence deepens, boiling with unbearable peace.

I am everywhere.

The voice echoes in my heart, with the gentleness of distant thunder. You are nowhere, my mind replies, unable to surrender bitterness.

Everywhere.

The ground beneath me stirs with life, casting shivers up my spine.

Everywhere.

I see once more the faces of my past. Menelaus and Agamemnon, Alexander and Aethra and Rhemnesia and

Parthenope.

Everywhere.

Leda and Clytemnestra and Theseus and Kalchas.

Everywhere.

I see myself, as I once was, young and vital and staring into a pond that has opened before me.

My own reflection looks back at me.

Everywhere.

"Are you well, my lady?"

A very real hand is upon my shoulder and I open my eyes to see the ghost of Parthenope.

"Who are you?" I croak softly.

The girl's eyes flash with a pride I remember. "I am Bateia, daughter of Parthenope," she replies. "These are my friends Eurythoe and Cylla, Cyane and Orsinome. We come here to worship the Goddess. We have permission," she adds defensively.

I smile then, wanting to disarm her fear. "Of course you do," I say quickly. "You have found Her."

Bateia smiles back uncertainly. "She is in our hearts, lady. How could She possibly be lost?"

"How indeed?" I say softly and notice she shares a puzzled look with her companions.

"Do you gather here often?" I continue, needing to know, needing to believe.

"Everyday," Bateia replies. "Though the priests would stop us if they could. We don't let them, of course. My mother used to say no one, no matter how powerful, will silence Her voice, for who can silence the voice of another's heart?"

"Only you can, if you cease listening," I reply, knowing I had.

The puzzled expression returns to Bateia's face once more. "Forgive me, lady, but I don't understand."

Of course not. How can she know of the tragedies that turn ears to stone and sever the disconnection to the self?

"It does not matter," I say. "Remember only She is within you — regardless of how far you journey."

Bateia bows her head respectfully, as if receiving a blessing. I know neither she nor the others comprehend my words. No matter. If they loose their ways, the Goddess will await them.

As She does me.